"Everyone loves a treasure hunt—pair it with a heroine you can't help but love, a hero you can't help but swoon over, and a family mystery that'll keep you on the edge of your seat, and you end up with *A Rumored Fortune*. This book is a treasure in itself and one you won't be able to put down!"

Roseanna M. White, bestselling author of the Ladies of the Manor series and Shadows Over England series

Praise for *Lady Jayne Disappears*

"In this delightful debut, a sweet romance, Politano pens a clever story-within-a-story full of Victorian intrigue and ghosts. . . . Older readers who miss the great gothic romances of Victoria Holt, Phyllis Whitney, and Mary Stewart will enjoy Politano's tale, as will readers looking for a chaste romance."

Booklist

"Witty, heartfelt, and elegantly penned, the story captivates readers from the first page to the last."

RT Book Reviews

"In depicting Aurelie's dogged pursuit of finishing her father's work, Politano also poignantly explores the rules (spoken and unspoken) of nineteenth-century English society in this excellent tale."

Publishers Weekly

A Rumored Fortune

Books by Joanna Davidson Politano

Lady Jayne Disappears

A Rumored Fortune

A Rumored Fortune

JOANNA DAVIDSON POLITANO

Revell
a division of Baker Publishing Group
Grand Rapids, Michigan

Published by Revell
a division of Baker Publishing Group
PO Box 6287, Grand Rapids, MI 49516-6287
www.revellbooks.com

Printed in the United States of America

Library of Congress Cataloging-in-Publication Data
Names: Politano, Joanna Davidson, 1982– author.
Title: A rumored fortune / Joanna Davidson Politano.
Description: Grand Rapids, MI : Revell, a division of Baker Publishing Group, [2018]
Identifiers: LCCN 2018007095 | ISBN 9780800728731 (softcover : acid-free paper)
Subjects: LCSH: Inheritance and succession—Fiction. | GSAFD: Christian fiction.
Classification: LCC PS3616.O56753 R86 2018 | DDC 813/.6—dc23
LC record available at https://lccn.loc.gov/2018007095

ISBN 9780800735197 (casebound)

Scripture used in this book, whether quoted or paraphrased by the characters, is taken from the King James Version of the Bible.

This book is a work of fiction. Names, characters, places, and incidents are the product of the author's imagination or are used fictitiously. Any resemblance to actual events, locales, or persons, living or dead, is coincidental.

18 19 20 21 22 23 24 7 6 5 4 3 2 1

This book is heartily dedicated to the two people
whose presence resounds through this novel.

First, to Rose,
dear friend and godly example.
It is her family history that was
the inspiration for this novel,
when she told me the captivating story
of her ancestors and their buried money . . .
and what it eventually cost their family.

Second, to my wonderful Vince,
who is the basis for this novel's hero.
I remember walking down the aisle toward you
and hearing the strains of a song
that has proven more true
than I even knew at the time—
"God gave me you."

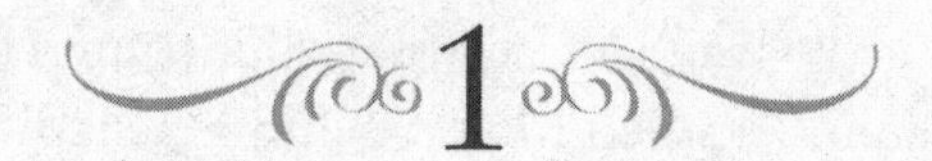

Never let common sense stand in the way of a great legend, they say, and there's wisdom in that. Because on occasion, those great legends turn out to be true.

—*Notebook of a viticulturist*

Somerset, England, 1866

"I say Tressa Harlowe's dead. It's the only explanation for it."

I didn't set out to eavesdrop, but some conversations are simply too interesting to avoid overhearing. Especially when the topic discussed by these strangers is me. In such cases, I had no choice but to absorb every word, for wasn't it my business even more than theirs?

I gazed from my shadowed corner of the dim room at the greasy little man who spoke these words and thanked my lucky stars I'd lost my way in the rain and wandered into this place.

The brutish man beside him tore off a hunk of bread and

plunged it in his mug. "Dead? Ach, no. She's too smart for that."

His mousy little companion hunched over his mug as if his frame couldn't support its own weight. "Either way, she's been away from the castle for months. It's the perfect opportunity, Hamish."

I could hardly wait to hear what opportunity my absence afforded them. I leaned forward and reached for my tea, drawing it into the folds of my cloak as I listened.

"So what exactly are you asking me to do, Tom Parsons?"

I breathed deeply in anticipation of the response, and my senses were flooded with the putrid scent of the place.

"I'm suggesting we avail ourselves of an abandoned treasure. No different than mining, simply digging for gold."

Hamish thunked two meaty forearms on the rough counter. "Look, you know how I feel about thieving from the rich. But this is different. I'll not go stealing from the likes of Tressa Harlowe. Much as I need that new horse, I won't do it. If that hidden fortune exists, and that's a mighty big *if,* well then, she deserves it."

"It seems everyone loves that little princess of the castle." Tom Parsons wrinkled his nose as if he could offer no suitable reason for this affection toward me. "Have you even met the girl?"

"Aye, a good many years ago, but you can tell who she is even from afar. Such a lot of life packed into a little mite of a girl."

"I daresay I'd be full of life if I stood to inherit 10,000 a year." The man's narrow lips pinched with resentment. "What does that girl need with a fortune anyway? Won't she have a hundred rooms all to herself one day? I've two up, two down, and ten people to fill them."

What did he know about rooms? Little good it did to have a hundred rooms or a thousand if they were mostly devoid of life.

Parsons spoke again, sniffing at his drink. "It'd be mad not to take such an opportunity. It's like a golden egg with no goose to guard it."

"Ach, you're a fool." Hamish threw his head back to down the last of his cider and then thunked the heavy mug back onto the counter. "She'll be back when she hears what's happened. Any day that fancy carriage of hers will come rattling down the road, spraying mud on all us common folk as she comes to claim her own."

I froze, straining to hear the rest. What? What had happened at my home? Father's summons now seemed ominous rather than exciting.

The proprietor strode through the crowd then and approached me, his sleeves rolled up to his elbows. "There's a man willing to take you to Trevelyan's outer gates, but no further. He's waiting by the door."

I stiffened as his direct address lifted my cloak of obscurity. "Thank you, sir."

"But save yourself the trip. With all the goings-on at Trevelyan, they won't be looking for help."

Me, in service? The mud and rain must have done more damage to my appearance than I'd thought.

Both men at the bar pivoted to face me as the man spoke, their two pairs of eyes seeing me for the first time. I fancied a light of recognition glowed from Hamish's face, but Tom Parsons merely observed me with a hint of annoyance at the interruption.

I rose and pushed back my shoulders, bestowing a gracious

parting smile toward them both. "Good evening, gentlemen." I moved past them, holding my breath as I squeezed between the tightly packed patrons, and then turned back. "You are most correct, by the way. The fortune does exist. I'll warn you though, it's guarded by the princess of the castle, and I suggest that you do not underestimate her." With a polite smile, I turned again toward the door and sailed through the crowds.

Outside, rain poured off the metal roof of the porch, creating a curtain between me and the waiting cart. I ducked and ran to the vehicle, where a man hoisted me into the dark chamber and slammed the door behind me. We only traveled a mile or two, for our own carriage had been nearly home when it had broken down, but the silent drive seemed endless. Perhaps by the time I reached Trevelyan and found help, the driver who'd stayed behind with Mother would have the carriage repaired.

Looking up at the impressive fortress before us, I wondered how those men could even doubt the existence of Father's legendary hidden fortune. I'd only glimpsed it once, but I'd always known of it, like one knows of the queen without ever meeting her. The idea of it had long haunted me, and I'd peppered Father with questions about it until one day when he'd given me his most direct answer on it. "I'll tell you where it is when I'm dying," he'd said with his usual gruff dismissiveness, and I'd accepted that answer.

At that time in my life, I believed him.

2

What you plant, you should harvest and enjoy without delay, for one never knows when his time will be up.

—*Notebook of a viticulturist*

Disembarking at the gates, I sprinted toward an abandoned barn and huddled under the eaves to wring out the ends of my sopping wet cloak and peer up at my destination. Trevelyan Castle's three towers sliced upwards through the curtain of smoggy rain, rising from the gray hills that embraced it, and I deeply dreaded what I should find there. *The matter is urgent,* said Father's missive that had called Mother and me home from abroad, and I couldn't imagine what would have made him write such a thing, or what would have made him write at all.

When the carriage harness had broken as we'd rounded the coastal road a ways back, Mother had of course seen it as a bad omen, for she could spot bad luck in a sunny day in July. But now, with the troubling words of that Hamish man from the inn sweeping through my mind, the whole world held an eerie chill that even I could not dismiss as I neared my home.

A shock of utter aloneness bolted through me as the cold wind penetrated to my skin. It was not the sort of isolation that lifted in the presence of others—it sat much deeper and longer-lasting than that.

The rumble of horse hooves thudded through my reverie. On the wooded path snaking through our woods, a black-cloaked rider leaned into his massive stallion, grasping his mane as they thundered toward me through the rain. A shiver convulsed me and I tucked myself into the shadows. What had that stranger been doing at our home? His beast panted closer, looming large and terrible. The rider turned to look at me, rain spraying off his dark curls under the hood, and I caught sight of nearly black eyes set in a strong, stubbled face.

Leaning back in one graceful move, the stranger reined in his horse and redirected him toward the barn where I crouched. A slash of lightning illuminated the wild eyes of the stallion as he pounded closer, and I shrank deeper into the shadows. Willing myself to be invisible, I watched them approach, and then the horse danced to a stop in the mud outside the barn.

"What are you doing here?" The rider's voice was low and harsh as the thunder. As if *I* was the invader on my own estate.

"Walking to the castle." I had to nearly shout above the storm.

"Not very effectively. Get on."

I hesitated at the sight of his rain-soaked leather glove outstretched to me, but this severe man was the only human

I'd seen since the driver from the Dark Horse Inn. He guided his mount under the eaves and gripped my hand, then lifted me easily behind him onto the horse at a precarious side-angle that thankfully kept me from straddling the beast in my skirts.

Propriety made me hesitate at the nearness of this stranger, but one glance at the steep hills before us had me slipping my arms around him and anchoring my hands on his chest. Dignity would have to make way for safety. I leaned my rain-drenched body against his back, sinking into its solidness, and the first jerk of the horse had me nearly squeezing the life out of the man. I moved close to his ear and shouted an apology over the sound of pounding hooves and thunder.

In response he covered my hand with his, pressing it to his rising and falling chest with a remarkable combination of strength and gentleness. "Hold on as tight as you need." That rare bit of masculine tenderness surprised and comforted me as I sat atop his horse and trembled.

Thank you, God, for the rescue. I shall accept this man as your hand in human form outstretched to me. Please let it be so.

I closed my eyes as the horse's hooves found solid ground at each stumbling step, and I relished the cool sea breeze on my hot face in unladylike surrender. My hair clung in wavy clumps to my cheeks, which were already slimy with mud, and a sense of urgency returned to my spirit. Mother, my little butterfly mother adorned in her own sort of gossamer wings, would be waiting in that broken-down carriage with our hired driver for me to send a rescue.

Bracing against a fresh deluge of rain, I clung to the rider and took in the familiar scents and sounds of Trevelyan

Woods. So many childhood memories, both sweet and lonely, hung about the castle and the land around it.

When at last we crossed the drawbridge and stopped under the red timber overhang, I relaxed my grip and peeled myself away from my rescuer. The urgent words of Father's missive swirled around me then, and fear gripped me anew. I glanced at the massive entrance for reassurance, that familiar arched doorway buried in the stone wall, and it was just as I'd left it. Nothing terrible could have happened if everything looked the same, could it? With a quick grunt, my rescuer turned and swung me to the ground.

"Thank you." My words were indeed heartfelt as I looked past him to the downpour we'd just galloped through. The barn that had sheltered me was nearly out of sight. "Mr. . . ."

"Vance. Donegan Vance."

The man's dark eyes engaged me from atop his horse, and I found it hard to draw mine away. He had quite an effect on me. I wished I could be indifferent toward this stranger, but he held a kind of horrible fascination for me. Rain dripped off the black curls that framed his face and traveled down his jaw.

"Thank you, Mr. Vance."

He gave a brief nod of acknowledgment, and then with one mighty yank of his arm, he spun the horse and galloped away in a splash of mud and rain. It was almost like a fairy tale, being rescued this way. Perhaps that's what made the man so handsome. Impossibly so. I watched the horse and rider charge back into the storm together, and then heaved a sigh and turned to my home and whatever awaited me there.

And suddenly, as I stood wet and chilled on the stoop of Trevelyan, hope flooded my breast. I remembered with billowing delight that this return was different—Father had sent for us. He wished us to be home.

I stepped up to the door and banged on the heavy wood. After a pause I repeated the effort. With a clank and clatter, the door opened. Framed in the glow from indoors stood our housekeeper, who remained as unchanged as the house.

"Margaret!" I leaped into her woolen-clad arms, a wonderful sense of home washing over me at the sight and smell of her. "Oh Margaret, how glad I am to see you." I pushed back and grasped her arms, words spilling out fast and breathless. "It's been a dreadful night full of adventures of the worst sort. The carriage has broken down and we should send someone immediately. Mother is waiting, and you know how she is. We'll have to fill her with five pots of strong tea and a tonic before she'll be able to tolerate life again."

Her crooked little smile stilled my words. "Oh, Miss Tressa. How sorely we needed you." She squeezed my arms affectionately, pulling me out of the storm and into the house.

As I stepped inside, I couldn't help throwing one more backward glance toward the darkened woods. To my surprise, the stranger and his massive horse had paused some distance away, watching the castle. As soon as I had stepped into the shadowy interior of the house, the man once again bent into his steed's neck and urged the animal to carry him farther away.

"We weren't expecting you this quick. Not at all." Into the warmth and muted candlelight of the narrow receiving hall Margaret guided me, and then to the dim gallery that needed three stories to properly display our collected portraits and statues. "This room's the only one with a fire blazing at the moment, miss, but we'll have that fixed for you."

I soaked in the warmth of the fire and smiled at this maid who had often created a sense of sunshine in my dreary life over the years, but trouble clouded her sweet face. I wondered why.

"It's perfectly all right if you haven't had the tart made yet for my homecoming, you know. We didn't tell you we were coming." I peeled off my gloves and handed them to her. "I should like to see Father at once. No, I shall need a thorough cleansing first. I'm afraid I'm wearing half the mud in the forest. Is Father in his study?" My numb fingers fiddled with the buttons of my traveling cloak.

She discarded the gloves and attended to my cloak with bustling efficiency, avoiding my gaze. "Let me just help you with that." She then busied herself with sending John the groom on his errand and caring for my poor cloak. Her high little voice seemed higher, more pinched than I remembered. "He'll have my lady brought up to the house posthaste, miss. Perhaps you'd like tea and a warming bottle for your feet." And without awaiting my reply, she hurried through the echoey room and disappeared through the service entrance.

Then the aura of Trevelyan Castle swirled around me as it always did when I set foot inside its great doors, distilling my bubbling excitement to a sense of awe and pure inspiration for my artist's heart. The very air seemed clouded with centuries of living, a sense of ancientness, and all the ghosts that went along with it. It was merely a house, yet I couldn't escape the feeling that the emotions, triumphs, and stories of generations had seeped into the walls and remained trapped there, their essence floating about the rooms.

With a deep sigh I spun in a slow circle, taking in the familiar portraits on the elaborate gold-and-blue backdrop of the walls, working hard to push aside the worry that insisted on settling around my heart. Margaret had looked tense, burdened. It was merely her shock at seeing me, wasn't it?

As I slipped down the stairs after a thorough cleansing and a relaxing toilette, a fresh life had returned to my spirit. I swept into the gold-domed drawing room with the familiar elegant furniture and hurried over to Mother, who had begun to recover from her ordeal. "Isn't it grand to be home again, Mother? How well you look already."

A spark of amusement flickered in her weary eyes. "It seems the old place has restored my daughter to me. I was afraid our trip had ruined the very essence of my little companion. You'd become so glum in those last weeks."

"We simply spent too much time indoors." Trapped in town as we had been, I'd begun to wilt as all the life inside me had been bottled far too long. The amusement and splendor of our social season abroad had excited Mother but utterly suffocated me.

Now I was home. Soon I would see Father and know the reason he had summoned us. I spun the little opal ring on my finger as I'd done so often of late. It was the only gift Father had ever selected for me, and it served as a reminder of those brief glimpses of tenderness in him, leaving me hopeful for more of it. We were so alike, Father and I, for he'd chosen the gem that most spoke to my colorful artist's heart, and one day he'd realize how much we could mean to one another.

Curling the band against my palm, I set aside my wandering thoughts and knelt before Mother with a smile. "Would you like tea?"

She touched her temples and closed her eyes. "Just my vials from the trunk before this headache swallows me. I sent Lucy to fetch them a quarter of an hour ago. Where could that girl—?"

Crash.

Metal banged and clinked on hall tile, echoing through the house, and Mother cast her eyes heavenward with a sigh of long-suffering. "Never mind."

My unfortunate lady's maid, Lucy, peeked around the door, her frizzy hair framing the wide-eyed face with tiny heart lips pursed to hold back a flood of ready excuses and apologies.

Mother waved her in with barely veiled impatience. Even though she never lowered herself to outright anger, no one failed to miss the disapproval of Trevelyan's mistress. "Did you bring my vials?"

"I have them here." The girl hurried in and handed her the case with a quick curtsy. "Also, tea will be a bit delayed." She lowered her blushing face.

In a beat I stepped forward and inserted myself into the incident. "How wonderful of you to protect Mother's vials in the collision with the tea cart. Not a one is broken, and that is admirable." I caught the girl's eyes and flashed an encouraging, conspiratorial smile upon her, for we were both victims of Mother's veiled contempt at times. Another curtsy and the dear, pitiable Lucy hurried away, her head down to hide her tears.

"I don't know why you insist on keeping the girl, Tressa. There are so many accomplished young ladies you might have as your lady's maid."

"But then who will have Lucy?"

Wind pelted rain at the windows. Still restless and haunted by the pallor that had touched Margaret's usually rosy face, I crossed the room to stand in the window bay that was now assaulted by the dying storm. "I wonder what drove Father to summon us home. I don't believe that's ever happened. Do you suppose he's changed a great deal?"

"In six and twenty years of marriage, he hasn't had the good sense to change yet. Why ever would he start now?"

The words pinched my heart. "Oh, Mother. Can't you at least try to like him? He adores you so." If only she knew how lucky she was.

"It complicates marriage so greatly, to have your heart tangled up in it. Besides, he does not make himself easy to enjoy."

Her words held truth, for Josiah Harlowe had not been one to lavish affection upon anyone. He doled it out as sparingly as he did his legendary fortune.

"Perhaps he misses you, and—"

"Oh for heaven's sake, child. He never sent for us, and I never should have let you believe it. The summons came from Amos. It was he who called us home."

The butler?

Finally the door slid open and our housekeeper scurried in with a fresh tea cart. "There was a Mr. Donegan Vance here just before you reached the house, asking that he be notified when you all return. He left no card, but he's staying in town."

She waved off the news. "Margaret, where is my husband?" Mother spoke from her graceful lounging position on the settee, her voice whisper-soft, as if even the effort of speaking drained her tired soul.

Margaret turned up the teacups and poured, nervous eyes

darting about, her pleasant face lined with worry. "Amos will have to tell you the news, my lady."

Mother straightened against the floral tapestry, her elegant head tipped with sudden concern. "What? What is it? Has he had business troubles?"

"No, my lady, it isn't that." Margaret nudged the poor butler forward with her elbow. "Amos will tell it."

"I . . . I wouldn't know how to say it." Amos's long fingers worked around the empty tray he carried as he faced us.

"Come now, one of you tell me what it is or I'll dismiss you both."

Margaret sighed, heaving her rounded shoulders forward. "He has died, my lady. Nearly a fortnight ago."

Disbelief tore through me as I struggled to grasp the truth. *Died!* The terrible word rolled around in my mind and settled like the steel of a knife, slicing the delicate thread of hope I'd held all this time. Stiff and regal, I held my composure like a calm pond on a summer's day. But beneath the surface, a tempest of the fiercest proportions roiled around, the power of it swaying me on my feet, leaving me weak and unsteady in its wake. A few deep breaths and the initial shock receded, but the pain had sliced deep into my belly, where it continued to turn.

Then I remembered Mother. I held my breath for a heartbeat as I awaited her reaction, one hand to my satin bodice.

A look of guilt and angst settled on the smooth planes of her face. "So, Josiah has died." She sank back into the settee. Her face had gone quite pale.

Margaret's lips pinched in her signature look of masked disapproval at the subdued manner of her mistress's grief. The nature of their relationship could not have been a secret among our staff, for the two seldom saw one another, yet this blatant acknowledgment of their detachment seemed rather vulgar, especially now.

"I'm so sorry, mistress. I offer the deepest sympathies of the entire staff."

When the housekeeper left the room, Mother turned to me with determination. "We must focus on the positives of this horrible situation. I refuse to be mired in grief."

"I'm afraid I cannot avoid it." Truly, the ache cascaded over me in waves, drenching my heart in loss and pain.

She reached out and grasped both my hands in hers. "I shall do all I can to make you feel better, as you always have for me."

I slipped my hands out of hers. "What good could possibly come out of Father's death?" It was so final, so utterly wretched, with absolutely no silver lining.

"Perhaps we should distract ourselves with pretty things to liven our hearts."

"You wish to shop?" The reality of our differences sliced cool and thin between us, intensifying my fresh grief. I ached even more for the father whose heart had been cut from the same fabric as mine, wishing for another chance to break down whatever barrier had kept us disconnected, for it seemed there was no one else in my life like me in the least.

"At last we can have all that fortune he's held so tightly and spend it as our own, with no one to slap our hands away."

I curled my hand into itself. If anger could be a noise, it whirred painfully in my ears. In some moments I found it difficult to empathize with her, but in this moment disgust speared any tenderness I may have felt. Her callous delight shredded my aching heart, and I turned away, unable to bear the sight of her.

"Oh come now, you can't tell me we must keep up a pretense. It's his own fault if he has no one to miss him, the way he lived like an angry hermit. Come, let's have the fortune brought out now. Where has he gone and put it?"

I turned back and looked about for whom she might be talking to, but she remained focused. "Why, I haven't a clue where it is, Mother. I assumed you . . ."

Her blue eyes froze into two orbs of ice and she dropped my hands. "He did not tell you?"

I shook my head, gladness and fear swirling through me that the fortune should be out of her reach, at least for this moment. "He said he'd tell me just before he died." I looked at Mother and the truth struck us both immediately. Here we were living in this immense castle with a lavish vineyard and a staff of nearly sixty-five . . . and barely a shilling between us. At Father's death, we were suddenly the poorest wealthy family in all of England.

Fear blanched Mother's face. "How could he . . . Oh this is the worst . . ." Then she paused with her chin out, a picture of courage as she rose from the sofa with effort and wobbled on her feet. "I suppose we must bear it."

Springing up, I steadied her and implored her to rest. Performing my usual service to her urged me on when I wished desperately to crumple into a heap of ashes and blow away in the wind. "Something will turn up. There's nothing we cannot better deal with after a good rest. I'll help you to your chambers and send a maid with eau de cologne for your head."

She allowed herself to be led out of the drawing room

and up the great staircase as I paused to lift a candle. Three steps up, she stopped me with a faint pressure on my arm. "You knew him best, Tressa dear."

I forced myself to swallow. If only appearances had translated into reality. No matter how often I followed him about the vineyard throughout the years, we'd shared no more than a handful of words. He'd addressed me in his gruffly tolerant way, occasionally sinking into true conversation for a fleeting moment, but otherwise he hastened me away.

"Surely you can think of some place . . . you must know something. *Something*."

I nearly said that I did not, but that would be a lie. I lowered my gaze as one image flashed through my mind so plainly I could nearly touch it. His notebooks. In those pages of his notes and observations on the vineyard, he had tucked pieces of himself that could be found in no other place. If one were to understand where he'd hidden the fortune that had been his lifeblood, the answer would be buried somewhere in those volumes.

Yet I held my tongue. The idea of Mother glimpsing the private words on those pages made me cringe.

"We'll think on it later, Mother. The only thing we'll discuss tonight is getting you to bed." Climbing alongside the leaping shadows of the candlelight, I glanced about the familiar house anew, seeing it as a cavern of mystery. For somewhere in these rooms lay the entirety of Father's fortune, the great secret of the man I'd barely begun to know. And unless I wanted to give up everything precious to me that still remained, I simply had to find that fortune.

"Here, miss, let me." Mother's lady's maid hurried up behind me and accepted Mother's weight, looping an arm around the woman's slender frame. Surprisingly sturdy, the girl bore the weight of her mistress without trouble, so I nodded my thanks and retraced my steps down the stairs. More tea would do wonders for the chill that had gripped me from the inside out.

In the drawing room, I paused as voices nearby arrested my attention. They wafted out from behind the service door.

"Will you tell her about the master?" Amos's voice warbled out in a fearful whisper.

It was Margaret's voice that snapped out a response. "You were there when I informed them of his death, weren't you?"

"That isn't what I meant, and you know it."

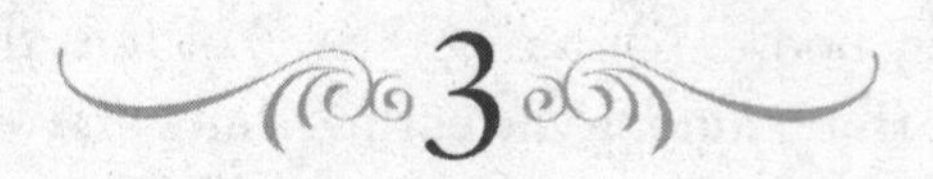

Each piece of fruit contains its own buried treasure that gives it limitless value—a seed.

—*Notebook of a viticulturist*

Squinting into the fog made orange by the rising sun, I strode through the sprawling vineyard in a nightdress and my tattered old garden cloak and pondered the odd whispers of my servant. What could she have meant? Shortly before breakfast and well before any sight of my mother, the early morning had wrapped itself around me in a cool, moist hush. The natural beauty around me dulled the edges of my pain, but the solid ache of it remained.

My dear blonde fur ball of a Spaniel dog, who had appeared as I'd exited the kitchen, followed closely, bumping my heels when I paused. Daisy's silent but eager company warmed my solemn heart as I strode among the vines ripe with poignant memories. Pausing amid the rows of spring leaves and gentle tendrils, I scooped up the little mutt and held her close. She nestled into me with jerky movements, as if nothing brought her close enough, and I hugged her gratefully. No one truly wished to be completely alone in such moments.

A black horse pounded through the yard just beyond the vines, heavy hooves scattering the veil of mist that lay over the field. I stood among the curling vines and watched the puffing horse round the corner and gallop across the open expanse toward me, subconsciously thinking it would be Father before I remembered with a stab of pain and loss that it could not be.

I twirled a fingertip idly through a cluster of hard little grape balls hanging from the wire beside me as Daisy wiggled down and scampered back toward the house. Finally the horseman rounded the stables and drew near. Only then did I recognize him as the man who had rescued me the night before.

The horse slowed to a high step and the rider held up a hand in greeting. I pulled the old gardening cloak more tightly about my frame, suddenly very aware that only my nightclothes covered me beneath it. Oh why hadn't I had the patience to dress? Here I stood before a man I didn't know, oddly dressed and with an uncovered head. My dark hair hung about my shoulders in thick, full waves, half of it pulled back in a knot behind my head.

"Hello there." He urged his horse closer and reined him in, springing down to stand before me in tall leather boots, black pants, and a faded white tunic open at the neck. Its fabric flapped in the open sea air against his chest. "It's you, is it? The little waif in the rain."

"I am eternally grateful for your help." The horse snorted and jerked against the reins, bending close to rub his nose on my shoulder as if relieving an itch, and my free hand rose to caress his face. What an enchanting animal, like a horse from a fairy tale. Beautiful feathering fell around his massive hooves, but he also possessed the tall, sleek appearance of a show horse. I smoothed my hand along his well-oiled neck. "A remarkable creature you have."

"He's a Shire I purchased from the Gypsies. I call him Gypsy."

"Fitting." I turned my face away to hide the shock at his admission. Had he truly met Gypsies? "What brings you back to Trevelyan?"

"A business matter to attend to." He glanced behind me at the rising sun, squinting into its intense orangeness. "And why are you out this early? The men should be ashamed that you have risen before they have begun work."

I inhaled and closed my eyes. "I am merely here to admire the artwork of dawn. My favorite artist happens to be God, and in my opinion his finest work is the sunrise. I cannot stand to miss a single unveiling."

His gaze bore into me, studying me as if confused or surprised at my words. If only I could eavesdrop on his thoughts. He shifted his attention to the thirteen acres of sloping vineyard beyond me before I could ponder any longer. "Perhaps you can tell me more about the master of this place."

I frowned. Just like the men in the pub, he believed me to be a maid. Before I could correct him, he spoke again.

"Were you on good terms with the master?"

His surprising question unsettled the delicate balance of my emotions. It felt invasive somehow, even though he could not know its true implications. I had been on painfully limited terms with Father, and I couldn't admit that I, more distanced from him than a servant, was actually his daughter. As my toes curled into the tips of my shoes, I looked up at him. "Not so close as some, sir." Like his vines. Throughout most of my life these plants had more right to call the man "father" than I'd had.

"You look poorly kept. Even worse than yesterday. Do they not dress their staff appropriately?"

Pinching my lips, I studied the hem of the cloak that had seen more years than I had. "These garments are of my own choosing. I've no one but myself to blame for their unsuitability."

Stepping closer with a squeak of his leather boots, he lowered his voice. "You can speak openly with me. I wish to know what sort of place this is." He smelled of deep woods and nature, and one look up into his deeply intense eyes told me he was a man who did nothing by halves. Passion sparked in their dark brown depths, and they were bright and expressive, although what they expressed I couldn't decide. "Tell me why they did not provide better for you."

"The house of Harlowe has blessed me with material goods beyond that of any maid. What reason have you to investigate this estate?"

He pressed his lips together, forming two long hollows in his ruggedly stubbled cheeks. "I'll be managing the vineyards."

I fisted my hands under my cloak and stared up at him. "I sincerely doubt that." My father had adamantly refused to allow his own daughter to join him in caring for them. A newcomer had no business working in—no, leading—the sacred endeavor.

"You must know little of the man, then, for he's offered me the position himself."

His words smote my tender heart, and I worked hard to brush them aside. Both palms clamped around the fabric of my cloak, but the hurt would not dissipate and my response snapped of it. "I assure you, sir, I know him well enough to know he never would have sought a stranger for such a position."

He considered me for a brief moment before releasing me from his gaze. "Where shall I stable my mount?"

"I suggest you verify your offer of work before doing that. I doubt you'll be staying."

With a crooked smile, he leaped astride his horse and turned the beast about in an anxious dance. "What the staff lacks in fine clothing, they make up for in airs." He winked. "At least, that is so of one little bird."

With a yank of the reins, horse and rider galloped toward the service cottages as if I hadn't said a word against it.

I watched his broad back, a strong upright figure moving as one with his horse, and frowned at his impudence. Even though he believed me a servant, he'd ridden over my words as if they hadn't been spoken. Nothing irked me more than unchecked confidence. I dearly hoped to be present when he was told to take his arrogant self from the premises. Despite his help the night before, an unreasonable dislike for the stranger arose in my heart, this man who deigned to pierce the privacy of our home and, in a fleeting moment, attempt to take over a position I myself could not earn in two and twenty years' time.

I knew in that moment I believed in love at first sight. But only because I'd experienced a twinge of the opposite just then.

Donegan Vance had never put stock in the idea of instant attraction, no matter how many new places he visited, but something about that girl in the vineyard haunted him like a mist that would not clear. She had an uncommon strength behind her eyes, likely from a life of hardship and want.

Surprisingly, though, it wasn't the strength but the weakness, the vulnerability and innocent hope playing so clearly across her features, that had drawn him. That hope shone out of her pure face with unusual frankness and provided a lovely color against the gray backdrop of Trevelyan Castle.

Ducking to enter the stone hovel he was to occupy, according to the terms of Harlowe's offer, he dropped his hat on the empty table and dust swirled up around it. Taking quick stock of the place, he chose the rafters as the safest spot to store his precious savings. To him, that money represented so much more than the mere merchandise it could buy. It meant restoration and freedom from the guilt that had dogged his steps for years. Shoving the bags safely out of sight, he exited the little cottage and led Gypsy to the stables where he found only a single worker.

"You there. I'd be obliged if you stable my horse."

The red-headed youth of about sixteen scrambled up from the straw-littered stall where he'd lounged, eyes two wide orbs of surprise. "Yes, sir. Of course."

"See to it that he isn't allowed to roam about the fields with the other horses. A stallion's temperament is unpredictable." Donegan yanked off the saddle and slapped the dust of the road from its surface. "Are you the only stable boy on the estate?"

"I work with the vines. I'm only here while I wait for the others."

Donegan clenched his teeth. No wonder Harlowe's vineyards needed help. "It seems I'll be your manager then, for I've come to look after the vineyards." He folded his arms across his chest. "What are your wages, boy?"

"Old Harlowe hired a manager, did he?" He stuck out his hand and Donegan shook it. "They call me Twig. Honored to meet you, sir. As for wages, I couldn't tell you straight off." The young man led the horse into the stall by the bridle and gave a few pats to his hindquarters. "There was no formal agreement between us, see. Some weeks I got eight shillings, some only six. Leastwise, we ain't none of us had any wages for weeks now. Excepting a clean place to sleep." He gave the horse another rub and hurried to add, "And we be grateful for it, you can be sure."

Donegan's heart sank at the familiar story and he immediately shifted into the mindset of a temporary stay at Trevelyan Castle. He could not do without a hefty income for even a single season. Tempting as it was to throw himself into this vineyard and unleash the life it was so desperately trying to release, images of what he'd left behind impelled him to maintain focus on his real goal—earning money. As much as this vineyard needed him, even more so did living, breathing people.

"I should warn you, though. The family's that particular about the staff keeping quiet about their secrets."

His eyes slid closed for a moment as he echoed the boy's word. "Secrets?" The situation grew worse by the minute. Although he should have known there would be secrets, with the ridiculous offer Harlowe had presented. The entire thing felt odd to him. Who on earth attempted to cultivate a vineyard in the South of England, anyway?

"The truth of it is, Josiah Harlowe weren't no well-heeled gent."

"You mean he didn't have a fortune after all?"

"Now I didn't say that. Sure, the man had more money than is good for most people, but he wasn't a gentleman in the way you or I think of one. It's rumored that he started out life common as the rest of us before he made his fortune."

"So did he come by his fortune through . . . dishonest means?"

"No one's quite sure where it came from or where it is now, but most believe he hides it away because he stole it. The rest is naught but rumors, since none of them up at the house was here when he was making his fortune. He brought over a whole passel of fresh servants when he bought up this place."

"I see." Donegan turned to look over the acres of perfect vine rows, sensing he would soon regret accepting this position.

4

> Force a vine to struggle and you give it a better chance at life. For any vine that has to reach its roots deep into the soil to find water and cling heartily to the guide wire against the wind will have a firm anchor to withstand any climate.
>
> —*Notebook of a viticulturist*

"I have a brilliant plan, Daughter."

Smoothing my gray cotton gown, I crossed the room to her, stifling my disappointment at her lack of grief. I'd known all my life what their marriage was, but in the face of Father's death it seemed more sharply evidenced. It was as if Father was merely a troublesome load from which she was now freed.

Forcing aside my pain, I smiled as I reached her. "It's dangerously early for one of those, Mother." I rounded the sofa and dropped a kiss on her powdered forehead. "By the looks of your face, I'd say your plan involved something quite devious."

"If your father did not see fit to share with us his money, *our* money, then we shall have to make our own fortune."

"I look forward to hearing what you have in mind." I fluffed her little parlor pillow with a placating smile and she leaned back into it.

"Later, Daughter." She whispered these words. Looking past me to something across the room, she smiled. "I merely wanted to awake your interest, but it wouldn't be seemly to discuss the details in the presence of our visitor."

Shocked, I spun to face a tall, finely dressed gentleman with a neatly shorn beard as he turned toward us in the window bay. I smiled politely.

"Dr. Caine, might I introduce to you my daughter, Miss Tressa Harlowe?" She indicated the visitor. "This is Dr. Roland Caine. He is the physician who attended your father recently while we were abroad."

He strode to us and looked down at me through spectacles that sharpened his frank blue eyes. Crinkles softened his handsome, well-chiseled face gently refined by age as he smiled and held my hand to his lips for a brief kiss. "Your mother has already spoken a great deal of your lively spirit, Miss Harlowe, and I'm glad to see her impressions are true. It's my honor to meet you."

I looked up into his face and found ample kindness there that drew me, invoking a companionable smile toward him.

Mother's voice rolled over the silence. "He's come to introduce himself to us and offer his condolences. Isn't that kind?"

The parlor maid wheeled tea service into the room, but the

doctor held up his hand in polite refusal. "I won't infringe on your hospitality any longer."

Mother smiled. "We were pleased to have our first caller since returning. Do come again."

While the scones on the cart momentarily captured Mother's attention, I hurried to catch the retreating guest just outside the room. "Pardon me, Dr. Caine, but . . ."

He turned to face me and my hands flitted about my cinched waist. Now that I had his attention, uncertainty gripped me. Did I really want to hear the details of Father's death? I looked down at the plush burgundy rug, then looked up at him helplessly.

"You wish to know how it happened." His sympathetic eyes spoke of many such encounters.

I gave the man a grateful half smile. "Perhaps." Then Margaret's whispered words swept over me. *Will you tell her about the master? That isn't what I meant, and you know it.* "That is, yes. Yes, I'd like to know." My chest tightened in expectation.

"I wish I could tell you, but I'm afraid I don't know much either. I merely treated his chronic condition. I'm a specialist of sorts."

"What sort of condition?" How little I'd known the man.

"Mainly scarring on his lungs. He must have lived near a factory or coal mine once, somewhere he breathed toxic air. I warned him against physical work in his vineyard, but . . ."

"He would not listen to anything that sounded like advice." I sighed, softening over the peculiarity I remembered so well. For all of his rejection in years past, he had been precious to me, and I'd built up a store of love for him that covered everything that had passed between us.

The man's face creased into a kindly smile. "I see you were well acquainted with the man."

Warmth flooded me as his words bandaged something in my heart, validating my place as my father's daughter.

He looked about the great entryway. "Even with all the visits your father paid my little clinic, this is my first time being inside Trevelyan Castle since he restored it. I must say, it fits the man."

"He would have been pleased to hear that. This castle symbolized so much for him."

He watched me with a look of deep understanding, melting my anxiety immediately.

"If you please, sir, I do have one more question. Was there anything peculiar about his condition? Anything odd that might have caused his death?"

He frowned. "What makes you ask such a thing?"

"It's just that, I've overheard some whispers among the servants, and . . ."

"Ah, that." He adjusted his spectacles. "Well, I'm sure you've heard of the Malvern legends, the early and sudden death of every master of Trevelyan. There's nothing like a good old legend to set tongues wagging, especially in a quiet house like this one."

"I know very little about the Malverns, but I do not suppose a family's legends are handed down along with their estate. They're nothing to us except the people who owned Trevelyan before us."

"Quite true." He smiled. "They've only dredged up such nonsense because your family has no legends to entertain their fancies. May I once again offer my heartfelt condolences, my dear, on the passing of your father. He was quite a man."

He bowed and turned to look for the butler to bring his

things. In the silence, the front door opened and a stranger limped inside with the force of his apparent anger, cane and hat tucked under his arm. Poor Amos the butler hurried after the intruder.

"Please tell the lady of the house I wish to speak with her. Mr. James Prescott." The man dropped the items on a chair as if he intended to stay.

I ran after him and stepped before him with authority. "I don't believe our butler admitted you."

But he brushed past me and crossed into the room to where Mother reclined, her lovely dress draped over the edge of the sofa in shimmering waves. I followed him in and hung about the fringes of the room.

Mother glanced up at me. "Tressa, won't you see about some tea for our guest?"

I hesitated, highly aware of the untouched tea settings still on the cart. Politeness forced me to leave this curious meeting as requested, but it did not keep me from listening in the hall. After sending a maid for an extra tea setting, I returned to hover outside the door.

Mr. Prescott's voice was low and unyielding. "I'm merely looking after my interests, you know. With your husband gone, I cannot count on the loan being repaid."

I shut my eyes and groaned inwardly. How many men would appear at our door with such a story in an attempt to wheedle our fortune from us? Loan, indeed. Not for a man with Father's wealth.

"I am a widow, but I'm still a lady. One who pays . . ." Her voice trailed off and I knew she'd be fanning her pale face. "A gentleman would make allowances for such circumstances, and I can see you are such a one, are you not?"

He shifted and clenched his fist. "One month. Not a minute more."

"If we cannot pay, what shall become of us?" Her voice had lowered.

Oh, the dramatics. I peeked around the edge of the barely open door.

"Your estate will become my property, to be reissued at will. You will have to clear yourselves from the place. Your husband signed a gentleman's agreement on the matter."

Clear ourselves from Trevelyan? But this was *home*. It vibrated with Father's presence, rang with his voice. The hills outside were laced with the vines he'd poured himself into for years. Leaving Trevelyan, leaving the vineyard, would mean abandoning all the pieces of Father remaining on this earth. I would simply have to find his fortune.

"Surely you would not render a widow homeless."

His commanding voice lowered. "I only aim to collect what is owed. No one may keep what they cannot afford. Not even a lady."

The fanning increased, as did Mother's breathing.

"I'm merely asking . . ." But the argument quickly disintegrated as Mother's breathing worsened. Her hand lay on her swiftly rising and falling chest, her face pale and eyes wide with alarm. The wretched man looked about awkwardly as the situation escalated.

"I—I can't—oh!" Mother wilted onto the sofa.

The man spun toward the door. "Doctor! Send for a doctor!"

I stepped into the drawing room and crossed to Mother in my usual way during these episodes. I propped her up and supported her until Amos appeared with Dr. Caine, his face a mask of efficiency. Fortunately he had not been hasty in taking his departure.

Dr. Caine knelt before Mother's slumped form and cupped her face. "Does this happen frequently?" He held her eyelids up and inspected each of her eyes. His other hand held her wrist to check her pulse.

I sighed. "Yes, often. But it usually passes quickly."

He frowned and adjusted his spectacles and continued to study her. "I'll send some pills 'round for you and they should help considerably."

The unwelcome gentleman spoke up from the doorway where he now hovered. "Mistress Harlowe, if I may just—"

I rose to face him, concealing all my seething irritation behind a mask of civility. "Please leave us in peace for the time being, sir. We shall handle all business matters when my mother is well." Which would likely be never, but he needn't know that.

"Perhaps I'll leave these papers here on the desk for—"

Dr. Caine rose to his full height and spoke with a menacingly quiet voice. "They've asked you to leave. Go now, or you'll have her death on your hands and I'll be the first to testify at the inquisition."

"But—"

"Out, now!"

The shorter man backed helplessly toward the door as the imposing doctor advanced on him like a bull. At last, Prescott turned and limped out, snatching his things from the chair as he went. As the invader's footsteps echoed toward the front of the house, Dr. Caine returned with a sigh, shaking his head.

"Thank you," I whispered as he neared.

A tiny smile toward me warmed his face as he knelt to attend Mother again. I glanced absently at the papers now residing on the table and noticed the red wax seal and the emblem at the top. Though I'd rarely seen formal documents, they looked genuine, and this thought tugged at my mind, refusing to leave it alone.

When Dr. Caine rose to depart soon after, he touched my arm. "A word with you, my dear."

I nodded and followed him out of the room.

"I'll have to keep a close eye on her, so don't be alarmed if I call often."

"So she is truly ill, then? Forgive me, but I'd always assumed her condition to be little more than exaggerated complaints and convenient fainting spells."

His solemn face said everything he didn't wish to voice. "I know this is a difficult time, but perhaps the good Lord has placed you here for this purpose. You're much stronger than she is. I see much of your father in you, and that's to your credit." He squeezed my arm. "Prove yourself his child and help her through this. You are the only one who can."

With a deep sigh, I nodded again. His words, meant to empower and encourage, merely settled a heavier burden on me and deepened my aloneness. God had created an awfully large load for my disproportionately small shoulders, and a tiny sense of betrayal snaked through me. God was to be revered, but not understood, it seemed. At least, not by me. I saw the doctor to the door and leaned against the metal-studded wood, wishing for someone to help me carry it all. Mother, the lost fortune, the debt . . .

You are the only one who can. The doctor's words echoed through my mind, inciting me to action. Of all the troubles that had settled upon me as we'd returned home, the lost fortune hovered over me with both the heaviness of importance and the draw of a puzzle. This endeavor had a definite goal, for the treasure existed somewhere in this house, and finding it was quickly becoming crucial.

I watched from the window as the doctor left, thankful for his sudden entrance into our lives. At least I had help with the medical aspect of matters. After speaking to the parlor maid and the houseboy about remaining ready to fetch Dr. Caine the minute I requested it, I returned to Mother, who seemed quite recovered.

She turned her sharp gaze on me. "Has that terrible Mr. Prescott left? I should tell Amos to never admit him again."

"You should have cast him out the second he said that vile word. Why ever would a man as wealthy as Father have debt? We must be wary of fortune hunters every minute now."

Mother fanned herself and closed her eyes. "You know your father and his many quirks. Perhaps he made such an agreement so he could have the pound notes in his hands, to amass an obscene amount of money and bury it in a hole in the ground like a dog with his bone."

"You cannot truly believe this debt is real."

"The documents are real enough, and stamped with your father's wretched signet ring."

I glanced toward the papers he'd left on the desk, my mind fanning out in possible explanations. "We should speak to someone about Father's investments. We may need to withdraw from them."

At the sound of carriage wheels rattling over the drawbridge, Mother's eyes opened, snapping with intrigue, which struck sudden fear in me. "Maybe we won't need to. It seems my plan is beginning."

"Mother, what exactly have you done?"

"I'm protecting my child. No matter your age, I am compelled to see you're not left destitute if the fortune does not exist."

"It exists, Mother. I'm sure of it. There must be another explanation for that wretched debt." I crossed to part the sheer curtains and watch a fine black coach draw up to the front. It looked slightly familiar, but my memory refused to match a name with the vehicle. Still, the sight of it brought an unnameable anxiety to my heart. Movement inside showed a man's black coat and hat moving about as the owner prepared to exit.

All at once, I knew whose carriage had arrived. I gasped when I saw the once-beloved face in the window. "Oh Mother, why? How *could* you?"

Her hands twisted anxiously in her lap. "There are no investments, Daughter. No bank accounts, no assets to sell. No debts to be called in or crops ready to sell. There isn't even a will."

"But *this?* Is this truly necessary?"

Her quick voice carried on, skimming along like a hummingbird lighting on flowers. "We shall be penniless if we lose this estate. We must take any chance to save what we can."

"This is a chance?" Determination to find that fortune poured through me, for it would save me from much more than poverty.

"And in the meantime we must recognize we only have one asset now, besides the property itself."

With a deep sigh I watched Andrew James Carrington III unfold his long legs from the coach and brush off his coat as he'd done so many times in our courtship. "And what asset is that, Mother?"

She studied me with a purposeful look. "You."

5

Bad weather can only harm the vineyard if one is unprepared for it, which is completely unnecessary. One can always count on bad weather, just not on its exact timing.

—*Notebook of a viticulturist*

I dealt with Andrew's arrival in the most logical way I knew how—by looking as stunning as humanly possible. As I pointed out my dark blue muslin and lace gown to my lady's maid, I recalled the smudged taupe-colored dress I'd worn when Andrew had rejected me years ago. I directed Lucy to pile my hair in meticulous sweeps and curls as I remembered the windblown wreck my hair had been that last painful time I'd seen him.

This day would be entirely different than that fated one I could never erase from memory.

"What a vision you are, Miss Tressa." Margaret spoke

from behind me, her face appearing in the mirror as Lucy stepped back to survey her work. "I can hardly believe you're the same girl I opened the door to, all soggy and dirty you were. Now look at you." She tilted her head fondly and touched a gold pin in my upswept hair. "Why, you could be Josiah Harlowe's legendary fortune yourself, a glowing pearl with strands of polished copper for hair."

My lady's maid, Lucy, swept the pins littering my dressing table into their tin. "All those treasure hunters came too early and missed the finest gem of the house."

"Treasure hunters have been here?"

"In droves, miss. Never have we had so many goodwill calls from neighbors and vendors and even strangers who never had a reason to care about Trevelyan before. The most brazen of them simply poked about the grounds on their own."

"Lucy, hush." Margaret brushed the girl aside. "You must learn when to button your mouth."

"Tonight's visitor is certainly no treasure hunter, at least." Mother swept into the room and hovered behind me, scrutinizing my face in the mirror as she might analyze the finer points of a gown she was selecting.

Lucy leaped out of Mother's way and the tin of hairpins tumbled from her hands, crashing and plinking across the floor.

Mother pressed her fingertips to her temples, then forced a smile toward the girl scrambling across the floor to retrieve the pins. "Be sure to do something about her face, Lucy. All that color from the sun will only remind Andrew of her oddities."

I couldn't help but wish to return to childhood, when my barefoot-running, outdoors-loving, energetic oddities were considered at least marginally appropriate.

With a delicate squeeze to my shoulders, Mother turned and swept out the door. Heaving a sigh, I looked at the blemished, rosy face of our housekeeper in the mirror, and the sweet tenderness there transformed it into a thing of maternal beauty. "Margaret, do you find me odd? Andrew must be coming because of the fortune, for it seems to be my one redeeming attribute."

"That wealthy man has all the treasure he needs, save one special pearl, which he hasn't plucked yet." She winked in the mirror and gave a final pat to the lingering stray hairs.

I spun on my stool to face the kindly woman I'd known all my life. "Margaret, what do you think of this scheme Mother's concocted?"

She pinched her lips, then took a breath. "I always say, those who marry for money earn it. And Andrew Carrington has nothing to offer you but money, I'm afraid. Now out you go, off to dazzle that poor man before you send him packing." She gave a tender pinch to my arm as I rose and glided toward the door.

I descended in gleaming black kid boots, idly wondering if my blue gown was dark enough to be considered mourning attire until the dressmaker could ready something in black. Perhaps I should have my maid dye one of my muslins. Before the thought had finished, I immediately smote it down. What did it matter if my clothes were one shade off? Father's death had already painted my heart an ashy gray. I would surely be mourning inside more than anyone.

"Clarissa, won't you see where my lovely daughter has hidden herself?" Mother's voice floated out from the drawing room.

With a deep, refreshing breath, I opened the doors and

stood framed there, a live portrait created in tandem with my maid to convey both the lovely femininity and hints of indifferent elegance I wished to display to this man who had scorned me. There he stood, that trim figure against the unlit fireplace, one arm leaning on the ivory mantel as he spoke to Mother in the dulcet tones that I could not quite remove from my memory.

"Welcome, Mr. Carrington." The words came out in one steady breath.

Andrew turned, his eyes taking in all of me in one brief, breathless moment. I held my breath and waited. His face softened and I saw my appearance mirrored in his glow of appreciation. He strode to me and took both my hands. I shuddered to touch them so casually, these hands that had been in so many of my waking dreams in our time abroad. I had gone through the hard work of forgetting him, and all those years of effort unraveled the instant he said my name.

"Tressa."

I focused on his wave of dark blond hair to avoid meeting the eyes that spoke volumes. How could one possibly grow more handsome with age?

A quiet smile lit his face and he lowered his voice. "I see you have not completely relinquished your feelings for me."

I dropped my gaze to his chest to hide my traitorous emotions, but that too was a mistake. For there, tucked just inside his suit, was the red silk cravat I'd given him years ago. The one he said he'd wear whenever he missed me desperately. How long after that moment had he stood in Trevelyan's courtyard and broken my heart? A week, perhaps.

I kept my voice low so only he would hear. "A woman can never be fully indifferent to the man she was to marry."

Mother swept toward us, her eyes alight with pleasure as her soft voice brushed my ears. "Andrew has come to help us through this dreadful ordeal. Isn't that wonderful, Daughter?"

Andrew smiled and turned back to me. "Mother and Father are in Paris so I've been at the London house alone. I simply had to come when your mother sent word. I took the first train here. And now I shall remain until you . . . until my presence is no longer required."

His voice, warm and familiar, wrapped itself around me like a pleasant memory. *I must keep up my defenses until he's gone*, my mind demanded. But with each passing second in his presence, I found my resolve melting and my feet slipping from their firm foundation.

The sound of echoing footsteps in the hall broke the tension, and I gladly looked away toward the door to await the new arrival, backing into the shadows to observe.

"We have more callers." Mother's airy voice seemed to smile at the notion as she moved toward the door, for she dearly loved visitors.

But it was not that sort of guest we found entering from the hall. The stranger who had deemed himself manager of the vineyards filled the doorway, looking over the room with a slight downturn of his dark eyebrows. I watched from the shadowed fringes of the room as he addressed Mother.

"I've come to offer my condolences to the lady of the house on the loss of its master." Standing there in all his rugged informality and heavy boots, Donegan Vance contrasted sharply with the delicate chintz and flower patterns of the room. Despite the roughness of his trade that clung to him, he exuded a compelling presence that made it impossible for anyone to ignore him.

Mother studied him without a blink. "Have we been introduced?"

"Not yet." He strode forward and took her hand for a moment, then released it. "Donegan Vance, new manager of the vineyard."

"But did you not enter through the front door?"

"I had been looking over the vegetation around that side of the castle. The front entrance was the closest."

"Naturally." Stunned and bright-eyed, Mother allowed her gaze to rove over the man before her. Not a single spark of welcome lit her face.

"Your late husband engaged me to help him with his vineyard before his passing."

She paused to consider. "I see."

"I'd like to discuss wages and negotiate a down payment before I begin—a small percentage of good faith money."

The corners of her mouth tipped down. "This is quite irregular. I've never paid my staff before they've worked."

"But you have neglected to pay them altogether at times, from what I've heard, and you will find that I am not as accommodating." His boots were planted on our lovely white rug.

A vague dread settled over me as I watched the conversation play out from the far corner of the room beside Andrew. Father, not paying the workers? He'd never do such a thing. Lacking as he was in warmth and affection, he had always been impeccably fair to a fault, even to the lowliest laborer. Yet this validated Prescott's claims of Father's loan. Unless they were both lying . . .

"What's he talking about?" Andrew whispered in my ear.

I flashed him a look that said *later*.

Mr. Vance continued. "You will also need to pay your field hands what is owed them."

Mother lifted her chin. "I'm afraid we haven't organized the household finances yet."

Or *found* them.

"They should be paid for their work."

"Of course." Mother's gracious voice fell from her mouth like a silky waterfall. "They deserve every farthing promised them, but there may be a delay."

The man frowned. "How long?"

"Two months will be sufficient, I'm sure." But she wasn't, of course. How could she be? "They'll only have to wait a little while."

"Wonderful. They'll simply wait a few months to eat as well."

Mother's eyelashes fluttered as she absorbed the shock of his directness. The man had the bearing of a feudal lord, one who elicited obedience from an entire village simply because they knew their fate rested on his whim.

"Now, I'd like to discuss a plan to—"

"You'll have to take this up with my daughter." Mother swept her arms gracefully in my direction, easily passing the argument along while she retained a shred of dignity before this man she obviously did not know how to answer. "I'm afraid I know very little about the vineyards, and she's better suited to managing the grounds."

He turned to me then, his passionate face framed by a square jaw, and I stepped out of the shadows toward him. Shock flamed across his features at the sight of me, darkening his eyes, but he recovered and extended his hand.

A smile flicked about my face despite my efforts to pinch

it back. I spoke in a low voice only he could hear. "At your service, one scrawny little bird." I lifted my hand gracefully to meet his. "With airs."

The look of shock that paled his tan face then was wholly satisfying and enjoyable to witness. His eyes snapped with something—irritation, or maybe the restrained desire to debate me, yet he accepted my hand for a brief moment like a civilized man. Either way, I had risen to the top of this situation and I enjoyed my view from there.

He stepped back and spoke again to Mother. "I shall follow your daughter's lead, then. I look forward to seeing her out in the vineyards with us as we work."

She straightened. "She'll do no such thing. We aren't as common as that, Mr. Vance. She will merely see to the paperwork and any questions you have."

I stepped forward and laid a hand on her arm. "I'll be happy to take part, Mother. It is an art form, really, balancing the perfect conditions and careful pruning to bring about the best grape, and you know how dearly I love art."

The stranger's gaze snapped to me, evaluating me with a glint of keen approval, but he spoke not a word. He offered a smile and a subtle kinship passed between us.

"Very well, if you wish. But Mr. Vance, I must request that you limit your access to the service entrance. It's more convenient from the vineyards." The polite order rang with warning.

I looked to the man before me to see if he'd received it, but his stony expression revealed little of the thoughts that passed below the surface.

"Mr. Vance," I said, "I hope it is agreeable to discuss payment in the coming weeks. Perhaps we can come to an arrangement that suits you."

"As long as that arrangement involves money transferring from your hand to those of your vineyard staff."

"We'll address the details later." Excusing myself, I made a graceful exit with the intent of retreating to my chambers, but Andrew followed close behind. I forced myself to stop and acknowledge his presence when we reached the hall where sunlight filtered through the tall windows.

"Tressa. Is it true, what they've said? About the hidden fortune?" Anticipation flicked in the depths of his eyes as if he'd been presented with a puzzle, a chase, that he couldn't resist.

His words deflated me immediately. "Oh Andrew. Is that why you've come?"

Regret flashed over his face. "Of course not. Forgive me for such a poor opening to the conversation I was too nervous to begin. What I should have had the courage to say is . . ." He glanced down at his polished boots, then back up to me. "I hope we may renew our friendship."

"Do you?" I looked over his fresh, clean-shaven face and forced the barely substantial walls to once again be erected between us.

"Isn't it what you want?" He swept up my hands in his eager ones. "Because if it isn't, if you've changed your mind . . ."

I withdrew my hands, and as the image of him on that final day, apologetic, pitying, dominated my thoughts. "No, I believe *you* changed my mind when you chose to end our courtship."

His face crumpled in regret. "Surely you know that isn't true. I was forced to do it. They would have disinherited me."

"You still chose to comply, did you not?" I spoke those words with all the pent-up sadness that had clouded those dark days. His parents had even sold their country estate near Trevelyan to keep us from happening upon one another, all because our name did not go back to ten generations of nobility. Father was part of the new wealth of England, his lowly heritage a millstone upon my marriage prospects.

"You're right, as always, Tressa. It took the death of your father for me to see what a coward I was. I should have pressed Father to reconsider, for I would be able to protect you now."

"I'm not suddenly rendered helpless, Andrew. I need no more protection now than I did before."

He inhaled deeply, a look of utter desolation crossing his features. "What I mean is, I should not have given up so easily before." His lowered voice wove through me, shaking my calm. "I can promise you, I won't make that mistake again." And with those words, he strode deeper into my home and climbed the stairs to the room where he would be staying indefinitely.

Disappearing to my bedchamber afforded me a chance to both quiet my mind and awaken my creative spirit. Desperately wishing to bathe my hurting soul in the lovely colors outside my window and capture them for the bleak days ahead, I pulled a rough handmade box from under my bed and flipped open the lid. My lovely bottles of color, the raw materials of my art, lay waiting for my eager fingers. "Hello, old friends."

Glancing about my bedchamber, which was already covered top to bottom, including most of the furniture, with bursts of colorful flowers, curling vines and ivy, and rich green leaves I'd painted, I decided to begin a new design in one of the many unused rooms about Trevelyan. It had to be some space no one would frequent, for anyone who saw that I had painted on the walls would think me mad.

My wandering brought me down into the arched undercroft, which had served as a sort of tinker area for Father. Taking a quick turn about the empty space, fear prickled my skin and I wished I'd taken someone with me. The eerie silence seemed robust and alive rather than a simple absence of sound.

A tall metal shield draped in cobwebs depicting a coat of arms caught my eye where it sat angled in the shadows, just past the single shaft of light streaming in the slit of a window. Then my attention was drawn to the splendid vineyard tapestry that always left me in awe. It was truly beautiful, this rendering. The solid vine trunk rose up from the ground between two posts and out at the top into heavily leafed branches that twined along their guide wire. Heavy grape clusters hung from the leaf-filled branches and tendrils burst out between the foliage. The center of the thick trunk had been filled with an iridescent gold filament that shone even in the dim light of this space.

The vineyard's secret scrolled along the top, always enflaming my curiosity, drawing me back to stare at this tapestry often over the years. Below it read, *the abundance lies within*. I'm not certain exactly when I'd decided this tapestry was a hint at the hiding spot for Father's fortune, but it had always been that in my mind. Perhaps words like *secret* and *abundance* led me to this conclusion, or maybe it was simply the glowing gold of the vine's trunk.

I stepped forward and traced the bold letters stitched across the bottom, and again I wondered at the name.

Malvern.

Father had been utterly fascinated by the grand family who had built Trevelyan centuries ago and worked against nature to bring about a vineyard in the part of England where one did not belong, yet he never wasted the few words spoken to us explaining the reason for his captivation. I turned away and pulled out a jar of deep red pigment, settling myself on a tall stool before the wall that would receive my touch of color. Somehow he felt he owed that family his fortune, but I never knew why exactly, for he'd died without finishing the story. Without finishing *our* story.

I closed my eyes against another wave of sorrow as images of Father played through my mind, and an odd notion swept over me as gently as the strokes of my brush: *It isn't over.* It was as if two parts of me warred constantly. One hoped for the impossible, and the other accepted reality and resounded the truth of it incessantly. Of course it was over. I was merely in denial. Father was dead, and that fact placed a cap on that part of my life forever. I continued my work.

But that story isn't over.

When the notion returned with gentle insistence, I wondered if these words were not of my own wishful thinking, but from God. I had drifted so far from the easy conversations of my lonely childhood in which he'd impressed various thoughts upon my heart. Had I mistaken this prompting? What could it mean?

Perhaps there was more to be uncovered about the story of Father's life—or his death. Dr. Caine's words about the Malvern legends niggled at my mind. When I'd finished, I cleaned my brushes and tucked away my jars, stepping back to look over my scripted painting of the word *Malvern* on the wall, and the doctor's casual words swelled to an overwhelming dread. Death, sudden and early. It had happened again to the new master of Trevelyan. But it was merely a legend. A silly superstition. Yet the chill of this space settled on me invasively. I looked about the room so full of Malvern relics and suddenly fancied it haunted.

Fear and excitement swirled through me in this forgotten space and compelled my feet toward the door. Wind moaned long, low notes outside the castle walls, and I scampered up the narrow staircase and burst into the servant's hall to catch my breath. Fortunately, the room stood empty. Most of the staff was busy repairing the dining room from the chaos of dinner. Setting my paints and brushes on the floor, I curled into my favorite deep windowsill that often held baked goods and closed my eyes, breathing deeply of night air.

Soft steps echoed around the corner and Lucy's nervous face appeared in the shadows. At my tired smile, my lady's maid entered. "Is something amiss?" Pity glistened in her eyes that went deeper than concern for the immediate moment. I'd rescued the girl once in her days as a chambermaid when Mother intended to dismiss her due to what she called chronic awkwardness. I insisted she become my lady's maid, despite her lack of experience, for it was the only way to keep her. Ever since then, Lucy had been my devoted personal attendant, complete with enough characteristic blunders and missteps to keep me sufficiently amused.

"No, thank you, Lucy. I'll be fine." I closed my eyes and forced myself to relax. Then my eyes flitted open and I studied the girl as I remembered the odd bits of conversation I'd heard in the hall the night we'd returned. "Lucy, there is one thing you can do for me."

"Yes, miss." She clasped her hands behind her back and stepped forward, her little black boots swishing in the empty room. For all her flaws and mistakes, her lust for gossip made her a wonderful source of information.

"There's more to this situation, isn't there? About my father's death, I mean."

Her features froze, eyes wide. "Of course not. What more could there be?"

I leveled a look at her, boring through her façade until it cracked.

She dropped her eyes. "I suppose you'll find out soon enough. It's the way he died."

"Go on." I spun around and dangled my legs down from the sill.

"It wasn't sickness that took him. It was the sea. The waves wrecked his boat against the rocks and he drowned."

I gulped, forcing away the terrible image. Yet, drowning was no great rarity in a coastal town. "Did they find something unusual about him when he . . ."

She looked away awkwardly. "He hasn't done it, miss. Leastwise, not yet."

Hadn't washed ashore? "You mean they never discovered him?"

She nodded, gaze still on the apron bunched in her hands. "I've no idea what you'll do about the rites and services, miss. Nothing can be done until . . ."

I studied the girl, her frizzy curls framing her face, and thought of Father. I shuddered at the image of him drowning.

Yet I was breathless at the thought, the farfetched notion, of him secretly surviving. *It isn't over yet*. As those words resounded in my heart, losing Trevelyan Castle became unthinkable, for it was the only place he'd return to if, in fact, he did return. It was not likely, and it only gave a shred of hope. But I found it was all I needed to feel immensely better and full of purpose.

"How do they know he drowned, then?"

"Amos said the fishermen saw him go out, and only his ruined boat came back. And why else would his boat come back empty?" She fidgeted. "I'm sorry, miss, that you cannot have the funeral yet. Really I am."

I touched her arm and smiled, glowing inside. "It's quite all right, Lucy. Truly."

6

The appearance of death in a vine does not mean the end has truly come. Every vine has its winter, but when you cut below the stiff surface, you'll find life.

—Notebook of a viticulturist

That sweet drop of hope still pulsed through me the next morning, pulling me from my bed before anyone else had risen. This secret would be mine to hold and savor, for I dared not suggest it to anyone else. Who would believe it?

Wearing a simple frock that I had saved for wandering in the vineyard, I burst out the back entrance and into the chilly field, wondering why on earth everyone seemed perfectly content to sleep through such an artistic display every morning.

After a refreshing run to the vineyard slope, I dropped to examine the soil, rubbing it between my fingers to check its loosely clumpy texture. I reached up to the branches that spun along their guide wire, extending out in both directions from the vine, and saw with satisfaction that Father's latest graft had held. New leaves burst forth along the length of each branch, and little green balls of fruit hid beneath the foliage. Standing to survey the gentle downward slope of the vast fields now in my command, I delighted in the lovely green color too vibrant to be bottled in my jars of pigment.

Along with the flood of color assailing my senses came a tidal wave of memories. The clearest recollection was a childhood conversation that had occurred near where I now stood.

"Father, I have the grandest secret to tell you." I twirled and danced down the fresh-leafed vineyard in the glow of early morning sunshine.

His answering grunt appeared to come from his worn hat, which was all I could see bobbing above the row of vines separating us. The man seemed empty somehow, as if his soul and body had separated at some point. My childish self believed that I alone held the ability and the obligation to catch that drifting soul and gently ease it back into the empty shell before me, and I forever persisted in that effort. Finally his face rose above the leaves, his wild beard blending in with the tangled vines that surrounded it.

"Don't you want to hear my secret?"

He blinked, as if remembering anew that I was there. "A girl of nine shouldn't have any secrets."

"I'm ten, Father. And I shan't tell you unless you tell me yours." Secrets were wonderful commodities, little nuggets to be grasped and then spent at the right moment. For years he'd kept the delicious mystery of his hidden fortune from everyone, but I had determined long ago that one day I'd be the solitary person who knew where it was. The one special person he trusted.

How I longed for that honor.

He squinted and removed his hat, the hair stretched over his balding scalp lifting in the breeze. I held my breath as I waited for what he'd say.

"What sort of grape draws the gnats, girl?"

I sighed, knowing I'd failed. "A broken one."

"Broken. Penetrated." He stood and shoved his fists into his back. "Any secret sweet enough to draw pests should always remain perfectly intact." We always talked of vineyards and grapes, Father and I, but in doing this, we spoke of so much more.

"But Father, I'm not a gnat."

"You're a *girl*." As if that rated even lower than gnats. Then he bent again and plunged his arms into the tangle of leaves and tendrils to count the clusters. "I will tell you where it is before I die."

Even now, years later, I still dwelt upon the possibilities, gazing over the perfect rows of vines. They seemed like an elaborate symbol of Father's life that might offer me great understanding of the man and his hidden fortune, if only I knew how to interpret what I saw.

Just then distant movement caught my eye. Even at this hour, I was not alone. Frowning, I stepped past the tangle of vines on wires and moved toward this lone worker. Father only hired the most faithful men, but their loyalty was reserved for the days he was present. None would be moving about this early if he was not here to compel it. The distant figure could be none other than Donegan Vance.

As I neared the man, my bare feet whipping slender grass blades, I squinted to see what work had drawn him out so early. His movements seemed odd. He grabbed and jerked, delving heavily into the work of destruction. But how could that be? Pruning in this season would kill the vines, and surely he knew that. Those fresh, delicate leaves, the tiny fruit buds . . .

Lifting my skirts, I charged toward him, weeds and loose vine tendrils whipping my bare ankles. "Hey!" My shout echoed in the fresh air of the morning, sending a flock of birds twirling up to the sky. "Hey, stop that!"

His tunic hung loose across his powerful back as he hefted up armfuls of free-hanging vines, yanked and tossed aside leaves, destroying the plants' springtime efforts. Then as I looked at the ground around his feet, what I saw nearly choked me with anger—perfectly formed little buds lay scattered around his dirty boots like debris. I grabbed his arm and yanked. "Stop. Stop this! What are you doing?"

He straightened, eyeing me. "Surely you've witnessed pruning before."

"Nothing as brutal as this. You are ruining our vines."

His hand glossed through his dark curls, pausing at the back of his neck. "That's already been done. I'm merely trying to repair the damage so we can give what's left a chance."

"By pulling perfectly good clusters that have just begun to form? You'll kill the plants if you prune them this way, especially before winter dormancy. Surely you know that."

His eyes met mine and a shadow passed over them.

Suspicion curled in me. "You're not here to improve the vineyard, are you? Father never hired you. What are your intentions, exactly?"

"I told you. I'm here for money. It's what draws most men from their beds in the morning, is it not?" He turned to the nearly bare plant and with deft hands plucked clusters of leaves from what remained, leaving a path of thinned-out vegetation in his wake. Each snap of new leaf shoot made me cringe, as if the man broke the very heartstrings of my father.

Seething inside, I controlled my words so they rolled out of tight lips. "I urge you to consider what you're doing. You will be charged for all the damage you cause."

Tossing down another handful of leaves, he turned to me and swiped his hand across his moist forehead. "We cannot wait for the vines to go dormant months from now or you'll have no crop this season. These vines are far too full of useless shoots to nourish the grapes."

What an arrogant man. "How little you know about vine dressing. The grapes are in their infancy, and they have plenty of time to grow."

"But they won't."

"Did they tell you that?" The drying dirt on my hands began to itch. "I do hope you move on before the constable lays fines on you that are too great for your meager purse."

He paused and stared at the sun behind me. "I believe you have company."

"What sort of response is that?"

"A truthful one." He nodded toward the house.

I spun to see a small black carriage rumble across the red drawbridge toward our house, horse hooves pounding the faded wood.

Company. Neighbors paying respects, most likely. But the single-horse carriage looked shabby, and desperately in need of a new coat of paint and a polish. None of our acquaintances would own such a vehicle, and none of the local villagers would own a carriage at all.

"I suggest you leave me to my work," said Mr. Vance as he paused to brush dirt from his hands, "and go tend to yours."

Lucy's words about treasure hunters rang a warning through my head. Helplessly pulled in two directions, I let out a sigh and sprinted toward Trevelyan. Past the rows of vineyards and up toward the house my legs pumped until I reached the back door.

I raced through the kitchen toward the courtyard, but Cook blocked my exit, hands on her abundant hips. "We need meat. The butcher has refused my market orders until his notes are paid, but your mother is demanding all this fine food for your Mr. Carrington. And now you have more guests."

"Have you enough for dinner tonight?"

What a mess this hidden fortune was making of everything. Had we truly fallen so far behind on payments in the short time since Father's demise?

She grimaced, nose twitching. "One last meal. Two with no guests."

"Serve what we have and we'll see to everything later." I held my poise on the outside, but fear and anxiety swarmed just below the surface. Only a fortnight Father had been gone, and already the damage had been great. *God, won't you help us? You wouldn't let a whole household starve, would you?*

I strode toward the front of the house and out a side door to the courtyard to assess the visitors, hoping they would not wish to stay. If the butcher had stopped serving us, the other vendors wouldn't be far behind.

Who were these guests, anyway? Slipping behind the roses that climbed the courtyard wall, I glanced about the open yard but saw no one. I breathed in the gentle perfume of flowers and leaned into the tangle of foliage, craning my neck for a closer look. Who on earth would—

"Hello there, little one."

I jumped at a voice nearby. A familiar-looking man in a bowler hat and faded suit peeked through an adjacent archway against which he lounged, watching me snoop. His jaunty smile said he enjoyed my shock. "Fancy that, you're woolgathering outdoors. Still your favorite pastime, I imagine."

"Cousin Neville!" The years dropped away and I was a child again. He had been my companion in many long summer months when Mother had insisted on visiting her family in town. My lively chum had almost replaced the vibrant hues of nature I'd had to leave behind. I flew to him with the abandon of youthful affection and threw my arms about him. "Oh, you've no idea how happy I am that you're here."

"Surprised to see me, little Tressa?"

"Delightfully so." How many years had it been, ten? Mother's family had distanced themselves from us over the years as their decreasing fortunes widened the chasm between us. This was especially the case with this only offspring of her brother, who was firmly planted in the working class as a junior clerk. "Have you driven all the way here from Kettering?"

"Of course I have." He pushed me back and held me by the shoulders, inspecting me as an older brother might. "You look well. But the question is, are you as well as you seem?" His words warmed my battered heart, breathing a little life into me.

"One is never well after losing a most beloved father." My shoulders trembled against my will beneath his grasp. "I'm glad you've come, though."

Behind Neville the carriage jostled and a large purple feather emerged, followed by the pert-nosed, stylish little woman who wore it. The lad perched on the driver's seat leaped down to assist her.

"You've brought your wife." My joy was briefly punctured by the arrival of this stranger who would witness my daily grief.

The newest visitor gazed about the exterior of my home with the sharp intelligence of one who had seen much of the world and had a great many opinions on it.

A grin lit Neville's face, which was clean-shaven below the mustache. "I couldn't well leave the little woman behind if I plan to stay any length of time."

"And what length of time might that be?" I dearly wanted my cousin to remain, but I wasn't certain about this ill-fitting woman he'd brought. I turned back to his eager face.

"Well, the respectable amount for a grieving nephew, of course. Which I expect will be plenty long." He tipped his head and winked. "It's been so long since I last saw you that all I remember is a little girl fiercely attached to some big dreams."

"Which is the making of a visionary." Neville's wife, a young woman with neatly arranged black hair and the poise of an elegant parlor chair, clicked up to the courtyard with quick, purposeful steps and summed me up in one keen glance. "I'm glad to find someone of like mind in this place. I was afraid I should find only provincial minds and antiquated ideas out here in the country."

I raised my eyebrows, wondering what thoughts I'd conveyed that led her to believe I was not those things.

She smiled and thrust a gloved hand toward me. "Ellen Langford. I've heard absolutely nothing about you, which is perfect. My opinions of you are a fresh slate ready for you to fill."

I pinched back a smile and took her fingertips for a brief touch, then released them. "How kind of you to journey into our remote little part of the world."

"But of course." She smiled as if we understood one another, but no one had ever felt more foreign. Our provincial country estate was, to me, more real than the big city where man-made creations rose and crumbled in a vain effort to overtake what God had made. Here, nature ruled supreme in bountiful, unrestrained richness.

She slid one arm behind my back and cinched me close as if we were sisters, leading me toward the doorway. "No man could provide the comfort a woman needs as well as another woman. I make sacrifices where I must."

We stepped into the dark hall lit only with the glow of overhead candles, and there Ellen stopped, her arm tensing about me. "Neville, it's like a medieval castle." Disdain leaked into her terse words.

"Ah, it's good to know your eyes still work, my dear."

"Did you know it would be like this?"

"Much as I can see through walls, dearest."

Such was my introduction to the newest members of our household, for it seemed they had come to roost upon Trevelyan.

Just then the door creaked open and Margaret peeked in. "Miss Tressa? You're wanted outside. Mr. Vance wishes to speak with you."

"Tell him I'll be along as soon as I've seen to our guests."

But the dear housekeeper's face puckered with worry, her hands wringing under her apron. "You won't want to keep him waiting, miss. He has a man by the shirt."

Weeds are merely misunderstood plants whose use the gardener has yet to uncover.

—*Notebook of a viticulturist*

Donegan Vance lunged for the man when he darted, catching him by the collar and dragging him back with a scramble of boots on loose rock.

"Mercy, Mister. Have mercy." The skinny intruder trembled in his oversized rags, his face paling under the sheen of dirt that covered his sun-scorched features.

"I haven't called the constable yet, have I? That's plenty of mercy." He had no plans to hurt the young man, but he had no patience for lazy workers and even less for those who stole instead of working. They denigrated everything he'd tried to do for underpaid laborers working an honest day. He wouldn't release him to continue pilfering, yet he couldn't bear to call the constable and see the man deported or hanged. Therefore, he'd leave it up to Tressa Harlowe, who was the one wronged. Part of him was desperately curious to see what that little slip of a girl would choose.

The sun bore down on the exposed soil in the fields, drawing an earthy smell into the atmosphere, as the slim little figure in gray swept out to pass judgment on the poor wretch now in his grasp.

Donegan shoved his prisoner toward her. "It seems you have a poacher."

"I see." She considered him with a look that revealed nothing. "To whom do you belong?"

His dark squirrel-like eyes darted about, flashing onto Donegan and back to the girl. "I'd rather not say." Donegan gave him a jerk again and the man's feet swished against loose rocks. He whimpered. "Old John Dowell is me father, but I'm me own man now. Clinton Dowell."

"What did your father do, Mr. Dowell? What's his trade?"

He gulped, tugging on the shirt that hung loose about his neck, and said, "Drink. Kicked me out years ago when I tried to sober him. Don't belong to no one now." Pity smote Donegan's wrath and his hold on the man's shirt loosened.

Tressa's lashes fluttered against pink cheeks as she absorbed those words, then her steady voice softened. "What were you attempting to poach from my land, sir?"

"Just a pheasant. There are so many of them and your woods are vast."

Amusement sparkled over her downcast features. "I see. And did you catch one?"

"Yes, miss."

Donegan glared at him and the lad cringed. "Three, actually. Please, don't call the constable."

"Three. How wonderful." She strode forward to stand before the poacher, arms folded across her chest, and inspected him with those glittering green eyes of hers. Like a queen she was, approaching a subject begging for mercy with no amount of indecision. Although her face revealed nothing of what that decision entailed.

The vagrant shifted back toward Donegan at her approach. The man's tattered clothing had an aura of trapped moisture and soil, marks of a drifter living outdoors—the sort who lived off what he could pilfer from other people along the way.

"Well, then." Tressa's delicate face glowed with composure as she faced the man, and Donegan held his breath in anticipation of the coming decision. "In punishment for your offense, you will work for this estate."

Shock rippled over Donegan. Now that was one answer he hadn't predicted. She kept doing that—yanking the rug out from under his expectations. He shifted and studied her face, so fresh and lively, glowing with keen intelligence, and wondered what sort of creature this was. Maybe mad, perhaps brilliant, but definitely unexpected. Wonderfully so. Her judgment was an interesting blend of mercy and resourcefulness that impressed him greatly.

"I have need of fresh meat, and it seems you are able to catch it for me. Do you also fish?"

Hope lifted the ragged man's chin and his bleary eyes looked at her with a flare of optimism. "All the time. All I need is a knife and a net."

"Will a space in our barn suit you for sleeping quarters? I cannot pay you, but I'll offer you food and lodging, if that will suffice, as well as honest work."

He merely stared in response, then bobbed his shaggy head. Moisture glistened in his eyes.

She offered a smile. "Well then, welcome to Trevelyan. Now you belong somewhere. Mr. Vance, please allow him to fetch his poultry bag so he may work. Then I'll have John show him to the barn."

Donegan simply stared at her, but he moved aside so the lad could scamper toward the woods and his bag. "You want him working for you?" The words came out with gravelly disbelief. He hardly knew what to think.

She lifted her chin. "At times, circumstances compel one to become creative."

"Be careful. He may not be what he seems. He might be—"

"A scrawny bird with airs?" Her rosebud lips tipped up at the corners as her soft-spoken jab once again unsettled him in a pleasant way, enchanting him nearly against his will. "Let's give him a chance and see what he does with it."

"You've released him now. He may scamper off into the woods and—"

"And what, continue to starve? Perhaps it's a risk, but I'm willing to take it. You see, I've just asked God for help in providing for my family, and I'm not about to go wasting his solution."

Yet another surprise that jolted him. What wealthy person had ever spoken so frankly about talking to God? Most of the ones he'd encountered merely seemed to politely acknowledge God on Sundays and at sewing meetings, without having much reason to actually converse with him.

"Ah, look who's coming over the hill—our scrawny bird, eager to work for his living."

Donegan pivoted to see the lad loping back up the hill from the woods with a purposeful stride, sack flung over one shoulder.

"You jump to an awful lot of conclusions, Mr. Vance."

He gulped. How true were her words.

Donegan turned once again to face the heiress he had planned to disdain when he arrived, yet the bright green eyes staring back at him began to melt the hard rock of dislike he felt for ladies such as her into something akin to admiration. She was wealthy and privileged, aristocratic in bearing and probably quite accomplished—everything a man of breeding would require in a woman. Yet he found himself growing to like the girl in spite of all that.

Dinner found us seated around the table with our guests, who were swiftly becoming acquainted with one another. Thanks to Clinton Dowell, we'd been saved the embarrassment of serving our guests stew, a meal so obviously made to stretch for days. His ill-gotten pheasants graced our table, with more to come.

Afterward we moved into the gallery and Mother retired to her bedchamber. I wished I could also make my escape. Yet when Neville and Andrew took themselves off to tour the gun cabinets, I found myself alone with my cousin's wife, whose very nature exuded opinions even if she did not speak them. Upon closer inspection, it was clear that her neat and trim dinner gown was merely cheap fabric expertly tailored to mimic the attire she likely could not afford.

The enticing draw of the treasure hunt beckoned me, yet politeness kept me firmly rooted in the room with my guest. I stood by the pianoforte in awkward silence, but she immediately filled the space with words.

"How well appointed this house is. Not at all what I expected when we first arrived." Ellen lingered near Mother's harp and ran a fingertip over it. "A bit dreary, perhaps, but there's an unmistakable air of magnificence and wealth." She spoke the last words tenderly as if savoring the name of a lost love.

"I've never loved any place half as much. Perhaps more for what it represents to me than the grandness of it." I tolerated our trips abroad, but every sweet and precious moment in my life had occurred upon this estate.

"But of course." She smiled across the room with perfect pink lips. "You are surrounded by endless possibilities. You may marry who you wish, or no one at all. Why, you are the master of your own fate, over any man. How delighted you must be."

"I believe that you and I are far more different than you've come to believe. I've never aspired to have any sort of power over a man."

She turned to face me as high emotion swirled behind her face and pinked her cheeks. "It's never about having power over a man, Miss Harlowe, but over our own lives, rather than giving it to a man. It's a luxury afforded to so few of us."

After nearly a half hour of such conversation, I excused myself under the guise of checking on Mother. I pondered Ellen's words as I slipped through the halls and glanced about at the cavernous rooms that had always been my home. Is that what its emptiness represented—freedom? How odd that it was the last thing I wanted, yet I seemed to have it in abundance. I was free of close attachments, drifting about an open sea, hoping desperately to connect to something or someone in a meaningful way.

I climbed the stairs and peeked into Mother's room. Dr.

Caine bent over her grand bed where the heavy velvet drapes were tied back. He turned at the sound of my entry and his face creased into a pleasant smile. "Miss Harlowe. Your mother was just telling me what a comfort you have been to her."

"Is she worse, Doctor?" Her slender form looked so insignificant in the large blue-and-gold tower room that rose to a grand cherub-painted dome at the top.

"Just a bit overtired from the visitors. Perhaps there should be fewer guests about for—"

Mother's quick hand on his arm arrested his words. "No, please. Don't send them away."

He patted her hand. "Of course. You should have people around you for now, until you feel safe. Those rumors about his death—"

Panicked, I caught the man's eye and interjected, "Are perfectly meaningless, yes? Of course they are." I swooped to her bedside and fluffed the pillow behind her.

He hesitated and Mother stiffened, drawing her crisp sheets up toward her chin. "What rumors?"

"Oh, they're just rumors passing around the staff. Nothing to them, really." The man had unwittingly walked into dangerous territory and now I'd have to sweep up his mess all night if Mother persisted in knowing more. A day did not exist when she simply accepted what happened to her without seeing a sign somewhere. "It's time you slept, Mother. It seems our visitors have settled in for a long stay, and you'll need your strength."

Her eyes flicked between us nervously, her face smoothing a bit when she'd held my gaze for a moment. "Rest. Yes, rest will be good. How thankful I am for you, Tressa. You always seem to know what I need."

"You have a fine daughter, Mistress Harlowe. Good day now, ladies." Lifting his bag, Dr. Caine strode out of the room.

I turned to escort the doctor out and ask more questions in the privacy of the hall, but Mother's hand held tight to mine.

"Stay with me, Daughter." The slender fingers contained surprising strength as they clamped over mine. "Are the rumors dreadful? What are they saying?"

I sank onto the edge of the bed. The woman took hold of every ghostly tale and rumor as truth, as one might latch on to the characters in a novel enough to light a candle for them in church. "Nothing you need to worry over."

She fumbled with her throw. "There's something odd about Josiah's death though, isn't there? I've heard whispering since we've returned, but no one tells me anything."

I sighed. She'd have to know sometime. "Mother, we did not miss the funeral because of our journey. There has been no funeral. Father did not die as one might have expected."

"Whatever does that mean?"

"They say he's drowned, but they only found his boat."

Her red-rimmed eyes stared at me. "They did not find him?"

I stiffened as her mind seemed to fly to the same conclusion that had lighted on mine the night before, but she did not find the remotest bit of joy in it. "You need warm milk." I slithered my hand from her grip. "I'll have Margaret fetch it and that'll put you right to sleep."

Without waiting for an argument, for there surely would be one if I gave her half a chance, I darted out the door and down the narrow hall. I glanced about for Dr. Caine, but the dark space echoed only with my own footfalls. Somehow the doctor had already disappeared. Emitting a deep exhale to match my feelings, I continued toward the stairs.

Yet Father's opened study on the second floor beckoned to me, tempting me with the sight of his notebooks neatly shelved behind his desk. Slipping into the cozy room of heavy furniture and an oversized fireplace, I pulled down one of the narrow volumes, preparing to hear Father's voice through his written words. But when I opened the book at random, the hard, angular writing on those worn pages was utterly foreign. How could I have forgotten?

Everything, all the deep thoughts and secrets of the vineyard, was recorded in Welsh.

Maybe I'd show them to Neville and see if he could make sense of the foreign lines. Perhaps we could return to the easy childhood camaraderie that had filled my days and my heart for a few brief weeks every year.

The sound of my name spoken in muffled conversation below drew me toward the peep, the skinny slit overlooking the drawing room that had been the haunt of my childhood. I hung back out of view while the voices below floated up.

Neville's voice came first. "You act as if you resent our being here to grieve my uncle."

"No, I resent you being here to fortune hunt." This came on the clipped voice of Andrew.

"Well, why dance around it? That's why you've come, isn't it? Because of the stories, the promise of hidden fortune."

"I'm sure your purpose here is far nobler."

My tender heart crumbled at the near-admission that came on the familiar voice of my childhood playmate. *Would you take even this balm of comfort from me, God?*

"That's no business of yours."

"Well, at least we've established why we're all here." Ellen's voice rolled over the tense words. "But Neville and I are the only ones entitled to it."

I'd been uncertain of how to label this woman who had swept into my home with her modern notions and quick approval of me, but these words firmly settled her into her proper position, further chilling my lonely heart.

"How can you be so vulgar?" This from Andrew, bless his heart. "The only one deserving of the fortune is the owner's heir, Tressa Harlowe. Or have you forgotten the man had a wife and daughter?" I could have cheered at the bite in his well-placed words.

"The money was never his to begin with." Ellen's voice came sharp and clear. "Has no one ever told you how the great Josiah Harlowe came by his fortune? It was because of Neville's father, Roger Langford. They were business partners years ago, and Uncle Josiah used Roger's money to invest in the mine that made him wealthy. Only he never repaid him. That's why the fortune was kept a secret—because it wasn't truly his to begin with. It was Neville's father's, and now it should be ours."

"You'll have a hard time proving any of that. I should tell Harlowe's widow what you're doing and see how quickly she sends you packing."

"Well, no one will have it if it's not found." Neville's careful voice carried up to me. "I suppose the only way to handle it is to work together. I'm sure we each have a piece of the puzzle, things we knew or heard from Uncle Josiah that would help us figure this out. Perhaps if we work together and share—"

"We will share *nothing*." Ellen spat out the words.

"Pardon my wife. What she means is—"

"I'll not listen to another word of this nonsense." Andrew's voice again rose above the others. "It'd serve you right if you left here penniless and disgraced, you miserable vultures." He stalked from the room and slammed the door, the impact of it vibrating the wall I leaned against.

Heartache threatened to engulf me. Why was I so surprised, though? The rumors of Father's hidden fortune had slipped into the background of our local life, but it seemed his death had brought them back to the surface and made fortune hunters out of everyone—even my dear cousin.

Ellen's low voice chilled the air in the room they now had to themselves. "Have you lost your senses? Are you truly suggesting we divide up the fortune that rightfully belongs to us?"

"We'll never find it without help, especially from Tressa."

"Tressa has less need of it than anyone. She has no debts or obligations. Soon she'll marry a wealthy gentleman and the fortune will be a mere afterthought to her. But if we lose out on that money . . ." Her voice tightened. "I cannot return to the Savoy."

The theater? She'd come from the theater?

Her panicked voice sped up and she clutched her throat. "I cannot go back, Neville. I cannot. Cannot. *Cannot*—"

"Don't trouble yourself, dearest. Let her help find it. Let them all help." Neville spoke with eerie calm. And then came the words that lit a string of goosebumps along my bare arms. "In the end it isn't about who finds it, but who wants it most."

I flattened my back against the wall. Suddenly I found myself in the most dangerous place I could be—directly between greedy people and the thing they wanted most.

8

It matters a great deal which vine a branch clings to,
for out of that vine flows the branch's source of life.

—Notebook of a viticulturist

Andrew, wait." I flew down the stairs toward him as he left the drawing room, for he seemed to be my only ally. I tripped over the rug at the bottom and stumbled. Landing with a soft thump against his chest, I instantly drew back and looked up into his shadowed face, tucking a loosened chunk of hair behind my ear.

"What is it? What's wrong?"

"I have to find my father's fortune." Panic tightened around me. "There are so many people about who want it, and I cannot risk losing it to them. I must figure out where it is, and I need to find someone who speaks Welsh, and—"

"Of course," he murmured as my voice trailed into utter despair. "Of course I'll help you." Pulling me close in a motion so familiar to me, his fingertips traced little patterns on my back between my shoulder blades. "I will always help you."

The soft voice pulled at my mind like quicksand. I pushed away to still the storm of feelings. The cool air that rushed between us tempered my thoughts and stilled my heart.

"I'm afraid you've read too much into my display just then. I should never have—"

"Yes, you should. I'm the one person you should be able to come to."

I placed a hand squarely on his chest, stiffening the arm that held us apart. "Perhaps that isn't the best idea, Andrew. Mr. Carrington."

Emotion pinched his features. "Don't call me that. Tell me what you need, Tressa."

"Do you speak Welsh? That's what I need most right now."

"What about Latin or French? I speak both of those fluently."

Steps thudded against the rug in the drawing room, then clicked onto the wood, and Andrew stiffened, glancing at the door. "Quick, back to your chamber. We'll speak later." He gripped both my arms and studied me with a potent look. "This is not over."

Turning, he leaped up the steps two at a time and disappeared around the bend at the top. The drawing room door opened and I slipped around the corner into a dark hall and flattened my back against the wall.

As I let out a breath, I became strongly aware of someone sharing the dark hall with me. A nearby shuffle, a low breath, the whoosh of movement. Eyes wide and searching, I waited.

A deep male voice rolled through the darkness. "I speak Welsh."

I gasped, prepared to scream. A hand came to rest gently, firmly over my mouth, and it tasted of the outdoors and the sticky sweetness of vine sap.

Keeping his hand in place, the interloper moved into the slant of light from the other room. It was Donegan Vance, of course, lurking about in the shadows of my home, as he always seemed to do. The man had the uncanny ability to be everywhere, even where he was not wanted. Which, in my mind, was most places on this estate.

Lowering his hand, he watched me. "Best not to alarm the household, but I thought you should know. I speak Welsh."

"What are you doing here?" I hissed out the words.

"Looking for you. It's time we spoke honestly."

"I do believe at least one of us has been doing that from the start."

"Certainly you do not refer to yourself, the girl who led me to believe she was a servant upon my arrival."

"You cannot blame me for your own hasty judgments." At his pointed look, I bit my lip and glanced away. "You happened upon me in a trying moment when I did not wish to discuss anything personal. Especially where it concerned being my father's daughter."

His voice softened. "All right, then. This time I want the truth. Why can't you pay the workers? What keeps such a wealthy family from providing the barest necessities to those who serve the household?"

"Obviously you've overheard the answer." I indicated the hall where Andrew and I had been talking.

He frowned. "You claim the rumors are true, then. Your father hid his fortune—even from his own family."

My jaw twitched. "It is so." Not only would he force me to

unveil every bit of exclusive knowledge I had on the subject, but he'd ridicule my answers as well.

"I don't believe a word of it. What sort of fool in this modern world hides his money?"

"The kind who tended his vineyards in a velvet smoking jacket and took soil samples with silver forks. I promise you the money is hidden and we have hardly a farthing to our names otherwise." We'd traveled about the country and even abroad, needing little more than our name as currency, and Father paid the notes as they came.

His dark, ominous gaze arrested mine and held it there in the dim moonlight. "Something odd is happening here. I will uncover it, so you'd best tell me straight out."

I wrenched my gaze from his face. "Before you were offering to help me find it, and now you don't even believe it exists."

"My offer remains. Perhaps it'll help me learn the truth. What do you need to read in Welsh?"

I hesitated. "My father's notebooks. All his notes on vineyards and grapes."

He raised one dark eyebrow. "Fascinating. I'll make a trade."

"What sort of trade?" Surely he wouldn't ask for immediate payment when he knew I had no funds.

"I'll work on translating the notebooks in the evenings if you'll work beside me in the vineyards. And not just as an observer as you've already offered, but as a worker, dirtying your hands."

I looked up at him through narrowed eyes. "You're mad. Why ever would you want such a thing?"

"Perhaps I enjoy your company." He shrugged, a smile

turning up his lips. "You are the first person to ever claim that field work is an art."

I narrowed my eyes. "You wish to humble me."

"If you find it so detestable an arrangement, I'll settle for 10 percent of the fortune."

I flattened my shoulder blades against the wall behind me. "You are merely here for money too, aren't you?"

"That's the reason anyone labors for anyone else."

"There's more to it than that, isn't there?"

A muscle pulsed in his jaw as he glanced away, and his silence told me more than any words could say.

It always amazes me what can be hidden beneath a grape's translucent skin. You cannot know for certain if a grape is as ripe and sweet as it looks until you have tasted it.

—*Notebook of a viticulturist*

What a foolish move, forcing a lady to work in a vineyard. Donegan threw down the end of the spade over and over the next morning with all the strength of his frustration. It seemed that his liking of her was directly proportional to her *dis*like of him. As his admiration rose, hers vanished with no effort on his part. Yet she lingered in the peripheral vision of his thoughts like the tart aroma of immature grapes that now surrounded him.

What she'd said about vineyards as an art form had especially remained in his mind, for no one else had ever put into words what he thought about his work. It was as if she spoke the same language as he, but she spoke it more fluently and gracefully than he ever could. Different as she was from himself, something about her resonated deeply with him, and the draw to her only grew with each encounter.

Yet she had made her position quite clear—she could not stand him. It would serve as a supreme torture to have her around all the time, especially with her distaste for him radiating off her very being.

Right now, though, the only task that mattered was proving to her that he had no intention of ruining her family's vineyard. Although why she felt such a personal tie to what most would deem a mere crop he couldn't fathom. It was another intriguing aspect to this princess of the castle.

"What do you know about the girl?" He tossed the question casually to the ragged youth hacking at the weeds one row away.

"The girl? You mean Miss Harlowe?" Tom stood and smeared his bare forearm across his forehead. "A nice sort, I've heard. Not that any of us speak with her."

"She doesn't associate with the laborers?"

"Wouldn't be proper now, would it?" Tom's silly grin stretched his narrow face.

"Hmm." With a breath, Donegan allowed that revelation to sink in, to churn his heart and destroy the infatuation he'd developed, but it failed. The words circled his brain, but before they could take root, they simply disintegrated and fell away.

In their place, the weight of a vague conviction settled over him, starting as a gentle pressure and then increasing to a substantial heaviness about his shoulders. Instantly he recognized the sensation, but this time it confused him. It was the weight of responsibility and calling. Toward her.

God wanted him to help *her*?

The burden settled firmly on his shoulders that were already sore from work. He stretched them and frowned at the sun high in the sky. Countless numbers of poor and struggling people had received his help as God had convicted him, but why her?

I am but a working man. What could a servant offer the master?

When he looked up from that thought, her regal figure strode toward him, the lift of her chin telling him she came somewhat unwillingly. Sea breezes lifted the fringe of tendrils around her face, softening the hostility that hardened her features. Her plain gown hung in the perfect lines that spoke of costly fabric, even for a work dress. Yet in addition to the expensive clothing, she also wore that same desperate, plaintive expression beneath the thin veneer of self-reliance. Whether she wore the ragged cloak in which he'd first seen her or this costly dress befitting her wealth, there was the same poverty in her spirit that had touched him before.

"I've brought one of the notebooks." I clutched the volume in the vineyard's midday heat as Donegan paused to wipe his brow and study me with unreadable thoughts in his deep brown eyes. I held the precious book to my chest for the barest moment longer before extending it to him. Perhaps I shouldn't do this. Who knew what the man might do with the information? If only I knew someone else who could read Welsh.

"It'll be a nice evening diversion when my work is done."

He accepted the book and tossed it into a wooden wheelbarrow, where it broke up loose dirt chunks.

I cringed but set my jaw. I needed this man's help if I had any hope of tapping into this hidden piece of my father. With all the treasure hunters about, these notebooks were the only advantage I might possess.

Finally he paused to fully look at me, an internal battle of some sort playing across his chiseled features. "I wish to help." The statement came out in one quick breath and was followed by a brief silence. "You need help finding this fortune, and I wish to help in the search."

I frowned. "For what purpose?"

This question clearly caught him off guard, drawing his brows together and causing his weight to shift. "What does it matter?"

"Your motives matter a great deal, Mr. Vance."

He heaved a sigh, cupping the back of his neck. "If nothing else, maybe it'll rid you of this fool notion that I'm out to ruin your vineyard."

"Or convince me you're only here to hunt for gold."

After a moment of hesitation, he lowered his hand and beckoned me deeper into the rows of winding greenery. "Come. I want to teach you something."

The man's arrogance really was trying. "Do you not think the daughter of a viticulturist would know vineyards better than almost anyone else?"

"Yes, I would." His mouth jerked up at the corner with a trace of humor. "It'll only take a moment. You did agree to help in the vineyard."

I studied him, this odd man who had appeared from thin air with unclear motives and all the manners of a bull. Had

I agreed? As I remembered it, I had yet to decide between his two options. I followed along the row as the scruffy workers looked on.

"The most important part of the vineyard is the sap, its life source. It is to the vine what blood is to humans." He knelt before a plant, his knee sinking into the soil as he traced a fingertip along the vine from the root base and up the rough bark to the branches. "That sap travels up from the roots and the vine pushes it out to every branch and leaf, every morsel of fruit. See how many paths it has to take, and how much plant it must fill?"

"I understand the concept of pruning."

"Your vines need far more pruning than they've had." He pushed against the ground and rose. "That's what I was doing the other day."

"My father has turned out many successful harvests without pruning them bare."

"And this vineyard's about to experience its last few, unless someone removes much more. For years the grapes have grown lush and healthy by sucking the life out of the branches. See how weak they are?" He flexed one branch with a single finger. "If you continue to allow this many grapes and shoots on your branches, they'll all be withered and dead before long. This year's grapes are already suffering because there isn't enough sap to go around."

I stepped back, watching him. "These are all just the theories of an amateur."

"As are any ideas you have to the contrary, but what does that matter? It's like they say about the two vessels—what's the difference between the *Tayleur* and the ark from Scripture?"

"The *Tayleur*? You mean the cruise liner that sank?"

"Yes. The only difference is the failed *Tayleur* was built by professionals and the ark by an amateur."

"So how do you plan to make it up to us if your theories, amateur or professional, fail like the *Tayleur* and our crop is ruined?"

"It can't be any more ruined than it already is." He brushed off his hands and turned back to the vines. "If nothing else, you've gotten everything out of me that you've paid for. Now, if you want to make yourself useful, start pinching off leaves. They should be spaced several inches apart. I assume you're not opposed to a simple springtime pruning of shoots."

Clamping my mouth closed on what I wished to say, what politeness dictated I not say, I merely smiled and said, "Thank you for the lesson on vineyards. I'll look forward to receiving your translation of the notebook." As I knelt in the dirt, I hesitated, then looked up. "I do hope I can count on you to keep the contents of the notebook . . ."

"Of course."

I turned to my task and he strode farther down the row. A fine mess I'd created for myself with this partnership. But had I any other choice?

Later, when I'd stretched my stiff back and wandered into the house, voices carried through the nearly closed door of the small front parlor. I spun at a tap on my shoulder just outside the door.

Margaret stood behind me with a round-shouldered posture of concern. "The greengrocer came to the door, miss. It gave your mother such an upset that we had to placate her with false assurances. But the truth is, they'll not give us supplies anymore without pay up front. We're counting our blessings that they haven't called in the past debt yet."

"You were right to bring it to me, Margaret." I bit my lip and glanced about the dim hall. "How much produce remains?"

"Enough for a few more meals for the guests and staff, but no fresh fruit."

"Tell Cook to scrimp where she can and that nothing is to be wasted. I'll think of something."

She nodded, but the tension that had pinched her face since our arrival did not relax. Making my escape past the open door and down the hall, Margaret's words swam around my mind. Perhaps I could sell something—but what, the furniture? I'd have to haul it to London to find a buyer for the ancient pieces, and besides, none of it was mine to sell. Calling it mine would mean admitting Father was dead, and I couldn't bear to do that. Hope felt too wonderful.

In my chamber, I leaned against the wall and shut my eyes. Everything depended upon me finding that fortune, and I had to do it alone. Everyone around me, even those supposedly here to support me, had the same goal. And only one of us could attain it.

Shoving aside the invading worry, I glanced about the room for empty space to paint, for I needed to brush off the dust of everyday life and steep myself in creative beauty. Only one blank canvas remained—the ceiling.

With the help of a houseboy, I arranged two ladders in the middle of my room and placed the cushioned lid of my window seat across them. They would have to find other ladders to light the chandeliers in the hall for a while. Setting my paint supplies on a ladder step, I climbed onto my perch and lay back with my hair tumbling down over the sides. I drew out a stroke of green paint and let the color trail across the white expanse of ceiling as my mind wandered in prayer. *God, this is a mess. A tangled mess like the vineyards. Can you not see how desperate this is becoming?*

The brief petition was uncomfortable and a bit frustrating, much like stretching a long-cramped muscle and realizing the severe disuse of it. Somehow I'd faded away from these conversational creative experiences, shelving God until the day I had need of him.

Now it seemed that day had come.

I need your help. We need a way to keep life going here at Trevelyan, and only you could accomplish such a miracle.

With each twirl of my brush, I thought over Donegan Vance's words about the importance of sap and pictured that gorgeous tapestry hidden away in the undercroft. The center of that vine had been filled with radiant gold. *The abundance is within.* Perhaps that was the vineyard's secret—the all-important sap.

But what did that mean? What exactly did the vineyard say about Father's fortune? I had to be overlooking something painfully obvious.

Won't you show me what it is, God?

10

> As I look over the vast vineyard my hands have cultivated, I think over the many small, repetitive, tedious tasks that, together, amounted in the glorious whole before me.
>
> —*Notebook of a viticulturist*

After a mostly quiet meal, we moved into the gallery, where Mother played the harp for the pleasure of her guests. Her long, slender fingers moved with grace over the strings.

Cousin Neville stood and clapped eagerly when Mother finished the song. "Wonderful. How talented you are, Aunt Gwendolyn." He cleared his throat and shot a glance toward his wife. "Now, I'd like to extend some news to you. I'm happy to tell you, Aunt, that we've decided to help you and Tressa."

I clutched the arm of the sofa.

Mother smiled, her lips pressed tight. "How kind of you."

"Yes." Ellen stepped forward, taking Mother's hand as if they were old chums and tucking it in the crook of her arm. "We're going to help you find Uncle Josiah's money so you don't have to worry about it, on top of all the grief you must be enduring." She guided her to a chair and helped her sit.

Mother turned to me with a watery look that said she was nearing the end of her strength. "I rather thought Tressa would find it by now. I suppose she'd appreciate your help, Ellen."

Not bothering to voice my opinion to the contrary, I merely stared at the abandoned harp, its polished surface glinting in the candlelight.

"I'm sure Miss Harlowe believes she doesn't need help," Andrew said in a low tone, "but she does. More than she realizes." His face, shadowed by the many candles lighting the room, stared at me, dark with hidden meaning.

"Unless the help costs her too much." I met his gaze with an equally weighty one of my own, thus answering his thinly veiled statement.

Ignorant of the subtle exchange, Neville unleashed a rolled-up drawing across the long table before Mother's chair and slid a vase over one curled edge to hold it in place. "I've begun a rough sketch of Trevelyan Castle's layout to aid in our search. Now, Aunt Gwendolyn, you know Trevelyan better than we do, so perhaps you can help us fill in any important pieces."

Mother blinked at the page, her wan face remaining smoothly impassive.

Ellen knelt in a poof of skirts between Mother and the

sketch. "It looks as though the walls on this side of the house are far thicker than on any other."

"That was merely to reinforce the castle. It's a well-known medieval building technique to prevent invaders." I leaned close to Mother and Ellen. "Unfortunately, it doesn't seem to work against modern ones."

Ellen lifted eyes of glittering cold steel to me, immediately labeling me her enemy without saying the words.

I continued softly, casually. "But you are more than welcome to begin digging into the stone walls if you wish." I smiled at her. "It's about four feet of rock, so you'd best bring tools. If you'll pardon us, I believe Mother needs to rest now." I slid between my kneeling cousin and her target, easing Mother up and guiding her toward the door. "I'm sure she'll address your questions another day."

When we had departed the room, Neville addressed his wife and traces of his voice carried out to us. "Can't you restrain yourself, woman? She'll tire of you before we've even been here a week."

"Stop treating me as the enemy, Neville. Sometimes I think you forget we're on the same team. Come, bring me the map."

Let the Langfords mark up their maps and poke into crevices. I would continue on my own path. Not one that sought to explore the house, but rather one pursuing intimate knowledge of the man who had hidden the fortune. Once the words of his notebooks were opened to me, I'd be rich in ideas.

In the hall, Mother sighed. "How desperately I was in need of a rescue, Daughter. I do hope you never marry and leave me. You'll simply have to drag Andrew here to live."

"You assume it is Andrew I will marry."

She paused and gripped the smooth walnut railing. "Why

wouldn't I?" She turned her poised face toward me. "Unless you are backing out of our plan."

"How can I back out when I never agreed to it in the first place?"

She laughed, releasing that breathy music with an oddly dismissive quality that had made me view her as a sort of queen in my younger days. "Perhaps I should send him to see you. It's time you spoke privately."

"I wish you wouldn't."

"Please, Daughter." She rested a slender hand on my arm. "It's the only way I have of protecting you. Of providing for you."

How vastly different we were. An entire valley of beliefs and values separated us, with no bridge to cross. We coexisted well and often functioned as a team, but we were two opposing beings who could never fully understand one another. It made me miss my simple vineyard-loving father all the more. "I'm not convinced we're that desperate yet, Mother."

When we reached her room, she sank into a chair by the window and closed her eyes. "I've given you a poor view of marriage, Daughter. For that I am regretful. How I wish my marriage could have been what it should."

I perched on a nearby chair and clenched my hands in my lap. "Father was not so terrible."

"Nor was he a delight." She sighed. "I'm sorry, Tressa. I know you held him in high esteem, but he did nothing but snuff the flame that I used to be. I was cut off from what makes me alive and left alone with a man who barely said two words on his best day."

"He adored you so."

"I adore this lovely hand mirror." Mother lifted a delicately carved silver mirror from the table and turned it over. "Yet I leave it sitting here most of its life and only pick it up for brief moments of time."

"I'd prefer a distant marriage to a difficult one. Think of poor Ellen, who already seems at odds with her husband. At least you did not have her marriage."

"Ellen is a different sort of woman, Tressa. It isn't so much the man she detests as marriage itself. While most of us naturally look to men for protection and support, Ellen sees it as bondage. She will never have a happy marriage, no matter which man she chose."

"Then why did she marry at all?"

"She believed it better than what she had, which was poverty and desperation. Neville has told me she was a gem among the rubbish of the theater, and he pulled her up and dusted her off, giving her a comfortable home and respectability. Yet she will never be happy while subject to a man, no matter the circumstances."

"Perhaps we have something in common after all, for I should never wish to give control of myself to anyone."

"You are not like her, Tressa. She thrives on living alone, making her own decisions, being her own resource. You're not the sort to delight in that life."

The truth of her words sank deep into my floundering heart that was desperate for connection.

"No, you will marry as I did, but hopefully your union will be different." She touched my shoulder. "Marriage is a woman's occupation, Tressa. Her method of support. Just as a man may choose the wrong trade, a woman may choose the wrong husband and find herself toiling in misery every day. Find the right one, however, and your life can be wonderfully rich." She sat forward and took my hand. "Right now you have more freedom than you know. Your power comes in choosing the man to whom you will give yourself, and that means everything."

"And Andrew is the wisest choice? Is that truly what you believe?"

"Look at all he's offering you. Beyond his fortune and rank, he makes a fine companion for my lively girl. He tolerates your quirks and enjoys your company. You could do far worse."

With those soft words humming through my mind as I hurried to my chamber later that night, I reached my room and shut the door against the world. It seemed so risky, throwing myself under the control of one person for the rest of my life. Yet what was the alternative, even for an heiress such as myself—lonely spinsterhood?

Daisy rose and scuttled across the floor to greet me, gladdening my heart. Here at last I was in the company of a faithful friend. "Come, girl. Let's sit and waste the evening gazing at the stars." But as I'd sunk into a chair near the window, a knock jolted through my calm. Daisy jumped down and ran to whimper and yip at the door.

I rose reluctantly and answered it. "Andrew." The man stood before me, seeming even taller when framed by the ornate arch of my doorway. He held a single daisy in his hand, and the sight of the small token tightened my insides. "Your errand is in vain, I'm afraid. I meant every word of my refusal. I'm sorry that Mother encouraged you." I backed into my room and started to shut the door, but in an instant he splayed his palm on the wooden surface to stop me.

"I'm not here to trouble you with my overtures. In fact, I didn't come up here to see you at all."

I raised my eyebrows, my hand still gripping the edge of the door.

"It's this daisy." He held up the single flower. "It seemed so lonely that I thought perhaps I should give it to a little dog with the same name." He threw a smiling glance toward Daisy, who sat at attention near my feet, dark eyes intent on the visitor. "Plain as it is, I find I can't resist its fresh white petals, its innocent charm, and . . ." his glance swept up to my face then, looking painfully lost, "the utter beauty of everything about it."

The evident despair in his features chipped at the edges of my resolve, but I would not let it go further. "Perhaps the poor daisy preferred to be left alone." I allowed my harsh words to slice through the thickness of the moment to keep my warring feelings at bay. It would be dangerous to give in to him, wouldn't it?

"It won't ever find out unless it experiences something else." A playful smile lifted the edges of his lips, charming the defenses out from under me. "A short walk for Daisy and me, with you to chaperone, of course." He offered his arm. "Come, I've something to tell you."

I hesitated. How easy it would be to fall into his delightful company and stave off the solitude of this night.

"Please, Tressa. Just a walk between friends. Bring your lady's maid if you like. I so long for your company, and I can see the same loneliness haunting your lovely face."

I looked back into my empty, shadowed room, my only other alternative for the night, and took his arm. "I suppose a turn about the gardens would be allowable. I'll find Lucy." What harm could a simple walk do, really?

He led me with long strides into the hall glowing with soft candlelight and toward the stairs. The sudden tensing of his arm at the sound of footsteps reminded me painfully of our youth, all those days pretending before others that we meant nothing to one another, despite the secret understanding between us. I should have known then that his love was only temporary when he felt the need to hide it so. I was thankful when Lucy joined us, even though she remained a few paces behind.

Once outside, awash in the cool, briny breeze of the Bristol Channel, we talked quietly and easily. A tentative friendship arose between us with traces of the old and flavors of something new as well.

Thus we ambled about, little Daisy pattering at our heels, and the experience nearly swallowed me in its beauty. But every time the moment threatened to engulf me, my thoughts returned to that tightening of his arm and the many times in the past we'd hidden from others to maintain his façade of obedience to his parents.

When Lucy fell asleep on a bench, we lost ourselves among moon-drenched foliage nearby and the memories of our youth. Unable to bear the weight of my hesitations, I turned to him and voiced my thought. "This does seem familiar, all this sneaking about."

His awkward laugh did nothing to set my heart at ease.

I sighed. "Nothing's changed, has it?"

He led me deep into the back garden, following the perfectly trimmed hedges to the fountain in the center. Moonlight lit the spray of water in the middle of the great stone piece. "If you refer to my feelings, surely you know the answer to that."

I slid my hand away from his arm and sat on the edge

of the huge fountain, leaning down to rub Daisy's head. "I mean the need to keep it secret. Your parents still do not approve of the match."

"It's this ridiculous peerage, and the lifestyle that accompanies it. My future is cared for like the crown jewels, but I'm hoping to convince them to change their mind in time."

"Why should your father's position affect your future, and your choice of a bride?"

He sat beside me on the fountain and took my hands. "It's the surprise I was hoping to share with you. You see, there's a position opening for me in Parliament, but only if I earn enough respect among the constituents to acquire the vote."

"And this constituency is . . ."

He heaved a sigh and dropped his gaze to our hands. "Mostly friends of Mother and Father. Stuffy overly pious types in Bristol society who aren't very accepting of ladies without an established heritage."

I fidgeted, tracing the edge of the stone base where we sat. "I suppose I should offer my congratulations. Bristol? I had no idea you planned to remain nearby permanently."

"I hope you'll say a great deal more when I ask you something else."

He shifted off the fountain edge to kneel before me and my chest tightened as he took both of my hands in his. Now that this moment, this blessed moment, had finally arrived, I feared it. Wanted it to be over. I looked past him toward the pink roses climbing a trellis and tried to breathe normally, willing him to ask a different question. He bowed his head, touching his smooth forehead to my clasped hands, then lifted his gaze to mine.

I looked into his earnest eyes and imagined the nature

of my life with this man, seeing it in fleeting images. It was warm and familiar and exciting all at the same time, vastly different than the emptiness I had now. Yet the past hurts lingered, tightening around my mind.

"You'd make a spectacular politician's wife." He traced my knuckles with one fingertip. "You're well spoken, gracious, and most of all, so utterly loyal. The way you maintained feelings for me in the face of . . . And your father—no one else would have put up with the man all these years, but you pursued him even when he ignored you time and again."

I licked my dry lips as I listened to this recital of my best traits, chief of which was that of an accomplished lackey of sorts to those I loved most. If I ever imagined a sweeping romantic speech leading up to this moment, the words now hanging in the air between us killed that.

"We can announce our engagement after I've secured the position, then think of what we can do together. With my ancient family name and your father's fortune, they'd love us and we will be unstoppable. And not just in Parliament, but—"

"Why would you need my father's fortune? Hasn't your family always had plenty of . . ."

My voice trailed off as his gaze dropped, hair falling in a boyish flop over his forehead.

"I see." And truly, I did. More than he knew.

"You know how Father is with his investments. Always these ingenious inventions that need money to back them and bring them to market."

And in that revelation, the dreamy night sputtered and died out into a heap of ashes, soon to be cold. I rose slowly, allowing this moment to burn itself into my mind and protect me from future temptation. Whatever he did or said, no matter how he charmed me in days to come, his efforts would always be tainted with the notion that he wanted my money. Perhaps he wasn't ready to give up on our romance, but he'd created a mammoth-sized wall to scale. "I believe it's past the hour of decency for Daisy to be out, and I should return her to the house."

I stepped toward Lucy to wake her, but he caught my hand and turned me toward him, his earnest face imploring. "Why are you so eager to label me a gold digger, Tressa? You know me. You know my affection for you. Plenty of other girls have fortunes, and I could marry any one of them if that's all I wanted, without all the hurdles and trouble of pursuing a girl who shuts me out." He swept up my hands and gently tugged me close. Closing his eyes, he bestowed the tenderest of kisses on my fingertips and laid his cheek on them. "I choose the trouble. The hurdles. Because I believe the fortune I'll find on the other side is worth the effort. And I don't mean the money."

My eyes fluttered closed as confusion burst through my heart and swirled about, tainting my firm decision with doubt. It always happened this way with Andrew. I decided against him, piling up my logical reasons, only to have him flood them away with his unexpected words that captivated and enticed, leaving the door of my heart cracked dangerously open, for in my loneliness I deeply wished what he offered.

As soon as I stepped away, reason returned to my poor mind. I looked at Andrew, this man who had once meant so much to me, and offered a polite smile. "Good night, Mr. Carrington. I thank you for the walk and hope we can always be friends."

"Of course." He smiled, the wan tip of his lips indicating he recognized defeat.

Perhaps now he would give up.

I roused Lucy and sent her back to her room. Leaving that encounter felt easy and surprisingly freeing, despite the fact that I walked away alone. Sometimes being in your own company fulfilled you more than sharing space with someone who intensified your aloneness with every word.

 11

Winter is deceptive because even when plants enter hibernation and appear dead, they are still working and preparing for the next season.

—*Notebook of a viticulturist*

Donegan dropped the blade of the oars into the murky water just off the shore and gave one more long pull with both handles, thrusting the bow of his boat into the wet sandy beach. With unease weighing on him, he rose and climbed onto the sand. He allowed himself one guilty backward glance toward the distant shore that held Trevelyan and wondered how Tressa fared.

Long strides carried him deep into that dark path through the forest, the way lit only by the moon glowing off the smooth stone border. Shivering against the chilly air, he lit his lantern and ran the remainder of the way to the hillside where a plateau held a perfect little cabin like a toy on its palm. Clenching his jaw, he climbed the steps and rapped on the door. He exhaled his impatience at the silence that followed and tried again, harder this time. The little windows shook with the power of his fist. He would not be ignored.

At last, a shadow crossed the nearest window and the door opened enough for a dim face to peer out. "Yes?"

"We need to talk."

The large, white-haired man inside hesitated, then opened the door for him to enter. "That was never part of the agreement."

"It has become part of it. I'll not continue in this bargain without a few explanations, especially why you are doing this to her." Donegan heaved the door shut behind him and strode deeper into the room. "She's become the target of all manner of possible treasure hunters, from wandering vagrants she hires as trappers to suitors and relations. She has a keen mind, but a soft heart that is in danger of overpowering it."

"So." The old man's shrewd eyes settled on Donegan's face as a smile tugged at his lips. "You've met my daughter, have you?" Shadows highlighted the cragginess of his features in the nearly dark room. He crossed the raftered kitchen and poured two cups of steaming liquid from the kettle already over the stove. "Tea, Mr. Vance?"

"I'm not interested in tea. I want answers." Donegan yanked out a chair and sat at the table, arms folded. "She needs money. Creditors are demanding pay, food is running out, and they have nothing save rumors of a hidden fortune. Tell me where it is so I may pretend to help her discover it."

"No." The man's massive paw clutched the little spoon and stirred before he lifted the cup to his mouth and sipped.

Donegan's gut clenched. "Have you any heart? You've left your family with nothing."

"I left them you."

"Then tell me where you hid it. Let me help them."

Silence billowed over the dim cabin for long moments where only a single oil lamp flickered. Then Harlowe spoke again. "How does the vineyard look to you?"

"Terrible."

"Salvageable?"

"Maybe." Donegan fingered the little cup. "I've torn out all the extra foliage and many of the failed grafts. I plan to dig a trench to—"

"*No.*" His massive hand banged the table's surface, rattling the cups in their saucers. "No. I want nothing changed." Tension stretched across his face. "Your only task in the vineyard is to perfect my soil composition and keep things running."

Donegan eyed his employer in the dancing lamplight. Only a threat to his vines elicited a strong reaction from him, it seemed. Pity for Tressa curled through Donegan as he looked at the damaged old man who was meant to be her protector.

No, *him*. She had him now too.

"Who's been to the house? I want names of everyone."

Donegan kneaded his forehead. "An older gentleman visited for a short time, and the servants called him Prescott, but I didn't catch the nature of his call."

"A greedy businessman. Who else?"

"A few family members, I believe. I'm not sure of their names, but one of them claimed you built your fortune on money borrowed from his father and never repaid."

He scowled. "I've done no such thing. I suppose if this

person believes me dead, there's no one to challenge his wild stories. Watch them. Anyone else?"

"A wandering vagrant named Clinton Dowell caught poaching in the woods."

Harlowe let out a low growl. "Who is this Dowell? Is he old or young?"

"Seems quite young. Skinny fellow who looks like he's lived in the woods for years."

"Has he asked about the fortune?"

"No, but everyone else is gossiping about it. Servants and guests and laborers. Everyone is speculating about where you hid it."

He looked down with a grunt and pondered something with great focus. "Has Tressa looked for the fortune?"

"She hardly knows where to start."

"But she's asking you for help? She trusts you?"

Donegan glanced down at the rough floor. "Not really. She's asked me to translate your notebooks so she can read them."

A string of unreadable emotions passed over Harlowe's face. "She wishes to read my notebooks? You must not let her."

"Why, did you write the location of the fortune in there?"

Harlowe stared into the tiny flame of the lamp. "There's more to my story than the fortune. Why does no one remember that?"

"I'm beginning to believe this fortune doesn't exist. That's the secret you do not wish her to discover from those notebooks, isn't it?" Donegan eyed the man hunched over his laughably small teacup.

He stared down into the liquid. "Fine, then. She can have the notebooks if she truly wants them."

"And the fortune?"

His jaw flinched. "Maybe. No."

Doubt wedged its way into Donegan's mind. Could this foolish old man have made up the whole thing? He narrowed his gaze at the silent mountain of a man with delicate lines of pride streaking across his aged face, and it all seemed plausible. "Tell me where it is, Harlowe. No more excuses. I'll be leading your family to the money or to you, take your pick."

"No." The great man rose and walked to the window, blocking the dying sunlight, and remained silent for several breaths. "If you tell them my secret, you'll get nothing. Absolutely nothing. I need more time."

"Then give me your reason."

He lifted his troubled eyes to Donegan. "Because I'm still not certain of who tried to kill me. As long as he thinks he's succeeded, we're safe."

"You're sure this killer believes you dead?"

"Truly, I should be. If not for a fisherman who happened to see me clinging to a remnant of my boat, I would have drowned as he intended."

"So when we first met in France—"

"None of this had happened yet." He sighed. "It was the fisherman who rescued me who gave me the idea to hide out for a bit, and his son delivered my offer to you. I needed someone to protect them and bring me food while I figured out who was behind it."

"Have you any suspicions? Is it because of your fortune?"

The aged face turned into the shadows in the characteristic move Donegan knew meant he would receive no answer.

Donegan rose and shoved the chair under the table. "All

right, I'll keep your secret a little longer. But at least let me give them a small portion of your fortune to tide them over."

"No." Pain shadowed his face. "That is all anyone ever wanted of me, and I'm tired of hearing about it."

Donegan hesitated at the door. "Why do you push her away?"

The man's jaw worked for a moment. "She married me for security. Not love. Don't make more of the marriage than what it is. I made that mistake for far too long."

"Not her. I mean Tressa."

He swung his heavy gaze to Donegan then, pain evident through the depths of his blue eyes. "Tell me, Mr. Vance. How soon after my death did she begin searching for my fortune? Did she grieve for even a day?"

"You left them with no money for provisions, no way to pay their workers. You left them nothing."

"Only if money is everything."

Donegan braced himself on the creaky second-story timber walkway on the courtyard wall and stared down the line of castle windows ahead. Hers was marked by the sheer curtains fluttering in the breeze, aptly matching her lovely feminine nature. He might have been able to recognize it as hers even if her lady's maid hadn't pointed it out to him. He strode across the rickety timbers, clutching the papers he sought to deliver, wondering if he was the only one to use this walkway in recent years.

It was not invading her privacy if she was not in the room, was it? He'd seen her slip out to the gardens with that dark-suited gentleman and her maid hours ago, and they hadn't yet returned.

Dropping through the window, he strode into the dim space belonging to the remarkable princess of the castle and looked around at what appeared to be the oddest wallpaper he'd ever seen. A glass lamp on a side table was the only light source. He knelt and heightened the wick, broadening the lamp's glow.

Rising, he blinked to adjust his eyes and froze, stunned. Awed. For there he stood in the midst of the grandest paradise ever created by human hands, and it washed his black-and-white, practical mind with flavor and beauty that he never realized he lacked until then. Vivid color and elegance had spilled out of the lively girl onto every bit of her chamber, with light being the most brilliant pigment in her palette as it covered every plain surface, crowding out any trace of blandness. What would it do to his mind, to his senses, to reside every day in the midst of this little haven that so refreshed him with a single glance?

There in the midst of her splendid creation, he was overwhelmed with a powerful desire to shield the girl from the unseen danger that lurked about, the cloaked killer who had attempted to strike down her father. He simply could not let that shadow of evil snuff out one who embodied such beauty. There was little enough of it in the world as it was.

Dropping the translated pages he'd brought on a linen-covered table, he spun in a slow circle to take it in, his worn work boots swiffing over the floor as he glimpsed the inner working of her imagination. Thoughts and impressions spilled about the canvas of her room as if she'd dipped her brush into her mind and spread them over the wall to see and analyze. How could this be the same girl who so craved her father's money? *"How soon after my death did she begin searching for my fortune?"*

Then his gaze struck upon a paper propped against a wall and he crossed the room to examine it. Lifting the wilted corner, he glimpsed the elaborate sketch of a face wrought with such delicate detail and emotion that he could nearly picture her passionate little face as she drew it. It was the face of Josiah Harlowe, transformed from the worn-out bear of a man he knew into a proud, legendary creature full of strength and nobility. Vines curled about the edges of the picture in artistic chaos, blending with his wild beard until they appeared to be one. Donegan lifted the page so it caught the glow of light on the other side of the room and simply absorbed the sight of this sketch and everything it told him about old Harlowe, the man who was one with his beloved vines and nothing else, and even more so what the picture conveyed about its creator.

Suddenly little pops echoed from the hallway. She was returning to her little garden world. Not ready to part with the stunning piece that revealed so much, he tucked it into his cloak and sprinted toward the window. Sailing through the room, he banged his shins against a tiny table and crumpled in pain. What a pointless little piece of furniture. He clenched his teeth to suppress grunts of pain. Before he was prepared, the door unlatched. Judging his distance to the exit, he dove behind the curtains of a closer window and waited, feeling the steam of his own breath trapped by the fabric. He tested it, but this window was firmly latched against his escape. She slipped into the room and sighed deeply.

Now it felt like prying.

12

You can tell the quality of a man's soul with one look at what he creates, for what he's poured into his creation has come from within.

—*Notebook of a viticulturist*

I eased into the sanctuary of my bedchamber, anxious to be alone in my own private space. But I found an unfamiliar stack of papers on the dressing table and felt an odd sense of having been invaded. Crossing to the table, I lifted the papers and focused on the scrawled words, squinting to make out the unfamiliar handwriting. It was translated pages of Father's notebooks, which meant Donegan Vance had been here.

A swish of boots on the wood floor startled me and the papers fluttered from my trembling fingers. The man's tall figure emerged from behind the curtain. "Good evening."

"Donegan." I placed a hand over my chest as if the motion would still my thudding heart.

"You finally used my Christian name."

"Only because you surprised me."

"I merely thought I'd act as a gentleman and alert you to my presence."

"How kind. How did you get in here?"

He jerked his head toward the open window and the timber walkway outside. "I didn't think you'd want anyone else knowing about the papers I brought. I meant to slip in and out before you returned, but I lingered too long in this surprising chamber." His gaze flicked over my personal haven. "It would seem you enjoy the outdoors. So much so that you brought it inside."

My neck warmed as I looked about the room painted with every possible element of a garden, both real and imagined, and saw it through a stranger's eyes. What lady in possession of her wits went about painting her walls? "You find it humorous." My mother and the household servants had come to accept my oddity, but a stranger happening upon this room would believe the worst.

"Unexpected." His look absorbed the entirety of the room in several long sweeps, then once again rested on me with a smile. "Yet utterly fitting."

"I appreciate your approval." I exhaled and knelt to collect the papers.

"I wish to help." His voice rolled through my chamber.

Rising, I brushed off my hands. "You're welcome to pick them all up then. It was you who startled me into dropping them."

He shuffled them together and rose to hand them to me. "I

mean, help with the search. With everything." Suddenly his overly masculine presence towering over me in my bedchamber rattled my senses, leaving me breathless and slightly off balance. "But I wish to be a part of the entire search." His glance swept around my room once again. "Who are the Malverns?"

I blinked at the name that he had no reason to know. "Why do you ask?"

"It seems they were important to your father. He talks of them in the notebooks but never says who they are."

I glanced at the pages on the table, yearning to read them. "They built Trevelyan many generations ago. It was their summer estate until my father purchased it."

"There's a stronger tie than that."

"Perhaps he inherited something from them. He believes them responsible for his fortune, although I've no idea why."

He nodded with a frown and dragged his palm down his stubbled cheek. "So his hiding place could be a sort of tribute to them."

Instantly my mind returned to the undercroft where that elaborate Malvern vine tapestry hung, yet I dared not voice my silly notions. "I'll leave it to you to come to your own conclusions on the matter."

"I need you to tell me everything you think of. And one other thing." He eyed me intently. "I'll need to join the family dinners to catch whatever information I can."

These demands drew my frown. I considered thrusting out my chin and declaring I could do it alone, but both of us knew that to be untrue, especially considering Father's notebooks were in Welsh. Besides that, some primal, empty part of me yearned to partner with someone, to share the burden so abruptly loaded onto my shoulders.

But this man? I surveyed his roughly stubbled face, the imposing stance, and the snapping eyes that matched his words. "I'm not sure I trust you. You've done nothing but ruffle feathers since arriving."

His eyes glowed with humor in the dimly lit room. "You've struck upon the finest reason in the world to trust me. I'm nothing if not honest."

Yes, painfully so. "I suppose that is true."

"Let me help you, then. Strength comes to the branch through connection, and that's what I'm offering."

Connection. The word resonated with the deepest parts of me, catching my interest immediately and stilling my doubts. It was a word with a lifelong significance that I couldn't explain, and his words folded over my objections, tucking them back for the moment.

I met his gaze. "I suppose you may join the family for dinner and glean what information you will. But I'll warn you that Mother prefers for the garden to remain outside. You'll need to dress for dinner. And I beg you, don't ruffle any feathers."

He raised his eyebrows. "Demanding, aren't you?" The curtains fluttered in the open window as a wet breeze swept through my room and ruffled the papers on my table. Donegan glanced toward the papers. "Why do you want to read these notebooks?"

Heat prickled up my scalp as I searched for words that would not invite his ridicule. "I'm hoping to find a clue there. You never know what might turn up."

His answering frown gave the distinct impression of disapproval. No matter, though. A mere frown was far more pleasant than exposing my heart. I could not bear to reveal to him the depth of my rejection, the utter devotion to a father who had all but ignored me.

Stony judgment settled into his gaze as it passed over me quite thoroughly. "I'll leave you to read for the moment, but we'll speak again soon."

Hopefully outside of my bedroom.

With a powerful leap, he jumped through the window and onto the timber walk outside. The man rarely used the appropriate entrance, it seemed. His footsteps thudded across the wood and down the outdoor stairs and he was gone, leaving only the filmy curtains blowing in his absence.

Heart pounding, I lifted the pages of translation and counted six in total. After clutching the papers to my chest for a moment, I breathed deeply and began to read in earnest the words that had been so long kept from me.

> In honor of the Malverns, I pour myself into these vines and coax life from the dead soil, drawing something good from bad.

I stared at the word *Malvern,* nearly resentful of the fact that their name had earned a place in his private thoughts while his daughter did not receive mention. As I read further, it became clear these notes were not strictly about the vineyard but about life. Just as he spoke in vineyard symbolism, so his notes were rich in story and wisdom told through the lens of a viticulturist.

> A wealth of potential lies within these fields, and I will seek to tend it well. Whatever it takes, I will find a way for this to flourish and bear rich fruit.

I am working against nature, growing a vineyard where one does not belong, but I will defy the climate just as they did and create something that will live long after I've seen my last harvest.

Ever since the last Malvern branch was pruned away from the vine, peace and new life exist in the vineyard now in my charge. A new vineyard will flourish where the old has fallen, and the harvest will be great and plentiful. Cassius Malvern has been neatly folded into the pages of Trevelyan's history, the final, early demise in the Malvern family with no one left to miss him, and the vineyard will now flourish freely.

I traced those final lines with my fingertip, wondering at this poor, forgotten Cassius who had been pruned away. What had made Father record such a thing? The way he spoke of Cassius left me unsettled, but I did not dwell on it.

From there, the lines rambled on and on about soil composition and the direction of the sun. The level of detail rang of Father and gave me a sense of his presence in the work. Dipping my pen into the ink jar, I underlined anything that seemed important. Harnessing the power of the sun—*maybe he hid his money in the chandeliers or candleholders*—and fully enriching the soil that fed the vines—*he could have buried it beneath the vineyard.*

Perhaps I was reading too much into his dry and practical notes. As the possibilities wove around my brain and tightened into frustration, I pushed the pages away. Yet the name Cassius Malvern had burned into my brain like an eerie shadow, lingering and enticing my curiosity. No one deserved to be forgotten, and it bothered me relentlessly that he should suffer such a fate.

I awoke the next morning to the patter of pebbles striking the house beside my window. Bunching an extra blanket around me, I ran to the window and peered down at Donegan Vance, who stood in his worn black boots and long cape. "I have news. Dress and come down."

Those few words lit a terrible, tumultuous excitement that spurred me through the first part of his command. I donned a cotton percale and muslin dress with Lucy's help, waved off her attempts to arrange my hair, and slipped my feet into worn ankle boots more suitable for gardening than meeting with a gentleman.

But Donegan Vance was not exactly a gentleman. At least, not one I cared to impress. Especially when he dangled the carrot of exciting news before me at this hour.

The orange of dawn infused the morning mist and warmed my face as I stepped out into the courtyard and sprinted through the archway to the vineyard. Already the field had filled with brown-clad workers bent over their labor, and I wondered at the remarkable sight. The new manager had proven effective, even if he was off-putting. Donegan stood with arms crossed and feet planted as he surveyed the work and waited for me.

"How ever did you manage to entice the workers out this early?"

"I promised them food." He said the words with his usual frankness, and I could not tell if they were meant to poke at me or not.

"Well, let's have it then. What is your news?"

"Come." With firm fingertips against my shoulder blade, he led me along the east side of the vineyard, down the embankment, and toward the woods. A sudden fear passed over me as we traveled away from the house, but I shook it away. Donegan had already had a number of chances to do me harm if he so wished. Taking long strides through the tall grass, I hurried toward the woods with this man I barely knew. Oh, the lectures Mother would unleash if she knew what I now did.

But of course, she didn't. No one ever did. And sometimes that was to my benefit.

"Can't you simply tell me what it is?"

"It's far more dramatic to let you see it for yourself."

A crow's yell startled me as we passed under the canopy of trees that blocked the sun and threw shadows in our leaf-littered path. "You aren't taking me to a dead body, are you? Oh, you're impossible!"

"I do try." A flicker of a smile passed over his face and he tucked my hand into the crook of his arm.

We crunched through the leaves of last year's autumn toward a thin shaft of light cutting through the branches. It lit upon a copse of trees so thick they resembled a small fortress.

"This hardly would have caught my eye had I not read your father's notebooks." His chest rumbled through my arm tucked against him.

"Why not just tell me where . . ." But my voice trailed away in the damp forest air as our destination came into focus. The copse was not a clump of trees but a thick mass of vines that covered a distinctly man-made arch. Struck with wonder, I approached the stones and touched their time-worn surface, imagining what they might have been. The masonry was exquisite, the stones perfectly shaped and smoothed to fit together. This was no temporary structure built by Gypsies.

"What is it?" I whispered the words in the hushed aura of these ghostly woods.

"Step back here."

Shaking a little from cold or from anticipation, I walked backward until I stood beside Donegan. My gaze climbed the stone arch along with the vines to the top, where a metal piece connected both pillars in an arch across the top. Cut out from that piece was the word "Malvern."

An involuntary shudder whipped through my body and I took a step toward Donegan. "What is this place?"

"It's the old gate."

I ran to it and yanked at the thickly woven vines to have a better look. Sure enough, a pair of rusted metal gate hinges hung from the inner arch of the stone. I ran my fingertip over them, wondering what had happened to the gate that had hung there.

"That was the first thing I found." Donegan crunched through the fallen leaves and kicked at the foliage beneath the arch. "I thought that was interesting, until I found this." His rough boot kicked at a few remaining rocks and leaves to further uncover a gray stepping-stone marbled with white. "Even more intriguing."

Kneeling before it, I brushed dirt from its surface and my fingers slid over crude etching. The name *Cassius Malvern* suddenly became clear and I jerked my hand away as if I'd come in contact with a ghost. My heart thumped and I scrambled to stand, staring down at the irregularly shaped stone.

"Is this a cemetery?" I felt light-headed.

"This is the only stone I found."

I continued to stare at the etching as chills raced up and down my back. Something seemed oddly alarming about it, as if I'd seen it before, but my mind merely circled around the truth without landing firmly on it.

"It occurred to me last night after reading this name in the notebook that there are many people in Welporth who might know what happened to the Malverns, so I began to ask about."

I turned my back on Trevelyan, that great cavern of dreadful secrets, and faced Donegan. "What did you find?" I'd once thought secrets a beautiful, enchanting thing. Now I wished there were no such thing.

"It seems that, after centuries of owning this land, they fell on hard times during the last generation, the final male heir."

"Cassius." I mumbled the name of the last Malvern branch.

"They summered here until the boy was about twelve, and his father tried to teach him to manage the vineyard so he might follow in his footsteps. The villagers say he wasn't the sort to associate with them. Even at that young age, they knew him as entitled and elitist, watching them from his high tower and only speaking to them when he must."

"Perhaps he was not allowed." I spoke from the experience of my own life.

Donegan folded his arms across his chest. "He was eventually deemed mad and his family stopped coming here, leaving the vineyard in the hands of various managers. Some believed

Cassius was violent, others say he was merely slow-minded. Either way, he made short work of the entire fortune when his parents died and never returned to Trevelyan."

I glanced down at the stone. Apparently he had, at least in death. My hand rose to my chest as Cassius's story pierced even deeper into some shadowed part of me. I could not bear to think about him, but my imagination created an image of his face, etched with the supreme loneliness I felt myself, and hung it firmly at the back of my mind to dwell there.

Donegan's voice broke through my thoughts. "So it was that they lost their wealth. When the debts exceeded the pound notes, according to the local villagers, your father swooped in and stole the land. Not with spears and cannons, but with money."

"Buying is hardly stealing."

"When you attempt to take something money cannot buy, it is."

I looked at the proud, strong name of Malvern atop the arch, now reclaimed by the woods the family had sought to subdue.

Donegan spoke quietly. "He wanted to *be* a Malvern. A name and a history isn't something one can purchase."

"Still, there's little harm in wanting such a thing." Like the graft rejected by the vine, Father had tried every way possible to graft himself in the Malverns' life, but he had died a Harlowe all the same.

"He would have done far better to begin his own legacy instead of borrowing the wealth and sins of another."

I stiffened at the insult. "What sins did he take from them?"

"The Malverns were known for abusing and underpaying their workers, asking much and giving little."

"My father did no such thing. His workers always had plenty, and he was a fair master. Even if they've not seen wages for a short spell, they live very well, I can assure you."

"Can you, now?" His casual tone was unnerving. "Don't forget, I have been inside Trevelyan, and I can attest to seeing what 'living well' is."

"You can't expect us to keep our servants in manor houses, can you? Even they don't expect such a thing."

He frowned, studying me before he spoke. "Do you know what it means to call a vineyard an investment crop?"

"It means you pour into it for years with only the expectation of a return in the future." My words spilled easily from my memory of Father's many lectures on the topic.

"It means you care for and protect the vineyard because you recognize it's a valuable asset." He glanced toward the distant fields. "Those laborers are your vineyard, Miss Harlowe."

"Are they not provided with every necessity?"

He hesitated, thoughts darkening his features. "Come. It's time you experienced something for yourself."

To care for the plant is to care for the grapes, for the fruit is nothing but the overflow of what a plant is fed.

—Notebook of a viticulturist

For the second time I perched atop the black stallion puffing from his massive nostrils, but now we climbed down the hill and daylight warmed our backs. I clung to the man before me for safety, only now he was not quite a stranger. Below us the road wound down into the village where it was lined by identical little cottages with a long stone fence.

"How long has it been since you've walked through the village?" His voice carried back to me over his shoulder.

"Long enough." The truth was, I'd *never* been to the village. My childhood days had been full of my governess and tutors, without a thought for the village lying just past our woods. Now, the idea of riding into the midst of this place, walking among the people now working in my vineyard for no pay, made me recoil.

We trotted down the ribbon of dirt road that separated two long rows of homes, and the scene was surprisingly pleasant. Sunlight glinted off the waters of the distant channel, and feathery mounds of wisteria spilled over the matching fences running along both strings of homes.

Donegan reined his horse in before a neat green door with hens pecking at the bare yard. A crooked flower box held a few sad flowers. Dismounting, he helped me slide off the stallion's back and then knocked at the door. A quiet greeting ushered us in. An older couple sat before an empty hearth, one working at a table and the other reclining in a rocker.

"This is Mr. and Mrs. Hagan. Their three sons serve in the fields, and the eldest rents this home."

I looked at the tiny cottage. "They live together?"

Mr. Hagan, a scrawny man in a faded shirt with a red scarf about his neck, sat at the table, painstakingly piecing together a chipped cup. His careful handling of those mere remnants squeezed my heart. "Had me own cottage when I worked in the fields. Over twenty years I gave this vineyard, but you'd never know it, the way I was cast aside as soon as my body gave out. Neatly tucked away in this here place with promises of my own cottage, but now that he's gone I've got nothing."

I bit my lip, eager to promise him a small pension for his service, but I couldn't. I had nothing to give yet.

The tightness inside me eased only when I determined that this man would receive the first outpouring of the fortune when I found it, after estate notes were paid.

"It isn't so bad, Mr. Vance." The old woman rocked in

and out of the shadows, her arms wilted onto the arms of her chair. "We did love that Master Harlowe. Like a father to the village, he was, and always fair. He'd have never left us out in the cold, at least. Besides, our boys are good to us and we manage."

I lifted grateful eyes to the sweet woman. They deserved much more than they had. Their weary bodies evidenced years of loyal service, which should be amply rewarded.

"No one who serves one master so long should have to simply *manage*." Her husband grumbled these bitter words.

"It wasn't always this way, Mr. Hagan. Don't forget that." Her soft voice blanketed the rough edges of her husband's bitterness. "He was good to us for many years, and we have plenty. Save your pity for folks like the McEvoys. Since the storm, they still set out a pot when it rains."

Donegan grumbled. "No one's been to repair the roof?"

Hagan shook his head. "Not since the master . . ." His voice trailed off as he shifted uncomfortably at the mention of death.

When we took our leave of the place and walked farther down the road, I followed Donegan to a house across the street and down a little. He knocked and called out as if he were a regular visitor.

"How do you know all these people? I thought you'd just arrived."

"I always make it a point to know the families I work with. Besides, I did stay here for a time while waiting for the ladies of the house to return to Trevelyan."

I hesitated behind him. "Where exactly did you come from?"

"I've lived in Newcastle, Scotland, Cornwall, East Sussex. Most recently, though, I've come from a vineyard in the South of France."

"That isn't what I mean. It's just . . . you seem to have walked out of the mist, yet it seems you've been here forever too."

I wished he'd answer my question, although I almost dreaded the dark secrets of his past that he might reveal. I'd come to depend on him in many ways, yet what if his character came into question? Did I keep him on, giving him the journals only he could interpret and entrusting him with the vineyard only he seemed able to save?

The second door opened to us. "Mr. Vance." A wiry woman with rolled-up sleeves and a strip of cloth securing her frizzy hair stood in the doorway, her stiff posture and lifted chin evidencing the respect that Donegan seemed to elicit wherever he went. He introduced me as a friend and the woman greeted me with a formal nod, but she asked no further questions about my identity.

She ushered us into the dim space full of children in patched clothing, all tumbling over one another. The scarcity I saw there twisted my heart even further, and I wondered at Father's stinginess toward them. Donegan hovered at the fringes with a deeply shadowed expression, but I moved toward our host and apologized for calling on her without warning.

"What a surprise to have company in the middle of the day." Her cheery smile doused my concerns with pleasant welcome. "Come, get yourself rested while I bring some food. Bread and honey? My Stephan won't touch it, so there's plenty. Says it tastes stale before it comes out of me oven." The delightful woman walked toward her cupboard and leaned in, still chattering. "Don't mind the little ones. Just push them aside if you need the space."

As the cupboard muffled her voice, my attention drifted to the children playing about, and their contagious joy began to lift my burdened heart. The youngest sat on the floor, baby feet spread, arms flapping in delight. One girl braided her sister's hair while chattering faster than her mother. Three boys tumbled as a cluster over the rug. Another gave the scene lively background music with his fiddle. When the baby fussed, his mother stooped to gather him and thrust the little being into my arms. Surprised, I anchored the tiny whining body to me, praying he did not slip out of my grasp.

The intrigue of something new seemed to capture him, for he abandoned his whines to tug on the cameo hanging from my neck. Within a brief moment, a natural instinct overtook my hesitations and I cradled the little baby close and kissed the feathery blond hair. As the hubbub of many bodies faded to a pleasant blur around me, I looked down at the impossibly tiny face and savored the weight of him in my arms, watched his chubby hands flapping against my chest, and breathed in his sweet scent.

When I exhaled across his face, his large brown eyes jerked up to meet my gaze, eyebrows arched with interest. I smiled at him, for I was capable of nothing else then, and his face melted into a crinkly eyed smile that nearly shattered my heart in a pleasant explosion of longing. Before I could stop it, desire crept in and began to dwell in my heart. In spite of the lack, there were traces of sweet loveliness in this place.

I jumped when I felt someone brush my skirts. A young girl of about fifteen hovered behind me, one slender hand extended to touch the skirt of my gown whose subtle sheen glowed in the dim cottage. She withdrew her hand into her shawl when she saw me looking at her.

"It's beautiful," she said in a soft, breathy voice. How she must disappear in this house bursting with noise and chaos. "You do look magical in such a dress, miss. Just like a fairy."

I smiled. "It's a favorite of mine."

Our hostess handed us each a slice of bread, and though it pained me to accept a portion of their meager store, Donegan downed his in a few bites.

"It seems you're running out of room, Mrs. Campbell." Donegan's voice broke the reverie as he grabbed a kitchen chair and tested it, frowning at its wobbliness. Could the man be anything but negative? I silently chewed the coarse bread that tasted of homey warmth despite its sad texture, and continued to clutch the baby. They lacked so much, but they had a great deal too. It was true that there was no room here for an excess of belongings, impressive decorations, or even privacy. There was only room for the family it housed, squeezing them all close together in one happy mess.

"I've been pestering my man to be more forceful about what he's owed, but he's afeared of losing his position over it. His anger is boiling hotter, though. One of these days it'll blow and someone will pay. Hopefully old Harlowe's widow."

Involuntarily stiffening at the comment, I buried my face in the baby's fine hair and hid my utter embarrassment. Donegan Vance had discovered a brilliant way to punish and torment me without saying a single word.

"Give me that over there, Mrs. Campbell." Donegan took the proffered tools and quickly strengthened the chair with a few well-placed nails. He drove them into the wood with sharp bursts of his hammer, as if each strike were a wordless condemnation of my part in their poverty. With one last test of its sturdiness, he rose. "I'll be sure to have Mr. Campbell home for supper tonight, so make plenty of food."

"Now didn't you find my bread wonderful? Come, tell me Stephan is a fool to not appreciate it."

"I'd never call the man a fool. Nor the bread wonderful."

I coughed and gulped all at once at his response, but the woman merely heaved a large sigh and let her shoulders fall forward. "Ach, I suppose not. But then I never promised I could cook when he wed me."

She bounced back to her cheerful self in a moment, even while my heart still smarted a bit from the comment. Maybe they were all used to such behavior, for it seemed natural to her, but I could at least offer a taste of refinement. "It was wonderful, Mrs. Campbell. Truly wonderful bread, and I thank you for it."

Donegan led me from the house after I surrendered the now-wiggly baby. "Now you've seen the state of their homes. I hope it's had an impact on your mind."

I glanced back at the sparse but cozy home small enough to be a sort of hug, holding the family close together in pleasant disarray, and recalled the feel of the chubby baby against my chest. "Indeed, it has."

"A bit different than your own, is it not?"

I shot a glance up toward Trevelyan Castle that looked with Malvern arrogance over the little village. I closed my eyes and took a deep breath to still the familiar emptiness threatening to engulf me. "Terribly different."

When we finally mounted his horse and turned toward home, my heart was full. It was not that I didn't see the pot on the floor to catch the leaks or the crooked table and chipped dishes. My heart had seen and been painfully broken by it.

But like Donegan had said in the woods, there were simply certain belongings money could not adequately purchase.

Near the top of the hill, the man's demeanor softened. "You've been accommodating, allowing me to bring you here and parade you before these people."

"It was good for me, truly." I spoke into the fabric of his shirt as I clung to him. The horse ascended the rocky hill with a wobbly gait, moving far more slowly than his usual gallop.

"So you learned something?"

A breath of time passed in silence before I could answer. "That I did."

We crested the hill that looked out upon the perfectly sloped vineyard, and I breathed in the beauty of my home. If my life was not rich in love and family, at least it was brimming with beauty.

"There is one other thing I learned about your father." He reined in his horse and slid onto the ground, reaching up to help me down. "It seems the general unspoken belief is that your father stole his fortune."

"But where would he have gotten it? That's utterly ridiculous."

"Is it, though?"

I clasped my hands into fists. "I will not believe such a thing. If he was suddenly wealthy, it's because he earned it somehow." I said the words with all the vehemence of one trying to convince the listener as well as oneself.

Evening settled over the estate with a light patter of rain and the distant rumble of thunder. All day, scenes from the village had been tossing about in my mind, pulling at me and making me anxious. Father could not have left them so destitute, for it was not in his nature to be unfair to them.

Yet my mind quickly drew up that image of the stone in the woods, and everything Donegan had said about Father. What did I truly know of the man and his past?

When I sought out Mother in her small receiving room that evening, the name *Malvern* had lodged in the shadows of my mind. As soon as I entered the little room, an odd sight caught my attention and tore it out of the clouds—Dr. Caine looked up and dropped Mother's hand as if it were a handful of stolen farthings and I the constable. I frowned. Had I imagined what I'd just seen? Mother watched me from where she perched in a darkly upholstered little chair by the window, and a forced smile replaced Dr. Caine's usual warm one, but I moved forward and greeted them with all the grace of one who had witnessed nothing unusual. Such diplomacy where Mother was concerned was as natural to me as taking a meal. "How is the patient this evening, Dr. Caine?"

"Doing well enough to render my visits meaningless in the near future." He moved away to collect his things and pile them into a bag.

"Oh no, Dr. Caine." Mother's voice wafted over us with a pleasant lilt. "I'd never call them that."

If Mother did not intend to expose her grief, she managed quite well. Not even the façade of grief did she display.

"I thought you were out riding with Andrew. He had plans to invite you, I heard." She leaned close to whisper. "Have you already abandoned him?"

"I don't believe Mr. Carrington is staying at Trevelyan any longer. I have . . . changed the nature of our association." I glanced at our visitor, wishing he'd leave, for surely he could hear this most intimate conversation even at a whisper. "I'm not sure he'll want to stay."

Mother's expression melted into an indulgent smile. "Oh, but he does. I spoke to him this morning and urged him to remain. I explained how distraught you have been and insisted he give you more time to come to the right conclusions concerning him."

I tensed. "You mean *your* conclusions."

"I know your mind better than you, my daughter. Don't think I've forgotten how you pined away in your room when he left."

I clenched my jaw as heat rushed up my neck and through my face. I glanced at Dr. Caine, who silently poked about in his bag, likely attempting to remain inconspicuous.

Clearing my throat, I pivoted the conversation to what I'd come to discuss in the first place. "I have a question for you, Mother, if you feel up to it." She looked up at me. "It's about the Malverns. Who exactly were they to us?"

She sighed deeply and toyed with a handkerchief in her hands. "Didn't your father serve in their fields years ago? I believe they were his first employers and they taught him about vineyards."

"How did he find the position, though? Had he some connection with them?"

"I have no idea, and why on earth should you care? It isn't as if it matters anymore."

"It merely seems a rather weak reason to be so entirely obsessed with them, especially for a man of strong principles like Father. The Malverns sounded like dreadful people, always destroying and overworking their staff, and it seems he became like them in the end. Why did he not attach himself to an honorable family?"

"Honor defined those people." The sharp assertion came from Dr. Caine, who had been quietly placing vials and tools in his black leather bag.

Mother and I both turned to the man and the clock behind us ticked in the silence. I looked then upon his distinguished, angry face as an untapped storehouse of vital information.

Mother's voice cut through the uncertain silence. "Let's not dwell on such matters. I'm glad to be done with that family now that Josiah is gone."

But I wasn't sure that we were.

I pondered this information as I walked Dr. Caine out of the room later. He did not seem comfortable enough to utter a word as we wound around to the first floor. The stairs were too narrow to allow us to walk beside one another, so we descended in silence.

However, there were many answers I needed from him, so I began as soon as we reached the landing. "You knew the Malverns." I kept my tone casual.

"Many years ago, yes. I served as their physician when they summered here. They were known as one of the wealthiest families in the south of England, once upon a time, but they were decent people too. I owe them everything I have, for it was the eldest Malvern who sponsored my education."

"Cassius?"

As soon as the eerie name slipped from my lips, I regretted it, for all manner of anxiety passed over the poor doctor's face. After a brief silence, he cleared his throat. "No, that was the son. It was Cassius's father, Edward Malvern, who so generously provided for my studies."

I hesitated. "I'm sorry for what I said of them before. They've been a bit of a thorn in my side, being this big secret Father refused to speak about."

His smile once again crinkled the skin around his eyes, but it appeared sadder this time. "Quite understandable, my dear. Pardon my behavior upstairs. It was improper of me."

I wondered which incident he meant.

"Did they perhaps sponsor my father's education too? Or a business venture?"

He sighed and rested a calming hand on my shoulder. "None of that matters now, Miss Harlowe. Your mother was right about that. I never should have said a thing about them. It's just that they were so kind to me, and being in this house again . . ." His voice trailed off as he glanced up at the high ceilings filled with gold trim and chandeliers.

"You must know how they were connected then, my father and the Malverns."

He stooped to collect his hat from the table. "Every man deserves to keep a few pieces of his past private."

"Surely you cannot mean Father wronged them. He was so upright and splendid, and . . ."

He lifted his eyes so full of gentle pity, and I could not stand to look at them. It wasn't like this man knew my father the way I had.

"The only perfect father is the one in heaven. Never forget that."

I clung to my loyalty with desperate tenacity, forcing the doctor's words from my mind. The human part of me couldn't be satisfied with having a vague spirit father in some distant realm, and the little-girl part of me refused to give up on my earthly father and the hope of a true relationship with him.

"I always tell my patients to focus on the next thing and nothing beyond that. Too many of them are carried away in worrying over the future—what the illness will mean for them, how they'll pay for care, all of that. In your case, it's the past that has you so distracted. It's time to let it go."

"But, Dr. Caine, I have to understand what happened so I can at least locate Father's fortune. It's becoming a matter of urgency."

He hesitated. "Miss Harlowe." The gentle face wrinkled with concern. "Has it occurred to you that perhaps it no longer exists? Forgive my intrusion, but I cannot help but notice the reduced financial position of the estate. Your father did take out a loan with that Prescott fellow, did he not? And he has neglected to pay his laborers."

"Well, yes, but—"

"You're too smart for this, Miss Harlowe. Only a young pup will sniff around the same place for his meat long after it's stopped appearing, while the older dogs are off looking for a new source."

"Then the old dog merely gave up too soon." My voice came out weak and soft. "Besides, the pup knows no other source."

"Where there is creativity and God, there is always another source." He squeezed my shoulder and took himself away.

I saw him out the courtyard entrance where his horse waited, then moved back into the house. *God, what sort of new source is out there for us? Truly you cannot expect me to follow Mother's advice and marry—*

Distant voices broke through, drawing me to the tall windows. A group of men with bobbing lanterns marched toward the castle. I flew through the hall toward the foyer. Amos rounded the corner from the servant's hall and nearly collided with me as we reached the front door at the same time. With a worried glance toward me, Amos grabbed the handles and yanked open the doors. There beyond our steps, a crowd of disheveled laborers crossed the drawbridge and approached the castle with swinging lanterns and a cacophony of voices lifted to the cloudy night sky. Two men toward the back sang loudly as they marched.

"Amos, who are these people? Are they vineyard laborers?"

He clasped his gloved hands behind his back. "A rather unseemly bunch, aren't they? Perhaps a bit too intoxicated to keep appropriate company with yourself, Miss Harlowe."

"Fetch Donegan Vance." Those whispered words dispatched my faithful butler into the depths of the dark house as I, having no alternative, went to meet the men myself. How on earth did they find money for the pub if they supposedly hadn't enough to feed their families?

"We're here to speak to the head of the house." The one in front, a tall, lanky man with overgrown blond hair, stepped forward and held his lantern aloft. "We've things that need saying."

Chin up, I stepped out the door and stood guard before it. "That would be me."

He swapped glances with the men standing on either side of him, then they all turned to look up at me, their eyes glowing in the lantern light. "We've come for our wages and we're not leaving without them."

I stared down the direct gazes of the men in front, wondering what had suddenly lit this fire in them. What had Donegan Vance said to them? "You'll simply have to wait. I'd be happy to give it to you immediately if I could, but circumstances beyond . . ."

The men grumbled among themselves, their voices echoing in the night.

One man in work-worn clothes and tall boots stepped forward, arms crossed over his chest. "We've a right to our pay. Unless you can supply it, we're on strike from the vineyard to have ourselves a treasure hunt." He marched forward. "Come on, men. Let's go find it."

Ragged villagers swarmed up the path and I ran down the steps, hands out. "Stop! You cannot trespass."

"Hold up." A single deep voice rolled like thunder over the crowd, stilling the chaos into low murmurs. "This is not the way to go about it." The motley collection of laborers shifted apart as Donegan Vance strode through their midst. He paused before the leaders of the strike and spoke in hushed tones. I strained in vain to hear what they said.

Finally he strode up the path to me, arms folded over his chest. "It seems you have run out of time to pay what is owed, Miss Harlowe. You will have to find a way to settle up or lose your vineyard to neglect and your possessions to the men to whom you owe money."

"It's illegal for them to simply plunder our house for the fortune."

"That is so." He unfolded a piece of paper from his pocket and held it between our faces. "The law offers about this much protection from a band of determined and hungry men, especially in the country. You'd best settle with them soon."

"With what? You know my position. I've nothing to pay them."

He arched one eyebrow and cast a glance behind me at the vast estate that was my home.

"What, are you suggesting I distribute candlestick holders and gilded mirrors?"

"I'm merely suggesting you settle with them sooner rather than later, however you must."

I pushed past him. "If they force their way in and steal from my family, I'll—"

He grabbed my shoulder to stop me and stepped close, lowering his voice so only I could hear. "Keep in mind who you speak to before you unleash your anger. They're hardworking men trying to protect their families just as you are. That one who spoke has six children and two aging parents. He works twice as hard as you do and lives on a fraction of what you have."

"As if you know what I have or do not have." The words slipped out of my tense lips before I could stuff them away. I remembered with vivid clarity the joyful little cottage full of children, the wonderful smells of baking, the chubby baby. With a deep breath, I lowered my voice and finished my statement as warmth poured over my skin, heating my cheeks painfully. "There is wealth and there is lack in everyone's life."

His hard look evaluated me thoroughly, but I did not wish to explain further.

Stepping past him, I approached the small knot of men. "I need a little more time. Set a date in the future and I will find a way to meet it."

"Friday." Donegan Vance strode toward me. "Give her until Friday."

Three days? I shot him a look.

"I cannot do without them in the fields longer than that. You'll simply have to find a way to give them something by then or they'll make good on their threat to search out the fortune themselves."

I forced a swallow and straightened. "All right, Friday."

But I had no idea what I'd have to offer by then.

As I slipped back inside, heart pounding and temples throbbing, I heard whispers. Amos and Margaret lingered in hushed conversation that ceased the minute my footsteps echoed on the floor.

"Bad news?" I forced myself into their conversation as only a lady of the house could.

Margaret fidgeted with her apron. "It seems there's been a fire at James Prescott's country house last night."

I frowned. "I do hope he's unharmed."

"We've not heard yet, but they did say everyone escaped."

I simply nodded as I passed through the hall to the stairs, wondering why on earth the servants thought the matter held enough weight to speak so secretly of it.

14

> No season in the vineyard is meant to merely be endured, for each is necessary for the grapes to grow.
>
> —*Notebook of a viticulturist*

You're doing it wrong."

I shoved back the cloth band restraining my hair the next morning and stabbed the shovel into the ground, wishing I'd located a hat to guard my skin from the penetrating sun. "It's manure. How could one possibly do it wrong?"

Donegan took the shovel and struck the dirt clods in my wheelbarrow, mixing it with the fertilizer. "Like this. Nice and even. Each plant needs a mix of both."

Perspiration tickled my skin beneath my work dress, irritating me almost as much as the man before me. "Would you like my help or not?"

"Not if it makes more work for me."

I dusted my hands against each other. If only I could convince the regular laborers to return to the field so I did not have to do their work nor tolerate their manager. "The roots will be covered, and that's the point, is it not?" The sun had begun to make my head ache, and Donegan's correction did nothing to ease the pain.

"Nutrition for the vineyard is the point. Grapes are nothing but the overflow of whatever you put into the soil."

Donegan's simple statement hovered in my mind hours later as I shifted on my rigged platform near the ceiling, a cool cloth across my sun-warmed forehead. *The overflow of whatever you put into the soil.* I dabbed brown and black onto my ceiling-wide mural, giving the pictured dirt texture and rich color like ground coffee to symbolize the valuable nutrients it provided.

Is that the secret, God? Is it the soil? And if it was, what sort of clue did that offer regarding the fortune? Frustration tugged at the edge of my concentration as possibilities circled and were discarded by my overworked mind. If it meant he'd buried his treasure, I'd no sooner find it on this vast estate than if he'd thrown it into the channel.

But no, it wasn't buried—I had *seen* it. Several times. In that instant, an image poured over my thoughts with such clarity that I could nearly walk through it in my mind. There had been a weathered black trunk with metal banding, and an iron keyhole on the front. It always sat open on a table in the window alcove of a workroom, amid piles of paper, while Father bent over his test tubes and soil samples. Beautiful old books on vineyards lined the fireplace mantel where the words *Legendary Harlowe* had been etched.

I remembered stretching onto my tiptoes until I could peer over the side of the trunk across the room and catching the barest glimpse of the chaotic pile of coins and pound notes that nearly filled it.

I blinked at the paint smeared across my bedroom ceiling. At least now I knew where to look. But where was that dirty little workshop? Where was that chest?

God, can you not just tell me where it is? It was like he wished to dangle before me all these images to remind me that the fortune did, in fact, exist, without actually guiding me to it. But why?

Why will you not let me find what we so desperately need?

Yet he remained as silent and distant as my earthly father had been.

A knock at the door made me jerk, a streak of brown appearing across my delicate swirls of green. "Yes?"

Lucy breezed in, frizzy dark hair framing her face. "Ready to dress, miss? Dinner will be upon us straightaway, and your vineyard manager said to tell you he'd be in attendance."

After dropping my brush into the tin of water and swirling it clean, I rolled to the edge of my platform and climbed down the ladder. "I'll wear the brown with gold trim tonight."

"Of course, miss."

At least by donning brown I'd be likely to match the newest dinner guest.

As she laced my corset, I held the post of my bed and aligned my spine to the familiar restraint. "Lucy, do you recall a room with books on vineyards? Something besides the library and the study. Lots of books, and a fireplace."

Her eyes rounded. "You've remembered something. Is it where the treasure is?"

I pinched my lips into a smile and shrugged.

"Oh, what a wonder! I do wish I could help you, but I don't

remember seeing such a place and I haven't the courage to snoop about the empty rooms. I scare too easily. I even have a whole stack of books I'm waiting to read until I'm married so I'm not sleeping alone with my thoughts."

"Have you set the date yet?"

"I'll be old and wrinkled by the time he's released back to me. The queen, she does love to keep her soldiers a good many years when they sign her contracts."

I smiled at how a simple mention of her intended softened her so. If only Queen Victoria knew what a torture such service was on her soldiers and the ones left behind, perhaps she'd limit their terms.

A sudden jerk cinched my waist, perfecting my posture and shortening my breaths, and my mind turned to the dinner for which I was dressing. "So you've met the new vineyard manager, that Donegan Vance."

"Yes, miss, he is rather . . . hard to miss." After securing the stays, she fitted the bodice and draped the gown over my body, tugging it into place and letting it hang in waterfalls of rich brown and gold material about my frame.

"And what do you think of him?"

Her fingers paused on a hook and eye closure near my waist. "I wouldn't know how to answer that, miss."

"Oh come now, speak plainly. You know you won't see trouble over it." Since my rescue of the girl years earlier, it had become our habit to speak frankly when we found ourselves alone. "Your brother Jimmy is among his workers, is he not? What does he say?"

Her fingers resumed their work, but her mottled face tipped down. "Jimmy doesn't get on with him, but he isn't known for hard work any more than I am for my charms."

"And you? You sound as if you like the man."

"Well, miss, I don't *want* to. He's rough and common, so I know I mustn't. But I can't help but enjoy his honesty. I'm not one to read people well enough to know when they're lying, but I never wonder with Mr. Vance."

Indeed, no one did. Not a single one of his opinions ever remained a mystery.

Despite my maid's approval of Donegan, worry trailed me down to dinner that night, tensing my body as I watched the great double doors. Andrew sat across from me with his usual good-natured countenance, yet there was a remarkable silence about him. I forced a swallow and focused on unfolding my napkin.

"Darling, you seem unwell." Mother's soft voice drew the focus of everyone at the table, as was its natural tendency.

I tore my gaze away from the door and planted it firmly on the orange-colored soup before me and the little green herbs floating on top. "Only a bit exhausted."

"You shouldn't be exerting yourself so. Is that horrid vineyard man distressing you?"

Footsteps clomped over the hall tile, jerking my attention back to the door. Then the carpet of the drawing room muffled the steps until the newcomer pushed open the adjoining door and Donegan Vance entered the dining hall. He'd replaced his tunic and trousers with fresh garments and every inch of him looked impeccably clean, but otherwise he looked much the same.

"I've invited Mr. Vance to join us for dinner." I turned to Mother, entreating her with my eyes. "As I'm sure you know, he is responsible for any future crops we hope to have at Trevelyan Castle, and we must keep him well fed."

Mother's face smoothed into the hostess mask she donned around guests who were necessary but slightly unsavory. "How thoughtful of you to join us, Mr. Vance. We hope you find our home comfortable."

He bent his body onto the laughably delicate chair opposite me and I tensed at his rugged presence in this formal room. How greatly he contrasted with Andrew, who sat beside him, from hair color and complexion to demeanor. "It would be a sight better if you had a little more cushion to these chairs, but it'll do nicely."

The frozen expression remained as Mother's eyes flicked over this intruder with refined judgment sparking behind the mask. "I trust these fine French dishes created by our highly trained kitchen staff will meet your expectations, at least."

I cringed at the quiet sarcasm, but Donegan merely nodded in her direction. "Anything that fills a body will do."

What an impossible situation, with both Donegan and Andrew at our dinner table and Mother passing silent judgment over everything. As a manservant discreetly placed a steaming bowl before our newest guest and stepped away, silverware clattered on porcelain and chair legs scraped against the wood floor. With neat movements, Donegan draped a linen napkin into his lap and lifted his glass. "May I compliment you on the spread of your table, Mistress Harlowe?"

"This is only the beginning course, Mr. Vance. It is meant only to whet your appetite for what will follow."

He raised his eyebrows. "What a show of extravagance."

"I believe our cook has prepared a specialty tonight. I do hope you've brought your appetite."

Murmurs of assent and approval filled the air.

Donegan's voice rose again. "If anyone is lacking in that area, I'm sure you'll have plenty to borrow from your field hands."

My spoon stilled in the lovely soup. I dared not look at Mother. Heat rolled over my bowed head down onto my shoulders. So, this is why he'd asked to join our table. The man wanted to guilt us into paying what we did not have to the field hands he so heartily defended. How greatly this man broadened our troubles since arriving, and I ardently wished that he'd never come. We ate mostly in silence through the rest of the meal.

After the main course had been cleared, Mother spooned jam onto bread and her silvery voice shattered the silence thick with tension. "Have you any news with the search, Neville?"

He nodded, taking a piece of bread and a generous portion of jam. "Progress is rather slow, but we've identified a few places to investigate."

I set a slice of bread on the edge of my plate and looked up at this invited enemy. "Where might that be? Perhaps I should join you when you search."

"Quite unnecessary, but kind of you to offer." He smiled around the crusty bread and jam that we could hardly afford. "Aunt Gwendolyn has graciously encouraged us to search where we will." He finished his assertion with a dab of his napkin across his crumb-dotted mustache.

"It's no trouble, I assure you." I pushed my shoulders back against the slats of the chair and prepared for a verbal spar.

Donegan replaced his spoon and looked directly into Neville's narrow little face. "I believe the lady is informing you that she will be accompanying you, regardless of your underhanded desire to search for her money alone."

Neville gulped and then coughed and hacked. Ellen shot him a look. Mother froze. I tried to stare Donegan into silence, but the ripple effect of his words tickled me. Donegan Vance proved a hard-nosed adversary, but an equally forceful ally. Interesting that he intended to be both to me.

When the conversation shifted to the other end of the table, I caught his attention. "I told you not to ruffle any feathers."

His mouth lifted in a roguish smile and he shrugged. "I don't listen well."

By the time we'd completed dinner, it had been decided that the treasure hunters should adjourn to the drawing room for further planning. I watched Donegan in my peripheral vision, trying to guess his next move. *Please don't follow us, please don't follow us.*

Mother lifted her voice with quiet command. "Mr. Vance, I release you from all obligation to accompany us beyond the meal. Please, feel free to return home and rest. I'm sure you work harder than any of us."

He rose with the other diners and placed the napkin beside his empty plate. "I thank you for the food. I find it did meet my expectations, my lady." With a slight bow toward the head of the table, he left through the same doors he'd entered.

When the remaining diners retired to the drawing room, Neville unrolled his working map across the table. "We'd thought to begin our search in the underground floor of the towers and see what we could find."

Mother glided to her favorite Queen Anne parlor chair facing the table. "I can tell you now with some certainty that the room you seek will not be in the lower levels. No books would endure the moisture."

Shock rippled through me as our guests exchanged looks.

"What books?" Ellen spoke for the group.

Mother spoke again. "The room we are looking for has rows and rows of books. None of the lower floors have any books at all."

Where had she heard this? I'd never uttered a word of my suspicions to anyone, except . . .

Lucy. My gaze flew to the little maid wringing her hands in the shadows of the room, watching me with apology streaked across her face, and my heart sank. The girl hurried over and slipped a teacup and saucer into my hands as she whispered, "I only let a tiny bit slip and then she demanded to know more. I should have known to keep my mouth buttoned, but I wasn't thinking."

With a pinch-lipped nod, I dismissed the distraught girl and turned back to my elated guests.

"Then we shall eliminate the lower floors from our search," Ellen said with a bright smile. "That should save a little time."

As panic tightened around me, the moon's glow through the long windows whispered a tantalizing invitation to escape into the fresh night air. It was bright enough to walk about outside and I couldn't bear to pass up the opportunity. Excusing myself, I moved toward the narrow passageway between the hall block and the keep tower, whipping a cloak around myself and exiting into the gardens that overlooked the vineyard. I wove through the hedges to a vine-wrapped pavilion at the top of the vineyard's slope, a nearly abandoned folly of raised platform and stone columns, and stepped into its shelter. From here I could look over the entire sea of vines rising and cresting along the hills in perfect rows bathed in bright moonlight.

For as long as I could remember, this view had held more wonder for me than all the castles of Somerset. An audible hush filled the air and a pleasant breeze ruffled my hair against my cheek. I tugged the cloak tighter around me and thought of secrets and legends and luscious vineyards.

Somewhere past the rows of green roared the Bristol Channel, dangerously beautiful and dark. What if the fortune lay somewhere in the great expanse of water? I tried to picture Father rowing out with that chest to drop it into its depths. The image of Father floating on those choppy waves, a little speck lost in that great darkness, wrapped a band of fear around my chest that rose to encircle my neck.

I closed my eyes. *I cannot bear it, God. Why can you not finish what you began to tell me? I'm trying to find him, but I need your help. Are you so far away that you cannot hear me?* It was as if he'd appeared ahead of me on the path to beckon me on, then he grew distant. *Why don't you answer? Am I not trusting those words from you?* My stomach knotted.

"Thinking of painting the night sky?"

With a cry I spun toward the voice, my cloak slipping from my shoulders. My breath came out in quick puffs as Donegan Vance stepped up into the little pavilion.

He retrieved my cloak and handed it to me. "It could use a little color."

His playful tone loosened my tongue as I accepted the cloak. "What are you doing here?"

"I merely came to thank you for allowing me to join you for dinner."

"Why do you insist on sneaking up on me so often?"

"I find it to be the least expensive form of amusement. And as I seem to be working for no pay . . ."

I glanced away, recalling the painfully awkward meal. "Is that why you've forced your way into our dinner, to investigate our financial situation?"

"I believe I attended as your guest."

"You know what I mean. I thought you wanted to come so you could learn something."

"I have. I learned that I strongly mistrust every single person in your home. You shouldn't tell any one of them a thing."

I heaved a sigh, the weight of the race weighing me down. "For once I agree with you."

"Miracle." The corners of his mouth twitched. "Now then, won't you tell me what has so captured your mind this night? You look as though you're pondering the height of the sky."

I rested my back against a pillar and looked out over the lush vineyard shaded in the lovely blue-black moonlight. "I'm trying to decipher a puzzle."

He stepped beside me and folded his arms, following my gaze. "What sort of puzzle?"

"It's something I call the vineyard's secret, and it's eluded me since childhood." I breathed in the fresh night air. "I've always thought Father would leave some clue related to the vineyard that would point to his fortune. He always spoke in vineyard riddles, and it seemed like he'd do the same for his biggest secret ever." It sounded foolish when I voiced it aloud. "It probably seems ridiculous to pore over an old man's notes and musings, but it's the only glimpse of him I have left. I could search for years in that big old house for the fortune, or I could peer into the mind of the man who hid it."

Silence rolled over the calm night, punctuated only by wind sweeping through foliage as he studied me with rapt interest, seeming to see beyond my words to something I hadn't intended to reveal.

"There's far more to you than anyone would ever guess, isn't there? You're quite remarkable."

The words stole my tongue for a moment, washing over me with surprising pleasantness. It seemed this man took me seriously in a way no one else ever had. From Mother's self-absorption to Father's annoyance and Andrew's gentle condescension, I'd begun to believe I truly had nothing valuable in my head.

I decided the man was pleasant to talk to at times.

Emboldened by his interest, I told him about the vine tapestry that hung in the undercroft, describing the gold-centered trunk and the words. "I've always thought of this as a sort of treasure map, like it was somehow supposed to portray where he'd hidden the fortune, but only to the person who knew enough about his beloved vines to understand what this meant."

His eyebrows rose in keen fascination. "What do *you* suppose it means?"

I looked away, eager to gloss over the fact that I had no good theories. After a moment I broke the silence. "Why do you always wish to know my thoughts?"

"You've built such an immense fortress around yourself, but I've often found the highest walls hold the deepest waters. Yours should never be concealed."

I glanced at this man, this stranger who seemed so anxious to hear my thoughts. "Your walls are higher than mine, for I know nothing about you. And I imagine there's much to know—much you are careful to conceal. You are not simply a vineyard manager, are you?"

His stricken look of guilt gave a more thorough answer than any words could. He looked over the vineyard, then back to me. "The work of one's hands does not always reflect the depth of his abilities."

I frowned at him, wondering if I should demand the return of Father's notebook. If I did, it would keep the information in it safe, but it would be utterly useless to me. And with pressures bearing down on me, I had to know what was in it. Instead, I merely asked, "Have you translated more pages?"

"That I have. I found this section quite compelling. Wait here and I'll fetch it."

15

> The best fruit arises from a hostile environment—harsh winters, dry soil, and unrelenting heat from the sun deepen a grape's flavor and heighten its sweetness. Bearable conditions bring only mediocre fruit.
>
> —*Notebook of a viticulturist*

Donegan covered the ground to his cottage and back again in long strides, appreciative of the cool, fresh air. Inhaling and shaking his head, he willed himself to brush off the heavy enchantment of that ivy-covered pavilion. No, it wasn't the whimsical structure, but the girl who waited there. Her nature unfurled in layers that surprised and impressed him, and he found it difficult to tear himself away. Even her sharp tongue drew him, as it so aptly displayed her keen intelligence.

In theory, he should detest her. Who could hope to find value in the offspring of a father and mother such as hers?

Both spoiled and selfish in their own ways, the lord and lady of the manor had earned his distaste immediately, and his feelings only increased as he learned more. The child they produced and raised should, by any logic, be even worse.

But like a gemstone tumbled to perfection by adversity, she had become smoothed and polished by her life. She seemed neither rich nor poor, stuffed full of material treasures like the wealthy nor drained of life like those in service. She hovered somewhere entirely different, on her own colorful, creative plane.

Yet the reality remained—she was the princess of the castle. Firming his jaw, he turned back and found her walking through the mist-shrouded vines. He strode out to meet her in the vineyard and held out the papers.

"I'm grateful to you for doing this." Hungrily she scanned the pages, a frown tugging on her features as she read. "Cassius. He wrote about Cassius again. He calls him slow-minded and simple, and without the business sense that all Malverns had."

"From what I can tell, Cassius refused to overwork and underpay the laborers. Either laziness or . . . mercy. I'm beginning to wonder if this man your father dislikes was truly so terrible."

She lifted her pained expression. "Father wasn't always the most affirming person, but he truly wasn't mean without cause. Cassius must have done something to Father for him to . . ."

Her voice trailed off and Donegan shifted uncomfortably, picturing the cynical lump of a man she now spoke of. If only he could hear her speak this way. Her vision of him seemed to be tinted with a sort of hero worship despite what

Harlowe had insinuated, and he couldn't bear to be the one to tell her the truth about the man. She'd learn soon enough if she persisted with these notebooks. Donegan bridged the uncomfortable silence with the first question that came to mind. "Did he ever speak of him to you before?"

"Never. Only of the Malvern family in general. But something happened between him and Cassius that caused him a great deal of sadness, it seems."

Donegan recalled the words of the skinny lad called Twig he'd met when he first arrived—no one knew exactly how Harlowe had come by his fortune. Did Tressa realize that? "Perhaps it's a private matter that is better left alone. People often have actions in their past they don't wish anyone to know about."

"But I wish to know everything. There's nothing that could ever make me hate him."

Her surprising words only solidified how wrong Harlowe was in his impression of the girl. As she once again buried her gaze in the words before her, he allowed himself the indulgence of simply watching her eager face. It seemed her inner nature was as lovely as her outward appearance.

How utterly absurd was his fascination with this girl. As an heiress and employer of underpaid laborers, she was the antithesis of everything he'd worked for in his life, and he must think on that every time he looked into the deep pools of her green eyes. Like multifaceted emeralds, they shone at him as she looked up. "Why do you always stare at me so?"

He broke the gaze and looked back to the sloping vineyards around them, keeping her face in his peripheral vision. "I'm wondering why you are so desperate to find that pile of money."

"One needs money to live." But her face shuttered, closing off something vastly more important than the little she'd revealed. After a moment of silence, she opened the shutters the barest sliver. "Sometimes money is merely a way to acquire what you truly want."

"Trevelyan, you mean?"

"Everything that's here. My father toiled for years over this vineyard, and no one else would see it as more than a field." She lowered the papers and looked out over the long rows of vines hanging off their guide wires. She traced a large leaf with her fingertip. "Sometimes I feel he's actually here. He's poured so much of himself into these vines that it's almost like I can experience him when I walk among his handiwork."

She closed her eyes and inhaled. "I can so easily hear his voice out here, mingling with the noise of rushing water and the insects. 'Tressa girl,' he'd say. Then some brilliant gem of truth would pour out. Something about vines, but also about life. I've stored them all up in my memory to pull out and use when I need them, but if we left here, I'm afraid they'd scatter like fog."

It struck him then what she was saying—Trevelyan Castle was a great cavern of all her most precious memories, the vineyard a field of her experiences, growing and green.

"There's so much about this place that I cannot even put into words. If I could, I suppose I would never need to paint it." Her voice came out whisper-soft and then she dropped her gaze, the spell of her reminiscence broken. "Not that any of this has to do with the fortune."

He laid a hand on her covered arm and found surprising warmth emanating from it. "No words are wasted on me, I assure you."

She threw him a grateful smile, her eyes glowing with a sort of kinship that gave him more hope than it ought.

The way she spoke of her father, as if his name were a precious pearl cradled in her palm, shed more light on her than on the man himself. She treated her self-absorbed mother with the same tenderness every day. He wondered at the girl as he attempted to attach label after label to her, discarding each with true confusion and sincere regard for her.

He brushed away the swelling admiration and cleared his throat gruffly. Forcefully. "It seems you enjoyed being with him."

The clouds drifted before her face again and she smiled in a tender way that drew him to her in spite of himself, urging him to move near, but he pushed against the inclination.

She shrugged in answer to his question. "I managed to make myself present whenever he was about the house. But I was a child, of course, with all of my foibles and silly questions." She turned to face him then, those emerald eyes shining directly at him with full intensity in the shadows of the pillars, reeling him firmly in until he had to nearly fight against the urge to pull her close and embrace all the color and life embodied in the girl. "You can imagine what an annoyance it would be to always have me near."

He cleared his throat, forcing himself to shift back and grasp the post harder. "No, I cannot."

With a light smile, she examined him. "Do you find it impossible to agree with anyone?"

"Only when they are wrong."

Her eyes sparkled in the moonlight. "I suppose everyone but you falls into that category."

Horse hooves rattled over the drawbridge in the distance,

but it was merely background noise pricking this surreal moment. Many formless thoughts swept through his mind in those moments of quiet.

She turned and looked toward the channel. "I cannot stop wishing to see his little boat come bouncing over the waves, returning to Trevelyan's shores as he did so many times. I used to sit here to watch when he took the boat out. I never dreamed of him drowning. To my little girl mind, he was invincible."

"You miss him a lot."

She closed her eyes and inhaled. "I think I've missed him all my life. I fear it might break me, for now I'll have to go on missing him forever."

Donegan cast his gaze out onto the shoreline and hardened it in place as he pictured the little island beyond, thankful she could not read his thoughts. His own secret lay perched on the edge of his tongue, ready to spill out into the night. He swallowed and clamped his jaw shut.

He jerked as her elbow tapped his arm when she shifted. "I should not speak this way to you. My grief is not your concern."

Oh, but it was. How greatly it was. In a moment, he could end her grief, change everything that was happening to her now. Yet what sort of grief would erupt over this family, this girl, if he revealed what he knew?

"Ah well, all I can do now is to see this treasure hunt through and find myself a fortune." Her lighthearted words were accompanied by a whimsical smile. "There's no finer remedy to grief than doing, and this hunt has kept me blessedly occupied. How greatly I need something to engage my mind in good, productive things. In the words of Marcus

Aurelius, the color of one's thoughts stain the soul and I dearly wish to have a lovely, colorful soul." A brave smile thinly veiled everything beneath.

Heart aching, nearly suffocating with anguish as he looked at her, he despised his position. How could he possibly continue to allow her to hurt so? Tenderness lay just beneath her veneer of strength, so easily penetrated by the sharp suffering of this world.

And her eyes. Those gorgeous jewels of radiant intelligence that took in everything and revealed just as much. How different they would look if he took her to the little island. But he couldn't.

Why? Why had he agreed to this? Why did he continue to be complicit in—

"You are staring again, Mr. Vance."

He turned his gaze away, grinding his teeth. "Donegan. Please."

After an airy silence in which she studied him intensely, her voice again filled the open space. "So why is it you are searching? Do you suffer the same obsession as the others who've come lately?"

"I'd hardly call myself obsessed over money."

But as soon as the words escaped, the truth sacked his already tense gut. *Money.* That was why he'd agreed to this—purely for money.

"Don't be ashamed. It seems to strike all men, this passion for accumulation of wealth. Even my father felt the need to hide his fortune away lest anyone—including his family—should remove it from his clenched fist."

Then, before he could respond, a powerful surge of conviction swept over him in that vast field of leaves and vines as he pictured his leather pouches. Of all the things he'd left behind over the years—jobs, clothes, languages, even family—that money had been his only constant attendant as he'd wandered, driven to increase it. And now it drove him into this secret he so detested. The condemnation that had gripped him earlier tightened its hold with fierce, relentless power.

He shifted. "Money has a surprising draw, especially when it can do so much good."

She turned to him, curiosity in her eyes, but a distant voice disrupted the deepening conversation. She tore her gaze from his to look back at the glowing windows of Trevelyan. Just like that, the spell had broken.

"I should go." And without another word, she whished past him and hurried between the curling vines. Exhaling the built-up tension of the encounter, of all his thoughts, he followed the girl out of the vineyard, through the gardens, and into the torch-lit courtyard, where he focused on trying to avoid the hem of her skirt gathering leaves across the stones. Together they ascended the timber stairs to the double doors and passed through them to find a small gathering in the grand room beyond.

"There! Ask her." A red-faced man limped toward them, the thump of his cane punctuating his angry words. "It was you, wasn't it? Thought you could scare me into forgetting about that little debt?"

"Mr. Prescott, please. No one here had any reason to set that fire."

"It's because you haven't the money. You and your sorry little mother have nothing, yet you cannot be without your gaudy castle. Your showpiece."

"I assure you we do have the money we owe you, and it shall be repaid as—"

"Prove it." He spat the words. "If you have the money, prove it. Pay me now."

Her little hand clenched at her side. "If you'll only give us time to—"

He growled, leaning heavily on his cane. "A week. You have exactly *one week* to come forward with this money you claim you possess or I shall call in the entire debt and see you sell every stick of furniture and polished stone you own. Is that clear? And I'll set the constable on you for arson. If I hadn't had the deepest respect for your father . . ."

As Donegan stood on the fringes of this scene, feeling even more an intruder than ever, he determined to protect her. Setting his jaw, he stepped between the irate man and the woman to whom he fired his angry words. "The lady said she'd pay you. Now take yourself home."

"There's no use hiding behind your bully, Miss Harlowe. The truth always comes out. And when it does, I'll have the constable descending on this house faster than you can blink."

The nerve of this pompous stuffed shirt. Squaring his shoulders, Donegan glared a powerful warning at him. "I don't like repeating myself."

With a snarling grimace, the unwelcome visitor slammed his hat onto the fine gray hair and limped toward the door. The man turned to shake his gold-tipped cane at the room. "Don't think I'll simply disappear. This is far from over."

Donegan winced, knowing it likely to be true.

Andrew Carrington strode toward Miss Harlowe with a protective posture and laid a hand on her shoulder. "He's only angry. This will pass, and he'll soon forget about it."

"I wish I could believe that." Miss Harlowe tipped her face toward her fine-suited guest and the storm of emotion in her eyes surprised Donegan. A palpable connection existed between them, thickly filling the narrow space between their bodies. That the girl felt something for this gentleman was obvious even to one as obtuse to these matters as Donegan. They had something between them—an established history.

Gritting his teeth, he turned away. What sort of man was he, wishing to keep this girl for himself in any form, when one of her own kind had already stepped in beside her? With bitter envy he forced himself to glance back at the pair, their perfectly matched countenances and clothing making it even more obvious.

No matter if she was intelligent and interesting, passionate and spirited, beautiful and bewitching to the extreme. She could be everything he'd ever hoped to find, but it mattered little if he was nothing of what she sought for herself.

16

A good vintner will not allow his vines to grow how they will in whatever way seems best to them, but he will work painstakingly to guide, redirect, and prune each plant so it may reach the full potential it cannot even imagine for itself.

—*Notebook of a viticulturist*

"How is the vineyard faring?"

Donegan dropped the sack of food on the rough cottage table and faced the owner of Trevelyan. "Surviving. For now."

"Did you complete the soil mixture?" Josiah Harlowe rose to retrieve a plate of bread and cheese and clomped back to the table.

"No. Soot will destroy the nutrients in the soil. I decided on a different mixture."

"Nutrients won't matter if the moisture is not controlled.

Mold will kill every one of my plants in a single season. You will do as I instruct. I hired you, after all."

"To *improve* the vineyard. Not ruin it."

With a growl, Harlowe kicked the chair and plunked down in it. "All these years I've worked. I know these vineyards, I say. I know them. Have you already killed them?"

Donegan's jaw twitched. "As I've said, they're surviving. So far."

"And Tressa?" The old man's haunted eyes lifted and searched Donegan's as he asked the question, as if he needed to know more than the words would tell him.

Donegan softened. "Also surviving. But she needs you."

"Hardly." Harlowe jerked his gaze away. "No more than her mother, who simply wants my bank account."

"Can you truly be so blind?" Anger pumped through Donegan, fueled by the haunting image of the girl's face as she spoke with such sorrow about this very man. An odd sense of protectiveness swarmed him for the girl so out of reach. "You have no idea what you have within your grasp, do you? Your daughter is a pure anomaly. She's the only grape that has ever flourished without any tending, the sweetest and most pure fruit you could ever taste, yet you let it rot on the branch while you throw yourself wholeheartedly into so many plain grapes that will give you nothing in comparison."

He watched Harlowe's shadowed face crumple as if his words were a physical assault and felt triumph that compelled him to continue, even as the old man turned away.

"She is brimming with every color imaginable, no matter what fills her life. Her outer beauty attracts so many, but her inner beauty simply captivates." He slowed the storm of words and lowered his voice. "And for some odd reason I cannot fathom, she is deeply devoted to you."

The muscles of his back worked, but Harlowe did not turn.

Finally, when no response was forthcoming, Donegan stood with a sigh of surrender and grasped his lantern. "I'll be back in a few days with more food." Treading across the room and out the door, regret pulled at his steps, weighing them down, but what more could he do?

He traveled down the steps, but before he'd turned onto the path, the door behind him opened, casting an orangey light over the ground. Clomps of footfall neared. Donegan paused at the base of the steps and waited.

"Her mother was that way once. So pure and full of beauty and light. I wanted to hold it all in my arms, to give her everything, and in doing so I broke her. All that light died, replaced by frivolity and pettiness. I couldn't bear for the same ruination to come to Tressa."

Donegan turned to look up at his tired face. "They're not the same sort of woman. What you said before about your daughter and the fortune—it isn't true. She cares nothing for it. Not like her mother does."

"Then why follow me about for years asking about it? Why all the fascination with its hiding spot?"

"I don't know. But I know she sees much more in you than money."

Harlowe stared toward the distant channel, his features hardening.

"Give her a chance. She needs your money, but even more than that, she needs you."

"There isn't much reason for her to love me. I'm a broken old man. I've never been fatherly toward her. And my past

. . . I can never seem to be rid of it. You don't understand—don't know anything of what I truly am. What a mess I've made of things . . ."

"Her affection is not based on what you do for her or what you've done before." Donegan strode toward the steps and slipped the folded drawing out of his cloak, holding it out to him. "Perhaps this will convince you where my words have failed."

Frowning, Harlowe unfolded the page. When he looked upon the portrait, awe and surprise unfurled in his face, light filtering through the creases of his features as his eyes widened to take it in. "I've loved her from afar for so long. My little butterfly, with the wings I dared not touch. Is it possible . . . ?" He stared for endless minutes as Donegan looked on, reading the hope upon his face.

Harlowe studied Donegan for a brief moment, then shifted it immediately back to the page and drank in his daughter's portrayal of him and all it conveyed.

The following evening, Donegan watched the sun descend below the horizon as he did every night and pondered his predicament. In a life of travel and constant change, it provided a sense of home to watch the same great ball disappear below the earth, no matter whose land he stood on as he did so. Shoving both hands roughly through his hair, he sighed and walked toward his cottage. But as he neared the little building with the crooked chimney, a lone figure appeared on the horizon. It was a child—one who walked with a remarkably familiar gait.

It couldn't be. How could she have come all this way?

Donegan squinted as she came closer, observing the halo of red curls framing her narrow face. The girl looked up as she neared, focusing on him with the unabashed directness of a true acquaintance, and he knew it could be no other. He uttered aloud the name he had not expected to say for some time. "Ginny."

With a weary smile, she trudged the few remaining steps separating them and threw open her arms to collapse against him. Donegan swept up the trembling girl wrapped in grimy clothing and tattered plaid shawls, holding her close. The slight weight of the nine-year-old's frame shocked and worried him, but he said nothing as he held her close and drank in her presence. Then Ginny leaned back and looked up at him with bright eyes sunken into a dark face. "I always knew you were telling the truth. That you weren't running away from us."

He hugged her close again, that dear, precious girl. "Why ever would you think such a thing? Have I ever lied to you before?"

"The whole village is saying it. Even Mama said it. After what you did, no one thinks you'll be back to right things."

Tucking her dirty tufts of hair behind one ear, he smiled at the girl. "Let me show you something." Adjusting her weight against him, he carried her to his cottage and ducked into the dark hovel. Placing her on the only chair in the little home, he reached up into the rafters and pulled down his leather pouches, dropping them one after the other on the table before her. "This is what I planned to bring back. When I had a little more, that is." He pulled them down in great clumps, never more proud of the vast sum he'd counted hundreds of times already. Only a glimmer of the earlier conviction concerning his money attachment tugged at his spirit.

She peeked into one bag and her eyes rounded at the bank notes that unfurled from its depths. "That's enough to fix almost anything in the whole world that's broke."

"Enough to fix our little corner of the world, anyway."

She smiled at him, lighting her wan features with just a trace of the former brightness he remembered. A bag dropped and he knelt to retrieve it, but the filthy boots beneath her dress caught his eye as she tried to slide them farther out of view. With a frown he grabbed one and pulled it toward him. Those boots, likely her brother's, had been abused down to their final days. The sole flapped at the toe and was worn nearly clean in other places.

"Ginny, did you walk here?"

Her shoulders collapsed and she bowed her head. "Only when I couldn't find a tinker to give me a ride. Your address was always on the envelopes when you sent those bits of money, so I thought . . ."

"So they could send *letters*. Not you!" He tugged at the laces and eased the boots off her damaged feet. "We'll soak these feet tonight. Then we'll see about sending you back."

"I can't go back. Not without you." She grabbed the edge of the chair with both hands and leaned forward. "Things is bad at home. I had to find you, because you're the only one who can fix it. Mum left and I'm alone."

He sat back slowly, looking at her face and absorbing the distressing information. "Sarah is gone?"

She nodded, red curls hanging over her face. "She had to go into town to find work because there's nothing left and the rest are sick. She left me with old widow Cromwell, but there's no room for me there. The old lady told me I should find you and see what could be done about things. We need you, Uncle Don."

A gusty breath of defeat whooshed from his chest as he sat back against the wall, his thoughts racing. Even his sister had left now. He had to have that money so he could buy back his family's land. There was no more time to waste. Harlowe would simply have to give him what he'd promised. No more games, no more treasure hunt.

"You'll stay with me, then. We'll send word that you're here and I'll find you a place in Trevelyan. Can you work?"

She pushed up her sleeve and flexed her scrawny arm with a smile.

He returned it with a brokenhearted one of his own. "You shall have a place here for a while then, while I arrange things. Surely one of the servants will spare a corner cot if you can scour pots." He glanced at the pages of translation work scattered across his table and determination settled over him. "This will be my last stop. When I've gotten what I've come for, we will return together. Then everything will be set right again for all who remain at Carin Green."

She cocked her head at a delightful angle and offered a smile of approval that emboldened him to the hilt. The bright face of Tressa Harlowe faded into the background of his mind as his larger task once again swelled and saturated his mind, calling forth every ounce of his determination.

17

> Pruning involves difficult decisions. It's about removing growth, even what is good and beautiful, to attain something far better.
>
> —*Notebook of a viticulturist*

I held the little opal ring up to the moonlight in the hall and watched the colors dance about, sparkling across its surface. *What happened to you, Father?*

I opened the door to my bedchamber and crossed to the little lamp to heighten the wick, flooding the great room with its glow. There on the little chintz-covered dressing table lay more pages, and the sight of them quickened my heart. I hurried over to them and lifted the pages, crossing to the open window to read. I settled myself into the wide windowsill and took a breath before plunging in.

Donegan's note was scrawled across the top:

I read further until I found more about the Malverns. I don't know how they're connected to the fortune, but I can't help thinking they are.

After a small space, the notebook translation began.

I've spent many years with this vineyard, nearly 25 of them in ownership of it, yet I still haven't learned the balance that will bring about the perfect grape. Perhaps that is what drives me back into it every year, especially when I finally had free reign of it.

We had another decent rainfall last week and the sulfur is no longer drying it out. My next step is to adjust the pH level of the soil, but I still must dry out the plants as well as the fruit.

So he *had* been involved with the Malverns before purchasing the estate. But he couldn't have been a field hand, could he? There had to be more to it than that, because there was no way a field hand could ever purchase his master's estate. I shoved away the horrifying possibilities that invaded my mind and skimmed ahead until I reached the section that spoke of the Malverns.

The only times I will think of the Malverns now will be as a model for how I should not live my life. We are attached to different vines, drawing life from a different source. Thus the fruit we produce, the life we experience, will be completely different. I owe them my fortune and my vineyard, but that is all.

I am glad to be done with them, glad that Cassius is gone. I do not regret what I did. A dying branch left to rot on a vineyard will only kill the whole plant.

The light flickered as a breeze whipped through the open windows and fluttered the papers about. I ran to force the windows closed and latch them, then I bent to retrieve the scattered pages that had sent my heart racing with panic and dread that I had no idea how to face. These lines proved nothing at all—did he even claim involvement in Cassius's demise? If only he hadn't written the word *regret*. What had he done?

My loyalty tried to swell over my dread, but it had weakened. I desperately clung to the hope that he'd admitted nothing specific, until Dr. Caine's words returned to me. *The only perfect father is the one in heaven*.

But I wanted the one on earth. So very much. One I could see and feel and hear.

Looking down at the condemning words scrawled on the now-wrinkled pages, I crumpled them into a wad and tossed them into the cold fireplace where I touched a lit candle to them and watched them burn. Cassius Malvern hovered about this castle like a ghost, haunting this search as if he had a stake in it. The closer I came to understanding Father's notebooks and finding his fortune, the more thickly Cassius seemed to descend until he nearly inhabited my dreams. Grabbing my candle, I exited the room to find my lady's maid and share tea with her. Perhaps that would help. Footsteps echoed somewhere deep in the house. "Lucy?"

I slowed when I reached the study, for the doors stood open a crack. Somewhere there had to be proof of his innocence, or an explanation—something that released me from this terrible feeling. I rummaged about the shelves and cabinets until I found the housekeeper's register and a new idea struck. Would I find Father's name among the workers? I looked about the desk but only found recent log books—nothing that was before Father's time as owner.

Suddenly I knew where to look. I scooped up my candle and flew out the door, through the hall and down to the abandoned undercroft, that great mausoleum of all things Malvern. It wouldn't be in Father's register anyway—it would be in theirs. Setting the candle on the stone floor, I knelt before a stack of crates and began to dig. I cast aside odd papers and other items until at last my fumbling hand found what I searched for—a leather volume tied with twine at the top, labeled with the name *Malvern.*

With trembling fingers I flipped through the pages. Season after season flew past my eyes, countless names of workers in every position, then at last it was there before my eyes, in black and white—Josiah Harlowe. Heart hammering, I traced the line across the page and read every detail about him:

> Harlowe, Josiah. Recommended by S. Hentsworth. Start: summer of 1835. End: Harvest of 1837. Reason: hostilities toward CJM.

I held my breath and reread the last section: hostilities toward CJM. Cassius J. Malvern.

Then my gaze lifted to the Malvern portrait hanging high up on the wall. I'd seen it many times and it had always fascinated me, but today I stared at it with new eyes, full of greater understanding of the family portrayed there. A finely dressed couple dominated the scene with darkly colored clothing and proud faces.

But there in front stood a tow-headed boy with the jeweled hand of his mother resting noncommittally on his shoulder. He stared directly at the artist who captured them, while the parents stared off into some dreamy space elsewhere. I met the painted gaze of the little boy I'd observed dozens of times on this canvas, seeing him anew. Here was the lonely, cast-off child, the one who had been sent away and forgotten. The last Malvern heir.

Cassius.

Refusing to dwell on it more, I strode out of the room and up the circular stairwell, away from the unblinking eyes of the painted child. There had to be a reason for Father's feelings toward the boy. Possibilities swarmed through my brain as I tried to crowd out the nagging ideas I could not bear to examine.

I knew, as my mind recalled Donegan's words about him, that the fault could not have been Cassius's. Everyone in Cassius's life and in mine had been filled with greed—yes, including my dear father who had so proudly clung to his mighty fortune—and they had all called Cassius a failure. As far as I could see, he'd only failed at one thing—greed.

When I slowed on the landing, I suddenly had the chilly awareness of being followed. The glow of a single candle bounced somewhere behind me, its light flickering in a hall. Footsteps echoed, and the name *Cassius* vibrated through my being. With one hand on the stone wall to balance, I hurried into the main part of the house.

Pausing at the well-lit entryway, I dipped behind a column and blew out my candle, watching the hall as my eyes adjusted to the dark. Light gleamed from its depths, growing brighter as it neared. Footsteps matched its bounce. When a boot clunked on the tile floor, I peered around the corner and up into the shocked face of Dr. Caine. Relieved, I ran to him and grasped his arm. "Dr. Caine, it's you. Oh, I've become such a child in this big old house. If only there were enough candles in the world to light every corner of this dreary place."

His shock melted into a warm smile and he patted my arm. "Nothing wrong with having a little fright now and then. This isn't an ordinary house." He lifted his candle and glanced around the hall, at the suit of armor watching us from the doorway. "I must admit to being rather captivated with the place myself. Something about the eeriness appeals to the mischievous little boy in me." He sighed. "It's silly to feel that way, but there's no escaping the effect of Trevelyan Castle."

No, I thought. *It isn't silly. The same spell has captured me for my entire life.* But I kept this to myself.

"Dr. Caine, I must know about Cassius Malvern."

Instantly the name drew his brow into a series of wrinkles.

"What became of him? Please, Dr. Caine. You must tell me."

"It's best if you don't ask about him. He was so unlike the other Malverns, and his story has no happy ending."

"At least tell me this—is he alive?"

The silence that followed nearly consumed me as the candlelight flickered over his troubled features. Then he gave the answer I expected yet dreaded. "No."

The depth of grief that hovered beneath the surface made it impossible for me to push further, so I merely offered a brief smile. "I suppose I should have assumed it was so."

He considered me for a moment. “Perhaps it’s time you and your mother leave Trevelyan. There’s little to keep you here now, especially with the debt over it. Forgive my rather personal advice on matters that are none of my concern, but I cannot bear to watch you sink the way they did. I know you see this fortune as your path to freedom, but perhaps greater freedom will come from releasing the idea of it. And Miss Harlowe, please realize—that’s all it is now. An idea.” His blue eyes glimmered like deep pools of wisdom, and my heart fluttered at the idea of release. “Cassius might still be alive now if he had learned to let go of such things in years past.”

With those words, the chill returned to my spirit again and the cold face of the boy in the painting loomed heavily over my thoughts.

With another squeeze of my hand, Dr. Caine removed his hat from the bench beside the door. He was preparing to exit, this man whose gentle nature served as a balm to my frightened spirit. How I wished he’d stay.

“Dr. Caine?”

He turned and offered me the easy smile of companionship, but I could not voice the request that hovered about my lips.

Instead, I smiled and said, “Safe travels.”

With a final nod, he set his hat on his head and took himself out to his waiting horse.

In the empty silence of the room, I found myself wishing for him to remain and protect me from my childish fears, for I knew they would only grow after this day, but I hadn’t been able to ask it of him.

Perhaps I should have.

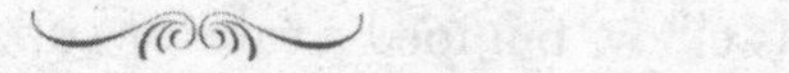

In that surreal moment between wake and sleep as I lay abed that night, my mind carried me back to the memories of that dark chest. The fortune had to exist—I'd *seen* it. I forced my memory to recall images and smells and sounds from that workroom, focusing on the table that had held the chest.

"Where did you get so much money, Father?"

He spun around and blinked at me. "You're still here? Why are you still here?"

"You told me I could stay."

His face twitched and he turned to glance out the window.

"Did you steal it like pirate treasure? Is that why you must hide it?"

"Who told you that?" He slammed the lid and locked it. "Who've you been speaking with about me?"

I trembled in the face of his anger. "Only the servants. They were gossiping in the kitchen."

Long, drawn-out moments of silence stretched through the warm air and hung between us. "They know nothing of where I came from, what I endured. Nothing."

Curiosity flamed through my mind then, the treasure forgotten in light of this little glimpse into Father's life. "Where *did* you come from?"

He shifted his gaze to me as if remembering once again that I was still there and studied me critically. "You'd best hang about with your governess and soak up your studies." He dusted his hands on his trousers. "Become an accomplished young lady and take yourself away from here."

"But I don't want to go away."

His elbow bumped a tube of soil, spilling rich darkness over the table surface, and he hurried over to it. He brushed it into a new tube and bent low to inspect his other tubes, lifting a notebook to continue recording. Once again I was invisible as his work swelled large and consumed his world. His pen scratched across paper and he lifted his spectacles off his eyes to see the details. I backed toward the fireplace to hide in the shadows so I wouldn't be sent away, remaining perfectly still, and then came the knocking.

At the sound, Father yanked the heavy trunk along the table, and the metal bands scraped along its surface. He was hiding it in this room.

A muffled voice came from somewhere nearby. "Get out of here." The voice was female, speaking in a strained, angry whisper. "Get out now." More knocking. My skin crawled.

Daisy's growl startled me from my drowsy little dream world. Forcing my eyes open, it stunned me to find I had been more asleep than awake as I'd walked through the past, for the voice was not in that room years ago, but outside my bedroom. Daisy growled again, and I placed my hand on her head. Then the voice that had intruded on my memory came again, piercing the last traces of drowsiness and plunging me firmly into the present.

"I said get out. Go away before you ruin this. Why is it so terribly cold in this hall? Did you open a window? Here, give me that lap blanket. Now go."

Again came the light thumps. Slinging aside the covers, I threw on a dressing gown and planted my bare toes on the chilly floor warmed only by a thin rug, then tiptoed across the room.

Nose to the crack, I opened the door and peeked out to see

movement in the little alcove across the hall. The glow of a candle illuminated the crouched, shivering form of Ellen in a white nightdress and black throw, her dark hair falling down her back and concealing much of her face. Rising with the candle, she thumped her palm against the wall, then moved to the right and repeated at intervals. Further into the darkness was the retreating form of cousin Neville, who must have eventually obeyed her orders to leave.

I studied her work, observing the strained, pale face and wondering at the appetite that drove her to grasp this fortune. I recognized in her expression the desperation, the hunger, to have that which always seemed slightly out of reach.

My door creaked and she turned and froze in the candlelit alcove, her face open and innocent. "I do hope I didn't wake you, dear. I had no idea your bedchamber lay in this section of the house." Shadows danced over her oddly placid face as she straightened to face me. "It seems I've lost my husband."

"In the wall?"

She glossed over my question. "You know how inseparable we are. I can never sleep without him."

"Naturally."

She smiled in the garish candlelight, her beady eyes piercing the soft glow. "I knew you'd understand. In the meantime, I thought I'd locate a book to help me sleep." Her slender hand indicated the shelves of my own books on vineyards that filled the little alcove. Ah, so this is what had led her to explore this particular spot. She must have thoroughly examined the library and every other room that contained books.

I smiled back. "I always find it lovely when a couple is so inseparable, even after marriage."

She stepped into the hall and slid an arm around me.

"Don't fret, darling. One day you'll be in that three-legged race yourself, and then you'll see exactly what it feels like. Come, help me find Neville."

We started down the hall, arm in arm. "I'm beginning to think I'll have to walk on my own two legs through my whole life. Falling in love seems far too complicated at the moment."

She paused in the dark hall, her eyes sparkling. "So many things can drive us into a man's arms, and very seldom is it merely love."

"What drove you into the arms of my dear cousin?" My vengeful little heart delighted in this trail of questions, but the splendid theater girl rose to meet them with confidence that surprised me.

"Cleverness. I wanted a house and income, so I convinced him he wanted me." With a gentle pressure of her arm, she led us forward again. "You see, little Tressa, when you are shopping for a husband, you must look past the man himself and evaluate everything he has to offer, for you are marrying a great many things along with him."

"And have you found it a worthwhile exchange?"

"Of course. I never live with regrets. I'll tell you a little secret about myself. I was a stage girl at the Savoy, but my time there ran out. Women can be petty, you see, and they decided the prettiest girl in the set needed to be pushed out of the way so the rest could have a chance. Lies and rumors earned me a quick exit, and that would have been the end for most girls."

"They tried to bury you, but lo and behold, they discovered you were a seed."

"Exactly." Her eyes sparkled at my summation of her story. "I made my way to the little café where I'd met a well-dressed gentleman who'd made it a point to seek me out for battles of wit now and then, and made sure he noticed me next time he stopped in. Within a week I had a marriage certificate with my name on it and a fine little home on Greentree Boulevard."

"What if you should someday fall in love, though? What then?"

This brought a heavy shadow over her lovely face. "Being in love is not all you'd imagine it is. It means someone else has control of you, and that's the end of one's freedom."

"Perhaps I shall be forever independent. I don't like the idea of being under the control of anyone."

She tucked her hand into the crook of my arm as we descended the wide, carpeted steps together. "My dear, we are all compelled by the force of something or someone. When you marry, at least you choose who is doing the controlling."

How her words echoed Mother's on the same topic. "Perhaps someday I'll be compelled by nothing other than my own convictions and desires."

She offered a wan little smile in response. "We can all aspire to such a life."

We reached the landing and the crash of metal sounded from the kitchen. "At last, it seems we've discovered the wandering husband."

Before we could make our way there, the intruder's swinging lantern departing from the rear kitchen door caught my eye. I paused to watch him from the window, yet it was not Neville's form we saw.

Ellen's perfect lips curved into a bewitching smile of amusement as she followed my gaze. "Ah, it is your Mr. Vance."

"I'd hardly call him mine." I watched the man stride quickly across the yard, a burlap sack over his right shoulder.

Irritation simmered along my skin that he should steal from our kitchen rather than simply asking for what he needed, but I set it aside. I turned back to Ellen for her opinion, as a matter of conversation, but my companion's face had quickly blanched to an alarming paleness.

She gripped the windowsill as a light panic tensed her features. "You must pardon me, but I do believe I hear Neville calling from our chamber." She spun toward the stairs we'd just descended. "I bid you good night." Lifting her blanket and nightdress, she sprinted full tilt up the stairs and out of sight. Yet when she reached the top, she turned left and flew down the hall away from her suite.

Turning from her odd actions, I returned to the window and searched for signs of Donegan Vance, but his light had disappeared. He must have reached his cottage already. I looked toward the front steps where I'd met the workers when they announced their strike, and with sudden panic, I realized that tomorrow was Friday.

18

> Focus merely on having a great harvest and you will have it—but only once. Focus on the lifetime of the vine and you will have a richer harvest every year after this one.
>
> —*Notebook of a viticulturist*

"I'm looking for Miss Harlowe." Donegan stood in the midst of the chaotic servant's hall as Friday's dinner preparations were fully under way. "No one seems to know where she is."

The rosy-faced housekeeper hurried over to him as she skimmed the night's menu and glanced over the clean serving platters laid out on the counters. "I'm sorry, Mr. Vance, but she left this morning and hasn't returned."

Shock silenced him for a moment. Gone? It was Friday—had she forgotten?

"Do you know where she went?"

This caught the maid's attention and she turned fully

toward him with a frown of concern. "No, I haven't heard." Her brow creased. "Truly, it isn't like her to simply disappear for an entire day. Perhaps Lucy knows." Hurrying to a slender scullery maid speckled with flour, she touched her shoulder. "Find out from Lucy where Miss Harlowe is, please. Quickly, now."

After a quick curtsy, the girl shot up the service stairs. Donegan paced before the window, dreading the moment he would see the mass of village men cresting the hill. They'd been absent from the fields since their threatened raid on Trevelyan, and surely they would not forget their delayed treasure hunt that was to take place that day.

When the little scullery maid returned with no news on Miss Harlowe's whereabouts, Donegan offered a quick thanks and marched from the room, slamming the service door behind him. Before he'd even reached the vineyard, he saw them. Led by Stephan Campbell and Lucas Fry, the ragtag band of laborers climbed the hill toward Trevelyan. Burlap sacks and pickaxes filled a horseless cart they dragged along with them.

Donegan strode out to meet them, his palm out. But what could he say to stop them? It was now Friday, the agreed-upon end of their patience after their time without pay, and Tressa Harlowe had disappeared.

"If you want your share, you'll have to help search." One of the men tossed Donegan a shovel, but he threw it back into the cart.

"I'll not let you do this. You've been faithful to the house of Harlowe for so many years, and what will it profit you to ruin them?"

A balding man spoke up. "Our own families will eat, that's what."

Laughter and assents followed.

Donegan grabbed ahold of their cart to prevent them from moving forward. Desperation and panic dug into him as he searched for anything that might stop them. "You are good and decent men who wouldn't . . ." His words trailed off as he glanced up to the grassy hill just beyond Trevelyan and saw a splendid sight. A proud steed pounded toward them, its bareback rider hunched low to clutch the animal's neck. Her dress billowed out behind her like a magnificent victory flag whipping in the breeze, her hair a long and tangled mess down her back. Never had she looked lovelier than in this eleventh hour.

As the horse huffed nearer, she straightened on his back and slowed him to a spritely trot across the field. Poised and elegant, yet flushed with a taste of the wild spirit that was constantly evidencing itself, Tressa Harlowe approached the little band with a look of rosy confidence. The group parted to receive the horse and rider.

When her horse danced to a stop among them, Tressa gripped the mare's mane and slid to the ground. Shaking out the fabric of her dress, she approached the men and opened a bag draped across her slender form. Donegan held his breath until she delivered her news.

"I have money for you."

Donegan exhaled all the tension of the day and the men gathered around her.

"It isn't everything we owe you, but hopefully it'll be enough to make your lives a little easier until all business matters at Trevelyan are completed."

Donegan smiled. What a diplomatic thing to call a treasure hunt.

"I do hope you'll be willing to return to the vineyard, for all of our sakes." She pulled coins from the bag and dropped them into waiting hands. "For if the vineyards perish, so does all of Trevelyan and Welporth with it."

When she had finished and the men shuffled away inspecting their money, she turned those sparkling eyes toward him with a light smile that made his heart leap. "Well, Mr. Vance, it seems I've beaten one fire to the ground. I've nothing left but to find the fortune."

"Where did that money come from?"

She met his look confidently. "It was rightfully mine to give, and that's all you need concern yourself with."

A change had come about Donegan Vance's face that night as he studied me from across the dining table with a touch of curiosity, but he remained blessedly silent.

Donegan was not the only one to come to the table with a marked change in demeanor, though. Mother presided over the meal with a rosy smile about her lips and a new inner strength held her poised in the throne-like chair as she addressed those seated around the table. Suddenly I realized what it was—the quiet confidence of one who knew herself to be loved, and it draped her entire person like satin. Being adorned in such assurance did wonders for her, and for that I could not hate Dr. Caine and his advances. Untimely as they were, they seemed precisely the remedy Mother needed.

"I have wonderful news for you all." She paused to sip from her glass and the chatter quieted. "I've made arrangements for all of us to attend the opening of a private art gallery at Lord Charles Standish Armitage's country estate in Bristol.

He's unveiling Franz Xaver Winterhalter's new portrait of Princess Helena in honor of her wedding this week. While the princess is married at Westminster, we shall be celebrating at the unveiling."

The silence that followed thickened in the air like a vapor. Neville raised one eyebrow, and the servers on the fringes of the room exchanged shadowed looks. No one dared point out what Mother, as the most well-bred of ladies, ought to know.

But after a few moments of quiet, Mother addressed the concern herself. "I do believe a mourning period begins when a death has occurred, but as my daughter has lately reminded me, there has been no certain death, no burial. No one expects a woman to remain captive in her own house indefinitely, and I intend to distract myself until my grief has a proper recipient."

Ellen's eyes glittered with judgment. Andrew focused his attention on his glass without a word.

I laid my hand on Mother's. "Perhaps we should discuss—"

"Tressa." Mother slanted her gaze toward my fingers resting on hers. She lifted her hand, grasped my fingers, and drew them toward her face. "You've lost your ring."

I tensed at the mention of the trinket now residing in the window of the exchange in Bristol and withdrew my hand. Parting with that little opal ring had cost me a great deal, but I'd rather have a chance at finding Father than a ring I kept merely to remind me of him.

She released it with a frown. "I suppose one of the servants found it lying about and turned your carelessness into their own stroke of good fortune." She lowered her voice. "You should be more cautious, especially now that we cannot replace costly little things like that."

Forcing back my stiff shoulders with the knowledge that I'd done what was needed, I lifted my gaze and met that of Donegan Vance, who studied me with rapt attention. Understanding dawned across his chiseled face as he watched my obvious discomfort with raised eyebrows, and I could not tell if he was pleased or not with what he'd discovered.

Ellen moved her attention to me. "I suppose you will accompany your mother, Tressa. Perhaps Neville and I will remain behind. Someone must monitor these servants with slick fingers or you shall return to an empty house."

Smiling over clamped teeth, I looked toward my cousin-in-law. "I wouldn't hear of it, Ellen. It's dear of you to offer, but I insist you go with us. Where else will you be able to wear that creation of yours with the peacock feathers sprouting from it?"

Finally we all rose to retire in the drawing room. I lingered just inside the doors, finding to my surprise that I desired the company of Donegan in that moment more than anyone else in the room. Perhaps if I'd been surrounded by a more likable crowd of people, he would not be the best company afforded me.

"You really ought to start telling the truth." Donegan's words immediately threw a chill on my brief moment of warmth toward him.

"When have I been dishonest?"

"You need to tell Ellen plainly that she isn't entitled to your money. It's the only method that will work with her."

I stepped close to keep my words private. "Spend one day in the society I keep and you'll see why I speak as I do."

"I doubt it."

"Plain speaking is for the villagers and working men."

"Well-bred society is too good for the truth."

I grimaced. "Stop twisting my words."

"I'm merely interpreting."

"Badly." I cast him a steady look. "Good night, Mr. Vance." I turned away and left the lingering party for the library, wondering why I even bothered talking to the man.

With sure steps, he followed me into the room of walnut paneling and perfectly kept books and touched my arm. "Truth isn't as dangerous as you think. Doesn't it say in Scripture that the truth will set you free? Well, maybe it will for you."

"It also says to speak the truth in *love*, which you seem to find impossible to do."

"So the way you speak to your cousin, that's loving?"

I hesitated, biting my lip as I recalled the jabs draped in silk. "No, it isn't."

"It would serve everyone far better if you spoke plainly. Once the sting of truth is dealt, it can begin to heal, but an unspoken truth festers for a long time."

"I see. Being cruel to be kind." I wandered along the wall covered in paintings, running my finger along the intricately carved frames. "There are so many colors and brushstrokes at our disposal, and each combination can paint the same scene in a different way." I paused before the recent addition I'd convinced Mother to bring home from France, a plein air painting of a seaside hill covered with wildflowers and people. It had been ridiculously inexpensive because it so departed from the classic style. "There are many ways to convey the same thing, and there's value in softening the harsher messages with love."

"You'll not convince me to speak anything but truth."

"Just like you did to Mrs. Campbell, that woman we visited in the village who offered you a share in the labor of her heart, which I believe you in turn said was terrible."

He looked across the rows of books, his forehead creased in a sudden frown. "I never said that."

"More or less."

The hardness melted rapidly from his features, leaving a broken despair in its place. He turned, looking directly at the intricately patterned rug. "You're right. That was foolish. It must have hurt her."

I gripped the edge of the desk and leaned against it. Could it truly be that easy to reach this man? The shell of callousness around his heart seemed to be paper-thin, with an abundance of tenderness just below the surface. Perhaps there was hope for him.

The look of desolation seared across his face drew my instant pity. With a sigh, I leaned over the desk and wrote a verse onto an empty page of the log book. It was one I'd been made to memorize when I was in the schoolroom with my tutors and had not yet learned to control my tongue.

> He that keepeth his mouth keepeth his life: but he that openeth wide his lips shall have destruction.

I tore the paper from the book and extended it to him with a smile of encouragement. "Perhaps this will offer you guidance when you need it."

He read it with a grim expression, then turned back to me with a troubled look and stumbled over his sincere question. "How should I soften the words, then? How do I speak gently and still . . . ?"

"There's always something you can find to compliment, no matter the food before you."

"Not at some of the tables I've shared."

"Then tell them kindly that you didn't care for it. Say it is not to your taste."

"Not to my taste. I can do that." He gave a firm nod.

Then his gaze roamed the paintings on the high walls. "Are any of these yours?"

Mine. As if my paintings were official and important.

"I've not painted a single one of these, if that's what you mean."

"You should display yours. You communicate a great deal through your work, simply by arranging colors so brilliantly. I don't believe I'd ever tire of staring into them, and I'm certain others would feel the same."

Jarred by the matter-of-fact compliment that carried no trace of false flattery, I closed my mouth and fingered the edge of the desk.

Amos rapped lightly on the doorframe and entered with a bow. "Tea is set out in the gallery, miss. The others are taking part already."

"Thank you, Amos. I'll be along presently."

With another bow he backed out of the room, again leaving me alone with Donegan. The man stepped forward and offered me his arm to escort me back to the waiting party.

We rounded the corner into the front hall with a swish of my skirts. "Will you be joining us for tea, Mr. Vance?"

His jaw flinched before he answered. "Thank you, but tea is not to my taste, Miss Harlowe. I prefer to fill my insides with solid food." He bowed over our clasped hands.

With a crooked smile I sank into a brief curtsy and departed into the gallery with the others, heart still simmering with amusement from the brief encounter. Tea and gossip seemed insufferably boring after the authentic, thought-provoking conversation I'd just left. My mind wandered and I glanced around the room and out the window.

It lingered there idly until a flash of movement caught my attention and drew me back to full awareness. As my mind filled with thoughts of treasure hunters and forgotten heirs, I excused myself from the waning gathering, leaving the room with a candle. I ran to a side door and pushed out into the night to look about.

A soft, pathetic whimper drew my gaze to the left. A scrap of a girl leaned against the kitchen tower's stone buttress, sobbing as if her very life flowed down her cheeks and onto the grass beneath her. I studied the unfamiliar child in tatters, wondering which servant was her parent.

As I neared, I felt as if I watched my childhood self crying. The suffering I saw in her bent posture, in the forward fall of her little shoulders, climbed through me with a familiar dull ache. Silently I strode toward her and placed a hand on the wild mass of red curls. She did not push me away, so I smoothed the curls with all the tenderness of empathy and understanding. She turned her face to me, those red-rimmed eyes studying mine, but she said nothing.

"Life can be a hard burden, especially with shoulders as small as those."

She sniffed, smearing her sleeve across her nose. "I'm older than I look."

Even the defiant thrust of her chin resembled my own years ago. Too often adults had made the mistake of speaking to me as a child when my heart had been far older. I knelt before her, leaning my shoulder against the buttress, and smiled at her. "Perhaps you only looked small because you were standing next to this gigantic tower. I can see in your eyes that you have the mind of a grown person. Has Mrs. Hodgson in the kitchen been cross with you? She used to scare the life out of me at times."

Her expressive eyebrows lifted and then turned down in a frown as she mulled over her answer. "I only wanted to smell the tarts. I wouldn't 'ave snitched any."

"That's unkind of her not to let you smell them. Perhaps she didn't know that's all you wanted."

In the moments of silence that followed, the little form under the cloak trembled slightly. I ached to take this little one and wrap her in an embrace, but I settled for rubbing small circles on her back. This simple touch unleashed a fresh flood of tears that pooled under her red-rimmed eyes, then rolled down her freckled face. "She ain't like me mum, that nasty old cook. Mum used to make tarts for my birthday and leave them in the windowsill." Her head drooped until her chin hit her chest.

"Is it your birthday?"

The lowered head nodded.

I squeezed her shoulder and rose. "Wait here."

I hurried into the kitchen where a startled Mrs. Hodgson spun to greet me. "Miss Harlowe. We weren't expecting the likes of ye down here. Was something the matter with your meal?"

"Dinner was lovely, but that isn't why I'm here. I'm afraid I'll be commandeering one of your wonderful tarts. And please fetch me a small candle."

I accepted the plate from the confused woman and lit the

candle after pushing it firmly into the little delicacy. Backing out the door, I smiled my thanks and cupped my hand around the tiny flame. When I rounded the tower's buttress where the little girl remained, those shadowed brown eyes widened in surprise at the sight of the platter.

I knelt before her and smiled warmly, bittersweet feelings pumping through my veins. "And now, you have to make a wish before you blow out the candle." I righted the candle that insisted on tilting sideways and extended the plate to her.

As I watched her, eyes shining in the candle's light, my mind was drawn back to a morning in the vineyard with Father. "It's a wishbone, Tressa girl. For making wishes." He held the dried V-shaped bone up before us. "You pull one end and I pull the other. Whoever gets the stem on top gets his wish."

He'd caught me staring at the sunrise from the kitchen and pulled me out into the vineyard for what he called a "front row seat." We sat against posts in the field, the soil rich and cool below us. I couldn't have been much older than six, yet I recalled every vivid detail of the rare glimpse into this tender side of Father. We had taken turns naming the various colors streaking across the sky when we felt a simple "pink" or "orange" would not suffice, then we sat in silence and simply delighted in the canvas of the sky. I thought it a most perfect morning. So when he pulled out the bone in that misty dawn hour and coaxed me to make a wish, I quickly said, "I already know what I'll wish for, Father. I want—"

"You can't tell me what it is, girl. But whatever you wish, make sure to ask for an abundance of it. If you take my advice, you'll wish for a good husband with plenty of love for you."

But at that time I cared nothing for a husband, good or bad. Pursing my lips, I silently stated the most ardent wish of my heart in one short phrase. *I wish for an abundance of this.*

Almost two decades later, I had nearly the same wish. Looking into the dewy eyes of the flame-haired girl before me, I smiled warmly and stirred the little flicker of hope that had smoldered quietly within me for days.

Please, Lord. Let that wish come true one day.

19

No one but the vintner can walk among his dead-looking crop at winter and know just how much abundant life is lying below the surface, just waiting for the spring to wake it up to vibrant life and glory in its season.

—*Notebook of a viticulturist*

Donegan planted his shoulder solidly against a beech tree as he watched the little scene unfold near the house. Her entire posture like a gentle caress, the princess of the castle knelt before his tiny niece and spoke words that, judging by the woman's expression, could only be the kindest sort. Watching her thus, bent in service to a small child so reduced in station, sparked waves of admiration that engulfed him. Despite who Miss Harlowe was, in this moment her loveliness deepened and intensified until he saw nothing but the beauty of a woman who would stoop to the level of a hurting child.

And in that soft twilight, with moonbeams casting down on them all, he began to yearn. Fervently, eagerly, and without the restraint of reason. The girl who had at once intrigued and drawn him had now burrowed so deeply into his heart with these newly revealed layers of beauty, that she would not easily be removed.

"For all your talk about being the manager, you don't spend much time gazing out at the fields." Lucy stepped near to him in the shadow of the great tree. "Leastwise, not the same way you gaze at other things."

Donegan crossed his arms and turned to smile at the maid. "Have you left your duties just to hassle me?"

Her plain little face grew serious. "You told me to come to you if I ever heard anything you should know."

"Something about the treasure?"

"No, it's that horrid cousin of hers, Mr. Vance." She hesitated, looking away. "Amos and I overheard him making plans. He's going to that painting show, and he told his wife he had a plan to keep the family away from Trevelyan."

Donegan glanced toward the massive structure that contained so many vile people, as well as a fortune that made them all even viler. "Did he say what it was?"

"No, sir. Only that his wife wasn't to fret about having to leave the castle with them. He said they'd be back alone to look about for the fortune soon enough. I'm afraid they won't let off until they've ruined her, or worse."

"Thank you, Lucy. I suppose I better go along, then. I can take my horse."

Her breath whooshed out in a sigh of relief. "I'm that glad to hear it, Mr. Donegan. She needs someone to protect her, even if she don't think so."

The moon lighted Lucy's lopsided mop cap as she followed Donegan's gaze to Miss Harlowe and Ginny.

"An odd sight, is it not?" Donegan kept his voice low.

"I'll say. I've not seen anything like that hair outside of a glowing hearth."

"I meant her. Miss Harlowe. Being so gentle and kind to a girl like that." He still couldn't wrap his mind around the many conflicting parts of her. "I've heard she isn't one to speak with common people."

Lucy folded her arms across her chest. "It's not as strange as you'd think, Mr. Vance. That girl always had a heart the size of the ocean. Only, she poured it out on one person at a time. Now look at her, learning to spread it out a bit, since her father's gone. I do pity her, losing him that way, but look what good it's done her."

He pictured the closed-off, bitter man that was her father. "She certainly chooses the hardest people to attach herself to."

"It's not because they are so great, Mr. Vance, but because she is. An uncommon love makes her uncommonly beautiful."

He couldn't help but agree.

A door opened near the pair kneeling over the plate, casting a square of light over the grass behind them, and Andrew Carrington stepped out into the night. Donegan squinted at the finely tailored black suit moving about, perfectly complementing the dusky blue of Tressa's gown that reflected the moon's light.

How foolish were those dreams of his. He must pull them out by the roots so they would never surface and unfurl their leaves. Miss Harlowe and the gentleman stood together, their long shadows joining into one. "What of that one? Won't he protect her? They seem so perfectly suited."

"What makes you say such a thing? Doesn't my lady deserve better than him?"

"What, is he a rung below her on the social ladder? Maybe not as wealthy or titled?"

"She isn't titled, Mr. Vance. And he's about six hundred rungs below her in every way. Got no character or backbone, that one."

Donegan squinted at the silhouette of the couple, at her sweet upturned face looking at his, and pictured those green prism eyes radiating with hope and tenderness. All of it was to be wasted on that stuffed suit, and no jewels as rare as emeralds should be wasted.

But reality chased his desire and smote it down—he was not the hero, either. Awareness of his massive secret hidden on that island, the big deception, turned in his gut like a snowball gathering weight as it rolled. If only circumstances had been different.

"I know he'll hurt her again, even if he does marry her this time. Mark my words, it will not end well."

Those words ricocheted through Donegan's mind and he glanced up at them again. Carrington had hurt her? Some primal instinct urged him to bound toward them to yank her away and shield her from him.

That was the exact minute that, despite everything, he decided to fight for her. What did Andrew have that he did not, anyway? Heartily shoving aside a growing awareness of all that stood between them, a plan took shape and blossomed in his mind and emboldened him. "Perhaps someone else should come and steal her from him, then." The demands of

Carin Green and the people waiting for him there niggled at his mind, but for the moment he was contractually obligated to remain on this estate. And in that contracted time, he would not deny himself the pleasure of her presence or the desire to pursue this girl he could not ignore.

A smile budded on the maid's tiny pink lips and spread over her face with sunny gladness and relief. "Well, it's about time you stepped up, Mr. Vance. I thought you'd never set aside that massive pride and—" She clamped a hand over her mouth as the last words escaped.

He merely smiled at her. "Lucy, what does that man have that I don't?"

"A lot of growing up to do."

"No, it's the clothes. Fine clothes, Lucy."

"That isn't much."

"So I assume you're prepared to assist me?"

A tiny smile returned to her lips. "Whatever you ask, Mr. Vance. I always knew a worthy man would come for her."

"She might not have me."

She rocked back on the heels of her worn black shoes. "Oh, she will. She might not know it yet, but she'll have you, sure as I stand here. And you have me on your side."

"Good. Because we have to overcome a great deal." Not least of which would be the class barrier.

Yet this girl did not travel the track laid out for her as so many of her set seemed to do. No, Tressa Harlowe had jumped the tracks long ago to run about as she would. Even her art poured out all over those gray walls when no one thought to give her a proper canvas for it. It was as if she couldn't help herself, so full of color and beauty she was, and that notion intrigued him to distraction.

Perhaps she'd disregard the bounds of society for one more reason.

Him.

I almost wished to remain at home when the day came for us to leave for the gallery opening. Neville's eyes sparkled in a dangerous way that worried me. Ellen even exuded a chilling calm. But when Dr. Caine appeared in the courtyard with those boarding the waiting carriages, my tension eased considerably.

Three carriages traveled to the Armitage estate in Bristol, for the Langfords would not fit in ours and Andrew insisted on taking his own. He might be called away at any time to attend to his father's urgent business matters. Neville and Ellen rode in their carriage with our two lady's maids and Mother and I rode with Dr. Caine in ours.

As Mother slept, her head lolling at an unladylike angle against the side of the carriage, I found myself clinging to the window with my face out in the breeze so I could watch the majestic woods as we rolled through them. The power of the huffing horses matched the grandeur of the towering pines and beeches bordering our path. Who needed a formal display of art when there were windows in carriages? When I finally eased myself back into my seat, Dr. Caine watched me with a sparkle of amusement.

I smiled awkwardly. "At times I forget I'm a grown woman."

"That's in your favor, Miss Harlowe. There's nothing in adulthood that outvalues the freshness of childhood."

I studied this man who had so recently come into our lives with such a large impact. Mother's cheeks shone with rosy good health, even in sleep, and it was all because of this man. "You know, I should resent you, but I'm finding it more and more impossible to do so."

His eyebrows rose. "Resent me?"

I merely nodded toward my mother. "There's something between you, is there not?"

With a crooked smile, he shrugged. "That something may soon dwindle to nothing. It is not for a poor sheep to possess a diamond."

"There are worse creatures than sheep, Dr. Caine, and things more valuable than mere diamonds."

We shared a smile across the carriage as it bounced over the rutted coastal road.

"Officially, I'm traveling with your party as her physician. Unofficially, I thought perhaps I might offer a little companionship and support while she's away from home. I won't attend the events, but I shall be present in the background in case she has need of me."

"You've nearly taken over my role." When his face formed the lines of apology, I hastened to add, "And I eagerly hand it over to you. I've been carrying the burden for years, and it's nice to have a small break."

He relaxed into his seat and my attention again drifted to the window. The sound of the sea gushed over my senses, making everything else pleasant in its own way. We spoke easily and freely on that ride, and the emptiness created by my distracted father filled just a little by this stranger who somehow fit that role better than Josiah Harlowe himself.

When our carriage rolled up to the magnificent entrance of the Armitage estate, lit with five gaslights and a glow from every window, a gentleman, tall and handsome, waited for us beneath the archway. Upon closer inspection, I saw in the man a familiar posture and stature. It was Andrew.

While the groom climbed down from his perch, Andrew stepped forward and reached for me with one gloved hand to help me down. What a handsome figure he cut, especially with the quietly confident smile tinged with boyish charm.

Suddenly his words echoed in my mind. *"I should not have given up so easily before. I can promise you, I won't make that mistake again."* It was only the challenge that drove him now, wasn't it? No matter how attractive he looked, how heartbreakingly familiar and dear, I must never forget that. What I saw now was not real. *Not real.* The way he looked at me, devoted himself to my care, it would all end the minute he no longer felt the draw of a challenge. Or when he'd acquired my fortune.

Still, I tucked my hand into his arm in that old way I once had and allowed him to escort me up the stone steps to the grand front entrance.

"You're a vision." He breathed the words so that only I could hear, his breath warm on my ear.

I dared not speak. With my free hand I fluffed the compressed fabric of my traveling suit and focused on walking as elegantly as my stiff legs would allow.

Soon Mother and I and our two maids met together in a lavish guest suite filled with large walnut furniture and the light scent of lilacs. We rubbed, brushed, and cleansed away the evidence of our travel and donned wonderfully fresh gowns in preparation of the evening. Now I touched the elaborate design of my hair sprinkled with tiny pink flowers to offset my sweeping dark-blue gown, wondering at the artistry of my maid. A woven choker dotted with pink roses rested against the pale skin of my neck, heightening the elegance of my appearance.

Dinner would be at eight, and the hours before then would be filled with walking among the fabled artwork I had glimpsed on the way in with delightful surprise. Much as I enjoyed great expanses of natural beauty in our vineyard, there was something awe-inspiring about seeing the work of legendary painters, men whose minds created images so amazing and full of life that they portrayed both the reality of their subject and the fanciful creativity of the artist's interpretation. How I longed to be downstairs among the color and artistry that would be merely a casual pastime for most other guests.

When I descended the gently curving stairs, the soft velvet gown brushing against my ankles, Andrew smiled up at me from the bottom, ready to escort me into the rest of the evening. How handsome he looked—tall and strong with a ready smile toward me. He would be hard to resist.

I find it difficult to prune flowers from the vines, but I must, or I will have nothing but a vineyard full of fading beauty in the end.

—*Notebook of a viticulturist*

The evening passed in a blur of well-dressed people floating about, while I studied the work of geniuses, wishing I could match their skill. An English flag stood proudly in each corner, and the royal Hanover family coat of arms was displayed at the head of the gallery.

Andrew elbowed me gently out of my haze of admiration. "The press is here."

"What? Who is here?"

"The press. The bald man there with the gold chain timepiece and spectacles is from the *Bristol Post*. We need to make a favorable impression on him, since most of my future constituency read the *Post*. One good word in that paper could do wonders for my career."

I looked over the sharp-eyed man who pointed at the paintings to his left with a cup of punch as he spoke with our host. Squinting, I assessed how I'd re-create such a face on canvas, with light gray shadows to bring out the wrinkles lining a neck that resembled a turtle's. I'd give his long mouth the little curve of a dubious smirk. Perhaps I should have learned to paint portraits—or at least paint on canvas—so that I might do something respectable with my art, as these other artists had done.

"I shall do my best to place you in a favorable light to him."

Drifting away from Andrew, I lost myself in a long alcove lined with paintings, daring to touch a few textured pieces when no one looked my direction. What sort of paint had created such a rich—

"Pardon, miss. You are Josiah Harlowe's daughter, are you not?"

I spun to face the newspaperman, his wrinkled face now in close view. He stood just outside the alcove, and I walked to meet him, filling my head with as many positive adjectives about Andrew as one could muster about a former suitor. "I am, sir. I believe Father had spoken to you a time or two about his harvest."

"That he has. I've always been fascinated by the man. Perhaps it's the legends of his hidden fortune that amuse this old man so. I'm quite happy to have run into you, although I must admit, I'm rather surprised to see you here tonight."

"I was on the guest list, I believe." I glanced about the large open ballroom filled with people, but Andrew was not in sight.

"Yes, of course you were." He adjusted his spectacles in the folds of his face and scrutinized me from head to dress hem. "I hardly expected you to accept, after all the . . ."

"We are not officially in mourning yet."

"Well, yes, but . . . I hear you've been in a spot of trouble." When I frowned, he filled in the missing pieces for me. "That fire at the Prescott estate that caused hundreds of pounds in damage and nearly killed two of his maids. Are you not the prime suspect in that case?"

My neck heated painfully as several well-dressed guests behind the man paused to eavesdrop with all the stealth of Guernsey cows. "Who has told you such a thing?"

"Why, I've heard it everywhere. I assumed it was general knowledge."

Panic washed over me, but he continued to watch me expectantly. It must be inherent in the nature of these men of the press to be relentless in their obtrusiveness. "I assure you, the truth will come to light and it will be proven that I was not involved in the fire."

"May I ask then how you explain the letter that was found?"

"Letter?"

"The one threatening him into releasing your family from the debt. The official word from the constable is that it was signed by you."

"M-me?" Fear piled over me in rapid waves. How could anyone believe such a thing?

He finally had the grace to appear uncomfortable. "My apologies, Miss Harlowe. I thought you'd already been informed. The *Post* has been following the story closely. It isn't every day a young woman, an heiress, is an arson suspect."

In the haze of my vision, I glanced around again for Andrew to come to my aid, but only strangers moved about. "I assure you, no officials have questioned me on the matter, and I'd tell them they were wrong if they did."

The newspaperman's eyes glittered with intrigue. "You're saying you have an explanation for it all, then?" His long fingers flexed at his side as if itching to pull forth his notebook and take down my words.

"Absolutely not. None is needed."

"I assume you can account for your whereabouts that night then, can you? That'll be the only proof that will convince anyone at this point."

"Why, of course." My mind spun. What had I been doing that night? Had I been among the family? No, I'd retired early. Briefly spoken to Donegan Vance in my room.

At last the familiar figure of Andrew materialized just ahead in my hazy vision, and in that instant it struck me what I'd been doing the evening of the fire, and who had been with me.

I straightened, looking the newspaperman firmly in the eye, speaking loud enough for Andrew to hear too. "I was out walking that night with a gentleman. Surely my companion could vouch for my presence." It had been the night he'd made that ridiculous excuse about the dog and the flower. I met Andrew's gaze and beckoned him into the conversation, but he returned my look with a severe one of warning, his blue eyes snapping in desperate communication. What was he saying?

"Which gentleman was out with you? I wasn't aware you'd attached yourself to anyone."

At these words from the newspaperman, my heart sank, for I knew what Andrew had been communicating. "*One good word in that newspaper could do wonders for my career."*

And any hint of impropriety could end it. Which was the thing he worried about—having his name attached to a lady of lesser heritage or being associated with an arson suspect? Memories pricked me then of hiding our attachment, of dropping hands when certain people looked our way, of him pretending he barely knew the girl he'd claimed to love. The insecurity and hurt from those times swirled around me now and thickened in the air until I felt they'd strangle me.

I lifted my gaze to Andrew's once more, searching for some sign that he would withdraw his silent request and help me, but the look had only intensified. Fear darkened the blue of his eyes. I looked between these two men, the eager news gatherer and the man I had once loved. This mess had grown like thick vines around me until I was trapped in its tangled branches.

"I cannot remember the details at the moment." Something delicate crumbled inside me and my heart ached.

Pulse throbbing, I excused myself and brushed past the man. Despite the plethora of artwork, the room had taken on a bitter aura and I needed to escape. Just outside the doors of the ballroom, Andrew burst upon me and spun me around by the arms in the empty hall. Breathing hard, I backed up and looked from his neatly tucked cravat to the clean-shaven face watching me earnestly.

"Tressa, I almost feel I owe you an apology."

"Almost?" Hurt poured over me anew.

"You behaved admirably, though. Sensational performance. I knew all along you'd make a fine wife to this government man." He took my hands and smiled down at me with warmth that made me sick. "I've never loved you more."

"I'm not an actress, Andrew."

"It'll only be around other people, don't you worry. At home you can be your own dear self. We shall be so happy, Tressa. Of course, we'll have to wait until I've gained the vote and this whole scandal blows over before we make any public announcement, but then nothing will stand in our way."

"This is only for the *Post*, right? When the constable comes to question me, you will tell him what happened that night, won't you?"

Andrew's face blanched. After a moment of horrible silence, he uttered a false, awkward laugh. "Tressa, I thought you understood. I couldn't possibly have my name tangled in any . . ."

I placed a trembling hand on his chest. "Andrew, you have chosen the wrong woman. I could never spend my days proving my integrity to others by lying. Do what you must to achieve your ambitions, but pray, do not include me."

With powerful steps beneath swishing skirts, I hurried down the hall echoing with merry voices and away from that face. When the tears threatened, I stepped into a quiet window bay in the grand entrance hall, secluded from the rest of the world. I slipped behind the heavy gold-trimmed curtain, tucked myself up on the curved bench, and closed my eyes. What a foolish, senseless girl I'd been. Knees to my chest, I curled around the ache inside and out of desperation connected my heart to the only One left to me in this moment.

Lord, please. Won't you close this wretched wound so it can finally begin to heal?

But it was more than Andrew's actions that had caused

this hollow space, for loneliness had traipsed after me most of my life, only being shooed away for moments at a time.

When footsteps plinked on the tile near me, I had collected myself and blanketed the hollow space with poise and determination to endure the remainder of the night with dignity.

"There you are, my lady. You're one for hiding, you are."

The friendly voice of Lucy lighted on my tender ears and drew me out from the bay. "One can only handle a roomful of strangers for a certain time before she must escape." I offered the girl a smile.

She tugged me out and poked at my hair critically. Her own frizzy hair and serviceable black gown remained unblemished. "They're about to unveil the princess's portrait, and then the dancing begins. Your partner cannot dance without you."

Dancing. The thought of being that near to Andrew made my stomach lurch. "I'm not certain I feel up to dancing tonight. Perhaps you can make my excuses and I'll simply retire to a guest suite."

"I'll not hear of it, my lady. What ever is troubling you on such a grand night?"

I released a sigh and looked at my maid, the closest thing I had to a friend. "I cannot abide the sight of Andrew just now. He's done something despicable, and I'd rather not speak to him just yet."

Her face brightened, delight smoothing its pale contours. "Good. Because he isn't the partner I mean."

21

> Appearances can be deceiving, but in the end, fruit does not lie. They make it abundantly clear the sort of plant from which they have sprung.
>
> —*Notebook of a viticulturist*

My eyes roamed about the crowded ballroom for Andrew despite my desire to avoid him. They were a magnet for the man when I knew him to be in the room. Yet his figure did not appear. Perhaps he had retired early. Then I looked about for the man Lucy deemed my partner, but I saw no one who fit. Violins drew out long notes in preparation for the waltzes and polkas to come, and a tickle of anticipation climbed my skin. Then the room fell silent.

Lord Armitage stood on a small platform addressing his guests, the curtained portrait behind him. Grand gestures accompanied the words I could not hear from the doorway, and after a long-winded speech he stepped to the side. Violins sang to accompany the sweeping movement of two servants drawing back the curtain, and there it was—the portrait of Princess Helena, the new bride, captured with elegant beauty in an off-shoulder gown with white roses. Exquisite beading looped about her hair among its chestnut strands. Oh to be in her place today, married and finished with the pain of the unknown, connected to someone forever.

Applause cascaded over the crowd, along with clinking glasses and "Here, here!" As the band swelled into "God Save the Queen," the room quieted. When the music ended, Lucy leaned close to whisper. "He's waiting for you." She tugged my arm and pointed. My roaming gaze passed over the people in the room and lingered idly on a man looking directly at me, through the crowd and chaos, before passing on. Then realization jerked my gaze back and locked onto his familiar form across the room. He remained still as a rock amid the waves of gowns and strangers, those dark, penetrating eyes focused firmly on my face.

It couldn't be.

But it was—Donegan Vance stood tall and stunning with masculine confidence, wild curls slicked back, and a heart-stopping cocky smile aimed at me. A dark cutaway jacket with velvet trim lay neatly against his chest, open at the top to reveal a crisp white cravat tucked in a stunning silver vest. His rugged appearance had always exuded a sort of raw attractiveness, but the sight of the restrained wildness and strength now standing before me nearly overpowered my senses.

"Well, go to him, then." Lucy urged me on with a gentle shove.

Breathless, intrigued, I steadied myself and moved forward. I reached him and simply stared up into his handsome countenance until he extended one hand. I took it obediently and watched this foreign yet familiar face.

When the instruments eased into the introduction of a waltz and other partnerships formed around us, I remained suspended in time for a moment, wondering what on earth this man before me would do as the dancing began. Holding our clasped hands aloft and placing his other firmly at my waist, he stared, brown eyes smoldering with untold secrets, lips still tilted up in a roguish smile.

The dance began in a whish of skirts and Donegan eased me backward with firm pressure against my palm. His hand at my waist steered me around the room, and I found myself twirling to the lively three-quarter tempo with the man who managed our vineyards. Matching our movements to the rhythm of the music intoxicated me, and the way we whirled about turned the rest of the room into a blur. I only saw the remarkable, captivating face of my partner. My delicate senses detected a new scent about him, but even that couldn't cover the lingering trace of vineyard and woods that was part of his very aura.

"You know how to dance." My voice came out surprisingly steady.

"I've acquired many impractical skills in my travels."

We spun until I was breathless, his gentle strength guiding my movements. Then the song drew to a crescendo and ended in another whoosh of skirts and chilly air against my arms that were bare above the gloves. We stood thus for a moment while I caught my breath, and then the strains of the next waltz swelled in the air. Pressing my shoulders back to create a steady frame of arms and torso, I again looked up to my partner as he led me into another dance, then another.

At the end of a German waltz we slowed, but his eyes remained firmly on me, as if no other person existed. “You are an artist in every facet of your life, it seems. You infuse your dance movements with the same loveliness and grace you pour into your painting.” The corners of his lips tipped up in a smile of amusement.

And that’s when I perceived a truth that made little sense—this man who was my complete opposite had decided to pursue me. Dizzy with the surprising realization, unsure of what to do around this stunning man who still held me close, I fumbled out my thanks. “Was this your first formal dance?”

“No, but the first time I enjoyed it.” His deep voice only magnified his striking appearance. He glanced over my shoulder as the music started again. “Come, I want to show you something.”

We slipped out of the crowd toward the fringes of the room and walked side by side to another alcove of artwork. Tucked back into this mostly hidden area stood a wall of large canvases, simply framed and unlit. Taking my arms, he turned me to face these nearly concealed paintings, and I gasped at the splendor contained in the plain frames. Bold, vibrant colors splashed across each scene, free of outlines or the dark, hard strokes that dominated the art world. These were not posed portraits of wealthy families but depictions of nature.

The fanciful watercolors portrayed natural scenes in a dreamlike manner that placed me behind the eyes of the artist who had rendered them. Rather than a direct transcription of his subject, this man had poured into his work the climate, his mood, and even his feelings on the beautiful subject he painted. That so free-form a painting would be worthy to hang in a private gallery stunned and fascinated me. I made note of the name etched in the corner—JMW Turner. What a lovely rebel this Mr. Turner seemed to be, deviating from classical styles with such bold work. No wonder our host had hidden these in the far corner of the display.

"These remind me of you."

"I cannot paint this well."

"I did not say it resembled your art. It reminds me of you. Colorful. Perceptive. Freely flowing."

Once again I allowed the frank compliment to wash over me and sink into my heart. "Yet I wear a plain dark dress. Not a single other person in this entire room would call me that when—"

"Then they're colorblind."

The rush of words stilled my tongue for a moment and I looked away to rein in my emotions at such a thought. "Perhaps they only see in hues worn on the surface, like my cousin in that stunning gown."

"Bright hues do seem to fit her."

I spun to face him with a playful smile to shatter the levity of the moment, but that proved to be a mistake. With my nose so near to his broad chest, I looked up into his finely chiseled face and met his warm, steady gaze that always seemed to be on me, no matter what room we were in or who shared it. "I daresay she's a peacock."

His eyebrows raised. "Like the bird?"

"Like the color. If she were a color, she'd be peacock blue."

A smile twitched his lips. "What makes her that specific hue?"

"She has a beautiful sheen that draws you in, but from close view, she's painfully startling. One can only be in the presence of such a color for so long."

"I believe I'd label this night *gold*. If it were a color, of course. One of those rare days that do not come often in life but one you know is worth holding on to."

I smiled, strangely touched at our exchange. It was not so much that he instantly understood the wanderings of my mind, but that he took the time to listen until he did, as if he knew he'd find something of value by untangling my mess of thoughts. I'd always had the sense that my oddities were merely to be tolerated—until now. It seemed this man delighted in them.

"What about you?" His rich voice spilled over my thoughts again. "What color are you?"

As I mentally sorted through several answers, a garnet-red gown entered my peripheral vision. I stepped back from him, out of the intoxicating aura, as if caught in an inappropriate act. "Mother."

Her sharp look speared into the moment, returning me to reality.

Donegan turned with all the casualness of one who bore no shame at our closeness. Mother drew me toward her with a hard stare at Donegan, sending a warning with her eyes. Donegan did not wilt under her silent condemnation, as nearly everyone did in the face of such a look, and a flicker of respect for the man took root in me.

"Mr. Vance. You must be enjoying yourself. Isn't this estate heavenly? So vastly different than what you're accustomed to, I'm sure."

I held my breath at the veiled insult. With a polite smile,

Donegan turned to me and studied my face, as if collecting specific words, and I couldn't wait to hear what he'd say. "It is not exactly to my specific tastes, my lady, but thank you for asking."

I coughed to hide the laugh that bubbled out.

Mother's tiny nostrils flared dangerously, contrasting with her pinch-lipped smile. "What a novel thing to say. Did the princess's portrait at least meet your high standards? Certainly you cannot find fault with Her Royal Highness."

"As I've not yet met her, I suppose I could not."

The woman eyed him carefully. "It's said she had first set her sights on her father's librarian. It would not be such a happy occasion to celebrate a union like that, but how fortunate for her that she has resettled her sights on that German prince and made a fine life for herself."

"I'm sure her sights had help resettling from her mother, who happens to also be her sovereign. Yet another reason I'm grateful for my mother of lower birth and higher caliber."

As my pulse increased at the climbing tension, I excused Mother and myself and steered her toward the long refreshment table, hurrying to speak before she could. "Mr. Vance looks quite refined tonight, does he not?"

She turned when we reached the table and surveyed me, her gaze lingering on my face. "Quite the picture of a gentleman. He could fool anyone . . . until he opens his mouth."

I thrust a cup at her and urged her to drink. At least that would keep her from speaking for a moment. "I hope you're not tiring yourself, Mother. Shall I take you up to our rooms?"

She studied me with those watery blue eyes. "I do believe I'm needed here, tired or not. Where's Andrew?"

His name smarted against my ears. "I haven't seen him lately."

"He said he'd be leaving soon to attend to some family business nearby. I hope he does not depart without a proper farewell from you." With a look that was clearly an order to find him, she pivoted and glided away.

Yet it was the presence of another—the eagle-eyed reporter—that tightened the room around me then and drove me to find fresh air and space. With purposeful steps I crossed the floor toward the three balconies extending over the front of the house, eager for air. I brushed aside the sheer curtains lifted gently by the breeze and stepped onto the middle terrace. Leaning gratefully on the cold stone railing that overlooked the lush gardens below, I took a deep breath and enjoyed the solitude. A light breeze played with the ends of my hair, tickling my face with pleasant coolness.

A faraway crunch on gravel disrupted my quiet, and my attention reverted to the glow pouring from the front entrance on the ground level below. A man in a dark suit emerged. My stomach clenched as I recognized Andrew's golden hair highlighted by the lanterns of the Carrington carriage. He turned back to the house and lifted a gloved hand in farewell to whoever stood at the front door before springing into the waiting vehicle. A sense of betrayal washed over me once again as I watched him leave, his recent words smiting my heart as they'd done when he'd left years ago.

It was probably wise of him to slip out this way, for who knew what might erupt once the news of my supposed guilt leaked out. I couldn't help feeling like I was an anvil about his neck, and that thought weighed on my heart.

As his carriage sped out of sight into the trees bordering

the drive, heavy footsteps swished against the stone floor of the balcony. I turned, knowing immediately whose dark form I would see. "Mr. Vance."

He stepped out of the shadows with a playful smile. "I thought we were past that formality."

"Not when you're dressed this way."

"Then I shall have to revert to my normal attire."

"I'm sure you will, the second we leave here."

As he neared, I gathered the courage to look directly into his eyes and what I found there surprised me. Past the intensity was unexpected softness. Not the sort that accompanied doe eyes and gushy words and weakness, but a gentle passion with great depth that glowed inside him and radiated out toward me. The welcome I saw there disarmed me, splashing cool waves of peace over the hurt created by Andrew.

When he stepped close, somehow emboldened by the elegant clothing he wore, I did not push him away. Instead I looked up into his face and saw appreciation and even admiration there, and delighted in it, allowing it to balm my wounds. I stood a breath's distance from him, allowing his eyes to search me and probe deeper than seemed proper. I couldn't speak for the nearness of him.

"I took your advice." His earnest voice captivated me.

"Which?"

"Kind words. To your mother."

"Ah, that. Yes, you used my exact words."

He paused, studying my face. "So how did I do?"

A playful smile twitched the edges of my mouth. "Surprisingly horrible."

"You've begun to speak the way I do. True and honest."

"You taught me well."

"'Tis a shame. I was going to suggest we work together. That verse you mentioned, something about truth in love. I say, we go everywhere together as one. I provide the truth part, you the love."

I smiled again at his playful words, enjoying the moment and feeling myself losing control of the situation like sand through my fingers. "Everyone should learn to speak lovingly for himself. I cannot do it for you."

His jaw flinched as he stared at me for several moments of surreal silence, and I desperately wished to peek inside his thoughts. Grasshoppers and frogs serenaded us quietly from the garden below. So many thoughts swirled in his dark eyes. "Then I must say, you are the most beautiful creature I've ever seen." His words gushed in a barely controlled whisper. "Full of color and life and passion that spills out of you and lights up the gray walls and people around you. Don a dark gown and it only accentuates the color inside you, like the sky is a backdrop for the stars."

He lifted my hand in his large one and tugged off the satin glove to run his fingertip over the barest of paint stains on my wrist, then his touch trailed down my arm, lighting little sparks of intrigue in its path.

"I thought to make you a canvas, but you're not that sort of artist. No, you will not be contained on a little white square simply because everyone else is. I watched you admiring the work of the artists in there, but the beauty in you is richer, grander, than they could even comprehend."

Like a needle and thread, Donegan's words sewed up the gaping hole carved inside me earlier that night, and I couldn't resist him.

When I did nothing to stop his ardent advances, he reached up and grazed my cheek with his fingertips and slid them back into my hair. In that brief contact I suddenly realized the severe lack of such tenderness in my life. It made me crave more with alarming intensity, and I closed my eyes, leaning into the caress. It was so innocent, that surface-level touch, but it had somehow plunged into the depths of my heart with its supreme gentleness.

"Do you know what I wish every time I look at you?"

I opened my eyes and looked past him to the curtains trembling in the slight breeze, my heart pounding.

"I wish to embrace all that life and spirit in my arms and hold it close, let it touch the gray walls of my life and splash all that color over me, because there's little so glorious, so exquisite, in all the world."

The gentle assault of affection crumbled my barriers, and I sincerely wished he'd kiss me with the lips that had just spoken those beautiful things.

He stepped close and whispered with a smile, "There. Now how'd I do?"

I lifted my eyes to his, where the glow had only deepened, and moved into his embrace, wanting more of it. "Absolutely wonderful." The man worked the fields with passion, and to my utter surprise he loved in much the same manner. I had never met a single person like him before in my entire life, and I wished this moment would never end.

I tipped my head up toward him, yet he came no closer. Instead, he remained in place like a stone wall bracing himself against what I knew he wished to do. I studied his familiar face until the enticing blend of friendship and attraction, coupled with the powerful restraint I sensed in his posture, dissolved my sense of propriety completely. "As long as you truly mean it."

He pulled me into his embrace, bestowing on me a kiss that matched the fervency of his words. Life flooded my parched heart and warmed me thoroughly. I wrapped my arms around him, returning the affection with all the passion pent up inside. Fueled by my utter fascination with this bold man and his powerful draw, I sank into the embrace and delighted in the feel of his arms about me. In that moment, hurt and betrayal raged around me in my life, but I had escaped into perfect bliss in the midst of it, and I savored it.

Finally he released me with a shuddering sigh before opening his eyes. Then, in a moment that should have been terribly awkward, we simply looked at one another, sharing a perfect silence that needed no words. Like the night I'd first met him, I felt supremely grateful for Donegan Vance. It seemed he truly had a habit of rescuing me at my lowest points, even before I realized how much I needed it. Andrew seemed a distant memory, his words like the meaningless patter of raindrops heard from under a protective roof. It seemed nothing could ruin this calm I now felt.

Ah, but there was one thing. Like a knife, reality sliced through the delicious moment. My muddled brain recalled the newspaperman with the beady eyes and painful questions. I pushed back. "Things are a disaster right now. You shouldn't be involved. It's . . ."

His smile disintegrated my attempts. "You aren't doing much to dissuade me." He kissed my nose tenderly, then my cheek. He brushed back tendrils that had come loose from my upswept hair and kissed the tip of my ear, his breath tickling my face.

"There's a huge scandal brewing and I have no alibi." The words pouring from my overwrought mind hardly made sense. Hopefully he understood.

"I suppose I'd no longer be welcomed into society gatherings. How tragic."

"I might be arrested when Mr. Prescott—"

He rested his forehead on mine and grinned wickedly. "Then I shall have to kiss you through the bars." Fingertips tickling my scalp under the upswept hair, he pulled me close and kissed me again with eagerness loosening his restraint. When we parted, my mind reeled, and I couldn't think of another thing to say. Somehow in his presence, it seemed the world would eventually right itself without any effort from me, and my worry would have been pointless. Again I delighted in the single moment of peace as our gazes held and his arms supported me.

"Prescott cannot have you arrested simply because he suspects you. There's nothing to worry about."

Before I could tell him about the threatening letter I'd supposedly sent, the sharp click of heels shattered the calm and I stepped back. Forcing my hand back into my glove, I turned to face Mother.

But it was Lucy who slipped onto the balcony. "She's looking for you, miss."

I exhaled. "Thank you. I'll be in presently."

With a powerful look of affection that fluttered my overworked heart, Donegan ducked through the curtain and disappeared. I moved to follow, but Lucy turned to me, eyes glittering with anticipation. "So what happened out here?"

"Nothing, really." What a lie.

I moved past her with a firm step, but the girl caught my

arm. "Just a minute, now." She stepped close and reached behind me, unpinning and twisting my hair back into place. "I have to fix your little bit of 'nothing.'" Her pinch-lipped smile and twinkling eyes promised to keep my secret, as she had so many other times.

Impulsively I hugged her. "You're more than my lady's maid, you know."

"Most lady's maids are."

With a quick squeeze of thanks, I dashed inside and scanned the room for that dreaded figure in red. She presided over a small cluster of women, speaking with graceful gestures and politely controlled smiles.

"What an unusual rumor. I wonder how it began." An older woman tapped her fan against her hand and studied Mother skeptically.

Mother laughed. "You know how rural servants are, with not enough to occupy their minds. Surely one of them misunderstood a simple message sent to the house and assumed the worst."

"It's a wonder she mistook a business trip for a fatal disappearance. I'm certainly glad to hear there was no truth to rumors of his death, though."

Accepting a cup of punch as I neared, I stepped up to the women surrounding Mother and touched her arm to ensure she noticed my presence.

"And here she is now, the vanishing beauty herself."

I offered a polite tip of my head. "The night sky is another piece of artwork in this lovely gallery. I merely wished to experience every display of beauty available tonight."

"She does find beauty in the most unusual of places. Even our field manager receives her attention at times." She leveled a dangerously calm look at me. "You'll excuse us, ladies. I'm so happy we've had this chance to enjoy each other's company."

Arm in arm, we stepped away from the crowds and out of earshot of the other guests. "Truly, Mother? Away on business?"

"It's as likely as anything else I've heard. Besides, it isn't as if him going off on his own, even in his own house, was not typical." Bitterness crystalized in her soft voice. "And you are growing like him, disappearing all the time lately, all thanks to that man who has taken over our vineyards. Is that vulgar man to lay siege to my daughter too?"

The woman with the fan frowned as she walked slowly past us again.

"It isn't seemly to speak of Mr. Vance that way."

She turned to face me, one gloved hand on the white linen tablecloth. "Nor is it seemly to parade this unseemly indulgence of yours."

"What on earth do you mean?"

"You've become far too familiar with the man, Tressa. I despise it occurring under my own roof, but it's a unseemly insult to me for my acquaintances to witness such behavior. If they only knew whom you'd danced with, where he came from."

"He's done nothing wrong."

Her look lingered on my face. "As Scripture says, a bad tree cannot bear good fruit, and fruit does not lie. No matter how he dresses, his true nature will be revealed."

"The only bad tree I saw tonight was the one who escorted me in."

Her nostrils flared. "You will not say a bad word about Andrew Carrington."

"How about two or three then?"

"It will only cause resentment after you're married."

"I can't marry him, Mother." I turned my face away from her accusing glare. She feared my marriage to a man who lived on a totally different plane than me. Little did she know how well that description fit Andrew.

"Then I truly hope you find your father's fortune."

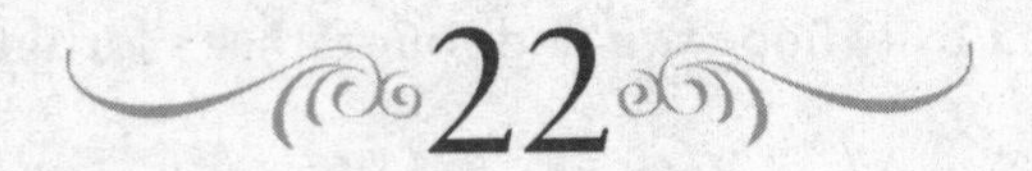

Only when the bad weather comes will it become clear that these guide wires to which I tie my vines are not a constraint but a rescue.

—*Notebook of a viticulturist*

Our stay at the Armitage Estate was cut short the following morning when news of my apparent guilt reached the ears of our host. We were politely excused from our previous plans to stay another night, seeing as we'd need to return home and attend to matters. In other words, Lord Armitage did not wish to have a scandal unravel in his tidy home.

I had slept restlessly the night before, my mind spinning with confusion and disbelief concerning Donegan and our shared moment on the balcony, and that morning I found myself exceedingly tired as a result. It had been foolish, kissing him only to find temporary comfort from what truly plagued me. Shallow attraction mingled with my broken pride, my smarting wounds, had driven me into that selfish interlude, not a true and genuine affection for the man.

What was I to do about him now? Part of me wanted nothing more than another balcony encounter, but I could not bear the dishonesty of it. Unless true, deep feelings blossomed in me, I had no right to such kisses, no matter how wonderful the moment.

I slipped into the morning room to snatch a few bites of food set out for the overnight guests and found Dr. Caine lingering at the sideboard. He sampled the cherry tomatoes and selected a hunk of crusty bread before turning to smile at me. "Good morning, my dear. Did you enjoy the evening's festivities as much as the open window of the carriage?"

I smiled. "Nothing could quite compare to an open window."

He turned back to the tomatoes, lifting and inspecting one. "Not even a certain man?"

I glanced away. In the light of day, I could barely believe I'd been so brazen—and with our field manager. "It was nothing, really." Yet as those flippant words spilled from my mouth, an engulfing heat invaded my body, climbing it and leaving awareness in its wake. Whether I loved or hated Donegan Vance, I could never quite be indifferent to him.

"With a man like that, it couldn't possibly be more." A muted warning light came into his eyes and he watched me, studying my reaction.

I frowned. "Dr. Caine, I thought you a higher man than one who judges a person by class."

"That isn't what I mean, child. It's the wanderlust. I see

the gleam of it in his eyes, and it'll only grow stronger with time. His lifeblood is change and freshness in everything, from scenery to work to . . . well, young ladies. He'll be on to the next before you can blink. You were merely a momentary fancy and he took it."

"There's more to it than that, Dr. Caine. You see, we've become friends. He's been kind to me."

He frowned. "A man admittedly in need of funds who has become friendly with an heiress. I suppose he's also offered to help you find your father's fortune."

"Well, he . . ." My loyal heart rejected Dr. Caine's words, but as his knowing eyes remained on me, warming patiently through my defenses, I wondered why I hadn't seen it this way before. His insistence on helping with the search, his ardent and focused attention toward a girl of the elite set he so despised . . . I'd truly been blinded—by a kiss.

Feelings of utter foolishness pummeled me as I worked to shove aside all memories of the previous night. Once the treasure was discovered and he received what he could of it, he'd pack up and leave without a thought, on to the next town and another girl he'd kiss with the passion that likely came from much practice.

Pain resurfaced as I recalled the sight of Andrew leaving in the garish light of the carriage lanterns. To be left so abruptly, so casually, had only widened the emptiness that had existed before him, and Donegan Vance's departure would be no less. This fortune tempted more men to my side than any woman's charms, and it would be the ruin of my heart before it was even found. I would not allow myself to be so blinded by any of them again.

Dr. Caine tilted his head with a kindly smile. "Have no

fear. He isn't the only man who will enter your young life. Just don't let him be the last."

After I donned my traveling clothes, I made my way to the foyer where my cousins already waited. We passed a few meaningless pleasantries that echoed off the gleaming tile floor.

"I cannot imagine why it is taking so long for them to bring our carriage around." Mother strode into the entry hall where our little group waited. "I asked a servant to bring some tea for your head, Tressa."

"I'll be fine, Mother." I rubbed my temples where they ached. "Just a bit tired."

"It's the bowls of dried lavender." Ellen glided toward me and placed a companionable hand on my back. "Someone is enamored with it and has placed it all over the lower floor."

"Perhaps they're trying to chase us out sooner, for I cannot wait to curl up in the carriage and close my eyes."

"Come, let's settle you in this chair." Ellen led me by the arm to a white-and-gold chair against the wall and urged me to sit. "I would stay and see to your comfort of course, but we shouldn't keep the groom holding our carriage any longer. I'm sure yours will be along in a blink, and we'll all be home by dinnertime."

"You would leave your relations waiting while you journey home?" Donegan Vance stepped into the hall, once again dressed in a tunic, dark pants, and tall boots. "Politeness would suggest you offer the first carriage to those who host you in their home, even if it is a sordid old trap on wheels."

My head pounded at his curt reprimand, and the stark light of morning beamed onto Donegan from the window, highlighting the blunt contours of his face. In that moment

I was even more convinced of my true feelings—or rather, the lack of feelings—for the man before me.

"I know of no such standard." Neville's smooth voice fell from his lips. "Besides, our trap on wheels, as you call it, isn't fit to carry these ladies who are obviously used to far better."

"I'm sure Miss Harlowe would forgo her usual standards of luxury to find relief for her headache. Why not allow Miss Harlowe and her lady's maid to take your carriage now and prepare the servants for the family's early arrival? I can accompany them and see to their safety, then you may both ride home in the comfort of the Harlowes' conveyance."

Regret flamed into traces of resentment toward this man who suddenly thought he could dictate what I wanted, what I would do, because of a kiss. What had I been thinking, allowing such liberties last night? For once, Mother had been right.

Neville spoke again. "You assume she wishes your company, even at the risk of her reputation. Enduring a ride with you—"

"Might not be entirely objectionable to her."

I frowned as my fate was laid out by these two men, neither of whom I cared for at the moment. Did Donegan Vance crave argument every second of the day? I took a bold step forward. "And then again, perhaps it might."

This time I steeled myself as Donegan's penetrating gaze swung to meet mine. His face flamed with surprise, but he said nothing. I dreaded watching his expression melt into hurt at my subtle rejection, but it remained unchanged.

I took the opportunity to end the debate on travel arrangements as firmly as possible. "I believe your horse can be brought around with a simple request to a groom, Mr.

Vance. There's no need for you to see us off. My cousins shall be leaving presently, and our carriage will not be far behind."

Like a gun firing a bullet, these words released Ellen and Neville out the door. I stood for several awkward moments watching the groom assist my cousins into their carriage, wondering what I should say next to Donegan. But what could I say, with Mother hovering over us? When the pair had been loaded along with our lady's maids, their conveyance jerked forward and started toward home.

As our carriage crunched around the long circle drive to the door soon after, Donegan leaned close enough for only me to hear his words. "I apologize if my company is now unwelcome. I suppose I was mistaken in offering it."

Mother stepped forward and tucked her hand in the crook of my arm, and I turned for one last glance at the man. "We all make mistakes that do not occur to us in the moment." The meaning of my words seemed to sink into the depths of his expression and harden his features.

So he would be angry at me now. It could not be helped, I suppose. I bound up the guilt in my heart by recalling what Dr. Caine had said. I was merely one in a long string of women and experiences for him, soon to be forgotten.

As the footmen piled our luggage onto the carriage, I tried not to think about Father's notebook in Donegan's possession and what might become of it now. I should have waited until returning home to speak this way, but I was no actress. I could not pretend to have certain feelings a moment longer than I truly possessed them. Wasn't it he who endlessly encouraged me to be honest?

In the carriage, when the lull of a long country drive had

put Mother to sleep, I once again met the smiling eyes of Dr. Caine seated across from me.

"It seems you've decided against Mr. Vance after all."

I sighed. "I merely had a weak moment, a crack in my common sense, and he was there to fill it."

He studied me with idle amusement. "You know, I'm not quite sure you belong at a dreary place like Trevelyan. You're far too bright and intelligent to be cooped up so. Have you considered going to London? It would give you a chance to excite your imagination." He offered an understanding smile. "And perhaps forget about certain young men."

"I'm afraid going to town does nothing but dull it. Trevelyan excites my imagination more than any other place on earth. I feel as if I'm only half alive when I'm anywhere else."

On the journey home, we spoke freely of many things from literature to marriage before falling into peaceful silence, and I couldn't help but respect this man who was, without effort, endearing himself to me greatly. For a flickering moment, I had the traitorous thought that he should be my father rather than Josiah Harlowe.

"I am grateful for your words of wisdom today, Dr. Caine. I hope you don't mind me saying it, but you've become like a guardian to me, in the absence of . . ."

His gentle face softened. "I only wish I could be your true father. What a blessing of a daughter you would be."

These words brought an unexpected prayer of thanks to my heart. Even though God had not yet revealed the treasure to me, he was caring for me in the background of my daily life. I lifted a smile to the man and wondered if, after everything, I'd end up with a father after all.

"I wanted you to know that if you are ever in need of

anything, I am at your service. Every girl needs a protector in whom she can trust, and you may freely ask of me anything you need."

I tucked his words into a sacred place in my mind, storing them there to be taken out and used in a dark time that likely lay ahead. "Thank you for the great kindness you've shown me, Dr. Caine. You are a life raft in stormy waters."

His weathered face crinkled into a pleasant smile and we slipped into silence. I rested my chin on my arm in the open window to watch the newly watered grass fly by, studying the few lone cottages and ruins along the way. We turned and the scenery became vast expanses of water on the left beyond the steep dropoff as we climbed a hill along a coastal road.

As my tired mind was lulled into a sleepy stupor, a slight tremor in the carriage disturbed my peace. Water roared far below us as we continued to climb the coastal road. Then the vehicle shuddered in earnest and panic jolted me upright. Mother awoke and braced herself against the side of the carriage as it jerked and banged over rocks and veered toward each side of the road in turns.

Wood splintered underneath us and the horses surged forward with grunts and whinnies as our damaged vehicle wobbled perilously toward either edge of the road. I couldn't even scream. Hot and cold chased through my body. I clung to the window, willing the carriage to veer right, away from the steep drop. It jerked hard to the left, discharging something heavy from the roof. I watched with horror as Mother's elegant blue steamer trunk hurtled over the cliff, banging down the rocks.

I clung harder. Dizziness overtook my senses.

With two final jerks that gave me far too clear a view of

the water below, the carriage lurched right and crashed into the side of the rocky hill. Horses bucked with a clink of reins against the dead weight behind them, but to no avail. We were stuck.

I forced breath in and out and closed my eyes, hand to my fluttering heart. The overhead clunk signaled the dismount of our driver. After a clatter and grumble, his round face appeared in the window beside Mother. "My lady, I'm afraid we cannot go on. The wheel has dislodged and the impact of hitting the road has broken the axle."

"Not go on?" Her breathless voice was thin with panic. "We're in the middle of the road! What shall we do, jump into the water?"

"We're a short piece from a little wayside inn, if it remains in business. We'll have to delay there while we see about repairing the carriage. The inn's a quarter of a mile or so."

"And what will become of our things still strapped to the carriage?"

His dirt-smeared face wrinkled into a frown. "You might have to go on without them. We cannot risk being struck by another carriage on this road, or we'll be—"

"Mother, it'll be an adventure." I clutched her hand and shot a warning glare at the driver to discontinue his dire projection. "We'll have our second night away from home just as you wished, in a charming seaside inn. It'll be lovely, and then we'll return home well rested."

Hopefully they would merely hand us a note for our stay here and we could add it to our growing debt when we returned home.

Mother straightened. "I shall remain here with my things. Who knows what sort of bandits lay about these parts."

I dared not glance down at the raging waters below or imagine what would become of her if another carriage thundered around that corner before we returned. "It isn't raining this time, and a walk will do you good."

The driver cleared his throat. "Dr. Caine, if you would be kind enough to take the ladies on to the inn, I'll warn off other drivers and see what can be done about rescuing the horses." Then he stepped close to me. "I'm afraid the carriage and belongings may be lost. I cannot manage both the baggage and the horses, miss."

"Save the horses, let the rest go."

Mother clutched my arm at these words. "My trunk! We must fetch it. Oh Tressa, I cannot leave it down there."

"Mother, we can't possibly climb down that rock face. They are just things, and not worth the risk."

She gripped my hands in her gloved ones, squeezing with the force of her frantic words. "They're all I have left. The only part of him."

"Mother, what are you talking about?"

"The beads from India. I've nothing else from my brother, and I shall never see him again." Great tears poured down her face.

"You brought *those* beads? What possessed you to do such a thing?"

With shoulders trembling, she looked at the ground and leaned on me. "He told me when he sent them home forty years ago that I wasn't to hide them away. That he wanted me to wear them whenever I could. No other jewelry is so precious to me."

My eyes slid closed in helplessness as I wrapped an arm around her delicate frame and turned her away from the cliffs, picturing my own little opal ring. I said nothing, for there was nothing to say. Any promises made would be empty ones, and words of comfort would fall short. Together we trudged up the hill, Mother's weary body leaning heavily on mine. She'd been crushed when her brother Roger, father to Neville, had been killed abroad in service to the queen. Watching her lose the last remnant of his affection toward her brought back the wretched memory of those days of grief, as if she'd lost him again.

The groom came panting up behind us, and I released Mother into Dr. Caine's care and fell back to see what he wanted. He spoke in a low voice. "Someone has tampered with the carriage, miss. That was not a mere accident. I just thought you should know."

I shuddered as I nodded, and forced my mind to remain on moving forward. I channeled every ounce of strength toward not thinking about who had done such a thing or about our four sleek horses still tethered to the carriage on that horrible winding road.

We did not arrive at the inn until we'd traveled twice the estimated distance, and by then we couldn't even see the carriage behind us. The three-story stone building with three chimneys and half a dozen gables sat atop a small hill, welcoming and full of life. I remained with Mother while Dr. Caine journeyed toward the inn to inquire about overnight lodgings. The sun had begun to descend, lighting the decrepit pile of fishermen's homes below us with a soft orange and pink glow. Storm clouds rolled over the dying light of day.

"Bad news, I'm afraid." The doctor approached with a posture of apology hunching his frame. "They've no room for us, and they suggested we journey back or toward home immediately. It does look like rain."

I looked to the doctor, pleading for him to offer a solution. "Haven't they a small back room they can spare us? Anything?"

He only shook his head. "Nothing but cider and tea and well wishes."

When rain began to drip from cloudy skies, we stumbled into the crudely appointed serving room for lack of any better plan. I sighed under the invisible weight resting on my shoulders as we settled at one of the thick wooden tables, wondering what should be done when nothing really *could* be done.

Mother spoke up to the woman serving our drinks. "I need to hire a man to fetch my trunk. Can you send someone around?"

"Aye, someone'll go after it, if you truly want them to. Be warned they'll be helping themselves to a large fee from its contents for their trouble." She cackled heartily.

"My beads." Mother gripped my arm. "My necklaces from Roger. I can't bear the idea of them down the cliff like rubbish."

I shared a glance with Dr. Caine and avoided voicing the response uppermost in my mind: better your beads than us.

Practical and somewhat crude, the lower level where we sat began to fill with plainly dressed working-class patrons. The place was somewhere between the elegance to which we were accustomed and the fishing shanties lining the beach below.

"We close up in a matter of hours. You'd best find lodging for the night." The server spoke plainly but firmly.

Mother looked to me with wide eyes of desperation that

begged me to fix the situation. I glanced about for an answer. Would they forcibly eject us if we lay down upon the benches along the wall?

When each of us had drained two mugs of cider, no solution had occurred to me. Rain dripped off the rotting eaves of the place, and all I could do was beg God for help. *Make a way when there seems to be no way, God.*

More time passed in which we silently waited for brilliance to strike.

The proprietor approached as closing time neared. "It seems it's time to leave, my lady."

"Where do you propose we go?" I straightened, preparing for a debate.

"Home, I suspect. Your carriage be out front blocking me whole entrance."

I jumped up and ran to the doorway, grabbing the white frame, and took in a magnificent sight. There stood our sleek carriage with four perfectly aligned horses, simply waiting to carry us home. I uttered a small cry and ran to touch it. The battered side attested to its recent misadventure, but everything on the underside, from the wheel to the axle, appeared perfectly positioned and firm. I stood before the rescued vehicle and closed my eyes, turning my face heavenward. *Thank you, Lord. Thank you.*

The rest of the party joined me and soon we were all packed inside and ready to depart. "Mother, who brought our carriage around from the road? Did they tell you?"

She pursed her lips with a smile around the answer that obviously delighted her. "It was Andrew. He found no one willing to repair it, so he fixed it himself in the barn. Isn't it perfect? His Tressa is in trouble and he comes to her rescue.

He's loved you all these years." She laid a hand on my knee across from her. "No one is perfect, you know. You can't expect to find anyone who is."

Biting my lip, I tried to rearrange my thoughts and final decisions regarding the man. It would not have surprised me to see him throw a bit of money at the problem and hire someone to repair it, but to climb on the ground and fix it himself? This was an unexpected turn. Perhaps he'd seen it as yet another puzzle to solve—or an apology for his cowardice last night.

"He got the horses to pull it up the hill all himself. The woman said he was simply covered in mud, head to boots. All for you, Tressa dear."

I met her gaze and spoke honestly. "I don't know how to return to loving him, Mother. He crushed all that when he left, and I cannot put the pieces back together again."

Her lovely eyes softened as she leaned toward me. "My dear Tressa. It's a man's task to love and a woman's task to accept it. Loving a man more than he loves you will only drive him to annoyance and resentment, but a marriage can be built on a man adoring a woman who remains just out of reach. He'll never cease trying to earn your affections, and believe me, with the right man that sort of life is not terrible."

Doubt filtered her words as they fell on my ears, for last night had made me aware of a vast wealth of passion waiting to be released upon the man I would marry someday, and I could not imagine merely doling it out in little drops for someone to chase. After a lifetime of bottling such passion, it would likely explode in utter chaos if it had no release.

Yet the thought of restoring the relationship whose loss had caused such pain enticed me. Perhaps it would repair what was broken and allow me to live as a whole and healthy person.

As the carriage lurched forward, I hung out the window for a final glance back. Perhaps the sight of Andrew covered in mud for my sake would ease my heart toward him. But a stream of light from the stables fell upon a different figure perched atop a proud stallion, black cloak flapping over muddy clothes that clung to his body. There in the shadows, Donegan Vance watched our little company depart as the wind whipped his dark curls over his masculine face. My heart somersaulted through all manner of confusion.

I breathed deeply of the moist air, then settled back into my springy seat. "Mother, who told you about Andrew repairing the carriage?"

"Why, the proprietor, of course. She said a handsome man from our party who was traveling separately was responsible. He must have completed his business matters speedily and come to seek you out. Can you imagine? All that he did for us, after the way you ignored him last night."

I watched that darkly cloaked figure and his horse until we rounded a corner and they were out of sight, and somehow it was fitting. More so than if I'd seen Andrew there watching from the shadows. "No, Mother. I can't imagine."

23

> A relationship between a vineyard and its vintner is one of long-term commitment, for a vintner must loyally tend his plants for three entire years before he has a single harvest to reward his efforts.
>
> —*Notebook of a viticulturist*

Just a few more steps. Donegan repeated that lie to himself several times on the trek up the darkened tower stairs. He hoisted his massive burden so it sat straighter on his shoulder, but the metal edges still bit into his flesh. A new respect for the servants of Trevelyan Castle surfaced as he slid the battered blue steamer trunk off himself and dropped it with a bang before the proper door. A deep breath filled his nostrils with the acrid smell of extinguished candles along the hall. At least the climb down would be without encumbrances.

Stretching his abused shoulder muscles, he thought of his quiet cottage with the inviting bed awaiting him. With one final rub, he descended the winding staircase. Finally, he could have a solid night's sleep. Then he would decide what must be done. Miss Harlowe now rejected the protection he'd been hired to provide, yet she obviously needed his help. And in truth, he wanted to give it.

Yet with each passing day, especially with the daily reminder of Ginny, Donegan's awareness of the need back home grew. It had been weeks and he'd not seen a single farthing of the promised fortune—nor had anyone, for that matter. He simply couldn't afford to remain so long without pay, to be at the mercy of a rich man's whims. Donegan sensed that, in the end, he'd likely leave without the money he sorely needed.

Unless he was the one to find Harlowe's fortune.

The temptation to make off with it tickled his mind, and he played out the idea. He needn't take it all, but only the ridiculously generous sum he'd been promised, which was enough to right the debts of his past. He could mount his horse with Ginny and ride away from this place for good, heading straight for Carin Green. There he could lavish upon the wronged people everything they needed and many of their wants too. Oh, to see those people blessed in such a way, all through his hand. Perhaps that would soothe the ache of guilt in his soul.

Maybe it would even be enough to erase from his memory the day he'd failed them all. It had seemed like a wise investment, that ship going to India. Captain Wright had made half a dozen treks between India and England, bringing back obscene amounts of wealth to his investors, and Donegan had decided to become one of them. Of course, that was the voyage that had ended in a tragic wreck at sea—and on land to those waiting for his goods.

Never a man to do things halfheartedly, Donegan had

invested nearly everything his family owned, including the equity in their land. The decision had cost his family, but so too did it cost the people living and working on their property. It had spiraled down from there with the typhoid outbreak and the closing of the bank holding his money. Landlocked and unattractive to outside buyers, the little village crumbled around his feet until he had run for help. Many months it had taken him, but this was to have been his last stop. Until he'd ruined everything.

That kiss never should have happened.

As he descended the narrow curve of stairs, he glimpsed movement out the window, far into the vineyard. A tall, darkly clothed figure moved about, sweeping down the rows like a ghost. Tensing for a moment to study the intruder, Donegan bounded down the remaining steps and burst out the side door. The family hadn't returned yet, and no one else would wander the fields this way.

Sprinting across the cool, dark gardens, he hurdled over a row of shrubs and slowed as he approached the vineyards. Moving closer, he studied the man until he was positive of his identity. Donegan exhaled and approached the vineyard's owner from behind, observing his tender affection toward the grape clusters. Perhaps after their last talk he'd returned home to set things right and the great lie would be over. "You've changed your mind."

Old Harlowe spun, whipping his cloak behind him. "How dare you sneak up on me that way."

"Better me than someone else. Imagine the chaos it would create in your castle to suddenly find its owner risen from the dead, especially for those so hoping to benefit greatly from your passing. What are you doing here?"

"I had to see how the vineyard fared. There's no opinion I trust so much as my own eyes." He crouched down in the soil and dug in, rubbing it between his fingers beside his lantern, then he tested the joints of several grafts. "I knew the moon would be minimal tonight so I took a chance. Especially after I heard nothing from you for a few days." He rose and stared into Donegan's face, brushing dirt off his hands. "Tell me, Mr. Vance. How are you caring for the things I've entrusted to you?"

Donegan averted his gaze, muscles tense as he remembered that breathtaking, terrible moment on the balcony. When the weight of guilt rolled over his aching frame, he sighed and relented to what he knew he must do. "I must confess something to you. And then I believe I must leave Trevelyan."

Harlowe's thick fingers disappeared into the wiry hair framing his jaw and traveled back through his hair. "All right, then."

"I'm afraid I've severed any trust I earned with your daughter. I stepped too close and was promptly shoved backward."

His bushy eyebrows arched and he dropped his hands. "Too close, you say? What have you done?" The words came out as a controlled growl.

Shifting his weight, hesitating for several breaths, Donegan forced out the three simple words he now loathed. "I kissed her."

Slowly Harlowe's brow relaxed and the man's face melted into a placid expression. "I do hope she kissed you back."

Shock jolted through Donegan's muscles. He stared at his employer.

"Well, she can be a little finicky in her tastes. She thought *Carrington* a worthwhile man, of all people." He turned to lift another clump of leaves and inspect more grape clusters buried within. "Unless you did not mean those impassioned words you spoke in my cabin when we last met. For truly it seemed you wouldn't be adverse to the idea of marrying her."

Donegan frowned. It seemed that rather than convincing the man of his daughter's value, he had only succeeded in conveying that Donegan made a promising suitor to take her off his hands. "If you wish to unload your daughter on some man, I'm sure there are plenty willing to relieve you of an heiress."

Harlowe frowned and plucked a little weed flower that had sprung up among the vines and twirled it, lifting solemn eyes to Donegan. "I was not hoping to push my daughter off on you, Mr. Vance." He lifted Donegan's hand and placed the tiny white flower in his palm. "Merely entrusting her to you."

He relaxed at this admission. "You care for her more than you let on, don't you?"

The old man considered this. "Like a butterfly I admired from afar but dared not touch. Too many times I've regretted drawing close to people, and I never thought to hope . . . yet she's different than most, it seems. She's a rare creature."

"And you wish her to marry a penniless vineyard manager?"

"Only one who recognizes the true loveliness of a thing has the ability to nourish that beauty into its full potential. Penniless or wealthy, you're the only one I've ever thought worthy of her."

"Unfortunately I don't believe Miss Harlowe agrees with you." He relaxed his hand, rolling the little blossom across the lines of his palm with his curled fingers. "All she sees is our differences, and she's right." He pictured the joined shadows of the genteel Miss Harlowe and her gentleman, and the little paper with her admonishing verse.

Harlowe studied him for a long moment, then bent over the branches that twined around the guide wire. "What a miracle grafting is. I take a branch from one type of plant over here, and attach it to a seemingly unrelated vine here, and somehow, if the bond is strong enough, they grow together into a new plant."

In response, Donegan pushed on the joint with his thumb and it bent easily, threatening to snap apart. "Some grafts simply don't take."

"I put much effort into choosing which plants to combine to make new breeds, because they each have something the other needs." He ran a finger over the joint. "Splices are always weak at first because they are foreign to each other, but all any graft needs is something powerful holding it together . . . and time." He gave one nod. "Now, come help me count." He lifted long curling shoots and touched each cluster.

Without anything intelligent to say, Donegan simply followed behind the aged vinedresser in the dark night, breathing in the steamy air and watching him look over his crops.

Time. That's all that was required for a weak connection to bond. Well, that and something holding it together. When it came to Tressa and himself, nothing short of God's own hand would be strong enough to bind two such different plants.

When a distant rumbling perked Donegan's ears, he laid a hand on his employer's arm. "They're returning. You should go."

Harlowe straightened like a deer in lamplight, watching his family's carriage approach through the woods and thunder over the drawbridge. With a grunt, he hunched over and flew like a wraith through the dark rows. Donegan remained in place and stared down at the little white flower lying tenderly on his rough palm. He wrapped his fingers around it protectively without crushing it as the courtyard filled with lantern light and voices.

He'd make one more effort for her. Since she would not have him, Donegan would merely ensure that the other man under her consideration was worthy of her. And in the meantime, he would love her from a distance as fully and passionately as he must, even if she never knew. He only hoped it didn't burn from his eyes when he looked at her.

He strode to the courtyard with eager steps until he neared the clamor of voices. He hung back until the women left, then slipped through the archway to prevail upon the gentleman he must speak to, but Andrew Carrington was not present. The only one who remained to glance his way was the physician who attended Tressa's mother, who now waited for his horse.

"Pardon me, I don't believe we've formally met. I'm Donegan Vance, manager of the vineyards at Trevelyan."

The man shook out his traveling suit and approached, hand extended. "Roland Caine. I've heard plenty about you, so I feel as if we've met."

"I've read a mention of you in Harlowe's notebooks, I believe. I'm translating the notes he's left on the vineyards, and he spoke of you here and there, but he also spoke of Andrew Carrington. That's who I've come to ask you about."

The man's face contorted and twitched as if Donegan had announced he'd been watching him through his private window, so he hurried on.

"I only intend to look after Miss Harlowe and ensure she's

safe with the man. Her father thought none too highly of his character."

Just then the groom approached, leading the man's chestnut-colored Arabian. The doctor took the reins and leaped astride, holding his hat in place and accepting a lantern from the groom. "I'm not one for gossip, Mr. Vance. You'll excuse me if I'm hasty in my departure, but it's been a long journey and I'm anxious to return home."

With a sharp jerk to the reins, the man spun his horse over the cobbled courtyard floor and urged him out into the night. He disappeared deep into the woods, the lantern bouncing with the horse's gait, leaving Donegan to stand and ponder the meaning of his abrupt reaction.

I held the lantern high in the garden and watched Donegan Vance trudge away from the house and toward the vineyard. I closed my eyes and exhaled. Tired as I was, I owed the man my thanks. Once I'd given it, I could sleep away the events of the last few days. After everything that had occurred, Donegan would likely make it hard to find a private moment in which to offer the words I needed to give him, but now he strode over the open field by himself. No one would see us speaking alone out here. Neville and Ellen had returned in the afternoon and were likely abed by now, and everyone else would be following suit.

Yet as I made my way toward him, my lantern swinging a glow where I stepped, the darkness ahead swallowed his figure until I found myself standing at the edge of the vine rows by myself in the nearly moonless night. With a frown, I turned down one row and walked between the vines, my white boots sinking into the soil. With each step I relaxed. Ah, how glad I was to be home. A familiar jingle echoed in the darkness and I turned to see Daisy flying toward me from the house. I dropped to my knees and set the lantern in the soil to greet my little dog, sinking my fingers into her soft fur and rubbing her wiggling body. I stood to continue my search and Daisy followed, bumping my heels and drawing a tired smile from me.

Down the row and up another I walked, breathing in the earthy scent of vines and leaves, wishing I could live among them forever. When I turned back and quickened my pace, something soft caught my foot and I stumbled forward, grabbing a post to catch myself. I bent to pick up the troublesome object, lifting it into the circle of lantern light, and found myself staring down at Father's old wool cap. I shook it out to be sure, running my thumb along its familiar fabric. But how could this be? I quickly batted down the hope that flared in me like fire on kindling, but it refused to be fully extinguished.

I tucked the hat under my arm beneath the cloak and held my light aloft, looking about the vineyard. "Father?" I spoke the dear name and waited as the sound was carried away on the wet sea breeze. My gaze spanned the entire vineyard as I turned slowly to take it all in, but no one lingered. Not even Donegan Vance.

Just then Daisy's sharp bark split the peace and I tensed. Her bark settled into a growl, then she took off toward the house.

"Daisy!" Sprinting after her, I batted down the unreasonable fear that had gripped me. The hat came loose and fell, but I kept running, my skirt whipping against my legs.

When Daisy fell silent and disappeared from sight, a flash of movement near the house caught my attention—someone in white moved through the softly lit garden. I strode toward the figure. As my boots thudded against the smooth path of the walk, I heard steps scuffing on the stones. Heart pounding, I slowed my pace and approached. When I peered around the tall hedge just before the house, I glimpsed Ellen in a billowing dress, her lantern glowing on a nearby bench. Daisy whined at her feet for attention.

Gathering her hair and twisting it back, she sank onto the stone garden bench beside her lantern and absently ran her hand down my dog, who had leaped up beside her. A sliver of garish moonlight cast a sickening paleness over her features that seemed gaunter than I remembered. Sympathy warred with the bitterness that had rooted in my heart regarding this woman. She looked desperately heartsick, and there in the darkness of night with sorrow painted over her features, I could not hate her entirely. Were we not all looking to cling to something that would bring us life? Ellen had grasped at the wrong treasure, but hadn't I done the same? I pictured Andrew's face with a sickening ache, then Donegan's. My father's face rose to mind, coupled with Dr. Caine's wisdom, but I shoved aside the thought.

Eventually Daisy jumped down and trotted toward the courtyard and Ellen drew up her knees and laid her face in her trembling arms, twirled hair untwisting along her back.

Hesitating for only a moment, I approached and laid a hand on her arm. "Ellen."

She jerked, and I stepped back. Her red-rimmed eyes studied me. Catching her thus, in her moment of despair and tears, stripped away her normal pretense of camaraderie. "So you've come back. Are you following me to ensure I haven't touched your precious treasure?"

The sight of the pain thinly veiled behind angry words affected my heart so that it was too soft to create a harsh response of any sort. "I merely wondered if I might help." When she continued to stare at me with open aversion, I pressed on. "I know what it is to long for something. To have the hope of it and never reach it."

She narrowed her eyes. "Don't act as if you understand anything about me."

"I understand poverty of a different sort, for I've been plagued with it all my life. I know the desire to be rich in something, to nearly grasp hold of it but never quite have what you want."

"Says the little rich girl with no worries."

"I may not wish for the independence and freedom you so greatly desire, but—"

"Is that why you think I want the fortune? To gallop around the countryside and live lavishly without care?"

"Perhaps 'unfettered' is a more suitable word."

She turned her face away. "You know nothing."

"I know that money offers a certain freedom, especially for a woman. There's no harm in wanting that for yourself."

"I don't want it for myself, you little fool." She spat the words out with a fervid anger. "I want it for my *child*."

I gasped. "Ellen." I couldn't stop myself from glancing down at her still-flat belly. "You are . . . but this is a happy thing. We should celebrate."

"Celebrate what, the start of another life in poverty?" A single tear cut a path through her mussed face powder. "I have nothing to give this child. I want to give him everything, but I cannot offer a blessed thing."

"Neville may not be wealthy, but he can surely keep you both out of poverty."

"He lost his position at the bank when they discovered my past in the theater. Just before we came here."

"Oh, Ellen." It was all my heart could squeeze out in response to this admission.

"Neville has possibilities, but only without me."

I frowned and studied her wretchedly pale face. "Surely he will not abandon you over it. You are his wife."

She hugged her knees. "You'll understand when you're in my position. Marriage isn't as certain as young girls believe it is. A man may not be able to change wives, but he can change his mind about the one he has."

"Is Neville . . ."

"Real marriage means worrying over money and the future and being worn down by everyday life. It ages you. After a few years, you look in a mirror one day and see a tired, worn-out version of the lively girl you were, and you wonder . . ." Her voice became whisper-soft. "You wonder if he sees the same thing."

"Oh, Ellen."

"He wants me to return to dancing until he decides what to do. It's my only asset, he says."

"But how can you? Certainly he doesn't expect you to do such a thing in this condition."

Her features hardened at these words and the truth of the situation sunk into my heavy heart.

"You've not told him yet."

She pressed her lips together as she looked into the distance, then spoke. "There's only a slender thread still binding us. Any little thing might snap it."

I lifted a tentative hand toward her and laid it on her shoulder, but she lurched off the bench and hurtled toward the bushes where she retched until she trembled. When she returned, blotting her white face with a handkerchief, the look of defeat on her face nearly broke me.

I recalled with vivid clarity the night she'd so abruptly departed from me, flying down the hall away from her own bedchamber with a face as gray as ash. "It is morning sickness that brought you out here."

She snorted. "Morning sickness. More like morning, noon, and night sickness. All-day sickness. Wretched, constant, pestering, overwhelming . . ." Her voice trailed off and she pulled her knees tighter to her chest and laid her cheek on them. Tears dripped down her pale skin and were absorbed by the fabric of her dress. "It's the worst. I've never cried so much in my life. I've no control over anything."

I breathed slowly, absorbing this moment with wonder, relishing in the unique connection formed by cuts and pain.

"Have you tired of him too?"

She turned her head away, resting the other cheek on her knees. Flickering lantern light highlighted the slender white neck exposed above her collar. "I wish I had."

The sorrow in those words wrapped itself around my heart and squeezed.

She refused to let me accompany her back to her room, but I couldn't resist making a cup of peppermint tea and leaving it outside her bedroom door with a little knock. She didn't answer my summons, but when I passed through the hallway again moments later, the cup was gone.

I wandered back to my own bedchamber and pondered the hidden stories that lay behind every polished face. The woman I'd labeled as cunning and selfish was merely desperate in her maternal efforts to care for a child she loved before it was even born. Her obsession with finding the fortune was merely a passion to provide.

And the wife who seemed to resent her husband was merely an insecure girl afraid to hope the man she'd married still returned her affection.

It was only as I climbed into my own bed, still throbbing with wonder at all that had transpired, that I realized I'd forgotten the hat I'd found in the field.

By morning it was gone, but my burgeoning hope was not.

24

> On the heels of every failed harvest comes the start of the next season, in which the vintner has the chance to put into practice everything he learned from the failure.
>
> —*Notebook of a viticulturist*

I unwrapped my garden cloak the next morning after a futile search for the hat and cast it on a stool as I entered my bedchamber. I hadn't imagined that hat the night before, had I? Perhaps my wishful thinking had carried too far. It *had* been dark.

The sight of papers on my dressing table caught my gaze then, capturing my attention. I perched on the stool and picked them up. In my haze of exhaustion I hadn't realized that they were new last night.

A line from my intrepid translator was scrawled across the top.

I read ahead until I found this. Tell me what you think.

Head resting on one hand, I pored over the translated notes.

My hands are black with the soot of my past, for I cannot escape it. My shoulders stoop with the weight of it. Like the residue that lines chimneys, it stains and tarnishes whatever it touches. I find it impossible to be close to anyone, for the awareness of everything that has occurred hangs about me even more thickly than when I lived it.

My broken heart absorbed his words as regret clawed at me, desperately wishing to reverse time and speak with him again. I grieved bitterly in those quiet moments, for Father and for everything we could have meant to one another. Oh, why hadn't he simply held out his hand to me and let me near? I would have come running if only he'd done that much, shame or no. What was it he couldn't bear to tell?

The rest of the notes were ramblings about mixing soot in with the soil as a moisture repellant and how it balanced with the nutrients the plants needed for food, but I could hardly focus on the inconsequential lines that came after the first paragraph.

When Lucy knocked on my door and slipped inside, I set a novel over the pages and shook away the private grief. Her sunny face greeted me with a smile. "Nothing like an adventure to make one appreciate an ordinary day at home."

"Adventures certainly have their value."

She shook her head as she dug through my armoire. "You've a funny way of thinking, Miss Tressa." Sliding a frock off its hanger, she draped it over her arm and approached me. "That Mr. Vance, I imagine he appreciates your taste for adventure, hmm?" Her coy grin drew mine in response, and I immediately welcomed the distraction.

"I suppose you'd like to know about the evening." When her face broke into the brightest grin, I told her in evasive language befitting a lady about the balcony encounter, the dance, and our conversation by the paintings.

The girl's cheeks glowed. "I knew you'd find one better than that Mr. Carrington. You always were too good for him, if you don't mind me saying it."

"What happened with Mr. Vance was a single night, Lucy. A dip into romance that I shouldn't have taken, and now it's over."

"You don't mean it, Miss Tressa. You truly won't have him? After the way he walked into that room, looking like a knight . . ." Her starry eyes lifted dreamily to the ceiling as she hugged my garment to herself, then flung it on the bed. "Is it because of Mr. Carrington's rescue? I don't care a whit what the mistress says, he only did it to impress you. If you wed him, don't expect rescues and gallantry forever, because it isn't him."

"You're right, it isn't." I couldn't bring myself to tell her what I'd seen as the carriage had pulled away from the inn, for that would only make her more persistent. I instinctively sucked in my torso, making it flat and narrow against the boning as she tied my stays. I let out my breath as she secured the corset, relaxing into the frame aligning my posture. "Yet

Donegan Vance isn't the man for me either. I'm nothing but a novel creature who piqued his interest for a moment."

"He looked to my eagle eyes like a man in love, nearly from the start."

I rested my hands on my abdomen as she secured the garment again. "Precisely. Any man who can fall in love that easily can fall out of it with just as much ease, don't you think?"

She frowned, her tiny heart-shaped mouth pinched together. "Not for a man who knows his mind. My Stewart knew the second time he saw me."

"Stewart? The one you wavered over for years?"

Her eyebrows shot up to the lace of her cap. "It's him who's quick, miss, not me. And once I saw him in that uniform, I near fainted dead away, and that cinched it."

When she'd finished dressing me, I sighed in relief at her exit. Silly girls and their notions on love. Yet the man did deserve thanks, and it seemed no one else would be giving it to him. I hurried out the back and through the garden to the slopes of the vineyard. A dozen men hacked away at the soil, and among them was the constant feature of the vineyard—Donegan Vance. Awkwardness tightened my limbs as I neared and I clenched my clammy palms into fists when I paused before him. Here was the man who had kissed me. And with those same lips he'd spoken some of the bluntest words that had ever stung my ears. Then he'd rescued me. I hardly knew what to think.

Despite my efforts to forget it happened, the balcony moment had remained in the background of my thoughts, called to the surface with the slightest provocation. Standing so near to him now made it impossible to think about anything else. What was it about the man's kiss that had so engrained itself upon my mind, in spite of the sort of man he was?

No, it was *because* of who he was that made the moment so indelible. Blunt and honest to a fault, the man did nothing falsely. If he kissed a girl, he meant it tenfold.

It was with these thoughts that I hovered behind him and watched his labor, my brain collecting the words for a conversation I had no desire to have. Again and again he brought the hoe down into the soil, carving a long trench beside the vines.

"I see you are making way for a new row of vines in between the old ones." I forced a teasing lightness into my words, but they hung dully in the air.

"Drainage. We've had a long, wet spring." He did not look up.

I twisted my fingers in the lace of my long sleeve. "I'm sure you heard about our misadventure. They say Andrew pulled our carriage out of the road and repaired it."

"Sounds like a lot of work."

"Mother truly was impressed by it." I dug the toe of my boot into the sandy soil. "I, for one, was shocked. I've never known him to be knowledgeable in such matters."

"People are often more than you can see."

I paused and pinched my lips, watching his repetitive work and the power of the arms that drove it. I couldn't decide then what he was meant to be—friend, enemy, or something else entirely. "That is why Mother was surprised." I cut a glance at him. "And why she'll be even more surprised at who actually rescued us."

He paused but did not look up. "Not if you don't tell her."

My pretenses fell away then, frustration rising. "And why

shouldn't she know the truth? It would change the way she sees you. Surely you know what she thinks. Perhaps this would at least entice her to be civil to you."

"Fortunately I'm not required to impress my enemies." He raised the hoe and brought it down again with a mighty swing. "Only to love them."

His words instantly stilled the argument boiling in me and turned it to guilt. Had I truly doubted him, this man who had been nothing but blunt and painfully authentic since his arrival? Perhaps he didn't make the finest dinner guest or stay in one place for long, but he was trustworthy and honest. He was not a suitor, but he was a worthy business ally and friend.

With one final blow to the soil, he straightened, leaning on his hoe, and looked down at me. "And what about you? What do you say I am? That matters far more to me. Do you also think me detestable?"

Under the powerful weight of his steady look, thoughts evaporated from my mind. A brief silence ensued in which I summoned my courage and reminded myself I was now talking to the man who spoke truth to a fault, so I was free to do the same. "Quite rough around the edges and distinctly opposite from me and everything I'm accustomed to." I offered a glimmer of a smile. "Yet not wholly unredeemable, it would seem."

His eyes searched my face, burrowing into the depths of my thoughts yet again. A small light of amusement settled in his face. "I'm glad I've found favor in your eyes, even if it's the tiniest sliver. I shall seek to increase it."

"You should know," I hastened to add, "that I still cannot ignore how dissimilar we are." I dropped my gaze, then forced it back up to his face. "I should apologize for the other night, for what happened on the balcony. It was foolish and impetuous of me. I do so value your friendship though, and I'm grateful for your help in this vineyard."

He squinted at me and dropped his hoe beside him. "Come then, partner. I've something to show you." He motioned with a sweep of his arm toward the plants farther down the row and I followed him. He knelt and dug gingerly through the foliage of one branch, indicating that I should look at it. "I'm afraid half of your crops are failing."

"What do you mean? What's wrong with them?"

He lifted the shoot of one branch with a single finger. "Many of the grafts haven't taken."

"How can that be?" I crouched beside him and inspected the joint. The branch burst toward us with leaves like an open hand. The shoots appeared strong and healthy.

"I've thought a lot about grafts over the last day or so, and a simple truth has struck me." Donegan ran his hand along the branch to where it fed into the vine and snapped it off with ease. The broken branch dangled from the guide wire it had wrapped itself around. "They are still two separate plants. It clung to the vine just enough to receive the life necessary for producing leaves and small grape clusters, but it'll never draw enough life to make decent fruit. The most you'll see is these hard little balls."

"But they're here, aren't they? If the grapes simply exist, we can make them grow."

He shook his head. "Every one of these branches appears attached, but it's not enough. A successful graft means the two plants meld into one. So much so that you cannot tell where the branch ends and the vine begins. They bear the same type of bark, the same coloring, and they cannot be easily snapped away."

"Have the men graft them better, then. We'll try again."

"It's too late. The vine is already healing over the joint, closing off the wound and moving its sap elsewhere in the plant. It's a slow but certain death, even if it is invisible to the outside observer."

I let out a gusty breath and dropped my forehead into my hands. "What went wrong? Can we even do it any better in the future, if we start over?"

"Actually, I do have a solution. Or rather, you do."

I frowned as he pulled out a roll of papers from his back pocket.

"Your father made an entire vineyard of new hybrid breeds by grafting heavily across the field. He knew a lot about the practice, but you knew one secret he missed."

I took the papers and unrolled them. To my surprise, it was my own sketches of grafting methods, pages torn from my drawing pad and given to Father years ago, when he'd declared me too old for playing in the dirt.

"Wherever did you find these?"

"They came to my attention as I dug through the notebooks. I was surprised to see them."

I shifted uncomfortably on the packed earth. "I fancied us partners of sorts, working together to invent a wonderful new breed. Foolish, I know."

"That isn't what surprised me." He shifted, resting one arm across his bent knee. "It was your incredible understanding of the way vines and branches are joined. I do believe your wisdom surpassed your father's."

"I hardly know more than a professional vintner."

"You remember what I told you about the *Tayleur* and the ark—the failed professional and the successful amateur? I believe that's the case here. If your father had simply followed your amateur method, we'd be looking at a completely different crop." He leaned over the papers and pointed at one diagram that depicted a deeply angled tip on the branch and a matching cut into the vine. "Here you show how these plants are supposed to fit together. It's meticulous and takes much extra work, but you see the results when you rush that part as your father did."

"Why does that matter so much?"

He shifted back and looked at me with a heavy gaze. "Because only two opposites make a perfect fit." He watched me expectantly as if awaiting my reply.

Heat swirled up into my face and suddenly the man felt far too close. I felt his breath on my skin and his scrutiny upon my private thoughts.

Finally we stood and he angled his face toward the sun overhead, releasing me from his probing stare. "Think on it and make a decision about this year's harvest, but no matter what, the faulty grafts will not last. You can count on that."

"Thank you. I'll consider what to do." I hesitated, fiddling with the hem of my sleeve. With a polite nod, I turned and strode back toward the house, but he called out to me.

"You never told me what you thought."

"Pardon?" I turned to face him again, the thunk of tools on sod in the background.

"The notes. I assume you read them."

The morning's pain jolted back to me. "Yes, I read them." I stepped closer again to shield our conversation from the others around us.

"The talk of soot, of the past. Did it strike you in any way?"

"It made me sad."

"Did your father ever talk to you about being a climbing boy?"

"You mean one who climbs from working class to wealthy?"

"It's a chimney sweep. What if your father swept chimneys?"

Chimney sweep. "That would explain so much, like the scarring on his lungs, and why he was ashamed of his past." Immediately all the details came together to form a clear image that made sense as a whole story. Father had been poor. Wretchedly poor. And he could not bear for anyone to know it. The stench of such a background would have stuck to him as indelibly as the name he was given at birth, and that's what he'd been so afraid would tarnish his family—his poverty.

Relief poured through me at the idea of Father's possible innocence. He hadn't done anything to Cassius or anyone else—it was his background that had caused him such shame.

"He told me when we met in France that he believed creosote from chimneys was a secret way to cure moisture problems in a vineyard, killing off mildew before it climbed the plants."

I turned those thoughts over in my mind and allowed all the implications to sink in. "A secret ingredient." Truth snapped into my mind and my gaze shot to my search partner, who watched me with serious eyes. "Donegan. It's soot, isn't it? That's the answer we've been searching for, the secret of the vineyard."

That meant the money was . . .

We said the words together. "It's in a chimney."

"We have to find the right chimney first, and it's not in any of the fancy rooms about the house." I stopped short of telling him about the workroom I'd seen in my childhood memories. As much as I'd grown to depend on the man, almost against my will, I knew now I couldn't fully trust him.

But as I turned away, the secret safely tucked in my mind, a departing figure caught my eye. Neville's hasty gait carried him quickly toward the house with purposeful steps.

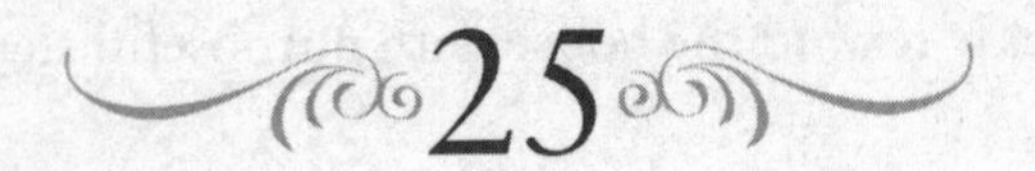

25

The vine's best protection against wind is not higher walls, but deeper roots; walls may crumble, but no amount of wind can move the earth.

—*Notebook of a viticulturist*

Sixteen. That was the number of fireplaces our home contained outside of the elegant front rooms, and I knew that because I madly searched every one—and found nothing. I'd eventually relented and had a bath readied so I could soak away the grit of my failed effort.

Donegan did not accompany us for dinner that night, and his empty place at the table seemed louder and more prominent than the man himself. I stared at the lone stack of china plates and the cutlery that bordered it. I felt as wilted as the dying branches in our vineyard that possessed only a trickle of sap—enough to preserve life in an endless game of striving, but never able to thrive. As yet another thing was plucked from me, my hope dwindled.

Are you still there, God? Won't you please help me before it's too late?

The waters of frustration and panic rose until I felt I'd drown in them. What was I missing? Which chimney was it in? And where was that workroom?

Andrew sat across from me, delicately poking at his food with a silver fork. "I find the gardens enchanting this time of evening. Don't you, Miss Harlowe?"

I stiffened. This was his coded way of requesting my discreet presence in a secret garden tryst, but my tattered soul could not bear it that night. I lifted a solemn smile to him. "I rather prefer seeing it in the bright glow of daylight, and in the presence of many, so that we may all appreciate the blooms."

"You look lovely in moonlight, you know." Andrew lowered his voice for these private words. His handsome face watched me earnestly, likely expecting me to change my mind.

"You will have to rely on your memories to prove that." With a hard look of politeness, I returned to my bread and smoothed butter across its spongy surface.

He leaned forward when the others became engrossed in their own conversations. "I've considered telling the constable you were with me the night of the fire. I'll make him promise to keep it out of the inquest and make it a private matter, but would that make you happy?"

A ray of hope beamed through my heart, spearing through the ice that had thickened there, but it passed quickly. I found I no longer wished for Andrew to redeem himself. Or perhaps I had given up hope that he truly ever would. Either way, his attempts fell dormant upon my ears and sank away without fanfare. "Let your conscience guide you, Mr. Carrington." Part of me simply refused to believe he would follow through.

The entrance of the butler then drew my mind away from suitors, vines, and all other trivial matters, for the ashen look on his face alarmed me. Amos leaned in to whisper to Mother, and when I heard the word "constable," I rose. The moment I'd dreaded had arrived. "Excuse me for a moment." But if my suspicions proved correct, my absence would be much longer than a mere moment.

I pushed out from between the table and chair and hurried into the drawing room beyond, then curved back through the hall to the stairway. Mother would take the constable's call in the drawing room most likely, the room built to impress anyone of consequence. The constable was, by virtue of his position, a man of that description.

I hurried up the steps as my pulse throbbed in my ears to the beat of my footfall. No one hovered about in the hall, and for that I was thankful. I unbuttoned and removed my ankle boots in the interest of silence and slipped up to the peep overlooking the drawing room, for I felt I must hear what was said. Soon Mother swished into the room below, her lavish skirts billowing around her like a bell, and a stocky man in a long buttoned coat followed as he removed his hat.

"I'm aware that I've come at an awkward time of day, and I thank you for seeing me."

"Of course, Constable. Have you any word of my husband?"

"I'm afraid not, but we do have a few suspects we'd like to pursue for his disappearance." He shifted uncomfortably, shuffling his hat between one hand and the other. "The first one is the younger mistress of the house. Is she at home tonight?"

The reality of his words slowly swirled about and took root in my understanding. It was me he spoke of. Me he suspected of involvement in Father's disappearance.

Her chin lifted. "Tressa? You cannot possibly believe that . . . No, you will not take my daughter."

"I'm not here to make an arrest just yet, Mistress Harlowe. I only want to make a few inquiries. Did your daughter enjoy a close relationship with her father?"

"Why, I—yes, I believe she did. Hardly a harsh word between them."

The evasive lie smote my old wound. Hardly a word of any sort existed between us, and well she knew it. Yet I could not deny the glimmer of warmth that lit inside me at her answer meant to protect me. Stubborn and demanding as she was, she did love me.

"Besides, we were both in London when this occurred. Tressa could not have been involved."

"One does not have to be physically present to be involved, but I appreciate the information. One other question, madam. Who was the beneficiary of the man in question, your daughter . . . or you?"

I held my breath at the veiled implication she could not have missed—who benefited most from Josiah Harlowe's death? Who would she choose to protect—herself, or me?

The pause lasted less than a second. "I'm certain everything would have gone directly to Tressa, with only a modest income for myself. She is his heir."

I sank down against the wall as her words descended into my soul and pierced me. The woman cared for me, it seemed, but not more than herself. Andrew's words at the fountain returned to me then and rang true—I was no more than a lackey to those I loved. Did anyone truly love me in return?

"Were you aware of her whereabouts the night of the fire at Prescott's?"

"No, I'm afraid I was not well and had retired early."

I would be arrested. And in my absence, the others were free to search out and seize Father's fortune, taking from me the ability to keep even this empty shell of his house.

"Now if you'll send Mr. Carrington in, I'd like to speak with him."

At the sound of Andrew's name, a tiny bubble of hope rose in me. He had agreed, only this night, to reveal the truth about me that would clear my name of the arson charges, at least. Surely that would help matters considerably.

Mother left the room and Amos returned with the news that Mr. Carrington had stepped out and could not be found.

Loneliness chilled me with the force of an arctic blast. Would no one speak up for me?

I pushed up and stumbled away from the peep. Andrew, my final hope, had flown. His absence screamed louder than any lie he had yet spoken.

Mother entered the room again and the constable approached her. "One other question, if you don't mind. Do you employ a lad named Smithy at the estate? Young boy about so high, usually wearing a green cap."

"I don't believe so, but then again we have so many people employed here."

"Yes, of course. Might I trouble your daughter for a brief interview, Mistress Harlowe? I have some questions for her.

What she has to say will be of great importance on both cases."

"Of course. Margaret, please find my daughter and send her in."

"Yes, mistress."

Panicked, suffocating, I sprinted down the hall. I tore down the stairs and into another hall to a lone window and glanced out at the vineyard, the tangled mess that resembled my own life. How would I ever untangle it?

Do you see, God? Do you see where I am? The mess my life is? Everything has been taken from me, and soon my freedom will be gone too. Why is this happening? I clenched my hands into fists and a tremble convulsed me, and the underlying thought slipped out. *Why are you letting it?*

I closed my eyes against the soft glow of the moon casting its light down on me, and the moment of silence brought recent words of comfort to my mind. *If you are ever in need . . . you may freely ask of me anything you need. Anything.*

Those words from Dr. Caine beckoned my aching heart, drawing me toward the open window where I leaned out into the night. I desperately needed the rescue of a father, but none stepped forward, except the man who wasn't even truly my father. He was the one ray of hope, as he had been often lately. He was to me what a father should have been, and now I would fly to him and beg his help as any daughter would. I drew a light wrap from the closet nearby and darted out, only to collide with another body. I recoiled, but it was Lucy's familiar form that stepped into the light of the hanging chandelier.

"I'm sorry, miss. I've come to see if I could help and I knocked into you instead. Oh, I always manage to do this."

Her hands fluttered and her brow creased. "Oh here, let me fix your hair. Look what I've done."

I stilled her eager hands. "It's nothing, Lucy. I'm so relieved to see you that you could have broken a hundred teacups and knocked me over in the same swoop and I'd still be glad it's you here in the hall."

Her body relaxed, shoulders slumping. "God almighty knew what he was about when he gave me to a mistress such as yourself. No one else would have stood me."

"You're a dear girl." I gave her a quick squeeze. "Now, you must help me slip out."

"They're looking for you downstairs, miss." Worry returned to her white face. "And there's more. Margaret sent the kitchen maid out to Haymarket to buy for the house and the people are talking in the market. The butcher and the milliner and . . . well, everybody. They're all cross that you aren't paying their notes, and they aim to do something about it. There was talk of marching up to the castle and demanding—"

"Tell them I've gone out, Lucy. I'm not at home to receive visitors."

Her worry multiplied across her plain features. "But you *are* home, miss."

And the front door would be properly guarded by the butler. The constable's groom would be in the courtyard, blocking an exit from the timber walkway, so my options were few. Noises sounded farther down the hall until it felt as if an army invaded from all sides. I leaned backward until I hit the wall and forced away the panic. My only help lay beyond the castle. I had to find Dr. Caine. I pulled myself up into the open window and looked down, judging the distance to the moonlit blue-green grass one story below. "Then I shall have to go out."

Before the whimpering girl could dissuade me, I leaned forward and tumbled out the window, watching the neatly shaped bushes below as I neared them. For a horrible second my mind felt suspended in the air, wondering if I was about to break my legs.

26

Pruning is the vintner's mark of hope upon a plant, for one only spends time pruning a vine he believes will be effective.

—Notebook of a viticulturist

Donegan Vance sat before his piles of pound notes and coins that had never looked so meager. He had hoped to nearly double the amount while at Trevelyan, but remaining any longer would cost him too much.

He raked a tense hand through his hair in the dim cottage that was to have been his final home away from home. How could he return to Carin Green after all those promises and the months away . . . bringing only this? He'd forever be mailing little bits of funds without ever accumulating enough to rescue the land. Frustrated, he slammed his fist on the table, rattling the coins. What a foolish man he was, thinking he could be a hero. He was anything but.

A small cry jerked him from his thoughts. "Ginny?" In a flash he bounded to the window and squinted into the dark yard. A creepy stillness hung about the garden made blue in the moonlight and he frowned. Whipping his cloak off the hook and throwing it around his shoulders, he marched out into the night and looked about. He froze when he spotted movement at the base of the castle. Moving forward with guarded strides, he watched the bushes bordering the hall block. A slender figure arose from the darkened greenery, her arms lifting to brush off debris.

He paused and watched, knowing who had dropped into his quiet evening. Turning this way and that, Tressa climbed out of the bush and limped toward the garden. What on earth had brought her out here at this hour? And into a bush, no less.

She hurried away from the castle and into the fringes of the dark woods, distress evident in her posture.

The weight descended again onto his shoulders until it anchored him to the spot, but he frowned. Why wouldn't this bothersome prodding go away? He'd done plenty to help her already, and received nothing but rejection in return. *What is it you're asking me to do, God? I cannot erase her father's secrets or tell her where the fortune is hidden. She will not let me be more to her than a mere acquaintance, so what exactly are you asking of me?* Her refusal stung yet again.

After only a moment of prideful hesitation, he pushed aside his feelings and strode toward her, approaching quietly from behind. "Being alone is overrated, I believe."

She wrapped her arms more tightly about herself but did not turn. "Not for me."

"It sounds like you're surrounding yourself with the wrong people."

She turned slowly to face him, and cast those bright, dewy eyes of emerald green toward him. "They're the only ones I have."

He looked toward the house, toward the people who deserved naught but a distant thought from this girl who loved so deeply and fully, then back to her. The stark pain he saw beaming out from behind her placid face overwhelmed and shoved aside all traces of his simmering hurt. "That is never the case." He uttered the words with all the feeling he dared not bare in any other way.

She turned fully toward him then, with a glimmer of a smile. "Thank you."

A sense of protectiveness blanketed him, and a desire to help and fix. How easy it would be to reach out and pull her close, to embrace her as he had once before. How perfectly they had fit.

When she turned her smile up at him, it crumbled every desire of his to leave this place, even though he must. As heart-wrenching as it was to be around her, to see her all the time, she had become the warm sunshine over his life and he found he needed a large dose of her every day. There in her presence, with her glowing face looking up at him, he ached for her. He cleared his throat. "What has driven you out here, Miss Harlowe?"

She dropped her gaze. "The constable is at the house to conduct interviews. I have been thrown to the wolves."

"Surely you know the truth will clear your name eventually."

"And then there are the dying vineyards, the unpaid workers, and the angry creditors. And . . ." Her voice trailed off as tears wet her eyes and she turned away.

"And?" He pressed the soft word into the air between them.

"And it all matters little anyway when Father isn't coming. He isn't ever coming. He's either dead or glad to be rid of us. I shouldn't have hoped . . ." She moved away from him to hide her tears and stumbled.

Donegan moved to catch her and she fell against him, immediately pushing back. He dropped his arms to his sides. "You do have an ally, you know. Are we not still friends?"

After a moment of silent hesitation, she wilted into him. Donegan's arms stiffened to keep from embracing her, for everything would unravel if he did. It seemed natural, almost necessary, to lift his arms and wrap them around her, but one tiny indulgence and he wouldn't be able to stop. And in this state, she might not either. So there they stood, the weeping girl leaning against his chest, her enamored yet rejected suitor holding her up like an oak.

Finally she spoke. "I can only take so much pruning," she whispered. "Why is God doing this to me? He's . . . he's pruning the very life out of me."

"No, he's bringing you to life. It takes a harsh summer to yield abundance in the vineyards. Perhaps this is your summer."

She pulled back to look up at him. "What am I to do then? How do I endure it?"

"When you feel you're dying in the heat of summer, all a branch needs to do is to hold on." He gripped her elbows and looked into her eyes to convey the importance of the truth he now uttered, for it was all he could offer her. "Cling with all its might to the vine. That's all, simply hold on."

In response she squeezed his hand, and the touch pulsated through him. It was not an exciting embrace of passion, but the deep and lasting kind that connected two individuals at a profound level. What Donegan feared was that the connection would, for him at least, be permanent. The urge to reach his arms around her and anchor her close nearly overwhelmed him, so he stiffened against her touch and she stepped back, hurt flashing in her eyes.

He hurried to cover the action with an explanation. "No man knows how to properly handle tears."

A smile broke across her face before she dipped it away in embarrassment. "How foolish I am, crying before my field manager. I take your friendship for granted."

He grinned. "It's nice to see the little bird without her airs at times."

She giggled and sat on the floor of the forest, rubbing her ankle. "You've an uncanny way of changing the atmosphere with your words, for better or worse."

He shrugged, grateful for the lightness entering their encounter. "I try." His boots shuffled in the dried pine needles underfoot as he too lowered himself to sit beside her. "So do you plan to finish that sentence?"

"Which one?"

"The one about your father coming back. It almost seems as if you don't think he's truly dead. Have you reason to believe it?"

She dropped her gaze, loose hair falling like a curtain across the side of her face. "Not a very good one, I'm afraid. It's just that, when my lady's maid told me they never found his body, it happened directly after an odd occurrence." She drew her knees to her chest, refusing to look at him, and again he felt he was on the cusp of hearing something very real and unexpected and lovely.

"It was a quiet moment in the house when I was thinking of how everything with Father was over now, that I'd never get a chance to see him again. Yet it seemed . . ." She hedged her words and looked about. "It seemed as if . . . that is, I had a strong impression that it wasn't over just yet. So when Lucy came in then and told me that his body had not been found, it was easy to jump to the idea that this was perhaps not the final chapter of his story. Then I found his hat in the vineyard one night, and my silly imagination took over."

He tensed at the mention of Harlowe's forgotten hat he'd swiped too late from the field, but forced his face to remain unchanged. "And now?"

Her jaw twitched. "Now I am allowing myself to accept that he's gone. Either he is dead or he chose to leave." She lifted her head with a wan smile. "At least I can always trust you, Mr. Vance. With everything that is confusing about this place, your bluntness offers a rare bit of honesty that's quite refreshing."

He gulped hard, the fire of his secret burning in his gut like a trapped flame.

"If you'll excuse me, I should make my way home." She rose and moved toward the house with ginger footsteps, pain hindering her movements.

He sprang up and touched her arm. "You've turned your ankle. You'd best let me look."

"No, nothing as serious as that. It's fine, truly." She took one more limping step and he scooped her up in his arms.

"It wasn't a question." The tenacity with which she clung to her dignity might just drive him mad. He settled her gently on the fallen pine needles of the forest floor and took hold of one foot, surprised to find it without shoes. He pulled the bare foot toward him despite her gentle reluctance, until he'd exposed the scarred and torn sole. "What sort of adventures have you been having?"

She pinched her lips, then released them into a small smile. "It seems those little bushes are surprisingly unsympathetic."

He lifted his eyebrows as he continued his inspection. He whipped off his scarf and dipped it into a tiny rivulet nearby and continued, cleaning the dirt of the woods from her skin. "Did you expect sympathy from them?"

"Apparently, for when I found myself at the height of trouble, I leaped into them."

A smile tugged at the corners of his mouth. "Probably shouldn't have done that."

Peaceful silence ensued for a moment. The noises of nighttime swelled to a pleasant echo around the empty woods.

She watched him work over her feet, face downcast. Levity once again darkened its pure contours. Her voice came out whisper-soft. "It isn't easy for me to let you do this."

"I know."

Silence enveloped them again as he smoothed the wet scarf over her feet, removing dirt and a little blood from the scrapes. He maintained a focused mind and gentle movements along her injuries, walking the narrow line of offering a gentle touch yet keeping himself closed off. Regardless, he relished in the simple encounter that seemed somehow sacred.

"I almost wish I could sleep out here tonight." Her whispered words lifted him from his thoughts. "Anything to keep from returning home."

He hesitated, then gave way to an impetuous notion. "Then why not at least put it off a bit longer?" He blotted her feet dry and moved back. "I've an idea, if you care to trust me."

"What sort of idea?"

He stood and brushed the debris of the forest from the knees of his trousers. "I call it my bad-day remedy. Treatment for a heartsick soul. That's all I'll tell you until you agree to do it."

She smiled up at him from the ground where her skirts spread around her like a billowing flower. "Mr. Vance, I accept your adventure."

"Wait here. I'll fetch Gypsy." He sprinted toward the stables and readied his stallion, who pranced in anticipation. He stopped long enough to retrieve a certain burlap sack from his cottage before leaping astride his horse and turning toward the girl who waited for him in the woods.

Perhaps this was foolish, including her in this, but he could hardly refuse to rescue her from her sorrow when the only one standing to be hurt was himself. That rationalization drove him on as his horse's hooves pounded the forest floor toward her. He leaned back to rein in his mount near her.

"What's in the bag?"

"Hard candy and brittle." He tucked it into the saddlebag.

She smiled. "What a curious remedy. I'm certain no chemist would prescribe such a lovely medicine."

"This isn't the cure. Besides, the sweets aren't for you."

She rose on unsteady feet, leaning against the tree. In one smooth movement he lifted her up into a sidesaddle position behind him, and the horse danced in place.

Again the slender arms slipped around him and he tensed. Yes, this had been a terrible idea. He closed his eyes for a moment and squeezed the reins before jerking his heels into

Gypsy's sides. They surged forward through the undergrowth that whipped at the horse's flanks and down the winding road to the village. If this girl was as much like him as he believed her to be, this would help her tremendously. And at the moment, that was all the reason he needed.

Gypsy clopped down the main street of Welporth before silent homes minutes later, but the girl's hold did not lessen. Directing the horse to the first house, he dropped large handfuls of sweets into a strip of cloth and tied it into a small bundle. He lobbed it onto the doorstep of the darkened home with a whish through the silent night, then urged his horse back to the road.

Down the row of simple homes they continued until the burlap sack was emptied and the sweets lay in bundles at the foot of each silent home.

"Where on earth did you get all those sweets?"

"Made them."

"You?"

"It's easy enough if you have the time to devote to watching it. There's little skill involved besides bringing it to exactly the right temperature. It may not be as magnificent as the sweets in the apothecary, especially without real sugar, but it's nearly free, with natural ingredients found about the woods."

"Yet you praise my artistry."

He turned to smile at his passenger, the saddle creaking below him. "Impressed?"

"Very." But the glow of her eyes expressed more than her single word.

He rotated forward again and clenched his jaw, mentally jamming down the hope that warred with reality in his chest. He had moved forward once and been stopped by her slender little hand almost immediately. If anything were to come of this, he must wait on her move.

Even if he waited forever.

"I almost hate to return home, even after delaying it so pleasurably."

"Good, because we aren't finished." He leaned forward and his horse responded, trotting toward the end of the street where the market square lay. In the center stood a rickety clock tower with an ancient gong, likely a relic from its medieval days. He led Gypsy up beside the gong and lifted the mallet from the stand. Turning once again, he handed the instrument to the girl who watched him with delight glowing on her face. "Would you do the honors?"

Pinching back a smirk, she accepted the mallet, leaned back, and struck the gong. Instantly he grabbed the mallet and dropped it back onto its pegs as the noise splashed through the empty air. With a powerful jerk of his arm, Donegan spun his horse to the left and dug his heels into the animal's sides. Gypsy leaped forward and sped away from the little line of homes as doors and windows flew open. Exclamations of delight soon followed and the girl behind him giggled and flung herself against his back.

Together they charged up a side street behind the village homes and up toward Trevelyan, Gypsy's powerful hooves pounding the packed earth. Up they climbed until the horse was heaving for breath and Donegan tugged the reins to slow the poor animal.

"Wouldn't it have been simpler to quietly knock on the doors before running?"

He turned and threw her a wicked grin. "Yes, but not nearly as much fun."

Her laugh warmed his heart and his enjoyment of the mission multiplied to the clouds. If only this could be his entire life instead of one brief evening, his happiness would be complete.

Urging the horse on at a slower pace, they finished the climb through the trees to the great castle that was, as he must remember, the home of the girl behind him. Drawing his horse into the shadows of the massive structure, he dismounted and lifted her down as well, reluctant to release her. “What color am I?”

She blinked. “Color?”

“You said if that cousin of yours was a color she’d be blue. What would I be?”

Those emerald eyes flashed over him, giving the question serious thought. “Black.”

“Am I truly as dull as that?”

“Black is deceptive, you see. It appears to be colorless, but it’s the most colorful hue there is. For you see, black is a mix of many things.”

He steeled himself against the charm of her reply, but her sweet voice curled into his mind and planted her words there. He lowered his gaze. “I’d carry you all the way to your bedchamber to save your injured feet, but I believe that if anyone saw it, my chivalry would cause you more harm than good.”

“I can manage.” She offered a crooked little smile with twinkling eyes. “I should sneak in the side door anyway, in case they’re still looking for me.”

He gave a nod and again squelched the rising hope with a firm hand. Clutching Gypsy’s reins, he stood beside Trevelyan’s towering walls and watched Miss Harlowe rub his horse’s nose. She seemed in no hurry to depart and he wouldn't urge her away.

She looked up to him. "There's something else I should tell you. It may be important or it may be nothing, but I did agree to tell you everything about the search. Every clue."

"Yes?"

"It's this memory from my childhood in a very specific room." Then she spoke of the workshop she so clearly remembered, with vivid descriptions of the dirty windows and rafters above. "And he'd carved something into the fireplace, so it couldn't have been a fancy room."

"What did he carve?"

She blew out a breath. "It was a title he'd given himself, in hopes it would become true one day, I suppose. *Legendary Harlowe,* it said." She paused to smile up at him. "Rather conceited of him, wasn't it?"

But shock silenced him. If only she had told him of this earlier, so much might have been different these past months. He lifted his eyes to the great stone castle behind her and steeled himself as the internal battle began.

For he knew exactly which chimney that box was in, and why old Harlowe had refused to tell where it was.

27

The best grapes are highest on the plant, in direct contact with the sun. The pity is that those are often the ones passed over simply because the effort to obtain them seems too great.

—*Notebook of a viticulturist*

Margaret, is there anything finer than fresh air?" I inhaled deeply, arms over my head as we walked along the high path over the cliffs the next morning. I'd convinced the poor housekeeper to accompany me here so that we might gather fresh mint leaves. It was another way to economize while still providing Mother with the delicacies she expected, but it had the added benefit of refreshing my spirit. "It's so rich with energy and life. If it had color, I daresay it would be a luminescent green."

"You seem terribly happy for a girl being hunted by the

constable. Your mother nearly sent out a search party looking for you."

"I told Lucy I was going out."

"Which she told us after we'd searched most of the house. He finally gave up last night, but he'll be back." She returned to her usual gentleness. "You cannot forever be slipping out when the constable comes, you know."

I scrambled up the highest cliff and looked out over the water, allowing my silence to answer for me. I had no idea what I'd do.

"I suppose you're counting on that Donegan Vance to come swooping in to rescue you again."

I allowed myself to think of Donegan Vance more often than I ought that morning as the phrase *bad-day remedy* tumbled about in my mind. I could learn to tolerate such a man.

Margaret huddled close as we crested the hill, and I turned to look down over the water before us. "Look, there's the pier. They're actually building it."

"Well, of course they are, miss. They do believe it'll be the magic fairy dust that brings all sorts of fancy people to our little corner of the world on holiday."

A powerful sea breeze flattened my skirt to my legs and unfurled it behind me like a sail as I held out my arms and relished the open sea air. "How could they stay away, once they discover our lovely little rock on the water?" Birnbeck Pier was sure to bring change to Welporth and beyond.

Turning my back to the wind, I looked down over the village in the valley and then at my beloved Trevelyan perched on the hill above it. "I daresay, Trevelyan looks even more splendid from this height, especially with such a magnificent backdrop." I breathed in the fresh air. "What if we made it a holiday house and opened it up to guests? Might that be a way to pay our debts and remain?"

"Only if you could afford fresh, modern furnishings. People will expect luxury on holidays. And you'd have to convince your mother."

As my gaze wandered from kitchen to keep tower and along the curtain wall, examining it through the eyes of would-be holiday goers, I saw something new. "Margaret, do you see that chimney on the well tower? Am I seeing things?" Hope tickled me at the idea that there was one chimney I had not yet explored.

"No, miss, it's there all right."

"But there's no fireplace . . ."

"I believe that may be the one your father had bricked up some years ago. The mortar inside began to crumble and he didn't care to repair it. Instead he walled over the fireplace and closed off the room."

Excitement and promise exploded in me as I grabbed Margaret's hands and tugged her forward. "Come, Margaret, let's hurry back. I want to explore it." Eagerness to share this with Donegan hastened my feet as I stepped down the steep embankment. If he'd warmed to my vague notions and silly ideas before, he'd be thrilled with this. At last, after all our searching and untangling, we had a solid lead.

Drying and wiping my sandy feet in the kitchen when we returned, I crossed the hall to find Amos poised at the banister and smiled at him. "Good morning. Have any of the other guests risen?"

"No, miss. But we did lose one last night. Mr. Carrington has asked me to relay his apologies for a hasty departure, and he left you this." The tall butler slid a folded note from his pocket and handed it to me with a grim look of apology.

"Thank you, Amos. I'm sure he has other business to attend."

> T—
>
> Things are escalating at Trevelyan, so I must escape home for the moment. This isn't over. The moment the fog clears from this scandal and I've earned the position, I'll be there to claim you as my bride, rest assured of that.
>
> Don't forget me.

I crunched the note in my fist. No, never would I forget him. Loneliness from the night before threatened to drown me once again until I glimpsed Donegan's profile through the cracked-open doors of Father's study. Here, at least, I should find a friend. I crossed to the room and slipped inside. "What are you doing in here? Mother has forbidden it."

He lifted his furrowed countenance from the ledgers he studied, but his mind seemed to remain tangled in the papers on the desk.

"Ah, that's right. You don't listen well. Not even to your employer, it would seem." My playful smile hardly moved him.

"I must inspect the accounts to know how desperate things truly are. There's a chance it might be wise to harvest the bitter grapes and make some use of them."

I stepped forward across the plush rug. "Perhaps we won't need this harvest, if we're as close to the fortune as I think we are."

He didn't even raise his head.

"I've another piece to tell you about. There's a walled-up chimney in the well tower—"

I spun at a noise behind me.

"Tressa, there you are." Cousin Neville spoke from the doorway behind me. "Have you forgotten about church? Your mother has been looking for you." Ellen stood behind him, watching me with eyes that always saw too much.

It was Sunday. How could I have forgotten? "I'll be along." The intruders departed and I dropped my voice. "We must speak soon, Mr. Vance."

Finally he looked up at me, that chiseled face blandly deflecting my earnest excitement. Tiredness rimmed his eyes as if he'd lost a week of sleep, and I wondered what had occurred since we'd spoken last. "I shall have little spare time until after harvest."

"Let the grapes rot for all I care. We can start fresh after this season."

"I never leave a project unfinished. Oh, you may also tell your cook that you will have one less at the dinner table. I cannot spare the time for a formal meal anymore."

"But . . ." With a frown, I backed toward the open doors. "As you wish." I turned and walked out slowly, willing him to look up at me as he always did, but he hardly seemed to notice my exit. Only then did I realize how much I'd come to depend upon being studied by that deeply intense eyes, for no one had ever seen me as thoroughly as he had.

Shoving aside a surprising depth of pain at this simple turn of events, I moved toward the well tower to explore, but Lucy caught me in the hall. The search would have to wait until a private moment that evening.

After my maid had dressed me for church and gone, I turned my attention to the new notebook pages left on the dressing table and wished dearly to find something comforting, something meaningful, in my departed father's words. What I found there only made everything tenfold worse. I sank onto a bench and skimmed several pages of dry notes until I reached a section in the middle that seized my attention and held it captive.

> I am not sorry I pruned Cassius Malvern off the vine, for one has little choice when a branch is rotting away. It was an act of mercy, and I'll never regret it.

Pain speared my heart, and I clung to the memory of my dear father as I remembered him, refusing to let my loyalty be corrupted. For if my father was wicked, who was left to me?

At least now I had an explanation for Donegan's distance. What a wretched end to this journey of discovery, in which I found nothing I ever wanted to know. The lonely, haunted face of that boy in the painting bore down on my mind, but I refused to believe what his accusing stare insinuated.

I grabbed my head in my hands and steeled myself against the hatred ready to slice through my tender daughter-heart, shredding it into an irretrievable mess. Everything—*everything*—had been taken from me, including the very ideal of my father. Reading this was nearly worse than hearing the news of his death.

Why, God? Why must you prune everything away from me? The word *connect* painted above the doorway claimed my reluctant attention. It seemed like the focal point of the entire room, mocking me in my haunting aloneness. *To whom can I connect, Lord? Who is left?*

The feeling of loneliness magnified when I took my seat beside Mother in the Harlowe family balcony box and set my open hand on the vacant space beside me on our pew, wishing with a powerful intensity. Rain poured down onto the roof as I looked down upon the sanctuary where a plainly dressed man guided his little girl into a pew below. How simple their lives were. They merely lacked money.

Together we rose as Vicar Davis walked to the front of the great stone church and stood behind the pulpit. His somber voice echoed about the huge empty space above the heads of the parishioners, silencing the last-minute shuffling and adjusting in the pews. Then we sat and my gaze flew again to the little family in the fourth row. The man had opened his Bible and laid it across their laps, one half on his leg and the other on that of his daughter, with his wife looking on from the other side. In that moment, my longing intensified to an unbearable level.

As the vicar's voice filled the air with his welcome and opening exhortation, thunder from the outside rolled gently across my senses. "Rise for the reading of the Lord's Prayer."

We stood as a single streak of sunlight beamed through the stained-glass windows, prisming into the dreary gray air with vibrant color that caught my artist's eye.

"Our Father, who art in heaven, hallowed be thy name."

We dutifully murmured the line in response, but the words began to dig into my consciousness, at once having a powerful effect on my thoughts.

Father.

What a precious, painful word. I couldn't help but stare at

the father below as the sermon began, and my imagination lent him every attribute I'd craved in my own. Why couldn't Josiah Harlowe have been like him, simple and noble and good? Someone who loved his daughter to distraction and doted on her, enjoying her presence, knowing all about her, protecting her?

As the rain slowed and the clouds passed away from the sun outside, the streak of light shooting through the stained glass expanded until I was suddenly blinded with color and warmth that bathed my dim thoughts. I blinked rapidly, then closed my eyes as light overpowered my vision. I was aware of nothing besides the beginning of the vicar's sermon that boomed and echoed through the air and into my mind as if spoken directly to me. "I AM, says the Lord, and that is all he has to say on the matter. Simply, *I am.*"

Instantly my thoughts pivoted. *Our Father, who art in heaven.* The words landed on my heart afresh, soaking into what had begun to turn stony and hopeless, warming it to life again. *I am,* he seemed to say to my pleas. *I am all those things you want.* A statement directly, personally, to my wrung-out fatherless heart.

My Father, who art in heaven.

My heart thudded at the possibility that God was reaching out to me in this moment through a blinding abundance of color, the language of my heart.

But this all-powerful, all-knowing Father continued taking things and people away from me. Things I needed. He could see the tangled, lonely life I now faced, so also could he see the hidden fortune.

Yet he did nothing to change any of it.

I took my mare out riding on the beach when we returned, giving her freedom to run across the packed sand. With a deep breath of muggy air, I soaked in the display of the receding storm's light reflecting off the waters, sorting through everything that had occurred that morning and allowing it to absorb into my spirit.

There must be an explanation for what Father wrote in his notebook—something that did not involve hurting Cassius Malvern. Or perhaps he had had a good and noble reason for what he'd done. I clung to those possibilities with relentless obsession, and the bitter feelings of betrayal dulled.

When I eventually turned my steed up the path to the house and trotted her across the yard, quiet blanketed the fields. This stillness did not strike me as odd until I led the mare into the stables and found no groom to attend me, no stable boy to take the horse. I slid off her back and guided her into the stall, reaching below to unbuckle her heavy saddle and tug it off. With a frown I slipped through the yard and wandered toward the house.

When I crossed under an archway into the courtyard, running footsteps greeted me, echoing in the closed space. Lucy flew down the steps with a speed that threatened to send her tumbling. "Oh, Miss Tressa, Miss Tressa. There you are." She fell into my arms and pushed back to clutch my hands. "You'd better come quick." She paused to suck in air.

"What's happened, Lucy? Slow down and let your brain catch up with your mouth."

"It's the fortune, miss," she gasped. "They've found it."

28

> The biggest danger of mold is simply its stealth. When it's significant enough to be seen, it has already done irreversible damage.
>
> —*Notebook of a viticulturist*

I followed my maid up the stairs of the well tower into the top room that now stood open for the first time in my memory. A crowd had gathered in the cramped attic space, from servants to guests, and the stale air filled with anxious chatter.

"Mother, what has happened? What is this?" Then as I stepped inside, my gaze locked onto the big black trunk of my memories, its presence consuming the room as it drew the focus of everyone. A few servants worked to clear splintered crates and debris off its lid.

"It was here all this time, buried under a great many crates and boxes beside the old chimney. I returned home from church this morning to find our dear cousins scouring the well tower because of some tip they'd had."

Because I'd told them where to look. Why had I spoken so openly to Donegan that morning in front of these people? Ellen must have overheard as they left the room.

Servants huddled in gossiping bunches on the fringes of the room, their words swirling and strengthening in volume. Through it all I merely stared at the box that had haunted my memories. I could barely breathe. I'd almost begun to believe it a fanciful idea from my childish imagination, but here it was in real life, before me and ready to be explored.

"Perhaps an even split between us," Neville suggested as he eyed the trunk.

"She'll be paying the local shops what she owes first. She's a lady of breeding." This from Margaret who hovered near the door.

"I'll need my kitchen stocked too," called Cook.

The chatter around us increased as the trunk was cleared of all debris, and then one voice cut through the mess.

"All of you, back away." Mother strode to stand before the coveted box and spoke in that deadly quiet tone that arrested every movement in the room. "How dare any of you lay claim to this fortune?" She paused to allow the power of her authority to humble them all. Even our guests watched submissively from the fringes. "This is a special moment that has nothing to do with any of you. It is for my daughter and I alone. I must ask the rest of you to leave."

The voices died out as our staff and guests filtered out of the room and onto the narrow stairway, many throwing backward glances as they left.

"Tressa, lock the door."

I turned the little latch and walked over to where Mother stood by the chest, an eerie calm blanketing her.

"And now, everything has come to this." She knelt in a poof of skirts and skimmed her fingertips over the top of the dirty box. "We shall see if it's all been worthwhile."

With nimble fingers, she worked the latches until they popped. I joined her and together we lifted the great lid. I held my breath and strained to see into the dark cavity as light filled it.

We gasped together. There lining the bottom of the trunk was a mere remnant of all the money I'd seen there years before, and the sight of it burst my anticipation. My heart pounded as I forced my eyes to assess the situation again and again, wondering what could possibly explain what we saw before us. "Mother, was the trunk ever out of your sight? Could Neville and Ellen have—"

Mother sat back with a cry of despair and trembled. "It's his final retribution, isn't it?" She turned to me with a humorless smile. "The man always did have to have the last word, and now he's done it again, even in death." She grasped the edge of the trunk and stared at the end result of her tumultuous years of marriage to Josiah Harlowe. "So this is the fortune he raved about for so many years. The great fortune befitting a great man." She released a dry laugh. "How right he was. Nothing better represents the man than this paltry sum he's left us."

"It's far more than a lifetime of wages for some." I forced my voice to remain calm. "If others can be happy with so little, I'd imagine we will do fine."

She turned her focus to me and tipped her head with a tender smile. "How young you are, to be so noble, so impractical. When you've lived as much of life as I have, you'll realize that money acquires more than belongings."

"What do you mean? What else can mere money possibly be used for?"

"Security." She reached out and cupped my face in her cold hands. "A woman with money will always have someone to love her. I want that for me, and even more so for the dear daughter who's always looked out for me. If there's one thing I could leave you with, it would be a vast fortune and the wisdom to use it well. For by it, all else in your life comes to be."

I moved my face away, my heart sinking again at our painfully blatant differences. "We'll not have much left to dangle before hapless men after we've repaid our debts and—"

"No." She stiffened. "We will leave this wretched place and its debts behind us. This fortune should be enough to at least afford us that privilege. I want to forget Josiah Harlowe and my entire life here."

I rose, turning away. Her indirect condemnation of him stirred up and magnified the chaotic thoughts I currently had concerning the man. "How can you hate him so? All he ever did was adore you."

She rose to stand beside me, slim and regal in the tower of her great castle. "That is the one thing I wish he had not done." She released a trembling sigh. "It wracked me with guilt and shame every time he lifted those mournful eyes to me, begging me to love him."

"Then why couldn't you? So much might have been different."

She dipped her face away from my anger, quiet for several moments. "I'd already bestowed every drop of love I had to give when I was seventeen. A man with a brilliantly beautiful smile and seven brothers and sisters to feed. He was a fisherman on the wharf, and I the only remaining child of aging parents who wished to see me wed into security. I could not deny them what they requested, especially with my brother Roger dead, so I married a wealthy husband. I grew to resent the man I slept beside every night, yet truly his only crime was that he was not David."

I watched this woman as she unfolded herself in surprising layers to me, peeling back the discontent and apathy to reveal something vivid and real. "And now? Do you regret pushing Father away?"

She exhaled, dropping her shoulders. "I regret everything about the way our life turned out." Turning her shining eyes upon me, she smiled and slid her fingers along my back to embrace me tenderly. "Except you, the sunshine I do not deserve in my life."

I squeezed her hand and rested my head on her shoulder. My dear, delicate little mother. With a glance back toward the trunk, something caught my attention. "Mother, look." Tucked in the fabric lining was a folded paper.

She picked it out and unfolded it, scanning with hungry eyes. "His will. He left his fortune, in excess of 50,000 pounds, to both of us."

She looked at me, then back to the meager amount of money in the trunk that was certainly less than the willed amount. "What are the chances the rest of the money is around this castle somewhere? Surely there's an explanation for this."

When we opened the door and beckoned two of our servants to carry the now-closed chest to the study, the crowd waiting on the landing below came alive. A path opened for John and the houseboy as they descended the narrow stairs with the trunk and reached the landing. Mother ran to Dr. Caine and leaned close to tell him what we'd found.

As the men passed the bevy of servants, a familiar little figure burst from the back of the crowd with a cry of utter despair. "That's my uncle's trunk. Leave it be! It isn't yours."

The flame-haired urchin flew across the landing and leaped toward the box, but one of the stable boys caught her up in his arms and swung her away. Limbs flailing, she struggled and grunted, planting a solid knee into the poor boy's abdomen, but he refused to release her. He whispered firmly to her as the space filled with mutters and shuffling.

Then the girl's wild eyes landed on me. "You'll help, won't you? Tell them this box isn't theirs." When the boy released her, she sprinted to me and collided with my legs, throwing her desperate arms about me. "Don't let them take it. It isn't theirs, truly it isn't."

I pulled her away and knelt to look into her narrow little face. "It belongs to the Harlowe family. Perhaps you've mistaken it for another."

Chin jutted, she smeared a sleeve across her angry face wet with tears. "No I haven't. I'm that sure. I've seen it only this morning when I stopped to visit me uncle. It was right in the middle of his table and I counted the money with him. Said that now we could go home. I don't care what that old piece of paper says. The money belongs to him. To us."

Breathless, speechless, I simply stared at the girl.

"You believe me, I know you do. You're a good sort, miss."

I grasped her by the arms and asked the question I loathed to voice. "Who is your uncle?"

"Donegan Vance, miss. He told me that the box belonged to him since he found it, and he never tells a lie."

At least he didn't take it all.

That was the thought pouring over my aching heart as I stood at the window in the long corridor of the hall block, tracing the lead crisscrosses with my fingertip. Servants had fanned out over the property to search for him, and soon we'd know for certain. Footsteps popped behind me and I turned to see Dr. Caine approaching, hat in his hands with a posture of apology. "Is everything all right?"

The simple words squeezed my heart, answering every desire I'd ever had for a father. The concern wrinkling his brow made his dear face even more so.

I gave a wan smile. "I suppose. We found the fortune, after all."

"And lost something more, it seems, in the process."

Donegan. I bit my lip and pressed back the hurt that rose at the thought of him. "It's just that I was beginning to . . ." My voice trailed off as I stopped myself from voicing the thought that I hadn't even acknowledged to myself yet. "I was beginning to think better of him," I finished lamely. "There must be some reason, some noble cause that made him take much of the fortune when he found it."

He stepped closer and laid a hand on my arm. "Miss Harlowe, it is strictly to your credit that you see good in everyone, but it's also to your detriment. I hate to speak ill of anyone, but I cannot bear to see him take anything more from you."

"But what sort of thief steals only a portion and then returns the rest?"

"The sort who hopes to cover his tracks. He left you a calculated amount that would lead you to believe you'd found the fortune so he could escape with the bulk of it."

Calculated amount? The log books. Donegan had been looking through the accounts earlier, trying to decide exactly how much to leave us when he took the rest. And that's why he was uninterested in my newest clue—he'd already found the fortune.

Doubt still tugged at the fringes of my hurt. "He did ask for 10 percent in return for helping me search. Then I suppose there were his wages for working. Maybe he took what we owed the vineyard staff as well. He has his own ideas of what is right and fair. He likely felt justified in the amount he took."

Hesitation played across Dr. Caine's aged features until he finally spoke. "Miss Harlowe, I hoped I wouldn't have to tell you this, but it seems you won't be convinced any other way."

My body tensed against the stone sill.

"He's what's known as a traveling con man. Not exactly dishonest, but cunning and underhanded. He swoops in with promises to save a dying crop and he often does, but he nearly scalps the owner in the process. Desperate landowners are, of course, willing to pay his high fees for his expertise, and he takes full advantage of that. Believe me, money was his only reason for spending any time at Trevelyan Castle."

His words echoed in my memory as I recalled what the man had said himself about his goals here. "He's admitted that from the first day, Doctor. He may have been selfish, but he's always been honest."

He looked down and cleared his throat. "There's one more thing. I happened to be at the Prescott estate more than once recently, and I saw something I never should have. I had been to see about Prescott's elderly aunt and . . ."

"Doctor, what are you saying?"

"It was Donegan Vance who set you up, Miss Harlowe. I was only waiting until I absolutely must to say what I knew. It was Vance who led Prescott to believe you had started the fire, he who sent him the threatening letter supposedly signed by you."

"No! He wouldn't do that. I'm positive he wouldn't. If you had seen what I'd seen of him, you'd know it isn't possible."

"Everything you saw was merely to charm you, to reach your heart. He knows what moves you. I've been investigating him ever since that night at Prescott's, and I'm certain of all of this. The man has a desperate need of money because of some large debts he's incurred, and now he's traveling the country and scalping landowners in desperate positions. He planned all along for you to lead him to the treasure and then get you out of the way by framing you. I have reason to believe he also is the one who—"

"Started the fire." I finished it quietly, looking at the dull gray stones of the windowsill. That would have happened the night we'd begun working together, just after I'd given him one of Father's notebooks. What might he have found there that he'd concealed from me? Maybe he'd even altered the notes as he translated to keep certain facts to himself. With every sentence from the doctor's mouth, new possibilities unfurled themselves in light of what I now knew.

"I urge you to verify everything with the constable. The note threatening Prescott was delivered by a freckled little urchin in a green cap who called himself Smithy."

I didn't need to verify anything, for immediately my mind

recalled that terrible interview in our drawing room in which the constable had mentioned a boy named Smithy. Dr. Caine spoke the truth.

He laid a gentle hand on my shoulder. "Everyone is flawed, Miss Harlowe. But you must learn to determine which flaws are acceptable and which are dangerous."

The truth momentarily crushed everything colorful and full of light in my soul, darkening it like Trevelyan. I forced out one final statement. "Thank you, Doctor."

Suddenly I understood how people became hermits. They were not overly negative about humanity—simply realistic. I closed my eyes as hot tears built up behind my lids.

He squeezed my shoulder and hesitated, then turned and walked down the hall into the shadows. I remained in that window alcove watching him go, as thoughts of utter desolation whirled through my mind.

"John, will you find Mr. Vance for me, please?"

The old groom gave a single nod and hurried away. Then, with a deep breath, I rose and went to do the only thing I could do. In my bedchamber I pulled the pins from my hair to let it spill down over my back and climbed up to my perch near the ceiling, selecting a brush. One dip in the yellow canister and I began painting, my heart again floating into prayer. God seemed to want to be a father to me, yet there must be something I was missing, something more I must do. Things seemed to get worse instead of better as time progressed, and he still did nothing to right the matter.

God. God, this is a tangled mess. Why oh why are you allowing this to happen? What purpose could you have for taking every person, everything dear, away from me?

Color swirled and spread across the white of the plaster

ceiling, long strokes drawing my focus and calming my mind. Then, as if the simple act of painting had brought me back to my childhood of informal intimacy with God, I spilled out my thoughts to him, matching the easy, free-form strokes of my hand. My heart unfurled in natural conversation as I worked. I expressed without speaking aloud my fear of the future, my utter discouragement at unfolding events. It wasn't pretty and eloquent as prayers should be, but it was raw and honest and real.

When I climbed down the ladder, doubt still tinged the edges of my mind concerning God and his plans, but my mind was calmer. My frustration had shrunk, but it solidified into a hardness in my chest toward Donegan that screamed for resolution. I only allowed myself a moment before the mirror as I re-pinned my hair, and then I flew down the stairs.

I hadn't any idea in my head of what came next, of what I believed, but I couldn't sit idle. The old half of me argued that Donegan was not capable of such deception or of hurting me. The new, mature half begrudgingly acknowledged that I knew what had happened to the rest of the money.

Now I had to prove it to myself.

As dusk blanketed Trevelyan in red and orange hues of the fading day, John the groom approached me at the base of the stairs. "I've found Mr. Vance, miss. He was in town all day, and he's just stabled his horse."

With a nod of thanks, I ran to meet the man and happened upon him sneaking about the kitchen. A white cloth lay spread on the rough table as he piled all manner of food onto it. When he'd finished, he tied the corners and gathered it in his arms.

So, he was planning a midnight escape. Where had he stashed the fortune?

As I hid in silence on the other side of the wall, he strode toward the door and slipped out into the evening. His form disappeared into the gardens and I moved to the window and watched him walk past his cottage and continue down the hill. As long as he didn't know I'd seen him, perhaps he'd lead me to the fortune. I grabbed a wrap near the door and flew on swift feet after him.

Past the vineyards he strode toward the beach. As I stood at the peak of the hill, I heard the swish of his strides through the water. I hurried down the path to watch him climb into a little boat and shove off with one mighty thrust of his boot into the sand.

I stood in the cover of the trees near the beach and watched his craft glide through the water, his arms pulling the oars over and over to carry him to some unknown destination. When his vessel angled into a little cave in the distance and disappeared into its depths, I frowned and clambered into my own craft to follow.

Curious, intrigued, I pushed off and drifted toward the rocks, slowing my craft to make the turn into the cave that had swallowed Donegan's boat moments earlier. Only seconds of floating through the dark cavern revealed light ahead. Soon I passed out the other end and found another vast expanse of the channel, utterly hidden from Trevelyan. I searched for Donegan's boat on the open water, but it had disappeared. Cool mist hovered over the water and the silence sent momentary sparks of fear up my arms. After all, I hadn't told anyone where I was going.

Rowing with long strokes and scanning the reddening horizon, I spotted a dark line in the distance. I steered toward it and forged ahead. I came closer and drew in a breath—for there before me, a small island languished in the channel, shrouded in foliage. As I coasted closer, Donegan's boat became evident on the beach. Forcing my oar down into the mud and seaweed when I drew near, I maneuvered the helm of my boat toward the shore a little ways down from his until it sliced a narrow path into the sand and held there. I lifted my skirts and stepped out onto a wet ground and glanced around at this bit of land I'd never seen before. Fear and cold wind swirled around me. Donegan's boat lay on its side on the banks, and farther up, another craft hid in the rushes. He was meeting someone. I quickly tugged my boat into the brush so it remained out of sight.

Hurrying along on tiptoes, lured forward with anticipation, I sailed through the cool woods past giant trees and whispering noises. Moist wind whipped hair across my face, tickling my skin. I brushed it back with firm hands as I slowed at the end of the path, and it was like drawing aside a curtain to reveal the last thing I'd expected. A set of stone steps wound up to a cottage built into the side of a hill.

I crouched in the bushes as my heart raced, my rapid breath making me dizzy. I hardly knew what to do. After long minutes of silence, Donegan burst out the door of the cottage and strode down the stone steps to the path, crunching past me over twigs and leaves. So this is where he'd hidden it.

As the sound of his footfalls faded into the deep woods, I sprang up and took the steps two at a time until I stood on the porch of the little cottage and looked into the dirty windows where a lamp glowed in some distant corner of the place. As I worked up courage, I inched closer to the window and peered in. A tidy little room lay beyond, sparse and crude and empty. Yet someone stayed here, that much was obvious. I moved stealthily back down the steps in search of another window, but in the dark I collided with the solid body of a bear-man.

"Tressa. What are you doing here?"

With a strangled cry, I jumped back and tumbled over loose rocks, sprawling across the walkway. Then I lifted my gaze to the shadowed man who had appeared from nowhere like a ghost, and breathed out a single word that contained all the shock and awe spiraling through me. "Father."

29

In the world of viticulture a cut means growth and a wound leads to long-term health, because through the wounds and cuts flow life.

—*Notebook of a viticulturist*

Bundled in a stiff wool blanket as if I'd come through some traumatic storm, I cuddled into the only cushioned chair in the cottage's open main room and tried to still my pounding heart as I looked at the man I had tried to grieve. I kept staring, as if my eyes couldn't fully absorb what I saw before me. Even though I had hoped for this, part of me had never believed it was true until this very moment.

Father sat on a short stool, poking at the dying fire in the stove. It was such a simple, everyday movement, yet so surreal. Shadows danced across his back as he broke the silence. "Have I ever told you, Tressa girl, which grapes draw—"

"The gnats. Yes, Father. The ones that are pierced." I adjusted on the lumpy chair. This was his answer to all my questions before I could even ask them—his secrets would not be breached.

"Sometimes it's best to leave a grape intact. That's the safest thing."

"Safest for who, for you?" The trials of the last weeks had rolled over years' worth of fear of this man, my tongue loosened more than ever before. Perhaps I owed Donegan Vance thanks for that as well.

He grumbled and leaned farther away.

"You owe me an explanation—you did a terrible thing and I want to know why. I cannot stop thinking about it and how dreadful it is." Cassius's face swam before my mind.

"I owe you nothing." His body stiffened, face closed off. "You're entitled to protection from me, and that's what I've given through Donegan Vance. Go back to Trevelyan and—"

"It's him we need protection from!"

He spun to face me. "Has he hurt you?"

The sudden surge of protectiveness surprised me and gave me undeniable delight, even in the face of his usual irritability toward me. With a deep breath, I told him about the fire at Prescott's and Donegan's double-crossing. "He has great need of money, and it seems he planned to find your fortune for himself."

The man's frown deepened as my story progressed. "And has he? Has he discovered it?"

"Yes." I breathed out the single word. "He made off with most of it, leaving only a little so we'd think we found your fortune."

He turned and frowned into the little flames glowing in the stove. "Hmm."

"Have you nothing more to say about this? He robbed us!"

After a moment of thought, he spoke. "Give the man grace. His intentions are good. He only wants to honor his word and restore his family's land. He had a massive debt to settle, and he needed the money."

I shook my head, hardly believing what I heard. "I don't care a whit if he needed the money—stealing is a horrible way to go about it!"

He shrugged and looked toward the window. "Such is the nature of humanity."

"Father, you cannot simply let him take all that money."

He heaved a great sigh that flickered the little light on the table. "Come. Let's walk and talk outside among growing things so I may speak to you about life and plants."

I dropped the blanket and followed him outside, my thoughts swirling, hope pricking in painful nettles. He led me down the stone steps and into the lush, mossy woods, whose coolness blanketed my overwarm senses with peace and calm.

"Everything in nature is always in process, either becoming more abundant through pruning or dying by neglect. Donegan Vance has merely pruned something from us." He stepped off the path, one boot planted on the smooth rocks bordering it, and held the lantern before a small tree. He pulled down on a branch the width of my finger, bringing its tip close to the ground. "Pretend there are heavy grapes weighing this branch to the ground. How long until a branch stretched this way begins to wither?"

"A week, maybe two."

"But if a vinedresser removes all these shoots and grapes, what happens then?"

A small trickle of betrayal wound through me as I so powerfully felt the pain of the naked branch that had been pruned of everything beautiful in its existence. "It's stripped of life."

"No, and therein lies the miracle." He released the branch and it snapped back into position. "Removing fruit takes the weight off this joint between the branch and vine so they can connect fully, and the branch can draw as much life as it needs. Enough to produce even richer, sweeter grapes when it's strong. The grapes are good, but a wise vinedresser will cut off as much as necessary for the branch to snap back and regain the connection it needs to live." He turned to look directly into my eyes. "So you see, when he prunes more and more from the branch, it is not a punishment. It's not a slow death. No, my daughter, it's an invitation."

"To what?"

He ran a finger along the joint holding the branch to the tree. "To connect. An invitation to connect and draw an abundance of life—from the right source."

The word swelled over me and I closed my eyes to absorb it all. *Connect*. I saw that word in my mind's eye swirling above my door, echoing in my heart for years. God had whispered it in my thoughts more times than I could count, but what did he wish me to connect with? He'd removed everything, one by one, until I had nothing left to cling to. No vine giving me life.

"The branch may be satisfied with a mere trickle of survival, but the vinedresser wants so much more for it." He stepped close and gripped my arm with gentle fervency. "I've always wanted so much more than mere treasure for you, Tressa girl. It's a grape hanging on your branch, but it isn't life. It *depletes* your life."

I studied his aged eyes. For him, though, that pruning had included removing Cassius. Had he pruned him away so that he might fully own the vineyard, attaching himself to the one thing that gave him life? I turned away from the glow of his lantern so he would not see my conflicting thoughts.

"It was Donegan Vance who taught me that, when he tried to teach an old fool like me how to care for his vineyard. What I thought he was trying to kill, he was actually saving from a slow destruction. What Donegan Vance did by taking that money, and what you call the terrible thing I did of leaving you without access to my fortune, they are both a matter of pruning that was necessary. Taking away what's good so you seek out something better."

I clenched my hands into fists in the darkening night. "That isn't the terrible thing I meant."

He paused on the path, watching me.

"Do you recall the name Cassius Malvern?"

Shock splayed over his features, then anger. "Where did you hear that name?"

I pushed back my shoulders and summoned courage to tell him about the notebooks, remembering that I thought him dead when I breached his privacy. "I've had Donegan translating your notebooks for me to read."

He paled in the moonlight to a sickening hue. "You deciphered everything from *those*?"

I offered a tiny smile. "I speak vineyard."

With a groan he sank to a large stone and plunged his fingers into his wiry hair.

"We also found the gravestone in the woods, beneath the old gate."

He remained still for several moments, shadows playing across his arched back.

"How could you have pruned him away like a plant? How could you be so heartless?" My skin prickled with the impact of the most direct words I'd ever spoken to him.

I waited for his reaction, my breath thin in the muggy night air. Distant birds called out and nighttime insects replied, joining into a chorus around us in those endless moments.

Finally he lifted his unreadable gaze and turned to me, his face intense in the shadows. "Why does it matter so much to you? It happened before you were even born."

The words poured out of me then, the culmination of all my thoughts on this boy who had so haunted me. "Because you snuffed out the only person of value in this entire household. He refused to overwork and underpay the laborers, which made him a worthless businessman in everyone's mind, but the only decent human being in mine. He may not have had keen business insight or your ability to be frugal, but that's to his credit. He was suffocated up in that tower, snuffed out by people who simply didn't see what he was because he wasn't what they wanted him to be. And rather than trying to see him, to see past whatever differences you had, you killed him."

He turned away, muscles jerking in his shoulders.

"Why, Father?" In the simple words lay a desperate plea for this once-beloved father to redeem himself with a powerful explanation, a secret reason for his actions, a denial of my words . . . anything that might ease the wretched ache I felt by merely looking at him. "Was it truly necessary?"

He raised his haggard face to look at me and said one word: "Yes."

He rose to his great height, towering over me in the dark woods, and I held my breath. What would he do to me now that I knew his secret? He took one giant step forward, his face contorted with emotion. I braced myself. Yet he simply bent down and planted a solemn kiss on the top of my warm head. "You see more good in everyone than they deserve."

A storm of thoughts and desires battled within me. "Please tell me you have an explanation for what you did. A very good reason." My heart ached as I awaited his reply.

He watched me with something sad glinting in his eyes. Regret? Tears left a narrow path down his cheeks. "I'll leave you to find your way back. Tell no one you've seen me. Not even your mother. Don't ever change, Tressa. Not ever. If you keep looking for good in the world, you'll find it. Never forget that." He handed me his lantern and turned.

"Wait, Father." I grabbed his hand. "You sound as if you're saying goodbye."

He turned to face me with solemn eyes. "I've given you what I most wanted you to have." With that, he trudged back up the path in the dark, his huddled form casting a long shadow that nearly touched my feet, once again leaving me behind as he had so many times before. When he was completely out of sight, I forced myself to walk forward toward the beach, my mind numb.

I rowed in solemn silence across the placid channel, slicing my oars into the dark water over and over. Water dripped from the paddles as they rose, mixing with the sound of nighttime water creatures chirping about me. The image of grapes weighing down the branch played again and again in my head. How many grapes had I clung to that had done nothing but weigh me down and drain life from me? Faces flashed before my mind, everyone and everything that had been slowly pruned away. As I pictured the branch snapping back up to its natural position, I couldn't help but wonder—what was left that I could even cling to? What was the vine that would provide life?

When I had beached my craft and slipped along the moonlit path toward the house, I spotted the lone figure of our vineyard manager striding among the vines in the soft glow of his lantern. I clenched my fist around Father's lantern handle and forced myself to remain calm, for it was the only way I'd gain answers. Perhaps Father could release so easily, but I could not. Donegan Vance had known all along my father lived, yet he listened to me pour out my pain to him day after day, encouraging me to lean on him, partner with him, open up to him. He'd insisted on standing in as my vine, yet in the end he'd merely sucked life from me like everyone else. With a word he could have ended my grief, but he bottled the secret that had been so important to me, all so he could find the fortune.

And then he stole that too. What a fool I was.

Swishing through the long grass bordering the vineyard, I blew out my light and approached from behind. I stood at the end of his row, watching him lift up great clumps of leaves to inspect the grape clusters while sipping steaming liquid from a dented metal cup. "I thought you didn't drink tea."

He spun around as if I'd caught him stealing, his white teeth gleaming in the moonlight. "Some occasions call for a hot drink." He sipped in silence, studying me down the aisle.

"Where have you been all day?"

"Making inquiries about obtaining new vine shoots from other regions, in case you must rebuild. It seems you do have one thing of value remaining in this vineyard. The trunks of the vines, I believe, will survive and sustain new branches, if we can bring them here. The current branches may fall away from poor grafts and the grapes will never grow, but the trunks are healthy. Like the true Vine of Scripture, it seems there's something rather eternal and rugged about your vines."

I watched him silently, this man who spoke of Scripture so casually, as if he were truly familiar with it, and tried to conjure the same sense of peace and forgiveness I'd seen in Father, but I could not.

Finally he looked at me and spoke again. "I believe congratulations are due. It's been said that you found your fortune."

"That we have. Just in time, it seems." I stepped toward him, my shoes sinking into the soil as the anger of the afternoon deepened in the presence of the one who had so deceived me. "You know exactly how dire the situation had grown."

"It's lucky you have the fortune, then." He lifted his cup for another sip and watched me, never showing a flicker of the many thoughts that must be brewing below the surface.

I stopped just before him, looking up directly into his eyes. "I suppose you'll demand your 10 percent now, for all the help you've provided."

He turned away, his face shuttering. "That isn't necessary."

And in that instant, that self-conscious look of utter guilt told me the truth.

"Don't you have need of it? I seem to remember you telling me you'd only come for the money. Isn't that true?"

He discarded the cup on a post and turned toward me, taking my hands in his. "It was at first, but surely you know it's more than that now. You can't possibly wonder at my feelings." His calloused hands enfolded mine, his thumbs exploring my palms with warm caresses. It was dizzying, this touch and his overpowering presence.

My common sense told me to shove aside the burgeoning delight in the moment, but it warred heavily with a deep-rooted desire I couldn't name or understand. What sort of hold did this man have over me that I wished to be passionately kissed by him and to slap him at the same time? My esteemed common sense would fail me when I stood before him in person and heard his deep, powerful voice so full of feeling. I felt suddenly that I'd believe whatever he told me in this moment, and that was dangerous.

His fervent words spilled out. "I've only tried to do as you wished and keep my distance, but only because you asked it of me. If you only say the word, give me one reason to hope—"

"Hope for what, another kiss? Marriage? What is it you want from me now, Mr. Vance? What more could you possibly hope to gain?"

A hundred thousand emotions flooded his eyes in that moment, shadow and light playing equally off the planes of his face. "Nothing but you." He grasped my arms with powerful tenderness. "I want nothing but you."

All the words in my head disintegrated as I struggled to keep straight everything I'd been so sure of a moment ago. It took every ounce of my conviction to plant my palms against his chest and shove him away with the force of my anger. Logic returned and I recalled the money he stole and the secret he'd kept. The only reason he still remained, pretending all this affection for me, was to cover his tracks so we would not follow him when he left with our fortune. No matter what good qualities he had, the man who would do those things was yet another thing weighing me down, depleting me. "Your first assumptions were absolutely correct. You have no reason to hope. None whatsoever."

Shocked, he blinked at me as pain seared across his face. My emotions teetered on the edge of victory and regret at the hurt I saw there, but this had to be done. He'd earned it, I reminded myself.

"Tressa. What have I done to make you so angry?"

"Do you think you're still fooling me, Mr. Vance? You have a large debt, do you not? And my father's fortune is how you planned to repay it."

Fresh guilt poured over his features, unmistakable and clear. "Perhaps I should have told you about the debts, but it hardly seemed important. If things had ever progressed between us such that—"

"That is something you'll never have to worry about. Nothing will ever progress between us except distance, Mr. Vance. I cannot tolerate dishonesty."

"I simply hadn't told you yet. That isn't dishonest."

"Hiding the truth is always a lie. Secrets come to light eventually, Mr. Vance. Even what is hidden away on an island."

He stared at me, speechless and stiff, the giant secret out in the air between us.

"Were you ever going to tell me he was alive? Or would you simply let me suffer endlessly?"

His jaw jerked and he looked down.

Yet I hadn't the patience for him to gather a worthless explanation. I wielded my final words as pruning shears, severing this man from me. "You will finish the week here and then go, and don't come back." In that time, I would have his cottage thoroughly searched and have him arrested, but he needn't know that now. Not while he was able to escape with it all. A small part of me hoped it would give him time to bring me the stolen money himself, proving his affection for me was genuine.

Something fierce and powerful flashed across his face for a single moment as he looked at me. As he opened his mouth to speak, I put up one hand to stop him, for my resolve was weak as it was. "Go. Just go."

"Are you truly that stubborn? You won't even let me apologize?"

"It won't change anything that's already happened."

With another deep, penetrating look, he clamped his mouth shut, moved past me, and strode into the night toward the stables. Moments later, he and his stallion pounded from the barn and tore down the path to town.

The loss left me unexpectedly weak, and I could not even rally to call the constable. Heartbroken, I sank onto the ground, leaning on a post as I'd done in childhood. Why did it affect me so? It wasn't as if it was the first time I'd felt betrayal. I looked into the darkness where he'd disappeared. Perhaps it was because he'd become my vine, whether or not I'd ever intended such a situation. Strong and true, and often my only friend, Donegan Vance had invited me to cling to him, and without realizing it, I had.

Now, with him so abruptly cut from my life, I felt cleansed and lightweight, yet empty. I was freed of entanglements and ready to cling to a single vine, but what was it?

What's left, God? To what am I even still connected that I might draw life? Who—

I grasped the thick trunk of the vine beside me as Donegan's flippant words returned to me with powerful force. *The eternal Vine from Scripture.* I clung to that vine as a band released from around my heart, exploding with understanding and exultation. Excitement and awe spiraled through me as I mentally stepped back to view all the brushstrokes of the last few painful weeks in one magnificent piece of art that told a deeply beautiful love story. All the pruning, the relentless removal of the seemingly good things, was an act of mercy and healing. A gentle pull on my heart away from what I deemed necessary, freeing me to cling hard to the only true Vine.

All while I'd conveniently shelved him.

The undeniable truth of God's pursuit engulfed me in a great awareness of love I'd never expected. That word *connect*—it was not a command from God, but an *invitation*. A lifelong one. The realization of this abundant love beamed onto me in glorious rays of lovely moonlight, solidifying his true position in my life.

My Father who art in heaven.

I tipped my face heavenward for a taste of life, my hand grasping the thick trunk of the vine beside me. I closed my eyes and breathed the word "Father," for once directing it heavenward. It flooded my prayer with a powerful sense of intimacy I'd never experienced before. Strangely unfettered, I poured out my frustration, confusion, even anger to the heavenly Father who seemed determined to make himself known to me.

Father, I'm so lonely. I've always been lonely. There's such a mess to handle, but I cannot do it alone. As everything slips out of my grasp, that truth is clearer than ever.

I continued, breaking the remaining pieces of my heart in forthright, earnest prayer and casting them before this Father in heaven and those broken pieces connected so instantly, so deeply, with his.

Then they slowly began to fuse back together into a messy whole. His presence settled about me more powerfully than anything in the physical world, filling me deeply in a way I'd never yet known. And I knew in that moment I'd never be alone again.

As I returned to the house, basking in the wonder of this undeserved love, the rocky hardness of my anger toward Donegan began to erode. Why hadn't I at least heard him out? The memory of my angry, self-righteous retorts made me cringe in the face of what I'd just received. I could have gracefully confronted him, requested that he return the money, and then worked on forgiving him. Yes, that's what I would do.

But when I went looking for him in the stable, John gave me the news. "He's left, miss. He took his stallion about an hour ago and said he wouldn't be back."

Of all the seasons, pruning is the one that finds the vintner working most intimately with the vine, involved in every detail of the plant.

—*Notebook of a viticulturist*

She's making inquiries, miss." Margaret smoothed the thick brush down my hair splayed over my back that evening. "Your mother is sending word to her contacts in London that she'll be in need of a property in town for a small sum. A widow's situation, she's calling it."

"So she's considering him dead." I closed my eyes as the brush smoothed the stress of the day from my scalp. "I suppose it won't be the end of the world to live in town." Yet the irony was that I'd just learned Father *wasn't* dead. What would become of him if we left? I could not leave him on that island.

Part of me wished to sing out the truth that Father was

alive, but his simple command stilled my tongue. "*Tell no one you've seen me.*" Whatever the secret he kept, I'd not be the one to pierce the grape and draw danger to him.

"He'd be so displeased, wouldn't he? Your father, I mean." Margaret softened her voice as she normally did when speaking of Trevelyan's master. "You and the mistress leaving this place. I cannot recall a time he ever truly wanted to leave, even on short trips."

"He'd despise so much of what has happened around here."

She ran her fingers through my hair as she looked at me tenderly in the mirror. "If only he were still here, he'd know what to do."

It was only as I lay in bed in the dark that night that it struck me once again that I had another Father from whom I could seek advice. For years I had painted my mental image of God with the same colors that made up my earthly father, fallible and distant, yet God had reached out to me so many times in gentle, personal ways.

I looked at the word *connect* painted above my door, then blew out the candle and burrowed under the blankets. Dipping my heart into the well of the rich conversation we'd had earlier, I cast up little arrows of prayer in these moments before sleep, connecting us yet again. I would never tire of such intimacy.

Father, help me submit to Mother's wishes with a glad heart. Release me from the hold of any resentment that might come about from this change.

I rolled over and then back again, my mind refusing to rest. Prescott's angry face loomed heavily in my thoughts, and the notion of ignoring the debt plagued me. I prayed again, but even more unrest sparked through my tired brain. Still saturated in the newfound intimacy with God, I prodded further into this conviction.

Father, would you have me pay the man? Is that your desire?

I remained still and silent in my bed, under the fluffy softness of blankets, and nothing happened. I turned onto my right side and gazed out the window, toying with the idea of using the fortune to pay Prescott what we owed. An unexpected calm stole over me, weighing me down comfortably in the soft bed. *Please, Father. Will you give me a firm yes or no? Mother will be so angry if I do this.*

No answer came other than the gentle release of obedience that relaxed my body and allowed me to sleep.

My conversation with God rolled into the next morning, stopping and starting as I thought through my decisions and actions. Dressing in a simple gray dress and upswept hair befitting the call I'd need to make, I bundled up the money in a much smaller box and ordered the groom to drive me to see Prescott.

After a short trip, the carriage wound up the spruce-lined drive of the wide brick house with white Greek-style pillars and crunched to a stop before the doors. John helped me step down and I surveyed the perfect house for signs of fire damage and, surprisingly, saw none. Fresh and clean spring air met my senses rather than the odor of burnt wood and brick, and wealth draped the oversized house. Why on earth would God ever want me to give all we had to this man? With a breath I climbed the steps and knocked with one gloved hand, my other clutching the little box.

I shifted the weight of the box as the door opened and handed my card to the housekeeper, who showed me in. "Mr. Prescott will be pleased to see you, miss."

I strode on plush carpet through glass doors that led into the drawing room and took in the sight of the overly red room with three clocks ticking just out of sync with one another. A distinct air of loneliness pervaded the enormous space, despite its sunny, open windows and light oak furniture.

"You've come into the lion's den, it seems." I spun at the sound of a deep voice as Mr. Prescott limped into the room, his cane popping against the wood. "I assume you have an excellent reason, since this is the first time you've granted me the honor of your presence."

"Of course." I approached the gruffly cynical man and held up the box. "I've come to pay what we owe."

He arched his eyebrows and pulled a nearby bell to summon his staff. "Constance, will you have tea sent into my study? Come, child, we will talk."

I followed him down a long hall and into a tall library studded with taxidermy where he sat at a desk. Books lined three of the walls floor to ceiling and the fourth wall was nothing but windows and little cushioned window seats. I perched upon the chair facing the desk and watched him.

"So, you are prepared to repay the debt."

"I am, sir."

He studied me for a moment with an expression akin to doubt. Placing spectacles on his nose, he frowned over several account books. When he motioned for the box, I placed it on the desk and waited, my heart pittering rapidly. "Eight hundred sixty pounds."

"The restoration expenses, plus interest, minus the portion

already paid . . ." He named the total that was within just a few pounds of what I'd brought. He tallied the numbers in the column of his log book. "Roughly eight hundred fifty-five pounds." He flipped open the box and thumbed through the mess of pound notes, then pushed the box aside with a grunt. "I'll have my solicitor count the money more thoroughly and draw up the papers. I'll have a copy sent to Trevelyan for you if all is well." He lifted a coin to the light to inspect it, then tapped it on his desk. "I suppose you are hoping this clears you of the charges of arson as well."

A white-capped maid wheeled a tea cart into the room and the pretty china rattled as it was transported over the wooden floorboards.

"Two millstones off my neck? I believe that's too much to ask of a single day, sir."

He frowned as the tea was poured and stirred sugar into his with rapid movements of the clinking spoon. "I'll release you from the debt, but do not attempt to make me like you, Miss Harlowe, for you'll find it a difficult task for even the most interesting and well-spoken people."

"I have reason to believe I was framed for this crime, and it is my hope that my innocence will be proven as soon as this man's guilt is cast."

"I see." He leaned back in his chair, the leather squeaking. "And who is the unlucky fellow who carries the weight of your suspicions?"

"Mr. Donegan Vance. A man we've had the misfortune of keeping on our grounds as an employee."

He raised his eyebrows. "I'd sooner believe you did it than the man you offer up to me, Miss Harlowe. I find you quite a wretched girl."

I rose, my hands gripping the edge of his desk as I faced him. "Mr. Prescott, let me remind you that the law has not yet found me guilty, so you have no reason to do so either. While I'm sorry for the inconvenience—for that's all the fire must have been, if you are still living in your home which shows no signs of a fire—I beg you to be a decent and civil person to me."

He met my gaze directly then and studied me for long minutes as his weathered skin wrinkled and scrunched. He raised a gold-rimmed teacup to his lips and sipped, never taking his eyes from me. "I'm not entirely sure what to make of you, Miss Harlowe. You've a fire in your spirit, but I cannot decide if it's dangerous or glorious. Perhaps both. Like your father, I'm never sure if I should trust you." He set his teacup in its saucer. "But it's become rather clear to me that you are most likely *not* the one who caused the fire at my home."

"You mean you're dropping the charges?"

A smile twitched his lips then disappeared. "Suspending, perhaps. For you see, this is *not* my house, Miss Harlowe, but that of Rumilla DuPlane. She has leased it to me while I decide what to do with my charred ruins. I would assume a person who had tried to burn my house down would know which one it was."

Hope unfurled in glorious layers. "Perhaps you can lend your keen perception to the constable when he interviews me."

Humor sparked in his eyes set in an otherwise pallid face. "It's awfully hard to go on despising you, although it has been my dearest pastime for weeks. You have that same quality your father had. That spark of wit."

I smiled then, and it was genuine. "Anything that likens me to him is the highest praise."

"Yet somehow, you are even more remarkable." He scribbled his signature across the bottom of a page and poured and stamped the wax with his ring. "This will do for now until my solicitor is able to draw up further paperwork."

"Might I trouble you for the box, sir? And the remaining money?"

He blinked. "There was only five pounds difference."

My chin lifted and I held out my hand as I rose, pushing my shoulders back into a poised bearing. "That may be so, but those five pounds belong to me."

He lowered his bushy eyebrows and studied me as he passed the box back, likely surmising exactly how much this repayment had cost me. "Right you are."

"Good day, Mr. Prescott, and I thank you for your time." I strode to the door of his study and paused, hesitating with my hand on the doorframe. "Why is it that you don't believe Donegan Vance guilty, Mr. Prescott?"

"Because, Miss Harlowe, it is he who came a week or so ago to beg your innocence in the matter. He spoke of your goodness and uprightness of spirit in terms so ardent I was nearly induced to believe him simply because of the passion with which he spoke. I'm not a man swayed by sentimentality, but Mr. Vance is not easy to brush aside." He raised his eyebrows. "Might I inquire what has caused you to believe that one of your truest allies was your enemy?"

Truest allies. Guilt tugged at my heart over our last encounter, but I shoved it aside and refocused myself. "Dr. Caine told me certain incriminating things he witnessed."

"This Dr. Caine must have the wrong man. Or perhaps he's mistaken in what he saw."

His words lingered in my overwrought heart as I left his

rented estate and returned to my carriage. Prescott almost spoke as if he did not know Dr. Caine. Perhaps he simply did not pay heed to the physician who attended his elderly relation, but it left a niggling doubt about the doctor's claims concerning our vineyard manager. The doctor might be growing feeble of mind and confusing facts. Maybe he had not been to Prescott's at all but another home with a family similarly named. I began to wish ardently that I'd thought to question his comment in the moment, but I couldn't concern myself with these matters now. Soon I'd have to explain to Mother what I'd done with our fortune and why it had been a good idea.

"Please tell me the servants are mistaken, Tressa." Mother intercepted me in the garden where I'd gone to prepare my speech to her.

I slowed on the brick walk and settled my gaze on her face shadowed by a pink-fringed parasol. "If they've told you about my visit to Prescott, they are correct."

Neville and Ellen flanked her as attendants would a queen. "Pray, tell me you didn't give it all to him."

"If I did, that would be a lie. It took nearly everything in that box to repay the debt, but now it's over. The debt will not remove us from Trevelyan."

Ellen came near and looked me over, that gaunt, pale face showing traces of the beauty muted by age. "I would *pay* someone to remove me from this ghastly estate. Can you not see I am withering in this wilderness? I need life and color around me."

I looked past her to the vineyard bursting with green, the

sparkling blue water beyond, and the sprinkle of red and pink wildflowers that accented the vibrant hues of our estate. What sort of color did she hope to find in town that was not present—and even magnified—in this glorious place? But I knew no such argument would find favor in her eyes. "It's far better to honor one's word and repay what is owed than to live upon borrowed funds anywhere."

"Whatever we're doing here is far from what I would call 'living.'" She spoke this final return with a posture of pride and disdain. "Was it that Donegan Vance who convinced you to do this? He's been the enemy of my days since he's come here, and I don't mind saying it. I'm glad to see the end of that boorish man, and I hope he hangs for his many crimes."

"One crime." Guilt pricked me again and wouldn't be shoved away this time. If only she knew all that Donegan had done for us. "He's committed only one crime, and I'm wondering if he didn't have a good reason for it. He's not as bad as you would believe, Mother." A man who had rescued us so many times would not simply steal most of what we had for selfish reasons. There had to be more to it.

"Oh Tressa, you'd defend Judas Iscariot himself if you'd met him." She frowned at me. "Perhaps we shall take a holiday. There must be a place to let in town that will accept credit on the Harlowe name. I'm sure our guests are equally weary of this provincial existence and would adore a change."

"Actually, Aunt Gwendolyn." Neville took one giant step forward to stand at Mother's elbow. "Ellen and I feel we've infringed on your hospitality long enough and should return home. We cannot remain indefinitely without, as you said, a definite object for our grief."

Or a dead man's fortune to be discovered. But I pinched my

lips over the thought as a vague panic tensed Ellen's pristine face. My glance dropped unbidden to her belly as her gloved hand unconsciously hovered there with a protective air. "I wish you both the best." I offered a quick nod, meeting Ellen's gaze that was heavy with many thoughts. "And you always have a home at Trevelyan, should you need it. Both of you." A warning light flashed in Ellen's eyes, and I merely smiled back. "I simply wanted you to know that."

Neville frowned as he looked back and forth between us. "I see you've told my little cousin about our talk, Ellen darling. Now you've given her the impression that we need charity."

"How silly, Neville dear." The words gushed out with far too much lightness as she snaked her gloved hand into the crook of his arm. "Why ever would she believe us in need of charity?"

I sighed and clutched my hands together, wondering what on earth she planned to do about the *other* secret. Pity for her nearly strangled me.

With a forceful stride, she pivoted them both and moved down the walkway toward the house. She cast the briefest glance back at me, and those dark eyes laid heavily into her pale face created an image that remained in my head well after the pair had disappeared around the bushes.

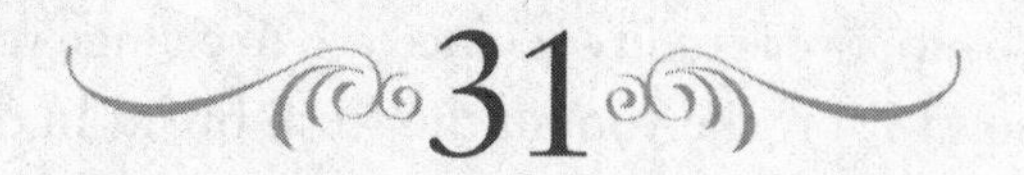

31

The only thing you must do for weeds to take over is . . . nothing.

—*Notebook of a viticulturist*

"What do you think of that Carrington man who hangs about Trevelyan?" Donegan thunked the mug onto the Campbells' table and looked at the village man across from him.

"Nothing that wouldn't be gossip, Mr. Vance, but he seems a bit untrustworthy to me. Never cared for him. Has he wronged you?"

"No, it's just something odd I heard about him once." Donegan hadn't managed to shake the impending sense of doom and utter helplessness heaped upon him since Caine's odd reaction to his questions about Carrington's character. "I thank you for your hospitality to me while I worked at Trevelyan."

"I prayed you'd never leave." Mrs. Campbell set a bowl of weak stew before Donegan. "Selfish of me, isn't it? You've brought naught but good to Welporth."

Donegan smiled up at the woman before shoveling a spoonful of food into his mouth. Tasteless as it was, the warmth of the watery meal made it inviting and satisfying.

"I don't suppose I could convince you to change your mind, could I now? I'll make you all the fresh bread in the world and drizzle it in honey. Or you can have Valerie. Sweeter than all the honey in the shire and pretty, besides. Isn't she a vision in that dress?"

Donegan eyed the girl hovering in the corner where she watched the hanging kettle, shyly avoiding his gaze. "I've never seen her look finer, Mrs. Campbell." The blue dress fit her well, even if it clashed terribly with the hovel surrounding her, and it brought a bittersweet smile to Donegan's lips. He knew immediately where the garment had come from. It seemed the color spilling forth from Tressa Harlowe could no longer be contained by the walls of her home, for it had leaked into the village as well. If it was possible, the ache for her expanded until he feared it would overtake his rational sense and keep him from leaving.

Yet he would do as she requested. Always.

"Come now, won't you stay? A man deserves to see the reward of his labors at harvest."

"I never stay in one village long. I do thank you for fetching Ginny and putting us up last night, though."

"'Twasn't a worry, Mr. Donegan." She smiled and turned to the counter where she began sawing bread into slices of wood. "Once you fit ten in a cottage, you don't notice two more. Won't you stay for a bite of bread?"

He hesitated, staring at the solid slices and remembering the taste of them. "I thank you for the offer, but we'd best get along before any more time passes. I could easily remain here forever, but my responsibilities lie elsewhere."

With a few final goodbyes, Donegan led Ginny out into the cloudy day toward his horse.

"Uncle Don, I don't want to stay here. I'm glad we're leaving."

"You enjoyed living at Trevelyan, did you not?" He leaped astride Gypsy and lifted the little girl in front of him, noticing her frame had acquired a little weight. "They said you were a good help."

"Oh yes, but it wasn't quite right. It wasn't home."

He sank into the leather saddle with a sigh and wrapped his arms around her little body. "I know the feeling." He'd never had strong attachment to the little glen until he'd had to leave it. Now every piece of Carin Green, including the precious girl leaning against him, seemed a treasure.

A patter of footsteps nearby drew his attention back to the Campbell cottage where their eldest boy waved as he approached. Donegan guided his horse closer and reined him in just before the lad who held out a cloth-wrapped package. "Mum insisted. It's an entire loaf."

"Please thank your mother, Sam, but I cannot take any more from your kind family."

But the boy shoved it into his hands with determination, meeting his glance with a desperate one of his own. "Please, sir. Please take it. Believe me, that'll be the kindness."

Biting back a smile, Donegan accepted the gift that had the weight of a stone and shoved it into his saddlebag. "Then thank you. And you're welcome."

The boy smiled. "It's been a real pleasure serving you, Mr. Donegan. The fields won't be the same without you."

Donegan hesitated, shifting in his saddle. It was finally time to depart, but a sense of unease had settled over him at the thought of leaving her with Carrington and it wouldn't lift. Dr. Caine's odd reaction to his inquiry had only strengthened it. "Sam, I need to speak to the local doctor about something. Could you tell me where to find him?"

"The closest we have in the village is old widow Carney with her herbs. I've heard there's a doctor in Haywood that old Harlowe saw, though. Same parish, just up the road a piece."

With a nod of thanks, Donegan shifted on his horse and nudged him into an easy gallop. They arrived in the bustling town of Haywood within the hour and easily located the little medical office on the east side of the main street. Slipping off his horse and tying him to a post, Donegan stepped up to the door and knocked. A tall and confident young man in a cheap suit and tiny spectacles answered the door.

"Is the doctor in? I'd like a word with him."

"I'm the doctor. How can I help?"

"I have the wrong clinic, then. I'm looking for the doctor who attends the Harlowe family."

"Ah, the Harlowes. Yes, I served Josiah Harlowe for years. I was his personal physician."

Donegan frowned. "You tended to Josiah Harlowe?"

"Yes, ever since I came here. I monitored his heart condition until his passing, even though he refused medicine for it."

"I thought he had a lung condition. Something to do with toxic air."

The doctor crossed his arms. "The man's lungs were

fit as could be. His only medical complaint was a severely weakened heart valve due to a childhood bout of rheumatic fever. I've been monitoring the condition for years, as did my predecessor Dr. Field before me. He staunchly refused to see any other physician, including specialists in London."

"Perhaps I misheard, then." Dread and indecision warred through Donegan as he thanked the man and left.

"Uncle Don, we're not going back, are we? You promised we'd go home."

"That we will, Ginny." He leaped astride Gypsy and turned him back toward the road. "I just have to send a message first."

32

Frost comes stealthily and silently to a vineyard, lacing it with beautiful, deadly designs in a single night, proving with all certainty that, despite his meticulous work, the vinedresser is truly never in complete control of anything he grows.

—Notebook of a viticulturist

Are you Tressa Harlowe? This is for you, from a gent in Haywood." A scrawny barefoot lad stood at the service entrance that evening where I'd been summoned to receive the note. "He said I'm to deliver it into your hands and no other." He thrust the smudged envelope toward me and I nodded my thanks, wishing I could drop a shilling into his dry palm.

When he scampered off into the sunset, I turned to shield the missive from the curious watchers hanging about the servant's hall and hurried from the room. Andrew? Father? My heart thudded. But when I reached the empty coolness of the entrance hall, I stared down upon the familiar handwriting of Donegan Vance. I froze. Pinching my lips, I stuffed the note in my pocket to read another time. I had no wish to hear the man's voice, even on paper. Confusion had overwhelmed me, and his words would be dangerously swaying, especially if they were as persuasive as his presence.

Abandoning the note in a wardrobe drawer in my room, I had the chambermaid redress me in an older serge frock. Releasing my hair from the twirls and pins placed earlier that morning, I shook out the waves and pinned a small section back and draped an old brown cloak over my arm.

I met the butler on the landing and he took in the sight of me without a word. One could always count on faithful servants for not reacting to their mistress's oddities. "Amos, have you done what we discussed?"

Dark eyes flicked back and forth in his long, somber face and he crept close to whisper his reply. "We've gone over every inch of the cottage, and nothing has been found. Not a single farthing."

I'd sent my two most loyal servants, Amos and Margaret, to scour the cottage for signs of the pilfered fortune, for I knew I could trust no one else.

"And no one intruded?"

"We were the only ones near the place. It's secured and I doubt even a mouse could gain entry." He leaned closer and slipped a large metal key into my hand. "You are now the only one with access to it."

"Thank you, Amos. Tell no one of this, and be sure to let me know if anyone snoops."

Swiftly flying through the servant's hall and out the service entrance, I breathed in deeply of moist air once I stepped outside. It was time to find answers. Bypassing the stables in favor of walking in the fresh air, I took long strides down the wooded path as the sun set, a basket dangling on my arm.

I dared not call on any of the field hands, for some might even have retired for the night, but stopped instead before the home of the one man I knew would be awake, one of the few I'd met when he came to the house for candles. The door of the lamplighter's home was answered by a slender woman with a pleasantly content face who welcomed me in before I gave my name.

"I hope I've not disrupted your meal."

"It would never be a disruption to have a guest." The older woman beamed as she ushered me toward a long, crude table.

Her large, pleasantly gruff husband whipped aside a long curtain closing off a small washing stand and stepped out into the room to agree with her. "Give the girl some bread, Maggie."

She settled me in a chair and brought me the softest bread I'd ever had the pleasure of tasting. What skill languished within this simple cottage.

I turned to the couple after a few minutes of pleasant chatter and dove into my mission with all the informality I could muster. If anyone knew of Donegan's activities, the lamplighter, an unofficial night watchman, would be the one. "I'm wondering if either of you happened to see Donegan Vance about with a trunk."

"Not long ago he brought that one into the square, didn't he?" The man frowned and looked at his wife for confirmation.

I sat forward. "Did you see what he did with it?"

"He merely came asking for help."

"To unlock it? Did he remove anything from it?"

The man's oversized brow lowered as he guessed my intentions, my suspicions of Donegan, but his little wife laid a hand on his arm and the motion exuded invisible calm over him. Husband and wife shared a look and the husband rose, sloshing back his mug of tea and clunking it on the table. "Come with me, Miss Harlowe. I must light the lamps. I'd like to give you a tour of our little village that you'll find quite enlightening."

A polite refusal rose with immediate swiftness to my lips, but a gentle awareness of my heavenly Father quieted my spirit, opening my heart to receive what this man wished to show me. Had I not lain awake regretting my harsh response to Donegan?

With a nod of thanks to his wife for the bread, I followed the man out the door. He paused to grab a pole leaning on the doorframe and light it in his own fireplace before he strode out into the dusky street glowing with the final traces of a red sunset. "We have five lamps in the village, all along the main street and into the square." He paused to reach his pole up to the wick atop the ancient metal light post, another relic of the village's medieval history, until a small gold flame glowed there.

He walked solemnly ahead toward another tall light post and again reached his pole up to light it. "When this one lights, you can see the McEvoy cottage just down the way. Their old roof was falling into the attic after a storm until it mysteriously found itself repaired by a man who took no pay. He simply came, mended, and left while they were out in the fields."

"How kind." I mumbled the words.

"Across the square is the Widow Kearney's place. Her two children have left the village, so Old Master Harlowe lets her stay in the little shack at the end of the road. Most of the village had quite forgotten about the old woman until a newcomer in town discovered her out on a chair clipping her grass with kitchen shears. She soon finds herself with wildflowers on her door every morning and her grass clipped."

On down the line he took me, interspersing each lamplighting with a story of someone Donegan Vance had rescued or aided. "There you see the old water pump. It brings water up to us so the women don't have to climb down the rocks to the channel to dip buckets. It was dangerous for them. It's been broken almost as long as I've lived here, until your Mr. Vance came to Welporth. Without a word he labored over it one evening and fixed it for us. He has an uncanny sense for how things work."

"Why did he do all these things?" The more I heard about the man, the more confused I became. These things had nothing to do with finding the fortune.

He studied me in the flickering light of the flames overhead. "Don't know, miss. Why do you delight in the vineyards or live in a castle? It's just who he is."

"I'm glad he's performed these acts of kindness, but—"

He waved aside my words. "Not a few acts. A way of life." He lit the final lamp and turned to face me in the moonlight. "Tell the man something doesn't work or someone needs help and it's like an official summons. It's as good as done, with no one around to witness or give him thanks."

The memory of his bad-day remedy speared through my

bitterness toward the man, leaving a crack in it. "Why would he do all this in secret?"

"It's what the Good Book says, isn't it? Don't let the right hand see what the left is doing. Do nothing out of selfish ambition or vain conceit."

"Donegan isn't the sort of man I would imagine knowing much Scripture."

He studied me with a crooked smile. "No, miss. He simply lives it out."

An internal battle tugged at my heart, but I pressed on. Didn't I know more than they did of the events that had occurred? I breathed a quick prayer, and the brief contact with God softened my words. "I'm glad he's helped the village, but he's been a great detriment to me. That trunk you saw—"

"Was the only thing we tried to dissuade him from doing. He insisted that the mistress have her belongings restored to her, though. He told us that she went on so to an innkeeper about some beads she'd lost, and he thought she should have what was so important to her."

My breath suddenly thinned, my chest tight. "What color was the trunk? Do you remember?"

"Blue steamer trunk with gold edges. Fancy little thing, but mostly a battered mess when I saw it."

"Mother's trunk. That was Mother's steamer trunk he brought into the square."

"Made us promise not to breathe a word of who fetched it back for her. He simply wanted her to have it. But seeing as you're thinking this way about him, I thought it best you know."

With aching clarity, his words tumbled over my senses. *I'm not required to impress my enemies. Only to love them.*

Including those who despised him. I shook my head. "And the strike? He knew very well I couldn't pay anyone yet."

"So did that little plumed creature with the beady eyes."

I frowned. "What plumed creature?"

"The one who marched her fancy self through the village one night and led all the men to the pub to pump them full of drink and notions about their rights."

Ellen. It was Ellen who had started the strike. Another wall crumbled and I forced myself to embrace the possibility that I'd been wrong about the man.

Father, what is the truth?

I took myself up the dark road alone and stared at the moonlight and its bright reflection on the distant waters of the channel. It was like Donegan Vance was two different men and I could not reconcile what I knew of him into one person. Every time he opened his mouth he was gruff and blunt, unyielding and prickly, but full of profound truth. He claimed his only goal was money, yet his every action was bursting with a selfless love so unusual I could hardly grasp the reason for it.

As the chill of the dark woods enveloped me, I threw the cloak around me and hurried up the road, the lantern I'd brought from home extended into the dark. The crunch of footfall nearby struck a light panic in me, and I increased my pace. As the footsteps neared, I broke into a run.

"Miss Harlowe."

Against my better judgment I threw a glance over my shoulder, but I relaxed when the form of Dr. Caine broke through the shadows behind me.

I slowed with an exhale and smiled. "Dr. Caine. I'm not accustomed to being alone in the dark."

He huffed up to me and took my arm. "If there is anything unsavory in these woods, it'd be no match for you, my dear." He patted my arm and strode beside me. "You seemed to be contemplating eternity. May I assume you were thinking of a young man?"

I lowered my face in the coolness of night and forced aside the image of Donegan Vance. "I suppose so."

"Are you deeply in love with him, then?"

I turned that question over in my head. "I'm afraid I don't understand him well enough to know. I hardly know whether he is good or bad."

"Don't write poor Carrington off because of a few faults, dear one. What heroine would ever truly want a flawless hero?"

I smiled, but did not correct him about the identity of the man stealing my thoughts just then. "Only every woman in existence."

"That's the trouble with women, and with romance for that matter. A flawless hero isn't as desirable as you'd think. He's only a man whose flaws have not yet been exposed, and let me tell you, that is far more dangerous than one whose flaws are known and understood."

I pondered then the exposed flaws of both Donegan and Andrew. The latter man seemed like a branch poorly grafted—connected enough to sprout an attractive show of leafy foliage, but unable to produce worthwhile fruit. Donegan seemed like an unadorned branch rich with fruit to offer others.

"One has only to determine which imperfections are excusable, and which are not."

We reached the clearing and crossed the drawbridge in silence, padding our way into the courtyard. At the sound of our footsteps, a small cloister of doves rose and circled into the sky.

"So have I sufficiently convinced you, my dear? Will you give your poor hero another chance?"

I stood in the cobbled courtyard looking up at the shifting gray clouds, but it was Donegan's face that came to mind, and I recalled the utter desolation on his face as I'd rejected him one final time. "I'm beginning to believe the question is whether or not he'd give me one."

His face melted into a grin. "If he doesn't, then I daresay he isn't worth having."

As we stood in the echoey courtyard draped in moonlight, I turned to face him. "Being quite frank, Dr. Caine, it is Donegan Vance who has so tangled my thoughts and feelings. I've heard terrible reports of his actions, but paired with what I know of him, I cannot bring myself to believe he acted against me so."

"It is a lovely problem to have, child—a blindness to the faults of others. You will simply have to rely on the guidance of those who know the truth. Which is precisely why I spoke up about Mr. Vance the other night."

"But you were mistaken about what happened with Mr. Prescott. Donegan did not go there to frame me at all. He went to defend me."

He laid a hand on my arm. "Trust me, Miss Harlowe. Vance will tell you whatever it takes for you to believe he's on your side, but I heard him myself when he came to speak to Prescott. He did not defend you, and you should never believe anything he says otherwise."

"Dr. Caine, it was Prescott who told me this. Not Donegan."

Silence ensued. His hesitation rang loudly in my head, shoving my mind toward a certain realization that simply could not be so. Was Dr. Caine lying? Why ever would he? "Is it possible you were mistaken on what you saw?"

Silence echoed through the courtyard again as my tension mounted to a nearly unbearable level. His soft voice broke into the night. "Come. I think it's time I show you something."

I looked into his face, those intelligent blue eyes that now resembled the dullness of a cloudy day. Fear mixed with a dangerous curiosity to see what he had to show me. I had the sense it would be very important. "What is it?"

His smile did not reach his eyes, but was a sad, solemn sort of thing. "You'll see. Just follow me."

I let him guide me out of the courtyard as I stole glances toward him and wondered what I would learn about Donegan. A vague mistrust warred with the heavy pull of curiosity.

"Let us go this way, around to the back of the house. This must be an absolute secret."

These words made me pause. Anxiousness stilled me and rooted my feet to the ground. Yet . . . what if there was an explanation? What if this thing he must show me would make sense of everything? The sound of waves colliding with the craggy rock face met my ears as Dr. Caine turned back toward me, waiting. As I swiped loose hair back, a distant voice drew my edgy attention. Was that my name?

Dr. Caine touched my arm. "We should hurry, before someone misses you."

Then the sound came again, closer. "Miss Tressa!"

I spun as Lucy flew toward us, her white apron flipping

wildly about in the coastal breeze. "Miss, you'd best come quick. There's been trouble."

"I'm sorry, Dr. Caine, but I must go."

Tension splayed over his face and he hesitated a moment before nodding. "I suppose it isn't time for you to see it yet. Another time. Soon, I hope."

33

Springtime is wonderful in the vineyards—weeds are small and manageable, the vines are trained and primed to grow, and next year's crop seems like a concern for a future time. But there is one terrible danger in this season of relative ease—complacency.

—Notebook of a viticulturist

"That Mr. Prescott is back, Miss Tressa." Lucy's breathy voice filled the courtyard as we stepped under the archway. "He says it's important and he won't speak to anyone but you."

I sighed and brushed my hair back. Even after finding the fortune, the troubles would not cease. "Thank you, Lucy. Help me repair my appearance and have Amos send him into the drawing room. Say nothing to Mother."

When I had smoothed my hair and changed my gown, I

swept into the drawing room with trepidation and greeted a stern-faced guest.

"Miss Harlowe, what is the meaning of this?" He hobbled to me and extended a small pile of pound notes. "I assume you will replace this foreign money with something valid."

I smoothed the papers on a small side table and looked at the foreign lettering, wondering what on earth I'd replace them with. With a big breath, I read the only words that were in English:

> This promissory note drawn by The Mounts Bay Commercial Bank, Cornwall, promises to pay the bearer one day after sight the sum of ten pounds sterling.

A quick count of the papers told me there were eight of them, for a total of eighty pounds. Not much in the grand scheme, but far more than the small sum remaining in the box when I'd departed this man's estate.

"Surely you will not bring trouble on us for so small a sum, will you, Mr. Prescott?" I dropped them on the table.

He sighed. "Young lady, no one can keep what she cannot afford. If you cannot produce even this small sum, then you have no business remaining at such an estate anyway."

"Please, sir. Give me until harvest and I shall have the rest of your money."

Indecision weakened the hard lines of tension on his face. "One week. And that's far more generous than I normally am."

I nodded, shoving aside the looming anxiety about where I would find the money.

When I thought he would depart, he merely lingered and watched me openly. "I do believe you'd make a fine couple, Miss Harlowe. That is, if you're wise enough to marry outside of our social class."

"Mr. Vance, you mean?" Heat flamed up my neck and spread across my face.

"Him with his strong opinions, and you with that pert little sense of determination . . . what a marvelous display of fireworks."

I willed my face to cool. "He was merely coming to my aid when he spoke to you on my behalf. His defense of me does not indicate any romantic intentions, Mr. Prescott."

He smiled in the way of a gruffly amused old man. "No, but accidentally confessing his love for you might."

Heat poured over my entire body then, up my limbs and into my scalp.

"You'll find no judgment on the differences in your situations from me, Miss Harlowe. Any field hand reckless enough to stand up to me might just be deserving of his heiress."

I forced myself to swallow as the man jammed his hat onto his head and limped toward the doors.

When our guest departed, I climbed the steps and brushed into the gallery where Mother was perched at a secretary. She looked up and smiled, but her expression dissolved into keen analysis. "Daughter, I do believe you look different." She rose and crossed the room, taking my chin in her fingertips to inspect my face flushed from the encounter with Prescott. "You look quite affected, and I find myself wondering who has breathed life into that overly serious face of yours and made it so rosy. The only explanation is that you are in love."

I jerked my face away, letting my hair curtain it. "You are

mistaken, Mother, for I have lately determined myself to be the worst judge of men and farther from the hope of marriage than I ever was."

Still, her critical gaze remained on me. "You forget how well I know you."

"What is it you want me to admit, Mother? That I think Donegan Vance a fine man? That I detest Andrew? Both of those things are true."

Her eyes snapped. "Donegan Vance, a fine man? He's taken far too many liberties with my daughter, then as soon as he gets his hands on our fortune, he disappears into the grimy smog from which he came. I know you kissed that odious man at the portrait unveiling, and I cannot stand to think of it."

She stepped close enough to lower her voice. "I thought to be mad at you first, then I later realized he'd seduced you. It was his plan all along. Did you know he attempted to follow us home from the gallery? Imagine, that man stalking us like a shadow. He asked after us all along the route, even after you stoutly refused his company before we left. What do you think of your fine man now, Daughter?"

Someone has tampered with the carriage, miss. I just thought you should know. The groom's words snapped back to my mind and brought the truth into clear focus. Somehow he'd known of the impending danger and that's why he tried to switch the carriages, tried to ride with me. And I, so wrapped up in my misjudgments of him, had refused—then he had rescued us anyway.

I looked at Mother's cold blue eyes. The woman who had nothing but malice on her tongue for him had received his generous help more times than she knew. I glanced at the beads from India that lay against her protruding collarbone, contrasting with the pale flesh of her neck. She hadn't even mentioned that she had them back. Had they been dropped at her door in the middle of the night? Had she tripped over the trunk and looked down an empty hall to see who had left them? She never would have guessed.

"What do I think of him?" I prepared the words in my head to tell her everything he'd done, but the memory of his bad-day remedy stilled my tongue. He wouldn't want her to know. Instead, I simply said with quiet confidence, "I like him even better now."

When night cooled the walls of my bedchamber, I curled into the windowsill to look out over the starry night. I couldn't erase Donegan's face from my mind, and the image brought an ache that wouldn't be dispelled. My confusion had only intensified after all I'd learned that day. I couldn't help but feeling I'd taken a gift that God had given me and tossed it out the window without understanding what I'd truly held in my hands. Like the faraway, unreachable stars that lit up the night sky, Donegan was lost to me forever in the great wide world.

I closed my eyes, wishing I could travel back in time simply by opening the glass clock face and moving the hands backward. I desperately wanted to go back to that night in the vineyard and hear his explanation for everything, for surely there would be one. The missing fortune, keeping Father's survival a secret . . . surely there was a reason for all of it.

A knock sounded on my door and I bid the visitor enter.

"Miss Tressa?" Margaret's rosy face peered around the doorway.

I smiled and she slipped into the room, closing the door behind her.

"What a wonderful night for gazing at the stars."

I smiled my assent.

"I'm glad to find you in." She approached and settled on the high-back chair near the window. "Your mother asked me to speak with you about that vineyard manager."

I turned my face away as my heart crumpled. "Oh, Margaret. Please."

But her quiet voice continued. "However, she failed to tell me what exactly I should say about the man."

I turned toward her smiling face that sparkled with mischief and took her hands. "I cannot hate him, Margaret. I've tried and it's no use."

"You have good reason to feel that way, my dear. He may not know how to craft a lovely sentence, but he's been naught but respectful toward you, and that does wonders to my mother-hen heart. He does treat you like the gem you are." She studied me then, tilting her face with motherly affection. "Do you love him very much, then?"

My shoulders drooped and I rested my chin on my knees. "I've no idea. When he left, I had no notion of love toward him, or even of tolerance, yet now that he's gone . . ." I lifted my head again. "Margaret, how can I fall in love with a man when he isn't even here?"

"Most women want a man for the way he makes them feel when they are with him. But you love who he truly is, and there's evidence of that spread all over this village, whether he's here or not. He's left little pieces of his servant heart all around, and you're discovering them like clues on a treasure map."

I lifted my head with an exhale and brushed the hair off my face. That's exactly what this resembled—a treasure hunt. There was a wealth of treasure hidden within a stony exterior, if only one knew how to remove the lens of the world to see what lay far deeper.

How vastly different was Andrew. That man lied and pretended, but he did it so poetically that the world lauded him. He resembled the deceptively sharp rocks covered by the soft, beautiful waves of the sea that lured you into danger by charming you into their presence before destroying you.

"How can you ever tell, Margaret? How am I ever supposed to know who is the good one and who the bad?"

She smiled and stroked my hair. "There's only one way to do that, and no one can do this better than you. You must eavesdrop."

"Eavesdrop?"

"Yes, love. For who a man is when he thinks no one is looking, that's who he truly is." She squeezed my hand. "I'll bring you some tea. And I've had Cook make up your favorite orange-iced scones. Perhaps that'll ease the pain a little."

I forced a weak smile. When the motherly woman slipped out the door, I leaned my head back against the window casement and looked over the shadowed vineyard below. Margaret's wisdom swirled through my mind and solidified into a plan far more powerful than eavesdropping. Why would I sneak about when I seemed to have direct access to the One who saw everything?

Father, what do you think of Donegan Vance? No amount of clandestine spying on the man would provide me with as much truth about his character as the One who had planted and tended him all his life.

As breeze from the open window lifted hair off my warm face, fragments of Scripture verses flittered back to mind and struck my heart. It was God's definition of love from the book of First Corinthians. I'd studied these lines years ago when the subject of true love had fascinated me to obsession and driven me to understand it however I could. Pieces of these phrases now swirled through my mind as I climbed down from the window and ascended the ladder toward the ceiling. Stretching out on my back, I dipped a clean brush in the black pigment and rendered in long, swooping letters the essence of the verse as well as I remembered.

Longsuffering
Others first
Content
Humble
Keeps no record of wrongs
Rejoices in others' blessings
Embodies truth
Endures being wronged
Values others
Perseveres despite adversity

My heart ached with the clarity this brought, and how well he fit these words. It was as if his name belonged at the head of each line.

I climbed down and rolled my brush through a bowl of water, turning it murky with pigment. Leaning against a bedpost to look over my work, I studied the list, focusing on the last line especially. *Perseveres despite adversity.* How often had he sprung to my rescue, aiding and supporting, even when I rejected him? Over and over again I'd cast him aside, only to have him tirelessly rescue, serve, and persevere. I sat on my bed and wrapped my hands around my scarred feet, remembering with profound clarity the gentle pressure of his hands as he'd tended this lowest part of me with such care.

Despite my dubbing him "black" earlier, the stark color did not fit the image I now had of the man. For when seen through the lens of my heavenly Father, the only color that described this man was love.

Regret touched me anew and the ache of longing filled me. I laid my cheek on my bent knees as the door creaked open and Margaret slipped back into my chamber, extending a rattling little teacup and saucer. "To warm your poor heart." She sat on a chair beside the bed and caught sight of the newest artwork adorning my room.

After a moment of silence, I looked at her with desperation. "What do I do now?" The words were a mere whisper, for it was all I could manage as my heart clogged my throat.

She leaned closer and wrapped an arm around my hunched shoulders. "Let yourself love the poor man."

A gush of admiration and desire released from my heart, yet it was chased by a wave of sorrow. What good did it do me to acknowledge the truth now? He had moved on to the next place to pour himself out for other people, his time at Trevelyan over.

And it was I who had sent him away.

Restless and distracted, I rose later that night and whipped my robe around myself. Thoughts of Donegan had poked at my sleep until I'd pulled my tired self from the bed. Hungry for a small taste of this man I'd only begun to know, I determined to visit his newly abandoned cottage and see what sort of place it was. Perhaps there I would find some condemning truth and release myself from this torment. Much as grief wrung a person out, the pain of regret was its own sort of torture.

After rescuing the long key from the bottom of my wardrobe and grabbing a candle, I slipped my feet into brown flats and stole out into the hall. Hurrying down the stairs and outside, I sprinted across the open lawn doused in moonlight and over to the cottage and fit the key into the door. I held my breath as I pushed the door open and extended my candle into the dim space.

Utter shock swept over me in powerful waves of disbelief and awe as I stepped into the cottage. The sight of it stole my breath and left me weak, my heart pounding. For here I stood in the room of my memories, the workroom where Father had hidden his fortune. It was *here*. I crossed the small space to the fireplace and allowed my fingertips to graze the words inscribed there—*Legendary Harlowe*. Yes, this was it.

My fragile heart didn't know whether to laugh or cry at this discovery. Everything made sense—including why Donegan had suddenly found the fortune on his own. It had been here all along, and when I told him of my childhood memory, he had found it in the chimney of this cottage.

The room was precisely as I remembered it except for a few scraps of the last occupant's trade—odd assortments of broken things in all stages of repair, crude yet smoothly clean tools, and bowls of sweets all made and ready to distribute. In all the years I'd lived here, I possessed little in great abundance except time and material goods, none of which had been spread to the people living right beside me in the village.

In the midst of that great, lavish display of generosity, a pathetic little strip of paper hung impaled on a crooked nail to one of the pillars supporting the structure.

> He that keepeth his mouth keepeth his life: but he that openeth wide his lips shall have destruction.

The verse I'd given him. How pitiful it looked, dwarfed in the rugged, oversized room so full of his overwhelming kindness. I walked over to it and ripped it down, cringing at the petty admonishment.

In that moment, I released my anger about the stolen fortune as my vision realigned to reality. He'd taken from a spoiled, wealthy girl who owed him for his work anyway to disperse among people who truly needed it. He'd also left me what I needed, for hadn't he counted out the amount of the debt and placed it in the hiding spot he knew I'd check next?

My heart softened even more. Yet the selfish part of me still hoped he'd return with the portion he hadn't earned and thus redeem himself fully.

34

If a branch wishes to survive a graft, it must become one with the vine, growing to resemble it so thoroughly that you cannot tell where the branch ends and the vine begins.

—*Notebook of a viticulturist*

I slept restlessly that night with the windows open, my limbs tangled in the sheets as much as my mind was tangled in facts concerning Donegan Vance.

By the time a pair of sparrows landed on my windowsill in the glow of sunrise, I recalled one more piece of Donegan in my grasp. His note still languished in the poor wardrobe drawer, utterly forgotten all this time and I hastened to retrieve it, wondering what his parting words to me would be.

You mustn't trust Dr. Caine. I've been to Haywood and he isn't known here. There's only one doctor in this entire area, and it isn't him. Yet he is somehow connected, because his name was in your father's notebooks.

Shock jarred me and I reread the note several times. If this was true, everything else fit into place, for all the accusations against Donegan had come from Dr. Caine. But how could that be? Dr. Caine hadn't asked a thing about the fortune, nor had I caught him snooping for it.

When I'd dressed in a simple linen dress and snatched a basket full of breakfast food from the sidebar of the morning room, I snuck out. I'd bring Father some food and ask him what to do about replacing Mr. Prescott's money too. Passing the study, I stepped in and I tucked the foreign pound notes into a little sack. Taking them with me would keep them out of the hands of any lingering fortune hunters. I still couldn't convince myself to place Dr. Caine in that category, but I must hold him at arm's length until I knew for sure.

"Amos." I touched the butler's arm in the hall and forced a cheerful smile. "The day is simply too beautiful to shield myself from it, so I believe I will soak it in. Tell Mother I've decided to take breakfast on the water. I'll return by the noonday meal."

The man nodded with an indulgent smile and extended a plain pink parasol to me from the stand near the door. "Yes, miss. Bring us any extra sunshine when you return."

Down on the windy beach, as the start of a storm rolled across the sky, I tied the little sack firmly to my belt to free my hands and gripped my parasol and basket. Settling myself neatly in the boat, I tucked the fabric of my skirt under me and took hold of the oars to push out into the water.

The wind magnified as I left the shore, threatening to rip my hat from my head. I tied my hat firmly onto my head and knotted the ribbon under my chin to hold the wayward accessory in place.

Struggling against the breeze, I rowed with sure, purposeful strokes toward the little cave. No wonder I'd never discovered the island before. Maneuvering carefully through the cave, I steered the hull toward the narrow green line in the distance. Nearly a half hour it took to row through the wind to the shore that I had so recently discovered.

After anchoring my little craft in the sand, I looped the basket over my arm and ran down the mossy path where the massive trees blocked the wind. The magical setting of this place enchanted me. Oh how I wished I could paint my entire room with the scene before me, and lay the moss on the floor as my carpet, so that I may always live and walk among this beauty every day, rising to see it in the morning and falling asleep in the midst of it.

I reached the cottage and pushed the front door open. "Father?" Lumps of leftover dinner remained in the chilled fireplace and messy stacks of papers crowded the tabletop. When I'd searched the tiny cottage, reality struck me with confusion and then horror—Father was not here.

But that couldn't be. Dropping the basket on the floor, I sprinted out the door and through the woods. At the beach I saw only crushed reeds where the second boat had been the night I'd found Father. The sky had turned an ominous shade of green and the air pulsed with the sense of an impending storm. Rain fell in torrents as the wind picked up. Panic clawed at my mind as I shoved my boat back into the water and clambered over the side, swaying it precariously in the powerful wind now sweeping over the choppy water.

Bracing myself inside, I grabbed the oars and stabbed them into the water, rowing myself forward with powerful strokes. After fighting the wind for a while, pain stretched across my chest and down my upper arms, anxiety driving me to a faster speed than I'd ever gone in a boat. I'd passed through the cave but could not yet see Trevelyan through the storm. With another searing pain, I lost my grip and the oars jerked from my hands with the pull of the water. I fumbled to grasp them in the twisting boat, but the left oar struck a rock and it wrenched away with a snap of metal and screws. As I cried out and lunged for it, I heard my name tangled in the wind on a masculine voice. I spun, hair whipping over my face, and saw Dr. Caine coming toward me in a large boat with a pointed metal hull and sails unfurled like dragon's wings.

Uncertainty clutched me at the sight of him, but he steered his vessel closer, determination hardening his features. He leaned over his steering wheel and waved me over, yelling over the waves. "Bring your boat closer."

"What are you doing out here? There's a storm coming."

"Looking for you."

Panic chilled my wet skin.

"Have you forgotten already?" He steered his boat closer to mine, navigating it through the choppy waters. "I needed to show you something. It's what you've been searching for."

"What are you talking about?"

"Now it's time to show you."

"Show me what?"

As his boat skimmed up behind mine, he leaned down,

cupping his hands to his mouth to yell, "How your father died." Then he spun his steering wheel with a hard jerk and angled toward me. I paddled with my single oar, but I struck rocks with a jarring thud.

Fear spiked through me like shards of ice. I shoved away from the rocks and paddled again, my little vessel sloshing violently about. "Stop!"

He spun the steering wheel again and I leaped overboard as he rammed my little boat with his metal hull. Cold and pain battered my body as I tumbled over rocks and waves, trying to catch at something. I pawed desperately at the remains of my upturned vessel when I found it, but with a groan and a slap it flailed, the hull tipping down into the water, and the waves began to swallow it.

In that moment, hovering alone in the vast channel and left for dead, the water's chill snaked into my bones. Fear squeezed with a constant pressure like the water that surrounded me. Dr. Caine's boat swayed and tossed in the distance as he sailed toward Trevelyan's shore. Despairing of survival, yet clinging to hope as I had for weeks, I dove under the frothy water and stroked with every ounce of strength, forcing myself forward by sheer willpower. Everything seemed to conspire to hinder me, from the skirt tangling my legs to seaweed that grabbed at my surging body.

When I broke the surface for air, I refused to look around. I merely ordered my body to sink back into the water after a few painful breaths and swim hard. I repeated the effort time and again, hoping I was close but afraid to look.

Then it happened. I reached the end of my endurance and it overwhelmed me at once. Pain pierced my side after the absence of regular oxygen and my right leg cramped to the point of torture. Reaching the surface again, I cried out. This time Trevelyan loomed within my blurry sight, the nearby trees bending toward me in the wind, as if reaching hands out to urge me on. The tide jerked my agonized body back and forth as I forced myself to stroke forward, angling to ease the stitch in my side.

As I swam toward the shore, glimpsing the detail of the craggy rock faces that held up my castle, a powerful, unnameable force tugged on me, growing stronger as I progressed and lighting panic in me. I'd reached the mudflats. I fought it desperately, dipping and rising again for more air and crying out in anguish, but it pulled me about effortlessly, as if I was mere seaweed. In a flash, an image of Father exploded through my mind. Dear, damaged Father, who had for a moment reached out to me. Oh, how desperately I wanted to survive so I could find him.

God! cried my desperate heart. *God, save me. You are bigger than all of this. Bigger than the channel, bigger than death.*

Water poured through my nose and mouth as I sucked for air and went under again. Blackness pushed against my consciousness. *Father!*

"Tressa!"

Deep, confident, strong—the sound of my name above the water.

"Grab on to me." The muffled voice commanded, but I couldn't comply. I hadn't the strength. Confusion and darkness swirled over me, overtaking my reasoning.

When you feel you're dying in the heat of summer, all a branch needs to do is to hold on. That's all, simply hold on. Those words spoken in some remote part of the woods poured through me with dreamlike beauty as I floated underwater.

"Grab on to me." The voice called again through the muddle of water. *God?*

Summoning every ounce of strength in my worn-out body, I surged mightily up out of the water and grabbed. My body crashed into something solid and wet and I wrapped my arms around it, crying as I realized it was a person who then caught me up when I could do no more. Powerful movements underneath jerked us forward through the water as I coughed, spewing salty water out of my burning lungs. I clung harder to the unknown figure and trembled, forcing myself to believe I was alive.

Soon the mighty beast under us found traction and fought through the mud flats with snorts and grunts that identified the creature as a horse, and all at once my foggy mind knew who had rescued me, to whom I now held.

"Don't let go, Tressa." Donegan's voice vibrated through his chest as I clung to him.

I forced my eyes open as the fight returned to my body and looked up at him. The rain had stopped, leaving only a chilling wind in its wake. I tried to speak, but directly behind us, I saw Dr. Caine's boat skimming toward us, the man himself bent over the steering wheel with determination. I inhaled to cry out, but fits of coughing wracked my body. When he was bearing down on us, a mighty yell came from the shore, carried on the wind, and terror ripped across Dr. Caine's features as he looked up, jerking the wheel in his shock. I followed his gaze to see what calamity awaited us, and there on the rocks overlooking the channel stood my father, big and burly like a bear, yelling a warning at us.

There was a splintering *crunch* behind us. I twisted around and saw Dr. Caine's boat had struck rocks covered by the choppy waves. The vessel tipped and bobbed, tossing its driver onto the floor as it rocked like a toy in the water. He rose as another wave slapped the side and knocked the unsteady man overboard with a cry, dumping him into the frothy waves. Panic and disbelief wracked my body, leaving it trembling and weak. My hold on Donegan loosened.

"Don't look. Keep your eyes on the shore." Donegan's hard voice cut through the wind and drew me to obey.

The shore—oh, the blessed shore that was almost within reach. I focused on it, and on the dark figure on its rocks who was now climbing down from his great height on the cliffs.

The stallion huffed against the power of the water as his hooves pawed at the rocky shore and pulled us onto the beach. Finally he leaped onto the sand and danced about, water pouring off his body. Donegan slid from his horse and lifted me down with him, cradling me in his great arms and placing me gently on the cool sand. For a moment I did nothing but experience the sensation of wind on my wet skin and bask in the realization that I had survived.

My body curled into ungraceful fits of coughing as more water poured out of my mouth and nose, raining down my neck. With a trembling hand I pounded my chest, willing the water to leave my lungs. Donegan held me up. When I forced my gritty eyes open and looked into his dear, dear face, the hard lines of worry melted into the most brilliant glow of joy I'd ever seen.

When I'd gained weak control of myself again, I blinked and looked up into his eyes that studied me with the familiar penetrating gaze. "You're here. After I told you to leave." My voice was a pathetic croak.

He thumbed wet hair off my face and gave me a bewitching smile. "I don't listen well."

I laughed, but it was overtaken by coughs. I forced myself to sit upright and he looped his arm around my back until the coughing receded. He was always like this, seeing me at my absolute worst and tenderly helping me anyway. How had I been so blind? I, who prided myself in my ability to see through the façade of half of London's elite, was blinder than the simplest socialite.

"Have you been hiding here all this time? Where did you stay?"

"I was summoned back, and I'm sworn to secrecy to protect my innocent accomplice."

"Lucy."

He shrugged and smiled. "I never break a promise."

I thought of his promise to Father to protect me. "So it would seem." I smiled up at him as he lifted me and strode across the beach.

"I hope you have no objections to being carried."

"I'm afraid I haven't the strength to walk. Or the desire." I offered up a timid smile that was something between a gentle invitation and an apology.

He smiled down at me as he moved with powerful leaps up the rocks toward Father. "It seems you do not hate me any longer. Have you forgotten all my sins already?"

"All I can seem to remember right now is that you risked your life to rescue me."

"Purely selfish on my part." Donegan huffed up the rocky shoreline toward Father where the rocks shielded us from the wind. I gazed at Father's beloved form in tattered clothing whipped about by the wind, the white hair like froth on his craggy face, and my daughter-heart thudded with hope again as he moved toward us with purpose, his face anxious.

Donegan set me on my feet on a plateau as Father reached us and he caught me up in his great arms, anchoring me to him with a low groan shuddering through him. Casting aside all protocol, everything of the past, I slipped my arms about his great form and embraced him with my entire heart. I held onto him thus for several moments of blissful relief, smelling the familiar leathery scent of him and delighting in his presence. I buried my face in his chest and sighed. "You're here. I'm so glad you're here."

"I had to come see how my little Tressa fared since she sent away her protector." He tightened his hold on me and kissed my head with great tenderness. "I couldn't leave you alone."

I smiled into his shirt and silently thanked God for everything that had happened, even the bad, for it had brought me to life. "I don't believe I ever was."

He pulled me back, massive hands framing my face as he frowned at me. "Such strength you have." The words were wrested from him like rusted metal forced into operation again, so rare were these praises. I relished them all the more for their scarcity. In that moment, I determined I'd never lose him again.

"You must have had a reason for killing Cassius, Father. I just know it. I know you were poor once and you wanted to be rid of that curse, but there has to be more to the story. Please, won't you tell me what it is? I wish to help you."

He slid his heavy hands down to my shoulders and moved me back to stare down at me with a solemn face. With a great sigh, he dropped his hands to his side and closed his eyes. "It seems I must finally tell you what I've done. But you must promise not to tell a soul."

35

Healthy branches aren't required when it comes to grafting—just a healthy vine. For it is from the vine that the life and strength flows, and a healthy vine can heal the weakest branch.

—*Notebook of a viticulturist*

Father led me to an alcove in the rocks that protected us from the dying storm as the breeze blew over my tired body. I dried myself as best I could with the cloak he handed me, then I waited, pulse thumping to the rhythm of the waves below. What could he possibly say that would explain everything?

Donegan cleared his throat, shattering the tension. "I should take care of my horse."

When he left, I turned to Father, looking up into his long-beloved face so worn and troubled. I couldn't imagine any scenario in which I could accept his violence against poor, forgotten Cassius, but I so desperately wished for it. I clung to his hand impulsively and begged. "Please, Father. Please tell me there is some reason for what you did. I cannot bear to think of you as a murderer. This has all been too unbearable, and I cannot—"

"Tressa." He stilled my avalanche of anxious words with a gentle squeeze of his hand. "Listen to me. You must understand that Cassius was a weak branch barely clinging to life, who was dying a slow death. What is it we do with weak branches, Tressa girl?"

Dropping his hand, I closed my eyes against the memory of Father lifting a branch with one finger and drawing out his knife. "Prune them off. Throw them on the fire."

"For some. But for others?"

Wind rustled the sand at my feet as my heart pounded harder, my mind then flooded with images of Cassius, his cold, silent eyes staring at me from the painting.

Father's voice cut through. "I regraft it. I attach it to a different vine."

I frowned. "What do you mean? What did you do to him?"

His blue eyes shone with intensity. "I gave him a chance at life. Cassius Malvern was pruned off and regrafted to become a new creation—*Josiah Harlowe*."

Shock turned my mind upside down, pulsing through my worn-out body, then slowly righted it as everything began to make sense in waves of understanding. Cassius. He was Cassius. I looked into the troubled eyes of this man I'd known my whole life, seeing traces of that same brokenness that existed in the eyes of the young painted boy. Time and change had faded the intensity, but it was there, hanging about the fringes of his expression, never fully erased.

"Dig up that 'grave' you found in the woods and you'll

find nothing but a little box of papers and deeds bearing the name Cassius Malvern. No body lies there, because it's right here."

Could it possibly be true? Staring up at him with wonder, I reached up to slide my fingers along his weathered cheek in a gentle caress. His expression melted at my touch, his eyes sliding closed. Here before me stood the forgotten, misunderstood, isolated boy—all grown up into a man who was just as lonely.

"I'm so glad, Father. You've no idea how I wished I'd had the chance to love that boy out of his loneliness." I placed my tiny hand on his massive chest where his heart thumped. "And now I can."

At those words, he gathered me close in his arms, fully encircling me with his massive frame, and bowed his head onto mine, resting his chin on my hair. He held me thus for several perfect moments, his heart thudding against my cheek.

I closed my eyes in disbelief. Was this truly my father clinging to me so? Even in my dreams it hadn't felt this wonderful, this engulfing. In that moment, I was wet and itchy with sand, poorer than the men who labored in our fields, and on the verge of losing the vineyard, yet all I could think of was little girl dreams and chicken bone wishes.

His embrace tightened, anchoring me to his warm body. "You are a greater blessing to this lonely, broken old man than you could ever imagine."

When he released me, I spoke. "Did you find life with the new graft?"

"Peace. I found peace. Which is as much as I could hope for. I borrowed the name Josiah Harlowe from a worker passing through the area who served in the vineyards for a few seasons. My father dismissed him when we got on well and he became my only true friend. Father made it out to be a disagreement between myself and the man, simply to have reason to dismiss him so I would not have a friend so 'beneath me.' I never had another."

"What made you so disconnected from everyone, Father? Why did you lock yourself away up in that tower years ago if you were truly so lonely? I'd thought from your notebooks that it was because you felt cursed with poverty, but you were never that."

"I do have a sort of curse over me. Yet it isn't poverty but wealth that has ruined my life, tainting every relationship." He brushed strands of hair off my face. "Tressa, since I've been gone, Trevelyan has been swarming with people wishing to help, eager to befriend. How has it felt to watch every one of them slowly reveal his true motive? To face danger from your friends? To constantly wonder what everyone dear to you truly wants? Now imagine your entire life being thus."

"Oh Father." I breathed the words from the pain in my heart. "How lonely you must have been. I understand all too well. Neville and Ellen, Andrew Carrington . . ." I glanced back over the still-choppy waters and trembled hard. "I even considered Dr. Caine a good friend, yet he—"

"Was a Malvern."

I gasped. "How could that be?"

"I'm not certain of it, but he claimed years ago to be my father's illegitimate son, born before me. Thus, the true heir. He pretended to befriend me in our youth, and later told me who he was. He was one of the many reasons I had to do away with Cassius. Yet somehow he must have found me again, found out who I really was."

I closed my eyes as a terrible ache rolled through me. "Poor man. What a wretched end to his life." I forced myself to look away from the deadly waters. "What of your parents? Your money was their money, so they wouldn't have tried to take anything from you. Weren't they—"

"Utterly consumed with their lives? Yes. Wealth is a jealous lover. When it turned out their son was not going to make an impressive showpiece among their peers . . ." His voice hitched as the thought trailed away on the breeze. "They tried to train me once, when I was young. They brought me to Trevelyan and taught me how to be stingy and overbearing with the laborers, but as you know I failed utterly. We never returned to Trevelyan after that summer of my thirteenth year. My parents labeled me slow-witted and eventually left me alone. Years later when they'd both died, I returned to this land of vineyards and life with a new identity and a lovely bride who, as it turned out, saw no more value in me than what I had in the bank."

He cast his gaze out to the water. "Most people eventually hurt you if you wait long enough, but vines never do. They can be scientifically managed and they require nothing but time and attention. People are selfish and unreliable." He smiled down at me. "Except for you, it seems. How I adored my little sprite of a girl who ran barefoot in my beloved vineyard."

"You shut me out." I said the words quietly, factually, despite the years of pain they represented.

"You asked about the fortune more and more. Asked about it until you seemed obsessed."

"With secrets and hiding places and . . . and *you*." I released his hand. "What changed your mind about me?"

Without a word, he reached into his shirt pocket and pulled out a folded piece of paper. With steady fingers he opened it and held it out as the breeze pulled at its edges. "What you said about Cassius the night you found me . . . and this."

There on the paper was the sketch that portrayed the dear father I glimpsed in those rare moments of connection. I gave a little cry and took the familiar drawing to look closer. Scars and wrinkles had been blended with the strong facial features and rugged handsomeness on the page. "Where did you get this?"

"Donegan Vance gave it to me just after lecturing me on the great inner beauty and virtue of my daughter."

I gulped.

"I believe he went on for six or seven minutes and he had no shortage of things to say on the matter."

"He truly does care, doesn't he?" I spoke the words with a sort of wonder, after all that had occurred between us. How many rejections had he endured before he delivered that speech?

"It nearly killed him to keep my secret, especially after meeting you. He stormed into that cabin, demanding to know why I'd put such a girl through the grief of my death."

"It was because Dr. Caine tried to kill you. You hid on the island, and Donegan . . ."

"Protected my life by keeping me hidden."

I frowned. "But then he stole from you."

"Don't let that money tear you apart from the man waiting for you up that path. It's been nothing but a curse to my entire life. I consider it a blessing that he's taken it from my grasp. As I said before, he did it for noble reasons."

I sighed. "It's amazing how one single trunk can wreak havoc on so many lives."

"Trunk? Which trunk is that?"

"Your treasure chest. The big black one with the fortune and the will."

He whipped his windblown hair off his forehead. "A black chest with metal banding?"

"That's the one." I huddled against the rocks as the wind chilled me. "Donegan found it in your old workshop. It was his—"

"Tressa." He looked down at me with the light of amusement in his face. "What exactly did you find in that trunk?"

"Your will, and the remains of your fortune."

"You're certain?"

"Yes, very." Then I remembered the little pouch with the foreign money. I fumbled about the wet yards of cloth until I found it, still tied to my belt, and pulled it open. "Here's a portion of it. This is what old Prescott wouldn't accept because they're foreign bank notes."

Father held out his hand for the wilted, wet notes and examined them. "Cornwall." He raised his eyebrows. "I hear it's a beautiful place, but I've never been. I believe it was Donegan Vance who told me all about the vineyards there, where he'd grown up."

I gasped, stiffening. "You mean this foreign money is his? But why would he—"

"That trunk you found contained my personal income, which grew or shrank with each harvest. A few months ago it ran out entirely and I had to borrow from Prescott. The last harvest failed and I wasn't even able to pay my staff. I was about to find a way to bring in more when Caine found me. So you see, when Donegan Vance found that trunk . . . it was empty."

"Empty." I breathed out the single word as understanding dawned in painful rays of truth. "And then somehow it had exactly what we needed to pay the debt. Oh Father, he must have given us nearly everything he had. And there's no fortune, so I can never repay him."

"Oh, I do believe you can." His tender glance shone down on me. "Do you recall that tapestry of the vine?" Taking my sketch and a small pencil from his pocket, he flipped the paper over and with the nub of the pencil he quickly outlined the same image that had captivated me—the twisting vine trunk and the long branches extending out like arms. The sight gave me chills. "Now step back here." Together we strode away from the rocks and back onto the beach where the wind had died down to a muggy breeze. My feet sank into the sand with each step until he stopped me and turned me about to face the rocks and Trevelyan beyond it. "Look up there and tell me what you see."

"I see the estate. The castle."

Then he held the rough drawing out before me, just under Trevelyan in the distance. Suddenly the outline of the vine and two posts melded in my vision with the three towers of Trevelyan. I gasped. "It's Trevelyan." I looked at Father, wonder making my head spin.

"And the source of all life is stored inside the vine." His pencil flicked over the paper again, drawing a little cellar door at the base of the vine, and steps below it. "Years ago, during the time of the Glyndwr Rising in the Hundred Years' War, Welsh rebels crossed the channel into the surrounding area and the Malverns decided to bury their fortune to protect it. Every generation was taught to mistrust everyone and guard the fortune with everything they had. My father invested some of it but removed it again in the bank crash of 1825 and returned it to its hiding place." When he'd finished, he held it out to me with a solemn smile and enfolded my hand over it. "Daughter, my dear, precious Tressa, I give you this great abundance of possibilities—the Malvern fortune."

Welling with emotion, I looked up into his aging face and hardly knew what to say.

"For the first time in its existence, this money has not broken a bond but proven it. And now, it will not crush but bless—through your hand. I could not bear to touch it all these years, the way it has destroyed so much that is good, but I believe you are strong enough to bear the weight of such a fruit. So now I give to you the great wealth of the Malverns, with my blessing. Take it and paint the world with the beautiful colors of your soul." He smiled tenderly and moisture gathered in the creases beside his eyes.

Overwhelmed, awed, I slipped my arms around his great body and embraced him once again. His arms came around me and he held me close. For that moment, the cresting waves and distant birds were the only thing to intrude. Then, in silence, we walked together up the path toward home. When we reached the top, the lone figure of Donegan Vance stood off in the distance, watching over the vineyard that was now empty of workers.

We veered toward the woods and Father stopped in its shadows, turning me toward Donegan. "Go and talk to your young man, Tressa girl. If I could wish anything for you in this life, it would be for you to marry well. To find someone who feels about you the way I felt about your mother when I met her. Just make certain of one difference."

"What's that?"

He laid a hand on my shoulder. "That you feel the same way." He smiled down at me with such tender sorrow that I thought my heart would break.

I lowered my gaze and sighed. "I'm overwhelmed with love for this man." Even his flaws, that direct nature that had so bothered me before, only evidenced further the absolute trueness of his whole being. Though he'd been so anxious to learn how to soften his words, I almost found the memory of his candor and bluntness endearing in that moment. The powerful authenticity of his very nature stood like an anchor in the shifting waters.

"Then go to him. Love him." When I stepped back, his lips twitched in a smile of amusement. "Now if you'll excuse me, I must break the news of my survival to my wife."

With one final glance toward Father's retreating form moving through the woods, I turned toward the sloping vineyards and Donegan. Overwrought and exhausted, my mind discarded so many unimportant things and allowed me to focus on the one task outweighing everything else—repairing what I'd broken.

My heart swelled at the sight of the strong, familiar figure in tall black boots looking over the vineyard he'd worked to bring back to life. Millions of words swirled in my mind as I approached, and any number of them might spill out when I reached him.

When I stood several paces behind him and he turned, a gentle welcome lighting that chiseled face, I couldn't voice any of it. Numerous thoughts clogged my throat. Here was the man I'd weighed and corrected, shaping him into what I deemed acceptable. Meanwhile he'd simply laid down himself and everything he possessed as a gentleman's cloak across the puddle of my troubles and allowed me to walk across it without ever knowing on what I trod.

I strode directly to him, planted my toes against the tips of his boots, and reached up to draw him down toward me. When he came near, I threw my arms about his neck and captured his lips with mine, kissing him with the passion of everything overflowing from my heart.

Immediately his arms slid around me, holding me to him as he deepened the kiss with gentle longing, and I was consumed then by the magnitude of his affection for me, the richness of the authentic love he offered me. When I thought I'd drown in the moment, he lifted me off the ground and spun me around with delight and rained kisses over my face. I pulled away and laughed, smiling up into his shining eyes. He said nothing, but his face revealed a great deal. Surprise and wonder had settled there, but most obvious was the glow of his deepest longings being realized. He set me gently on the ground, still staring at me with that powerful gaze.

I lifted my hand to the stubble on his face and his jaw twitched under my fingertips. "It seems I have made you quite poor."

"Perhaps. But in doing so you've made me richer than I ever was." He kissed my open palm that had caressed his cheek. "I feared losing it until the moment I chose to give it up. Since then I've walked in such freedom I cannot explain it."

"What on earth made you do such a thing?"

For several moments, only the distant sound of the waves

hissing over sand filled my senses, and then he spoke a single word. "God."

I shifted back to study his face. "God?"

"I knew he wanted me to help you with something. For weeks he prodded me, but I didn't understand what he had in mind. Eventually he made it clear that he was asking me to give up my money so you could keep Trevelyan." He looked down and kicked at loose soil. "I didn't understand it at first. Why would I give the small fortune it had taken me years to accumulate, the money I so desperately needed, to a girl who lived in a castle? It made no sense, but the order was clear, so I finally obeyed, trusting him for what was needed. It was only in the act of giving it up that I realized how tightly I had been holding onto it, and it brought me freedom to let go."

I smiled and rested my face against his chest, embracing him tightly. God had a way of pruning off anything that came between himself and his children, it seemed. I'd experienced it too and somehow I was grateful for it. "So. You truly have nothing?"

He looked down at me and brushed my cheek with his knuckles. "How do you feel about living in a poor little cottage?"

"Does it at least have a door?"

Relief flooded his face and he smiled with overwhelming tenderness. "My, but you're demanding." He reached his solid arms around me again and held me close for a long minute, then stroked my damp hair down my back. "I cannot bring you into my poverty and debt. There are so many problems I must deal with before I have any right to ask you to join me."

"Don't be foolish." I smiled against his chest. "Was it

your money that came alongside me every time I had need? Did it care for my injured feet in the woods or fix that roof in the village?"

"Poverty is not as romantic as you think. You've never experienced it."

I slid out of his arms and caught up his hand in mine, tugging him along. "Come." I led him solemnly up to Trevelyan, through the courtyard, and down the five steps into the base of the well tower, lifting a candle from its holder along the courtyard wall. In the privacy of the dirt-floored pump room, I fumbled for a box of matches and lit the candle, holding the soft light between us in the dark. "Follow me."

"Where are you taking me?"

"You'll see." I unfolded the paper and held the light up to Father's rough sketch. We walked through the room to the little water closet in back. There in the tiny space was a cellar door disguised to blend in with the rough wood floor, exactly where Father's diagram said it would be. Donegan wedged it open and together we climbed down the narrow cellar steps slick with moss, the candle's glow gliding over the crude walls hugging us on both sides.

When at last we reached the bottom, we stepped into a great dungeon of a room and I clung to Donegan's hand. "This is it. This is what we didn't even know to search for. It's the legendary Malvern fortune." I lifted the candle, shoving it farther into the room, and the sight captured my breath. The meager glow highlighted giant piles of coins and valuables, glinting off polished surfaces. I ran to a low-hanging wooden chandelier and lit it with my candle, magnifying the room's light. Together we stood among greater wealth than I'd ever imagined possible. Heaps of coins, crates and barrels filled with all manner of money and valuables, all winked back at us in the light.

I turned to Donegan, who stood genuinely agape at the display. It pleased me immensely to surprise him this way, and I returned to stand beside him. "All this time we were looking for the wrong fortune—a mere chest with a few piles of pound notes that would have run out too quickly. Yet here is an abundance that is all ours."

He strode in a slow circle about the room, taking in the sight of it. "So this is the fortune that has destroyed relationships and ended lives. Perhaps it truly is a curse, a source of greed and poverty on the deepest levels."

"Is that all you see in it? What a shame."

"You can do what you like with it, I suppose, but if you want to keep it . . . well, I'm not sure wealth and I are compatible. I've found such freedom in releasing the little I did have that I cannot tie myself again to large sums of money."

I offered a playful smile. "Mr. Vance, are you judging me by the size of my fortune?"

But he remained sober. "If this were my fortune, I'd be tempted to leave it down here and forget I ever found it."

"Then perhaps it's best it isn't your fortune. No, I will not simply walk away from it. That would be a waste of a perfectly good secret."

"You plan to spend this money, then?"

"All of it. Why keep it buried? And you realize I'll need the help of my faithful partner."

"I'm not interested in managing a fortune, if that's what you're suggesting."

After blowing out the leaning candles of the chandelier, I slipped my hand into the crook of his arm and smiled up at him as we walked toward the stairs and again ascended into daylight. Once outside, I blew out the candle and we walked together toward the vineyard. "What I'm suggesting is a lifetime of bad days, for I suddenly find myself with an abundance of bad-day remedy."

He glanced down at me, his masculine face softened with admiration. As we paused at the top of the vast slope overlooking the rolling acres, his fingertips trailed along my temple, calming the tension of the day and replacing it with pleasant sparks of hope and delight. I leaned my face against his chest and savored the moment.

"I intend to bring home an indentured soldier whose fiancée has waited far too long for her wedding." I pictured Lucy's face at the surprise reunion. Then my thoughts turned to poor Ellen and the terrible smiling mask over her tortured heart. "Then I must attend to an enemy or two. I do believe I know of an expectant mother who could use a little help. From there, who knows?" I looked up at him.

Hesitation tugged at his handsome face as he dropped his hand and I stepped back. "You know about the debts I have, the way I lost everything my family owned. I'm not a skilled money manager, Tressa. Especially with so large a fortune. I wouldn't know how to handle it all."

"Mr. Vance, do you recall what you told me about the two ships, the *Tayleur* and the ark? Well, I'd like to amend that." I took his hand and smiled. "The difference between the ships is that the failed ship was built by a professional, and the successful one by an amateur . . . *and his God.*"

He folded me into his arms then, his rough chin brushing against my forehead, and he kissed the top of my head like a solemn blessing. "More than anything, I want you beside me. As soon as I've paid off the debts and set things to right, I'll be back for you."

I pushed back to look up at him. "If that's all that's standing between us, then don't be surprised to find your debts disappearing faster than you can pay them. After all, I intend to repay your money, as well as give you what my father promised you."

"No, Tressa." He grasped my hands earnestly, but I interrupted his refusal.

"Don't take it for yourself. Take it for the people you intended to rescue back home. They will have their lives restored, and you . . ." I looked up at him. "You will have no more excuse to be rid of me."

He swallowed and studied me, those powerful eyes searching mine as his heart overflowed from their depths. "You should not spend your money that way. I'm no expert, but that's my firm advice. I'll pay the debts and return for you when they're cleared."

"Suit yourself." I leaned into him and looked out over the vineyard so alive with color and the sunset streaking soft hues behind it. "But I will warn you, Mr. Vance. I don't listen well either."

I am the vine, ye are the branches: He that abideth in me, and I in him, the same bringeth forth much fruit: for without me ye can do nothing.

John 15:5

Read On for an Excerpt of

JOANNA'S

Next Intriguing Romance . . .

I do not truly wish for all my dreams to come true.
After all, nightmares are one type of dream.

~Diary of Countess Lovelyn Shaughess

Spitalfields, London's East End, 1871

For one blessed moment I was actually beautiful. I rested one smudged hand on the bodice of the luscious gown belonging to Mrs. J. B. Hollingsworth and waltzed like a princess down Church Street in the dark, the little jeweled shoes clicking as I spun on the broken cobblestones. Gowns had a sort of magic hemmed into their yards of cloth, enough to change a girl's heart and appearance just by the wearing of them.

I paused under the gaslights to glimpse my reflection in a window, gasping at the vision of loveliness framed on the grimy pane of Bryn and Saunders Textiles. I twirled my hair up and gazed with wonder at the whole of me—shapely, trim, and utterly feminine. For the first time in my life, my willowy little body was fitted in a garment with actual shape and form.

Mercy gracious, I looked like a normal woman.

A flash of vanity lighted through my heart, but it was snuffed by chilly fear a moment later. The grim reflection of a fine-suited gentleman lurked behind my image in the window, moving steadily toward me. He must be coming for the gown and shoes.

With a shiver, I dropped my upswept hair and slipped into the shadows of the building, heart thudding with powerful force as I hurried away. The stranger's shoes clicked on the damp street behind me, splatting over little rivulets of rain-water as they moved toward me with purpose. I had only meant to borrow it and return it before it was missed, but what could I do now—strip down to my dirty chemise and run through the streets?

"You there." His low voice thudded through my senses, sparking me into action.

I sprinted past my rag cart and down a narrow, unlit street. I never should have touched the thing. The gown had been lying across a chair in the Hollingsworths' laundry cellar, and the maid had left me alone with it while she'd gone to fetch the castoffs. Once I glimpsed the ivory organza, and the little jeweled slippers cast under a stool, I hadn't the strength to leave them alone. I'd intended to return them within minutes. An hour at most.

Yet there was no point in stopping for explanations, for I was a rag girl, as much a castoff as the rags I peddled. People called me Ragna, a cruel twist on my real name, Raina. I sprinted with all my might, loose rocks skittering under my feet as I ran awkwardly through the shadows on pointy heels, dodging the yellow glow of streetlights. I stumbled as one of the ridiculous jeweled shoes came loose, and I kicked it off, darting on one shoe and bare toes into the first alley I saw. I slipped into the dark and *thunk*—my shins collided with something wooden, sending me sprawling over the broken cobblestones in a pile of crinoline and dirt.

Miserable crates.

My pursuer turned the corner into the alley too, and I glanced back to find myself in a dead end with walls surrounding me on three sides, the man blocking my only escape and closing the distance between us. Cornered, I wrenched the other jeweled shoe off and held it aloft. The long, dark shadow of the man approached with steady confidence, and I realized he'd kill me and *then* drag my dead body to the constable. Gripping the accidentally pilfered shoe, defeat stole over me. I'd survived twenty-two years in this slum, fought off every evil around me like a cornered tiger, only to be hanged for this—a mere moment of weakness.

I gulped in more air and steadied my nerves for a defensive attack. I lay in that spot, rooted by fear, praying to God that the foreboding stranger would somehow overlook me in the shadows and disappear.

Yet it seemed God had other plans, for the man strode up to me, the tips of his shiny leather shoes coming to a stop before the muddy hem of the once-white gown. I looked up into the finest face I ever remembered seeing inside of Spitalfields as the lights along the main street highlighted his confident features. I watched him, fear drowning my voice into silence. Then the fine gent knelt there in the street and held out the shoe I'd abandoned.

"Pardon me, have you lost a glass slipper?"

His handsome blond curls caught the moon's glow as a kind smile warmed across his face and my breath caught in my chest. I forced myself to breathe. He reached toward my dirty bare foot and his nearness sent me scrambling upright. I moved back, leveling a glare at him as I tried to avoid brushing off my dirty bare arm. Men grew uncomfortably brazen as the sun set over this cramped little section of town.

"Thank you kindly, sir, but if you'll excuse me." I felt the unnecessary sting of my words, but I'd lived long enough to know that kindness from strangers must be clearly snubbed. Anything less would find a girl helpless and ruined.

"You are excused." But he merely rose before me and remained in my path with arms crossed over his chest, watching with gentle amusement.

I smoothed the limp dress over my body and attempted to duck around him, but he stepped easily in front of me.

"If you'll give me but a moment, I have a proposition for you."

So he hadn't come about the gown. He was merely some well-dressed loon who'd lost his way and found a girl out alone at night. "You're blocking my way."

"Or perhaps just enticing you to take an entirely new one."

I frowned, breathing hard and poised to exit at the first chance.

"Won't you give me but a moment of your time? It's a splendid opportunity."

"I'm not in need of one." I shoved past him and limped toward the main street on one shoe, leaving this darkly clad stranger with as much poise as any highbred lady might. Don't run and they won't chase—every Spitalfields girl knew this, but this was my first chance to test the old adage.

But even as I walked away, the fleeting word *opportunity* settled into my mind and ignited a bloom of colorful daydreams and fanciful notions. They came almost unbidden, for I had been born with both a spirited imagination and a life that demanded regular escape into it.

I snuck another glance behind me and decided that the odd stranger appeared both sober and sane. His dark air of mystery fit the mood of the gloomy alley we shared, yet his trim gray tailcoat with perfect black buttons contrasted so sharply with the surrounding grime and decay. This made me both suspicious and terribly interested in whatever had driven him to pursue me.

I strode on with my head up, some wicked part of me willing him to catch up and quench my curiosity. A few paces later, he did at least grant the first part of that wish. His shoes splat-splatted over the rain pooled in the ruts of the cobbled road, and he again stepped before me, halting my progress.

"I noticed you did not say no." The defined *M* of his upper lip curled into an enticing smile as he once again held out the little jeweled shoe he'd rescued from the alley.

"Only because I cannot bring myself to take you seriously."

"No, it's more than that. Admit it—some little part of you desperately wants to hear what sort of adventure this stranger is attempting to offer you."

I dropped my gaze to the uneven cobblestone street, for surely my entire personality must be in vivid display upon my face. How else could he have spoken so directly into my secret heart? His smoothly spoken word "adventure" inflamed a desire in me so great, it tempted me to cast aside everything I knew to follow him.

"A girl with such remarkable beauty should have the gowns

and life that reflect her lovely face." He paused when I remained silent, cocking his head at a charming angle. "You seem to doubt the sincerity of my admiration. Shall I tell you more specifically what I find so stunning about you?"

My fickle heart struggled to remain aloof. "I'll not believe you. You're either lying or . . . or mad."

"What a monstrous thing to say to someone who's just paid you a compliment. Your punishment is that you must endure my company for the duration of your walk home." He offered his arm with a smile.

Unease sliced through me at these words and I stepped back. The man would not come near the flat I occupied alone. "I bid you good evening, sir."

Tingling with something—fear, or maybe excitement—I turned, but he laid a hand gently on the wall beside me, as if touching my arm without actually making contact. The effect was surprisingly arresting.

"What if I offered you a fine position at a magnificent estate, among the finest gowns and fields of flowers for your hair, and all you had to do was come with me and step into it?"

His words pulled at me at the heart level, where a love of beauty was buried, yet I resisted with all my might. If only he knew how he tortured me. "I couldn't simply walk away from—"

"From what, all this?" He lifted his arms to indicate the dank alley that was thick with the odor of trapped moisture. "Come, what would you be leaving behind, truly? Have you a family at home? A respectable man waiting for you?"

In an instant, images of the man I loved engulfed my hurting heart, twisting it in a familiar pain. I saw his precious face as he was years ago, swinging playfully upside down from the rusted stair rail, mock-curtseying with twinkling eyes and a lopsided grin, saluting his farewell from the crew deck of the *Maiden Faire* as it sailed into the fog. That familiar face and the marvelous personality behind it.

Oh yes, I had a respectable man. A splendid, bighearted, gallant man fueled by music and joy who was no less mine simply because he was dead. The lurid image of Sully's sinking ship tore across my imagination. I clenched my jaw and fisted my hands, forcing myself to answer over the wave of fresh pain. "I suppose not."

Now there was only Paul left to me—my poor, sickly, tenderhearted brother who had signed onto a ship's crew like Sully for lack of other opportunities, yet no one belonged on solid ground more than that boy. If I left, who would work to bring him home? The mere thought of him engulfed my heart in an overwhelming loyalty, a firm resolve to remain for him.

The man's voice interrupted my thoughts. "Nothing cleanses away the dusty taste of everyday life like adventure." His smile revealed perfect white teeth. Too perfect. "There's nothing here that you can't have tenfold at Rothburne Abbey. The position pays forty pounds."

I coughed. The enormous number nearly choked me, and my brain immediately sifted it into a time frame of how long it would take to pay off Paul's ship contract and bring him home. I could no longer save Sully, but I still had Paul, and I desperately wished to fill my little hovel with the presence of my sweet-natured brother. Ever since Sully's ship had gone down, I'd been that determined to rescue Paul. It had always seemed a distant hope to bring him home, but with this amount I could taste the possibility of it. "Paid every month?"

"Every week." He gazed confidently into my eyes, daring

me to turn away from his offer. "The worn path of everyday is safe, but precious little grows there. Come now, little Cinderella, have an adventure."

My lashes fluttered at the weight of the temptation before me. I could work endlessly and never see reward, or I could step into this opportunity and fill both my pockets and my soul.

"Now that I have you sufficiently intrigued, I'll leave you to your normal routine and see if you still find it worth holding so tightly. At noon tomorrow I'll be at the train. I pray the night will not torment your mind to a great degree with indecision." With a sweeping bow, he handed me the little jeweled shoe and strode back into the darkness from which he had come.

With a powerful shiver, I put on the shoe, hugged the sagging dress to my frame, and paced home. All manner of rationalizations and logic flooded my tired brain, tugging me this way and that. My final decision alternated as often as my sore feet crossing back and forth over the drain gutter running down the center of the rain-drenched street.

Soon I ducked beneath the flapping sheet strung across the alley and stood before the broken shutters and ugly chipped brick that was my home. I was hemmed in by buildings beside and before me in the narrow space, with no evidence of God's creation around except the starless sky above, but it was my life. My reality. What right had I to hope for more?

With a sigh I lifted my skirt to climb the steps and glimpsed the jeweled shoe he'd left with me, inviting me into a Cinderella story. I somehow found myself surprisingly immune to his charm, having already spent my entire heart on one man with no desire to retrieve it, but the hope of his offered adventure flared through my eager mind with powerful force. I looked up and somehow my building seemed ten times more wretched and grimy than it had when I'd left at dawn. With a whole world of possibilities offered to me outside this cramped district, it suddenly felt impossible to remain here.

When I'd climbed the stairs and settled before the window with a view of the distant train station, I thought about the many hours spent here, watching for Sully. If I left, that meant admitting he wasn't coming home. Tears trailed down my cheeks as I traced the window frame cradling my face and forced myself to recall the bold notice in the paper about the sinking ships off the east coast in a storm they called the "Great Gale." My finger had trembled uncontrollably as it skimmed through the names of the lost ships until it slid over the one that had once brought precious sparks of joy—*Maiden Faire*.

I looked out at the night, smiling sadly at the thought of his bright countenance, always playful and ready to smile. How I missed that dear face, and would forever. He'd be my most treasured memory, captured in my mind like a miniature in a locket. The images of wide smiles and a jaunty blue cap overwhelmed my poor mind. I'd made that cap for him when he'd taught me to read years ago. How much of the world he'd opened to me since our shared childhood.

"Hallo there!"

I jerked as widow McCall's voice carried through my flat from the open door, and I lifted my face, swiping madly at my tears. Her shrunken form sailed through the room to where I sat, and the frown that contorted her warted features only made me smile.

"And just what is my li'l lass doing out after dark? Only

God is invincible, you know. Ach, you and trouble ought to be the closest chums, the way you always go together."

"I've not seen trouble from anyone. At least, I don't think so. But something odd happened." I unleashed the tale into the room, and with every turbulent sentence that poured out, the encounter seemed more and more unbelievable. I told her about the opportunity at Rothburne Abbey and showed her the remarkable little slippers, wondering if I'd ambled into the pages of a fairy tale on my way home. What other reason would a gentleman have for so imploring the woman who sold castoff rags to follow him to a life of splendor?

"I shouldn't do it, should I? It's too odd. Too risky."

Her eyes glistened as one reliving youth and excitement. "Precisely why you should, love. This place holds you in its grip, but it doesn't define you. It's as if fate is plucking your pretty little self out of this mess and placing you where you belonged from the start."

"Oh no, I—"

"Now, now, don't argue with an old woman. I have eyes, don't I?" She reached out and rubbed the ends of my long hair between her gnarled fingers. "A sort of queen is what you are, stepping through the rubbish like you was balancing a crown on that pretty head of yours. I suppose it's in your blood, being one of them wealthy Huguenot weavers."

"That's long over for us, and we've been nothing but rag vendors since I was small." If only those merchants who'd grown wealthy by importing silks knew what their prosperity had cost an entire community of local artisans. The Huguenots were no longer a respected immigrant community spinning silks from behind tall, sunny windows and likely never would be again.

"Ah, but you've got a touch of the old blood in you, coursing through like a vein of gold. The way you talk, the look of your face . . . There's something about you, lass. Finally someone else stood up and took notice of it too, and you'll not refuse the brilliant man who's had the sense to see it." She lifted sharp old eyes to meet mine. "I'll miss you something fierce, but don't you ever come back. You've always belonged somewhere better'n here."

I sighed. "What do they want with the likes of me at an abbey, anyway? It's a strange place to find a position."

Her eyes sparkled beneath the frizz of gray hair. "You'd best go and find out."

When she took herself away to her own flat later that night, I again looked out toward the distant station. For years it had symbolized Sully's return, but now it meant the exact opposite. Leaving on that train would sever the last connection we had—a lifetime of memories in Spitalfields. Could I give up that dream to risk another?

It struck me then that I'd never see the great love he wrote of on his face, never hear him say it in his own voice. Once again I drew out the stacks of letters and flipped open the first one.

My dear Raina, it began, and that was enough to saturate my heart, for his every action since I'd known him had proven I was exactly that. He was one of the few who called me by my true name, and the use of it always touched me. The rest of the letter was doused with words from a poetic, passionate heart that had lain hidden behind the playful, lively exterior I'd always known. Why had he never spoken these words aloud before he'd left? He couldn't have feared rejection from me, for I'd loved him ardently before I even understood what the word meant.

What would I do, come morning's light? I could go two ways—one was bleak, offering nothing, and the other was beckoning me away to adventure, which had been my weakness since childhood. It lured and fascinated me, causing me trouble and disrupting the ruts of life. Though for the first time in memory, there would be no Sully to rescue me from my scrapes.

But neither would there be if I remained in Spitalfields pining away after his memory.

So it was that I found myself taking one final walk through Spitalfields the following morning as the sun dawned over a new day and a new life, a limp carpetbag swinging against my leg, anxiety and excitement chasing each other through my veins. I slipped the carefully freshened gown and slippers back into the laundry cellar of Mrs. Hollingsworth without being observed and turned toward the station. Widow McCall had made the situation seem so natural, almost inevitable, but now that I'd come, the oddness of it all pricked me again.

As the noonday sun heated my skin, I stood on the platform and the throng of travelers parted to reveal the man that had slipped into my life and upended my future. I shivered at the sight of such a handsome man smiling at me. What was that odd sensation he elicited in me with a mere look? I couldn't tell if it was pleasant or scary. Either way it was addictive.

He strode over and, with a small smile of victory, scooped up my bag. As I watched him stride away with the bag containing everything I owned, panic unfurled inside. I hugged my old patched shawl about me, a tangible reminder of who I truly was, because it seemed I'd forgotten. I dreamed so often of normal clothing and a world of acceptance, yet I still awoke every morning—including this one—as Ragna the rag vendor. Something was not right about this.

I caught up to him as steam huffed from under the train. "I don't even know your name."

"It is Prendergast. Victor Eugene Prendergast." He considered me with amusement and extended his hand, which I did not take. "Would you also like to see my character references?"

He had no reason to treat me as an equal when we both knew I was far from it. I looked up into his tolerant face. "What is Rothburne? What could I ever do at an abbey?"

"It's a monastic fortress renovated into a private estate. It's now the country home of the Countess of Enderly."

A countess. He wished me to work for a countess? I pressed my lips together and watched hundreds of more appropriately dressed people swarm onto the train ahead of us, wondering again why he'd chosen me. With one more powerful billow of steam pouring across my vision, I followed him and glanced back for the last time at everything I was leaving behind.

"Final boarding!" A red-coated man hung out of the door of the train car before us, urging us on.

I hesitated, waiting for the steam to clear for my final view of home, but my new employer tugged my arm. "Come, Cinderella. It's time to go."

"Raina. My name is Raina."

When I glanced back again, uncertainty weighting my steps, a blue cap descended into the steam, the black boots of its owner landing firmly on the solid wood platform. Heart exploding in my chest, I braced myself against the doorway, willing the steam to clear so I could be sure of what I saw. It couldn't be him, but I had to know before I left. Through the haze I saw a lanky sailor with a jacket tossed over one arm, bag in hand. How well I knew that stance—but it was impossible. Impossible! If only I could see his face.

"Doors closing."

I gripped the metal bar outside the train but strong arms lifted me from behind into the narrow doorway and I cried out, fighting back. "Wait! Stop!" The chaos of the station drowned out my cries.

At my cry, the sailor's wandering gaze lifted to mine through the steam, catching and holding it, but before I could cry out again, the train door shut and latched before my face.

Discussion Questions

1. Throughout the book, Tressa regularly shows loyalty for those she loves, even Donegan eventually. Some deserve it, others do not. Do you think this is foolish or admirable? Would you do the same?
2. How did Tressa's relationship with her earthly father shape her perceptions of God? How have people in your life shaped your idea of God?
3. When Tressa meets Donegan, she's not impressed. How did you feel about his blunt speech and informal attitude? Did your opinion of him change throughout the book?
4. In the beginning, Tressa feels alone and depleted. What or who does Tressa attempt to cling to throughout the book in order to draw life, and how does each one turn out? What do you feel keeps you anchored, something with which you could never imagine parting?
5. In vineyards, a fruit tells the truth about the entire plant. How would you describe the fruit that we saw come

from some of the characters? Which character's true "fruit" ended up surprising you? What fruit do people see coming from you?

6. How did you feel about Tressa and Donegan's balcony scene at the art gallery? Did you sympathize with Tressa's ache that drives her into that moment or did you feel she was wrong? In what ways do we try to heal something that is only meant to be fixed by God?
7. The verse "speak the truth in love" (Eph. 4:15) was mentioned in this book. At which part do you excel—truth or love? Who in your life teaches you the other part?
8. In Tressa's quest for buried treasure, she finds it in one surprising place—Donegan Vance. Even her mother shows surprising depth toward the end. Who in your life might contain buried treasure that you've overlooked? What can you do to draw it out?
9. How do you imagine the scene playing out when Tressa's father walks into Trevelyan and sees the servants? His wife?
10. The vineyard setting contains a lot of symbolism, from grafting of opposites to clinging branches, depth of a plant's roots to fruit produced, and many others. Which one stood out to you and why? How does it translate into something in your own life?
11. Tressa's father knows a lot about vines, but he has never clung to the true Vine. Now that Tressa has gone on this journey of pruning and abiding with God, and she has a brand-new relationship with her father, how do you think she might explain to him how to have the peace and love he's always sought?

12. The love story in this novel is a romance of polar opposites, yet they have some important similarities too. What do you think their marriage will be like? What difficulties and joys might they have, and what aspects remind you of relationships in your life?
13. Donegan and Tressa are now in possession of more money than most people will ever see. What do you think will become of the treasure, and how do you see them using it? How would you spend a fortune like that?

*Acknowledgments*

I give the deepest heartfelt thanks to the entire fiction team at Revell for choosing to publish another book from me and for pouring their talents so generously into its success. From the editors to the designers to the promotions coordinators, you all go above and beyond in every way. You amaze me so often! I'm thankful for you all and the talent and enthusiasm you invest in your authors' books.

Secondly, I wouldn't have a finished story without the people who read it and made me rewrite, gave suggestions, and talked me through some of the stickiest plot points: my dad, Bob Davidson, who reads everything first; Allen Arnold; Susan Tuttle; Dawn Crandall; Crystal Caudill; and Stacey Zink. This book took a ton of reworking and rethinking, of which you all played a huge part and gave of yourselves to help me. Thank you all so much for pouring into me and my writing. You all help me live and write better. Each of you added your own brushstrokes to this rough sketch to make it far better than it was when I sent it to you.

Also, I know I dedicated this book to you, Vince, but I just wanted to thank you again for loving all the parts of me—including the part that is a neurotic, scatterbrained, slightly crazy writer. I love you dearly.

Joanna Davidson Politano freelances for a small nonfiction publisher but spends much of her time spinning tales that capture the colorful, exquisite details in ordinary lives. Her manuscript for *Lady Jayne Disappears* was a finalist for several contests, including the 2016 Genesis Award from ACFW, and won the OCW Cascade Award and the Maggie Award for Excellence. She is always on the hunt for random acts of kindness, people willing to share their deepest secrets with a stranger, and hidden stashes of sweets. She lives with her husband and their two babies in a house in the woods near Lake Michigan and shares stories that move her at www.jdpstories.com.

MEET JOANNA

JDPStories.com

Joanna Davidson Politano

@politano_joanna

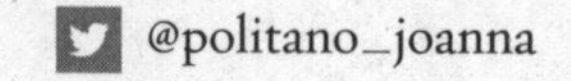